The
PUFFIN BOOK
of
CLASSIC CHILDREN'S
STORIES

The
PUFFIN BOOK
of
CLASSIC CHILDREN'S
STORIES

Edited by
HUMPHREY CARPENTER

Illustrated by
DIZ WALLIS

PUFFIN BOOKS

Text has been omitted in some of the extracts in this anthology. This is indicated by […].

PUFFIN BOOKS

Published by the Penguin Group
Penguin Books Ltd, 27 Wrights Lane, London W8 5TZ, England
Penguin Books USA Inc., 375 Hudson Street, New York, New York 10014, USA
Penguin Books Australia Ltd, Ringwood, Victoria, Australia
Penguin Books Canada Ltd, 10 Alcorn Avenue, Toronto, Ontario, Canada M4V 3B2
Penguin Books (NZ) Ltd, 182–190 Wairau Road, Auckland 10, New Zealand

Penguin Books Ltd, Registered Offices: Harmondsworth, Middlesex, England

First published by Viking 1996
Published in Puffin Books 1997
1 3 5 7 9 10 8 6 4 2

Filmset in Monotype Garamond

Made and printed in England by Clays Ltd, St Ives plc

British Library Cataloguing in Publication Data
A CIP catalogue record for this book is available from the British Library

ISBN 0–140–36815–9

CONTENTS

INTRODUCTION

'I don't recall reading *The Wind in the Willows* as a child, or indeed any of the classics of children's literature,' writes Alan Bennett in the introduction to his play based on Kenneth Grahame's book. His local public library bound all its books in dark leather, so that they looked boring. And the very idea that they might be 'classic' put him off.

As it happens, I remember exactly when I read *The Wind in the Willows* for the first time. I was eighteen, and sitting in a café, in a break from a summer school of music I was attending. For some reason I'd brought the book with me: a 1926 Methuen edition with no illustrations – I still have it on the shelf – which doesn't look like a children's book at all. In fact, you could argue that, like many so-called 'children's classics', it *isn't* a children's book. The poetic descriptions of the River Bank and the Wild Wood belong more to adult Edwardian fiction than to bedtime stories. Indeed, the one compulsory qualification for classic status in the genre is, paradoxically, that the book can be fully appreciated only by adults. Maybe this is a mistake, and this anthology should really contain those stories which the present generation of children regard as classic. In which case most adults wouldn't have heard of them.

Yet, written in the front of that copy, in my handwriting, dating (I'd guess) from my eighth or ninth year, are the words: '*The Wind in the Willows* can be seen as a play under the title of *Toad of Toad Hall*, adapted by A. A. Milne.' I hadn't needed to sit down and read the book because I knew it already, or at least thought I did, thanks to the play. And I *did* read the whole text of *Alice in Wonderland* at about the age of eight, much earlier (I believe) than many people do, because I had decided to adapt it as a 'shadow play' for performance by myself and two older cousins who were staying with us. I remember making the caterpillar's mushroom by placing a cushion on top of a cardboard tube, and using my hand to create the shadow of the caterpillar itself on the suspended sheet which made our screen, with two outstretched fingers as its antennae. My cousin Kate, who had short hair, played Alice in a wig made for her by my mother, consisting of strands of wool attached to an old tie of my father's, which she tied around her head. It created the perfect shadow of long hair.

Today's children still make up plays based on children's classics. *Peter Pan*, happily still appearing on the stage nearly a century after its publication (and omitted from this collection only because it is not a 'story' but a stage text – none of the various novelizations can equal the play), still inspires bedtime representations of Hook swashbuckling, the crocodile tick-tocking, and of course Peter and the Darlings flying. But mostly, of course, children now make their acquaintance with classics through television, at the cinema or on video. I don't think there is a single book or story represented in this collection which hasn't been filmed or televised or musicalized or cartoonized, in some cases many times over.

So why gather them – or, in many cases, bits of them – into this volume? To show you that the original isn't quite the same as the TV or stage or screen version. In most cases, the texts themselves are tougher and more full of life and surprising meanings than the adaptations. After reading even the first chapter of *Little Women*, with its multiple ironies about family life, you'll never again be fully satisfied with any dramatization. The passage from *The Wind in the Willows* in which Mole rediscovers his abandoned home is more full of painful resonance than the equivalent scene in even Alan Bennett's loving stage version.

The stories, and excerpts from stories, are arranged in chronological order. I tried arranging them by subject, but that was too arbitrary. *The Water-Babies* could, after all, be categorized under 'water', 'natural history', 'chimney sweeps' or for that matter, I suppose, 'babies'. And chronological arrangement does tell you something about the development of children's fiction if you read the book right through in order; but of course nobody is going to do that. The collection is for dipping, like any other anthology, and chronology has the advantage of not getting in the way of that.

I have begun early, with Aesop (whose *Town and Country Mouse* turn up again about 2,500 years later in Beatrix Potter's *Johnny Town-Mouse*); and I have ended early, with *The Borrowers*, published in 1952, because I am not confident about granting, or withholding, classic status to books more recently published than that. Nor indeed can one have cast-iron confidence about inclusions and exclusions from the earlier periods.

All decisions must be arbitrary, and I know there will be readers' letters passionately disagreeing with some of my choices or omissions. Please regard the selection as no more than a subjectively chosen hors-d'oeuvre; and having tasted them, you will, I hope, be drawn to those main courses – the books themselves – which you do not already know. (Almost all of them are available in Puffin Classics or Modern Classics.) And if you know most of the main dishes already, treat this collection as a pleasurable reminder, a bran tub of literary memories into which you can dip at will. And who knows? If they're not put off by that word 'classic', maybe the Alan Bennetts of the next generation will have a seed or two sown in their minds.

Humphrey Carpenter

AESOP

'The Town Mouse and the Country Mouse'
FROM *Aesop's Fables*

(ABOUT 6TH CENTURY BC)

A country mouse invited a town mouse, who was a close friend, to pay him a visit and share in his country living. As they hunted about the bare plough-lands, eating their wheat-stalks and roots pulled up from the hedge-row, the town mouse said to his friend: 'You live here the life of the ants. My house in town is a horn of plenty. I am surrounded with every luxury, and if you will come and visit me, you shall have an ample share of our fine food.'

The country mouse was easily persuaded, and returned to the town with his friend. On their arrival, they went to the pantry and the town mouse placed before him bread, barley, beans, dried figs, honey, raisins, and, last of all, a delicious piece of cheese. The country mouse was delighted at the sight of so much good food, and complained about his hard life in the country. Just as they settled down to eat, however, someone opened the pantry door. Both the mice ran off squeaking as fast as they could to a hole so narrow that the two of them could only just squeeze through. After a while they came out again, but they had scarcely begun their feast when someone else came to the pantry for some food. The two mice, more frightened than before, scampered away and hid themselves once more. Hardly a moment passed when they were not interrupted. At last the country mouse, almost famished, said to his friend: 'Although you have prepared for me a very fine feast, I must leave you to enjoy it by yourself. It is surrounded by too many dangers to please me. I prefer my bare plough-lands and roots from the hedge-row, where at least I can live in safety and eat without fear.'

JOSEPH JACOBS

A RETELLING OF *Molly Whuppie*

(TRADITIONAL)

Once upon a time there was a man and a wife had too many children, and they could not get meat for them, so they took the three youngest and left them in a wood. They travelled and travelled and could never see a house. It began to be dark, and they were hungry. At last they saw a light and made for it; it turned out to be a house. They knocked at the door, and a woman came to it, who said: 'What do you want?' They said: 'Please let us in and give us something to eat.' The woman said: 'I can't do that, as my man is a giant, and he would kill you if he comes home.' They begged hard. 'Let us stop for a little while,' said they, 'and we will go away before he comes.' So she took them in, and set them down before the fire, and gave them milk and bread; but just as they had begun to eat, a great knock came to the door, and a dreadful voice said:

> 'Fee, fie, fo, fum,
> I smell the blood of some earthly one.

Who have you there, wife?' 'Eh,' said the wife, 'it's three poor lassies cold and hungry, and they will go away. Ye won't touch 'em, man.' He said nothing, but ate up a big supper, and ordered them to stay all night. Now he had three lassies of his own, and they were to sleep in the same bed with the three strangers. The youngest of the three strange lassies was called Molly Whuppie, and she was very clever. She noticed that before they went to bed the giant put straw ropes round her neck and her sisters', and round his own lassies' necks he put gold chains. So Molly took care and did not fall asleep, but waited till she was sure everyone was sleeping sound. Then she slipped out of bed, and took the straw ropes off her own and her sisters' necks, and took the gold chains off the giant's lassies. She then put the straw ropes on the giant's lassies and the gold on herself and her sisters, and lay down. And in the middle of the night up rose the giant, armed with a great club, and felt for the necks with the straw. It was dark. He took his own lassies out of the bed on to the floor, and battered them until they were dead, and then lay down again, thinking he had managed finely. Molly thought it time she and her sisters were off and away, so she wakened them and told them to be quiet, and they slipped out of the house. They all got out safe, and they ran and ran, and never stopped until morning, when they saw a grand house before them. It turned out to be a king's house; so Molly went in, and told her story to the king. He said: 'Well, Molly, you are a clever girl, and you have managed well; but, if you would manage better, and go back, and steal the giant's sword that hangs on the back of his bed, I would give your eldest sister my eldest son to marry.' Molly said she would try. So she went back, and managed to slip into the giant's house, and crept in below the bed. The giant came home, and ate up a great supper, and went to bed. Molly waited until he was snoring, and she crept out, and reached over the giant and got down the sword; but just as she got it out over the bed it gave a rattle, and up jumped the giant, and Molly ran out at the door and the sword with her; and she ran, and he ran, till they came to the 'Bridge of one hair'; and she got over, but he couldn't and he says: 'Woe worth ye, Molly Whuppie! Never ye come again.' And she says: 'Twice yet, carle,' quoth she, 'I'll come to Spain.' So Molly took the sword to the king, and her sister was married to his son.

Well, the king he says: 'Ye've managed well, Molly; but if ye would manage better, and steal the purse that lies below the giant's pillow, I would marry your second sister to my second son.' And Molly said she would try. So she set out for the giant's house, and slipped in and hid again below the bed, and waited till the giant had eaten his supper, and was snoring sound asleep. She slipped out and slipped her hand below the pillow, and got out the purse; but just as she was going out the giant wakened, and ran after her; and she ran, and he ran, till they came to the 'Bridge of one hair', and she got over, but he couldn't, and he said: 'Woe worth ye, Molly Whuppie! Never you come again.' 'Once yet, carle,' quoth she, 'I'll come to Spain.' So Molly took the purse to the king, and her second sister was married to the king's second son.

After that the king says to Molly: 'Molly, you are a clever girl, but if you would do better yet, and steal the giant's ring that he wears on his finger, I will give you my youngest son for yourself.' Molly said she would try. So back she goes to the giant's house, and hides herself below the bed. The giant wasn't long ere he came home, and, after he had eaten a great big supper, he went to his bed, and shortly was snoring loud. Molly crept out and reached over the bed, and got hold of the giant's hand, and she pulled and she pulled until she got off the ring; but just as she got it off the giant got up, and gripped her by the hand and he says: 'Now I have caught you, Molly Whuppie, and, if I had done as much ill to you as ye have done to me, what would ye do to me?'

Molly says: 'I would put you into a sack, and I'd put the cat inside wi' you, and the dog aside you, and a needle and thread and a shears, and I'd hang you up upon the wall, and I'd go to the wood, and choose the thickest stick I could get, and I would come home, and take you down, and bang you till you were dead.'

'Well, Molly,' says the giant, 'I'll just do that to you.'

So he gets a sack, and puts Molly into it, and the cat and the dog beside her, and a needle and thread and shears, and hangs her up upon the wall, and goes to the wood to choose a stick.

Molly she sings out: 'Oh, if ye saw what I see.'

'Oh,' says the giant's wife, 'what do ye see, Molly?'

But Molly never said a word but, 'Oh, if ye saw what I see!'

The giant's wife begged that Molly would take her up into the sack till she would see what Molly saw. So Molly took the shears and cut a hole in the sack, and took out the needle and thread with her, and jumped down and helped the giant's wife up into the sack, and sewed up the hole.

The giant's wife saw nothing, and began to ask to get down again; but Molly never minded, but hid herself at the back of the door. Home came the giant, and a great big tree in his hand, and he took down the sack, and began to batter it. His wife cried: 'It's me, man'; but the dog barked and the cat mewed, and he did not know his wife's voice. But Molly came out from the back of the door, and the giant saw her and he ran after her; and he ran, and she ran, till they came to the 'Bridge of one hair', and she got over but he couldn't; and he said: 'Woe worth you, Molly Whuppie! Never you come again.' 'Never more, carle,' quoth she, 'will I come again to Spain.'

So Molly took the ring to the king, and she was married to his youngest son, and she never saw the giant again.

ROGER LANCELYN GREEN

From a retelling of *Sir Gawain and the Green Knight*

(14TH CENTURY)

King Arthur's adventures did not end when he had
defeated the Saxons and brought peace to Britain: for
though he had set up the Realm of Logres – the land of true
good and piety, nobleness and right living – the evil was
always breaking in to attack the good …

But year by year the fame of his court grew, and spread
far and wide, and the bravest and noblest knights in the
world came to his court and strove by their deeds of
courage and gentleness to win a place at the Round Table.

Many stories are told of these knights also – of Launcelot
and Gawain, of Tristram and Gareth, of Percivale, Ywain,
Marhaus, Cleges, Agravaine, and many, many others – and
more adventures that befell the most famous of these than
may possibly be told in one book.

One of the first and bravest of the knights was Sir Gawain – and it was said indeed that only Sir Launcelot, Sir Galahad, and Sir Percivale could surpass him. He had many exciting adventures: but now only one of them can be told.

King Arthur held his Christmas feast at Camelot one year, with all the bravest of his knights about him, and all the fairest ladies of his court – and his chief celebrations fell upon New Year's Day. Queen Guinevere, clad in fair, shining silk, sat beneath an embroidered canopy studded with gems: fair was she to look upon, with her shining eyes of grey, and each knight bent in reverence before her ere he took his place. Beside her sat King Arthur, well pleased to see the noble gathering and the joy that was in the hall; but he would not begin the feast, for such his custom was, until he had been told of some knightly deed, or set before his knights some strange or terrible new quest.

The minstrels had stopped playing and the whole company sat quietly in the great hall, only the roar and crackle of the log fires in the wide hearths breaking the silence – when suddenly there rang out the clash and clang of iron-shod hooves striking upon stone. The great doors flew open, and into the hall rode a strange and terrible figure.

A great man it was, riding upon a huge horse: a strong-limbed, great-handed man, so tall that an earth-giant almost he seemed. Yet he rode as a knight should, though without armour, and his face, though fierce, was fair to see – but the greatest wonder was that he was green all over. A jerkin and cloak of green he wore above green hose gartered in green, with golden spurs; in the green belt round his waist jewels were set, and his green saddle was inlaid richly, as were also his trappings. But his hair, hanging low to his shoulders, was bright green, and his beard also; green was his face and green his hands; and the horse was also green from head to foot, with gold thread wound and knotted in the mane.

He had no weapons nor shield save for a great axe of green steel and gold, and a bough torn from a holly tree held above his head. He flung the branch upon the inlaid floor of the hall and looked proudly on every side; at the knights seated about the Round Table, and the ladies and squires at the boards on either side, and at Arthur where he sat with Guinevere above the rest. Then he cried in a great voice: 'Where is the governor of this gang? With him would I speak and with none other!'

All sat in amazement gazing at the strange knight; some dire enchantment it must be, they thought, for how else could there be such a man sitting there on his horse, as green as the grass – greener than any grass on this earth?

But at length Arthur, courteous ever, greeted the Green Knight, bade him be welcome and sit down to the feast with them.

'Not so!' cried the stranger in answer. 'I come not to tarry with you; and by the sign of the green bough, I come not in war – else had I clothed me in armour and helmet most sure, for such have I richly stored in my castle in the north. But even in that land have I heard of the fame and valour of your court – the bravery of your knights, and their high virtue also.'

'Sir,' replied the king, 'here may you find many to do battle and joust if such be your will.'

'Not so,' cried the Green Knight in his great booming voice. 'Here I see only beardless children whom I could fell with a stroke! Nay, I come rather in this high season of Our Lord's birth to bring Yule-tide sport, a test of valour to your feast. If any man in this hall is so brave and so courageous as to exchange stroke for stroke, I will give him this noble axe – heavy enough truly to handle as he may desire. Yes, and I myself will stand here on the floor and receive the first stroke of the axe wherever he may smite me. Only he must swear, and you, lord king, to give me the right to deal him such another blow, if I may, a twelve-month and a day from now.'

More silent still sat the knights; if they had been surprised before, now their amazement was greater still. But none dared answer his challenge, so terrible was the man and so fearsome the great axe which he held in his hand.

Then the Green Knight laughed aloud in mockery: 'Is this indeed the court of King Arthur,' he cried, 'and are these the far-famed Knights of the Round Table? Now is their glory laid low for ever, since even to hear tell of blows makes them all grow silent in fear!'

King Arthur sprang up at this. 'Fellow,' he cried, 'this foolishness of yours shall have a fitting answer. If none other will take your challenge, give me the axe and make ready for the blow!'

But at this Sir Gawain rose to his feet and said: 'My lord king and noble uncle, grant me a boon! Let this adventure be mine, for still there is my old shame unhealed; still have I to prove my worth as a Knight of your Round Table, still to fit myself to be a champion of Logres.'

'Right happy I am that the quest shall be yours, dear nephew,' answered Arthur. And the Green Knight smiled grimly as he sprang from his horse and met with Gawain in the middle of the hall.

'I too am overjoyed to find one brave man amongst you all,' he said. 'Tell me your name, Sir knight, ere we make our bargain.'

'I am Gawain, son of King Lot of Orkney, and nephew to royal Arthur,' was the answer. 'And here I swear by my knighthood to strike but one blow, and bravely to endure such another if you may strike it me a twelve-month hence.'

'Sir Gawain,' cried the Green Knight, 'overjoyed am I indeed that your hand shall strike this blow. Come now and deal the stroke; thereafter shall I tell you who I am and where you may find me. Take now the axe and let us see how well you can smite.'

'Gladly will I,' said Gawain, taking the axe in his hands and swinging it, while the Green Knight made ready by kneeling on the floor and drawing his long hair on to the crown of his head to lay bare his neck for the stroke. Putting all his strength into the blow, Gawain whirled up the axe and struck so hard that the keen blade cut through flesh and bone and set the sparks flying from the stone paving, while the Green Knight's head leapt from his shoulders and went rolling across the floor.

But the knight neither faltered nor fell; swiftly he sprang forward with hands outstretched, caught up his head and, turning with it held in his hand by the hair, mounted upon the waiting horse. Then, riding easily as if nothing had happened, he turned his face towards Gawain and said: 'See to it that you keep your oath and seek me out a year hence. I am the Knight of the Green Chapel, and as such men know me in the north. Through Wales shall you seek me, and in the Forest of Wirral; and you will not fail to find me there if you be not a coward and a breaker of your knightly word.'

With that he wheeled his horse and galloped out of the door, the sparks flying up round his horse's hooves, and away into the distance, his head still held in his hand, swinging easily by the hair.

But all at the feast sat astonished beyond words at this strange adventure, and it was a little while before the hall was filled once more with laughter and the joy of that festal season.

The year went by full swiftly – the trees grew green with spring; the leaves, fading through the bright summer days, turned to red and gold in the early autumn – and upon Michaelmas Day King Arthur held a feast at Caerleon with many of his knights in honour of Sir Gawain, who must on the morrow set forth upon his dreadful quest. Ywain and Agravaine and Erec were there; Launcelot and Lionel and Lucan the Good; Sir Bors and Sir Bedivere and Baldwin the lord bishop; Arthur and Guinevere to bless him and wish him God-speed. Gawain donned his armour, curved and shining and inlaid with gold; he girt his sword to his side and took the Green Knight's axe in his hand; then he mounted upon Gringalet, his war-horse, and rode into the forests of South Wales, the shield held before him with the device of the Pentangle, the five-pointed Star of Logres, emblazoned in the midst.

So Sir Gawain set out, and rode through the realm of Logres, seeking for no joy but a deadly danger at the end of his quest. After many days he came into the wild lands of North Wales, and fared through lonely valleys and deep forests, forced often to sleep out under the stars by night, and to do battle by day with robbers and wild men.

Grim winter had closed upon him when he came to the northern sea, left the islands of Anglesey upon his left, and came by Clwyd to the Holy Head, near Saint Winifred's Well on the shore of the wide River Dee. Near to the mouth he forded the stream at low tide, and came across the desolate sands into the wild Forest of Wirral. Here were many more robbers and evil men, lying in wait by forest path and lonely stream, by rocky defile and by green valley – and he must fight with all who stayed him.

Everywhere he went he asked tidings of a Green Knight and of a Chapel also of Green near which was his dwelling, but none in the forest could help him in his quest. Only a brave knight could have passed that way, and Gawain endured all – foes to overcome, and the bitter weather of mid-winter.

On Christmas Eve he rode upon Gringalet through marsh and mire, and prayed that he might find shelter. And on a sudden he came through open parkland to a fine castle set on a little hill above a deep valley where flowed a wide stream. A fair lawn lay in front of it, and many great oak trees on either side; there was a moat before the castle, and a low palisade of wood.

'Now God be thanked,' said Sir Gawain, 'that I have come to this fair dwelling for Christmas, and may He grant me to find an honourable welcome herein … Good sir!' he cried to the porter who came to the great gate when he knocked. 'Grant me entrance, I pray you, and tell the lord of this castle that I am a knight of King Arthur's court passing this way upon a quest.'

With a kindly smile the porter opened the gate, and Gawain rode over the drawbridge and into the courtyard. And there were squires and serving-men waiting who helped him to alight, led Gringalet away to the stable, and brought Gawain into a goodly hall where a fire burned brightly and the lord of the castle came forth from his chamber to greet his guest, saying: 'Welcome to my dwelling, Sir knight. All that I have is here at your service, and you shall be my honoured guest for as long as it shall please you to remain in this castle.'

'I thank you, noble sir,' said Gawain. 'May God bless you for your hospitality.' With that they clasped hands as good friends should; and Gawain looked upon the knight who greeted him so warmly, and thought what a fine warrior that castle had as its lord. For he was a tall man and broad of shoulder, with an open, honest face tanned red by the sun, with red hair and beard, a firm hand-clasp, a free stride, and a straightforward speech: just such a man as was born to be a leader of valiant men and a lord over wide estates.

The squires led Gawain next to a fair chamber in the keep, where they helped him to lay aside his armour, and clad him in rich, flowing robes lined softly with fur. Then they led him back to the hall and set him in a chair near to the fire, beside the lord of the castle. They brought in the tables then, set them upon trestles, covered them with fair white cloths, set thereon salt cellars and spoons of silver, then brought in the dishes and the goblets of wine. The lord of the castle drank to Sir Gawain, and rejoiced with all his followers that chance had brought so far-famed a knight to his lonely dwelling.

When the meal was ended the two knights went together to the chapel of the castle, where the chaplain celebrated Evensong and the whole service for Christmas Eve.

Then the knight brought Sir Gawain into a comely closet and sat him in a chair by the fire. And there the lady of the castle came to visit him, accompanied by her handmaidens – a very lovely lady, fairer even than Queen Guinevere. So the evening passed in jest and joy, and they brought Gawain to his room with bright tapers, set a goblet of hot spiced wine at his bedside, and left him there to his rest.

Three days were spent in feasting and in Christmas rejoicings – dancing and carol-singing, and much merriment. And even the lady of the castle sat by Gawain, and sang to him and talked with him, and attended to his comfort.

'Tarry with me longer,' said the lord of the castle on the evening of the fourth day. 'For while I live I shall be held the worthier because so brave and courteous a knight as Sir Gawain has been my guest.'

'I thank you, good sir,' answered Gawain, 'but I must away tomorrow on my high quest. For I must be at the Green Chapel upon the New Year's Day, and I would rather keep mine oath than be ruler of all this land. Moreover, as yet I have found none who can instruct me as to where the Green Chapel is.'

The lord of the castle laughed happily. 'This is indeed good news!' he cried. 'Here then you may stay until the very day of your quest's ending. For not two hours' ride from this castle you shall find the Green Chapel – a man of mine shall bring you to it upon the first day of the new year.'

Then Gawain was glad, and he too laughed joyously. 'I thank you, sir, for this news – and greatly also for your kindness. Now that my quest is achieved, I will dwell here in all joy and do what you will.'

'Then these three days,' said the lord of the castle, 'I will ride out hunting in the forest. But you, who have travelled far and endured many things, shall abide in my castle and rest at your ease. And my wife shall attend on you, and entertain you with her company when I am out hunting.'

'I thank you indeed,' said Gawain. 'And in no other wise could I pass with greater joy the three days before my meeting with the Green Knight.'

'Well,' said the lord of the castle, 'so let it be. And as this yet is the festive season of game and jest, let us make a merry bargain together, I vowing each day to give you whatever I may win in the wood, and you giving in exchange anything that may come to you here in the castle. Let us swear to make this exchange, for worse or for better, whatever may happen.'

'With all my heart,' laughed Gawain. And so the oath was sworn.

Next morning the lord of the castle hunted the deer

through the forests of Wirral and Delamere; and many a hart and hind fell to his keen arrows.

But Gawain slept long in a soft bed hung about with curtains, and dreamt of many things 'twixt waking and sleeping, until the lady of the castle, stepping silently as a sunbeam, came and sat upon his bed and talked with him merrily. Long they spoke together, and many words of love did the lady utter; but Gawain turned them all with jest and courtesy, as a true knight should who speaks with the lady of his host.

'Now God save you, fair sir,' she said at length, 'and reward you for your merry words. But that you are really Sir Gawain I misdoubt me greatly!'

'Wherefore do you doubt?' asked the knight anxiously, fearing that he had failed in some point of courtesy.

'So true a knight as Gawain,' answered the lady, 'and one so gentle and courteous unto damsels would never have tarried so long with a lady and not begged a kiss of her in parting.'

'Faith, fair lady,' said Gawain, 'and you bid me to it, I will indeed ask a kiss of you; but a true knight asks not otherwise, for fear to displease you.'

So the lady kissed him sweetly, and blessed him and departed; and Gawain rose from his bed and called for the chamberlain to clothe him. And thereafter he ate and drank, and passed his day quietly in the castle until the lord of it came home in the grey evening, bearing the spoils of the chase.

'What think you of this game, Sir knight?' he cried. 'I deserve thanks for my skill as a huntsman, do I not, for all of this is yours, according to our bargain!'

'I thank you,' answered Gawain, 'and I take the gift as we agreed. And I will give to you all that I won within these walls.' And with that he put his hands on the lord of the castle's shoulders and kissed him, saying: 'Take here my spoils, for I have won nothing but this. If more had been mine, as freely would I have given it to you.'

'It is good,' said his host, 'and much do I thank you for it. Yet would I like to know whence came your kiss, and how did you win it?'

'Not so,' answered Gawain, 'that was no part of the bargain!' And thereupon they laughed merrily and sat down to a fine dinner.

Next morning the lord of the castle went forth down the hillside and along the deep valley-bottoms to seek out and slay the wild boar in the marshes.

But Gawain abode in his bed, and the lady came once more to sit by him; and ever she strove to wheedle him into speaking to her words of love unseemly for the lady of a Knight. But Gawain the courteous turned all into jest, and defended himself so well by his wit that he won no more than two kisses, given by the lady ere she left him laughing.

'And now, Sir Gawain,' said the lord of the castle when he came home that night and laid the boar's head at his feet. 'Here is my spoil of the day, which I give you according to our bargain. Now, what have you won to give me in exchange?'

'I thank you,' said Gawain, 'for your just dealing in this game. As truly will I give you all that I have gained this day.'

Thereat he took the lord of the castle by the shoulders and gave him two kisses, saying: 'Now are we quits – for this and no more have I got me to-day.'

'By St Giles,' laughed the lord of the castle, 'you will be rich in a short time if we drive such bargains!' Then they went to the feast, and sat late over their meat and wine, while the lady strove ever to please Gawain, making fair, secret glances at him which, for his honour, he must not return.

The morrow would be the last day of the year. Gawain was eager to ride forth in quest of the Green Knight; but the lord of the castle stayed him with hospitable words.

'I swear by mine honour as a true knight that upon New Year's Day you shall come to the Green Chapel long ere the hour of noon. So stay in your bed to-morrow and rest in my castle. I will up with morning and ride to hunt the fox; so let us make once again our bargain to exchange all the winnings that may be ours to-morrow. For twice have I tried you and found you true; but the next is the third time, and that shall be the best.'

So once more they swore the oath, and while the lord of the castle went forth with his huntsmen and his pack of music-mouthed hounds, Gawain lay asleep, dreaming of the terrible meeting with the Green Knight so close before him. Presently the lady came in, blithe as a bird; she flung up the window so that the clear, frosty sunshine streamed into the room, roused Gawain from his slumbers and claimed of him a kiss.

She was fairer than the sunshine itself that morning, her hair falling each side of her lovely face, and her neck whiter than the snow gleaming between the fur of her gown. Sweetly she kissed Gawain and chid him for a sluggard.

'Surely you are a very man of ice that you take but one kiss! Or is it that you have a lady waiting for you in Camelot?'

'Not so,' answered Gawain gravely. 'No lady yet has my love. But it may not be yours, for you have a lord already – a far nobler knight than ever I shall be!'

'But this one day we may love,' she said. 'Surely it may be so? Then all my life-days I may remember that Gawain held me in his arms.'

'Nay, for the sake of mine oath of knighthood and the glory of Logres, I may not do so, for such were shame indeed.'

Then she blamed him and besought him, but ever he turned aside her words courteously, and ever held true to his honour as a knight of Logres should. At last she sighed sweetly, and kissed him a second time, saying: 'Sir Gawain, you are a true knight, the noblest ever. So give me but a gift whereby to remember you, that by thinking of my knight I may lessen my mourning.'

'Alas,' said Gawain, 'I have nothing to give. For I travel without baggage on this dangerous quest.'

'Then I will give you this green lace from my girdle,' said the lady. 'Wear that for my sake at least.'

'It may not be so,' answered Gawain, 'for I cannot be your knight and wear your favour.'

'It is but a little thing,' she said, 'and you may wear it hidden. Take it, I pray you, for it is a magic lace and while a man wears it he may not be slain, not even by all the magic upon earth. But I charge you to hide it, and tell not my lord.'

This proved too great a temptation for Gawain, and, mindful of his ordeal with the Green Knight next day, he took the lace and promised never to reveal it. Then the lady kissed him for the third time, and went quickly away.

That evening the lord of the castle came home from the hunt bearing with him the skin of one fox. In the bright hall where the fire shone warmly and the tables were all laid richly for dinner, Gawain met him merrily.

'I come with my winnings, and I will be the first giver this night!' he cried gaily; and with that he kissed him solemnly three times.

'By my faith,' cried the lord of the castle, 'you are a good merchant indeed; you give me three such kisses – and I have only a foul fox-skin to give you in return!'

Then with laughter and jests they sat down to the feast, and were merrier that night than on any of the others. But

Gawain spoke no word of the green lace which the lady had given him.

The day of the New Year came in with storm: bitterly the winds howled and the sleet lashed against the window-pane, and Gawain, who had slept but little, rose at the first light. He clothed himself warmly and buckled on his armour, setting the green lace about his waist in hope that its magic might protect him. Then he went forth into the courtyard; the squires brought out Gringalet, well fed and well groomed, and helped him to mount.

'Farewell,' he said to the lord of the castle. 'I thank you for your hospitality, and pray Heaven to bless you. If I might live a while longer I would reward you for your kindness; but greatly I fear that I shall not see another sun.'

The drawbridge was let down, the gate flung wide, and Gawain rode out of the castle, with a squire to guide him. Through the bitter dawning they rode, beneath trees dripping drearily, and across meadows where the wind moaned as it bit them to the bone, and they came to a great valley with cliffs at one side of it, all filled with mist.

'Sir,' said the squire, 'go no further, I beg of you. Near here dwells the Green Knight, a terrible and a cruel man. There is none so fierce or so strong in this land – and no man may stand against him. Over yonder at the Green Chapel it is ever his custom to stay all who pass by, and fight with them, and kill them – for none can escape him. Flee away now – and I will not tell ever that you fled for fear of the terrible Green Knight.'

'I thank you,' said Gawain, 'but I must go forward. I would be a coward and unworthy of knighthood if I fled away now. Therefore, whether I like it or not I must go forward … And God knows well how to save His servants if so He wills.'

'Well then,' said the squire, 'your death be your own doing. Go down this path by the cliff, into the deep valley, and upon the left hand, beyond the water, you will find the Green Chapel. Now farewell, noble Gawain, for I dare not come with you further.'

Down the path rode Gawain, and came to the bottom of the valley. No chapel could he see, but only the rugged cliff above him, and high, desolate banks in the distance. But at length he saw, under the dripping trees, a low green mound beside the rushing stream; and he heard a sound as of a scythe upon a grindstone coming from a deep hollow in that mound.

'Ah,' said Gawain. 'This must be the Green Chapel! A very devil's oratory it is, and green indeed – a chapel of mischance! And within it I hear the knight himself, sharpening a weapon to smite me this day. Alas that I must perish at his hands in this cursed spot ... Yet will I go on boldly, for my duty is so to do.'

Gawain sprang from his horse and strode down to the streamside.

'Who waits here,' he cried, 'to keep tryst with me? I am Gawain, who have come to the Green Chapel as I vowed.'

'Wait but a little,' came a mighty voice out of the hollow beneath the mound. 'When my weapon is sharp, you shall have that which I promised you!'

Presently the Green Knight came out with a new, shining axe in his hand. He was as terrible as ever, with his green face and his green hair, as he strode down the bank and leapt over the wide stream.

'You are welcome, Gawain!' he cried in his great voice. 'Now will I repay the stroke you dealt me at Camelot – and none shall come between us in this lonely valley. Now off with your helmet, and make ready for the blow!'

Then Gawain did as he was bidden, bending his head forward, with his neck bare to the stroke.

'Make ready to strike,' he said quietly to the Green Knight, 'for here I shall stand and do nought to stay the blow.'

The Green Knight swung his axe round so that it whistled, and aimed a terrible stroke with the sharp blade of it; and try how he might, Gawain flinched at the sound of it.

'Ha!' grunted the Green Knight, lowering his axe and leaning on the handle of it. 'You are surely not Gawain the brave, thus to fear even the whistle of the blade! When you struck off my head in King Arthur's hall I never flinched from your blow.'

'I shrank once,' said Gawain, 'but I shall not a second time – even when *my* head falls to the ground, which I cannot replace as you have yours! Come now, strike quickly; I will not stay you again.'

'Have at you then!' cried the Green Knight, whirling his axe. He smote once more, and once more stayed his hand ere the sharp blade drew blood. But Gawain stirred not a jot, nor trembled in any limb. 'Now you are filled with courage once more,' he cried, 'and so I may smite bravely a brave man. Hold aside your hood a little further; I am about to strike my hardest.'

'Strike away,' said Gawain. 'Why do you talk so much? Are you perhaps afraid thus to smite a defenceless man?'

'Then here is the blow I promised!' cried the Green Knight, swinging his axe for the third time. And now he struck truly, yet aimed with such care that the blade only parted the skin at the side of his neck.

But when Gawain had felt the wound and the blood over his shoulders, he sprang away in an instant, put on his helmet, drew his sword, set his shield before him and said to the Green Knight: 'Now I have borne the blow, and if you strike again it is beyond our bargain and I may defend myself, striking stroke for stroke!'

The Green Knight stood leaning on his axe. 'Gawain,' he said, all the fierceness gone out of his voice, 'you have indeed borne the blow – and no other will I strike you. I hold you released of all claims now. If I had wished it, I might have struck you a crueller stroke, and smitten your head off as you smote off mine. The first blow and the second that struck you not – these were for promises truly kept, for the one kiss and the two kisses that my wife gave you in the castle, and you truly rendered to me. But the third time you failed, and therefore had the wound of me: you gave me the three kisses, but not the green lace. Oh, well, I know all that passed between you – she tempted you by my will. Gawain, I hold you to be the noblest, the most faultless knight in all the wide world. Had you yielded to dishonour and shamed your knighthood – then would your head be lying now at my feet. As for the lace, you hid it but for love of your life – and that is a little sin, and for it I pardon you.'

'I am ashamed,' said Gawain, handing him the green lace. 'For cowardice and covetousness I betrayed my oath of knighthood. Cut off my head, Sir knight, for I am indeed unworthy of the Round Table.'

'Come now!' cried the Green Knight, laughing merrily, so that Gawain knew him indeed to be the lord of the castle. 'You have borne your penance, and are quite absolved and forgiven. Take and keep this green lace in memory of this adventure; and return to my castle and end the festival in joy.'

'I must back to Camelot,' said Gawain. 'I may not bide longer. But tell me, noble sir, how comes this enchantment?

Who are you that ride in Green and die not when beheaded? How come you to dwell, a noble knight in a fine castle, and also to strike axe-blows, the Green Knight of the Green Chapel?'

'My name is Sir Bernlak, the Knight of the Lake,' answered he. 'And the enchantment comes from Nimue, the Lady of the Lake, the favoured of Merlin. She sent me to Camelot, to test the truth of the renown that is spread abroad concerning the valour of the Knights of the Round Table, and the worth of Logres.'

Then the two knights embraced one another and parted with blessings. Gawain rode back swiftly through the Forest of Wirral, and after many more adventures he came to Camelot, where King Arthur welcomed him, marvelled at his tale, and set him with honour in his place at the Round Table. And of all the knights who ever sat there, few indeed were so worthy as Gawain.

ROGER LANCELYN GREEN

From a retelling of *The Adventures of Robin Hood*

(FIRST PRINTED ABOUT 1500)

Although there was so much to do in Sherwood, where nearly all of the food they ate had to be hunted, trapped, or shot, and they were always in danger of surprise from the Sheriff of Nottingham, Sir Guy of Gisborne, and the rest, Robin Hood occasionally found time hang heavy on his hands.

On one such occasion he and Little John were walking by the high road to Nottingham where it runs through the forest, when they saw a Butcher with his cart of meat come jogging along on his way to market.

'Yonder comes a proud fellow,' said Little John, 'who fancies himself a master with the quarter-staff. He comes through the forest twice every week, and nothing gives him greater pleasure than the chance to thrash someone with his big stick.'

'Twice a week,' said Robin, 'and he has never paid any toll to us! It is long since I fought with the quarter-staff, except in friendly wise with you or Friar Tuck. I'll go and have words with this Butcher – and see if blows come of it!'

'I'll wager a piece of gold he beats you!' said Little John.

'Done!' smiled Robin, and, laying aside his weapons, he cut himself a good oak staff and strode down the road until he met the Butcher.

'Now then!' cried the Butcher sharply, as Robin laid a hand on the horse's bridle. 'What do you want, you impudent fellow?'

'You have haunted these ways long enough,' said Robin sternly, 'without paying the due toll that you owe to me! Come, sirrah, pay up at once!'

'And who do you think you are?' cried the Butcher. 'A Forest Guard or what? I serve the good Sheriff of Nottingham, and he'll make your hide smart for this, after I've tanned you myself, and broken your head into the bargain.'

'I am of Robin Hood's company,' was the reply, 'and if you will not pay tribute in gold, get down out of that cart and pay it in blows.'

'Right willingly!' answered the Butcher, and, jumping out of his cart, he charged at Robin, whirling his staff about his head.

Then there was as good a fight, and as pretty a play of skill with the quarter-staves as ever one might see; but the long and short of it was that though Robin suffered a sore clout over one eye, in the end he brought the Butcher to the ground with a last stunning blow.

'The piece of gold is yours,' said Little John coming up.

'This is a fine fellow,' said Robin as the Butcher sat up and looked about him. 'Give him wine, Little John. I'll warrant his head is ringing even louder than mine!'

'That it is!' groaned the Butcher. 'By the Mass, you are a bonny fighter. I think you must be Robin Hood himself, and no other!'

'That I am indeed!' said Robin.

'Then I think no shame at being beaten,' said the Butcher with a sigh of relief. 'And I'll willingly pay any toll you may ask of me.'

'No, no,' answered Robin, 'you've paid toll enough with that broken head of yours. Come now to our camp and see what good cheer we can make for you.'

When the meal was over, Robin said suddenly to the Butcher: 'Good friend, I have a mind to be a butcher myself. Will you sell me your horse, your cart and the meat now on it for ten pounds – and stay here in the forest with us?'

'Right willingly,' answered the Butcher, and the deal was made.

'You go into danger for no good cause,' said Will Scarlet doubtfully as Robin donned the Butcher's garb.

'Nevertheless I go,' answered Robin. 'I grow weary of this unchanging forest life – and also I would have news of what passes in the world outside. It is said that King Richard is a prisoner somewhere in Europe, and Prince John makes no effort to find and ransom him. I would know more of this. Never fear; not even the Sheriff will know me!'

With that Robin fixed a black patch over one eye, climbed into the cart and went rattling away through the forest and on to the Nottingham road once more. In the afternoon he came to Nottingham, drew up his cart in the market-place and began to cry: 'Meat to sell! Fresh meat to sell! Fresh meat a penny a pound!'

Then all that saw and heard him at his trade said that he had not been a Butcher for long, since at that price he could not expect to earn a living. But the thrifty housewives gathered round him eagerly, for never had they bought such cheap meat before.

Among them came the Sheriff's wife, and seeing that the meat was good, fresh and tender, and most unusually cheap, she invited the Butcher to bring his cart up to the Sheriff's house, sell to her what was left, and then sup with her and the Sheriff.

Robin accepted with delight, and as evening fell he stabled his horse and empty cart in the Sheriff's stables and sat down to dine as an honoured guest at the Sheriff's board.

At dinner that night Robin learned many things which he wished to know. He heard that King Richard was in truth a prisoner, but that Prince John was giving out that he was dead so that he himself might become King.

'But a pestilent fellow called Blondel,' added the Sheriff, 'has gone in search of Richard. He is a minstrel, and so can pass unmolested through the most hostile lands. May the plague take him speedily!'

'Will the great Barons and the Lords and Knights accept Prince John as King?' asked Robin.

'There the trouble lies,' said the Sheriff, shaking his head sadly. 'Many, like the Earl of Chester, oppose him. But many more will be won over …'

Later in the evening the Sheriff asked Robin if he had any horned beasts that he could sell to him – meaning live cattle rather than joints of meat.

'Yes, that I have, good Master Sheriff,' answered Robin. 'I have two or three hundred of them, and many an acre of good free land, if you please to see it. I can let it to you with as good a right as ever my father made to me.'

'The horned beasts interest me most,' said the Sheriff. 'Good Master Butcher, I will come with you on the morrow and make you a right fair offer for the whole herd, if they please me.'

Robin Hood slept well and comfortably in the Sheriff's house, and ate a fine breakfast in the morning before they set off together, accompanied by only two men, to see the horned beasts.

The Sheriff seemed in high spirits when they started out, jesting and laughing with Robin. But presently as they went deeper and deeper into Sherwood Forest he grew more and more silent.

'Have we much further to go, friend Butcher?' he asked at last. 'God protect us this day from a man they call Robin Hood!'

'The outlaw, you mean?' asked Robin. 'I know him well, and have often shot at the butts with him. I am no bad archer myself, if it comes to that; indeed, I dare swear that Robin Hood himself can shoot no better than I.'

'Know you where he lies hid in Sherwood?' asked the Sheriff eagerly.

'Right well,' replied Robin, 'even his most secret place of hiding.'

'I would pay you well if you were to bring me thither,' said the Sheriff.

'That will I do,' answered Robin. 'But hist now; we draw near the place where the horned beasts are to be found. Stay a moment, while I wind my horn so that the herdsmen may drive them hither.'

So saying Robin set his horn to his mouth and blew three blasts. Then he drew a little behind the Sheriff and waited.

Presently there was a crackling in the thicket, and a great troop of red deer came into view, tossing their antlers proudly.

'How like you my horned beasts, Master Sheriff?' asked Robin. 'They be fat and fair to see!'

'Good fellow, I wish I were far from here,' said the Sheriff uncomfortably. 'I like not your company ...'

'We will have better company anon,' Robin remarked with a smile, and even as he spoke out of the thicket came Little John, followed by Will Scarlet, Much, Reynolde, William of Goldsbrough, and many another of the outlaws of Sherwood.

'What is your will, good master?' said Little John. 'Come, tell us how you fared in Nottingham, and whether you did good trade as a butcher?'

'Fine trade indeed,' answered Robin, pulling off his eye-patch and the rest of his disguise. 'And see, I have brought with me the Sheriff of Nottingham to dine with us this day.'

'He is right welcome,' said Little John. 'And I am sure he will pay well for his dinner.'

'Well indeed,' laughed Robin. 'For he has brought much money with him to buy three hundred head of deer from me. And even now he offered me a great sum to lead him to our secret glade.'

'By the Rood,' said the Sheriff, shaking with terror, 'had I guessed who you were, a thousand pounds would not have brought me into Sherwood!'

'I would that you had a thousand pounds to bring you *out* of Sherwood,' said Robin. 'Now then, bind him and his men, blindfold them, and lead them to dinner. When we reach the glade we can see what they have brought us – and by then I will have earned every penny, ha, ha!'

So the Sheriff and his two trembling followers were blindfolded and led by the secret paths to the hidden glen, and Robin feasted them there full well. But afterwards he bade Little John spread his cloak upon the ground and pour into it all the money the Sheriff had brought with him, and the sum came to nearly five hundred pounds.

'We will keep the three good horses also,' said Robin, 'and let Master Sheriff and his two men walk back to Nottingham – for the good of their health. But let Maid Marian send a present of needlework to the Sheriff's lady, for she entertained me well at dinner and set fair dishes before me.'

Then the Sheriff and his two men were blindfolded once more and taken back to the Nottingham road, and there Robin bade them farewell.

'You shall not defy me for much longer, Robin Hood,' cried the Sheriff, shaking his fist at Robin in farewell. 'I'll come against you with a great force, depend upon it, and hang every man of you from the trees by this road-side. And your head shall rot over Nottingham gate.'

'When next you come to visit me in Sherwood,' said Robin quietly, 'you shall not get away on such easy terms. Come when you will, and the more of you the merrier, and I'll send you all packing back to Nottingham in your shirts!'

Then he left them and returned to the secret glade where the Butcher, whose name was Gilbert-of-the-White-Hand, was waiting for him.

'Here are your cart and horses back again, good Master Butcher,' said Robin. 'I have had a fine holiday selling meat in your stead, but we must not play too many of such pranks.'

'By the Mass,' swore Gilbert the Butcher, 'I'll sell meat no longer, if you will have me as one of your merry men here in the greenwood. I cannot shoot with any skill, for see how my left hand was burnt white with fire when I once shot a deer to feed my starving family. But you have had some little proof of how I can smite with the quarter-staff.'

'Proof enough, good Gilbert,' cried Robin. 'I am right glad to welcome you as one of us … Come, Friar Tuck, propound the oath to him. And then to dinner, and we'll all drink to the health of our new companion, Gilbert-of-the-White-Hand, the jolly Butcher of Nottingham!'

CHARLES DICKENS

From *A Christmas Carol*

(1843)

Scrooge took his melancholy dinner in his usual melancholy tavern; and having read all the newspapers, and beguiled the rest of the evening with his banker's-book, went home to bed. He lived in chambers which had once belonged to his deceased partner. They were a gloomy suite of rooms, in a lowering pile of building up a yard … It was old enough now, and dreary enough, for nobody lived in it but Scrooge, the other rooms being all let out as offices. The yard was so dark that even Scrooge, who knew its every stone, was fain to grope with his hands. The fog and frost so hung about the black old gateway of the house that it seemed as if the Genius of the Weather sat in mournful meditation on the threshold.

Now, it is a fact that there was nothing at all particular

about the knocker on the door, except that it was very large. It is also a fact that Scrooge had seen it night and morning during his whole residence in that place; also that Scrooge had as little of what is called fancy about him as any man in the City of London, even including – which is a bold word – the corporation, aldermen, and livery. Let it also be borne in mind that Scrooge had not bestowed one thought on Marley, since his last mention of his seven-years' dead partner that afternoon. And then let any man explain to me, if he can, how it happened that Scrooge, having his key in the lock of the door, saw in the knocker, without its undergoing any intermediate process of change, not a knocker, but Marley's face.

Marley's face. It was not in impenetrable shadow, as the other objects in the yard were, but had a dismal light about it, like a bad lobster in a dark cellar. It was not angry or ferocious, but looked at Scrooge as Marley used to look: with ghostly spectacles turned up upon its ghostly forehead. The hair was curiously stirred, as if by breath or hot air; and though the eyes were wide open, they were perfectly motionless. That, and its livid colour, made it horrible; but its horror seemed to be in spite of the face and beyond its control, rather than a part of its own expression.

As Scrooge looked fixedly at this phenomenon, it was a knocker again.

To say that he was not startled, or that his blood was not conscious of a terrible sensation to which it had been a stranger from infancy, would be untrue. But he put his hand upon the key he had relinquished, turned it sturdily, walked in, and lighted his candle.

He *did* pause, with a moment's irresolution, before he shut the door; and he *did* look cautiously behind it first, as if he half-expected to be terrified with the sight of Marley's pigtail sticking out into the hall. But there was nothing on the back of the door, except the screws and nuts that held the knocker on, so he said 'Pooh, pooh!' and closed it with a bang.

The sound resounded through the house like thunder. Every room above, and every cask in the wine-merchant's cellars below, appeared to have a separate peal of echoes of its own. Scrooge was not a man to be frightened by echoes. He fastened the door, and walked across the hall, and up the stairs, slowly too, trimming his candle as he went.

You may talk vaguely about driving a coach-and-six up a good old flight of stairs, or through a bad young Act of Parliament; but I mean to say you might have got a hearse up that staircase, and taken it broadwise, with the splinter-bar towards the wall and the door towards the balustrades – and done it easy. There was plenty of width for that, and room to spare; which is perhaps the reason why Scrooge thought he saw a locomotive hearse going on before him in the gloom. Half a dozen gas-lamps out of the street wouldn't have lighted the entry too well, so you may suppose that it was pretty dark with Scrooge's dip.

Up Scrooge went, not caring a button for that: darkness is cheap, and Scrooge liked it. But before he shut his heavy door, he walked through his rooms to see that all was right. He had just enough recollection of the face to desire to do that.

Sitting-room, bed-room, lumber-room. All as they should be. Nobody under the table, nobody under the sofa; a small fire in the grate; spoon and basin ready; and the little saucepan of gruel (Scrooge had a cold in his head) upon the hob. Nobody under the bed; nobody in the closet; nobody in his dressing-gown, which was hanging up in a suspicious attitude against the wall. Lumber-room as usual. Old fireguard, old shoes, two fish-baskets, washing-stand on three legs, and a poker.

Quite satisfied, he closed his door, and locked himself in; double-locked himself in, which was not his custom. Thus secured against surprise, he took off his cravat; put on his dressing-gown and slippers, and his night-cap; and sat down before the fire to take his gruel.

It was a very low fire indeed; nothing on such a bitter night. He was obliged to sit close to it, and brood over it, before he could extract the least sensation of warmth from such a handful of fuel. The fire-place was an old one, built by some Dutch merchant long ago, and paved all round with quaint Dutch tiles, designed to illustrate the Scriptures ... hundreds of figures, to attract his thoughts; and yet that face of Marley, seven years dead, came like the ancient Prophet's rod, and swallowed up the whole. If each smooth tile had been a blank at first, with power to shape some picture on its surface from the disjointed fragments of his thoughts, there would have been a copy of old Marley's head on every one.

'Humbug!' said Scrooge, and walked across the room.

After several turns, he sat down again. As he threw his head back in the chair, his glance happened to rest upon a bell, a disused bell, that hung in the room, and communicated for some purpose now forgotten with a chamber in the highest storey of the building. It was with great astonishment, and with a strange, inexplicable dread, that as he looked, he saw this bell begin to swing. It swung so softly in the outset that it scarcely made a sound; but soon it rang out loudly, and so did every bell in the house.

This might have lasted half a minute, or a minute, but it seemed an hour. The bells ceased as they had begun, together. They were succeeded by a clanking noise, deep down below; as if some person were dragging a heavy chain over the casks in the wine-merchant's cellar. Scrooge then remembered to have heard that ghosts in haunted houses were described as dragging chains.

The cellar-door flew open with a booming sound, and then he heard the noise much louder, on the floors below; then coming up the stairs; then coming straight towards his door.

'It's humbug still!' said Scrooge. 'I won't believe it.'

His colour changed though, when, without a pause, it came on through the heavy door, and passed into the room before his eyes. Upon its coming in, the dying flame leaped up, as though it cried 'I know him! Marley's Ghost!' and fell again.

The same face: the very same. Marley in his pigtail, usual waistcoat, tights, and boots; the tassels on the latter bristling, like his pigtail, and his coat-skirts, and the hair upon his head. The chain he drew was clasped about his middle. It was long, and wound about him like a tail; and it was made (for Scrooge observed it closely) of cash-boxes, keys, padlocks, ledgers, deeds, and heavy purses wrought in steel. His body was transparent, so that Scrooge, observing him, and looking through his waistcoat, could see the two buttons on his coat behind.

Scrooge had often heard it said that Marley had no bowels, but he had never believed it until now.

No, nor did he believe it even now. Though he looked the phantom through and through, and saw it standing before him; though he felt the chilling influence of its death-cold eyes; and marked the very texture of the folded kerchief bound about its head and chin, which wrapper he had not observed before; he was still incredulous, and fought against his senses.

'How now!' said Scrooge, caustic and cold as ever. 'What do you want with me?'

'Much!' – Marley's voice, no doubt about it.

'Who are you?'

'Ask me who I *was*.'

'Who *were* you then?' said Scrooge, raising his voice. 'You're particular – for a shade.' He was going to say '*to* a shade,' but substituted this, as more appropriate.

'In life I was your partner, Jacob Marley.'

'Can you – can you sit down?' asked Scrooge, looking doubtfully at him.

'I can.'

'Do it then.'

Scrooge asked the question, because he didn't know whether a ghost so transparent might find himself in a condition to take a chair; and felt that in the event of its being impossible, it might involve the necessity of an embarrassing explanation. But the ghost sat down on the opposite side of the fire-place, as if he were quite used to it.

'You don't believe in me,' observed the Ghost.

'I don't,' said Scrooge.

'What evidence would you have of my reality beyond that of your senses?'

'I don't know,' said Scrooge.

'Why do you doubt your senses?'

'Because,' said Scrooge, 'a little thing affects them. A slight disorder of the stomach makes them cheats. You may be an undigested bit of beef, a blot of mustard, a crumb of cheese, a fragment of an underdone potato. There's more of gravy than of grave about you, whatever you are!'

Scrooge was not much in the habit of cracking jokes, nor did he feel, in his heart, by any means waggish then. The truth is that he tried to be smart, as a means of distracting his own attention, and keeping down his terror; for the spectre's voice disturbed the very marrow in his bones ...

'You see this toothpick?' said Scrooge ...

'I do,' replied the Ghost.

'You are not looking at it,' said Scrooge.

'But I see it,' said the Ghost, 'notwithstanding.'

'Well!' returned Scrooge. 'I have but to swallow this, and be for the rest of my days persecuted by a legion of goblins, all of my own creation. Humbug, I tell you; humbug!'

At this, the spirit raised a frightful cry, and shook its chain with such a dismal and appalling noise that Scrooge held on tight to his chair, to save himself from falling in a swoon. But how much greater was his horror when the phantom, taking off the bandage round its head, as if it were too warm to wear in-doors, its lower jaw dropped down upon its breast!

Scrooge fell upon his knees, and clasped his hands before his face.

'Mercy!' he said. 'Dreadful apparition, why do you trouble me?'

'Man of the worldly mind,' replied the Ghost, 'do you believe in me or not?'

'I do,' said Scrooge. 'I must. But why do spirits walk the earth, and why do they come to me?'

'It is required of every man,' the Ghost returned, 'that the spirit within him should walk abroad among his fellow-men, and travel far and wide; and if that spirit goes not forth in life, it is condemned to do so after death. It is doomed to wander through the world – oh, woe is me! – and witness what it cannot share, but might have shared on earth, and turned to happiness!'

Again the spectre raised a cry, and shook its chain, and wrung its shadowy hands.

'You are fettered,' said Scrooge, trembling. 'Tell me why?'

'I wear the chain I forged in life,' replied the Ghost. 'I made it link by link, and yard by yard; I girded it on of my own free will, and of my own free will I wore it. Is its pattern strange to *you*?'

Scrooge trembled more and more.

'Or would you know,' pursued the Ghost, 'the weight and length of the strong coil you bear yourself? It was full as heavy and as long as this, seven Christmas Eves ago. You have laboured on it, since. It is a ponderous chain!'

Scrooge glanced about him on the floor, in the expectation of finding himself surrounded by some fifty or sixty fathoms of iron cable; but he could see nothing.

'Jacob,' he said, imploringly. 'Old Jacob Marley, tell me more. Speak comfort to me, Jacob.'

'I have none to give,' the Ghost replied. 'It comes from other regions, Ebenezer Scrooge, and is conveyed by other ministers, to other kinds of men. Nor can I tell you what I would. A very little more is all permitted to me. I cannot rest, I cannot stay, I cannot linger anywhere. My spirit never walked beyond our counting-house – mark me! – in life my spirit never roved beyond the narrow limits of our money-changing hole; and weary journeys lie before me!'

It was a habit with Scrooge, whenever he became thoughtful, to put his hands in his breeches pockets. Pondering on what the Ghost had said, he did so now, but without lifting up his eyes, or getting off his knees …

'But you were always a good man of business, Jacob,' faltered Scrooge, who now began to apply this to himself.

'Business!' cried the Ghost, wringing his hands again. 'Mankind was my business. The common welfare was my business; charity, mercy, forbearance and benevolence were, all, my business. The dealings of my trade were but a drop of water in the comprehensive ocean of my business!'

It held up its chain at arm's length, as if that were the cause of all its unavailing grief, and flung it heavily upon the ground again.

'At this time of the rolling year,' the spectre said, 'I suffer most. Why did I walk through crowds of fellow-beings with my eyes turned down, and never raise them to that blessed Star which led the Wise Men to a poor abode? Were there no poor homes to which its light would have conducted *me*!'

Scrooge was very much dismayed to hear the spectre going on at this rate, and began to quake exceedingly.

'Hear me!' cried the Ghost. 'My time is nearly gone.'

'I will,' said Scrooge. 'But don't be hard upon me! Don't be flowery, Jacob! Pray!'

'How it is that I appear before you in a shape that you can see, I may not tell. I have sat invisible beside you many and many a day.'

It was not an agreeable idea. Scrooge shivered, and wiped the perspiration from his brow.

'That is no light part of my penance,' pursued the Ghost. 'I am here to-night to warn you that you have yet a chance and hope of escaping my fate. A chance and hope of my procuring, Ebenezer.'

'You were always a good friend to me,' said Scrooge. 'Thank'ee!'

'You will be haunted,' resumed the Ghost, 'by Three Spirits.'

Scrooge's countenance fell almost as low as the Ghost's had done.

'Is that the chance and hope you mentioned, Jacob?' he demanded, in a faltering voice.

'It is.'

'I – I think I'd rather not,' said Scrooge.

'Without their visits,' said the Ghost, 'you cannot hope to

shun the path I tread. Expect the first to-morrow, when the bell tolls One.'

'Couldn't I take 'em all at once, and have it over, Jacob?' hinted Scrooge.

'Expect the second on the next night at the same hour. The third upon the next night when the last stroke of Twelve has ceased to vibrate. Look to see me no more; and look that, for your own sake, you remember what has passed between us!'

When it had said these words, the spectre took its wrapper from the table and bound it round its head, as before. Scrooge knew this, by the smart sound its teeth made, when the jaws were brought together by the bandage. He ventured to raise his eyes again, and found his supernatural visitor confronting him in an erect attitude, with its chain wound over and about its arm.

The apparition walked backward from him; and at every step it took, the window raised itself a little, so that when the spectre reached it, it was wide open. It beckoned Scrooge to approach, which he did. When they were within two paces of each other, Marley's Ghost held up its hand, warning him to come no nearer. Scrooge stopped.

Not so much in obedience, as in surprise and fear: for on the raising of the hand, he became sensible of confused noises in the air; incoherent sounds of lamentation and regret; wailings inexpressibly sorrowful and self-accusatory. The spectre, after listening for a moment, joined in the mournful dirge; and floated out upon the bleak, dark night.

Scrooge followed to the window, desperate in his curiosity. He looked out.

The air was filled with phantoms, wandering hither and thither in restless haste, and moaning as they went. Every one of them wore chains like Marley's Ghost; some few (they might be guilty governments) were linked together; none were free. Many had been personally known to Scrooge in their lives. He had been quite familiar with one old ghost in a white waistcoat, with a monstrous iron safe attached to its ankle, who cried piteously at being unable to assist a wretched woman with an infant, whom it saw below, upon a door-step. The misery with them all was, clearly, that they sought to interfere, for good, in human matters, and had lost the power for ever.

Whether these creatures faded into mist, or mist enshrouded them, he could not tell. But they and their spirit voices faded together; and the night became as it had been when he walked home.

Scrooge closed the window, and examined the door by which the Ghost had entered. It was double-locked, as he had locked it with his own hands, and the bolts were undisturbed. He tried to say 'Humbug!' but stopped at the first syllable. And being, from the emotion he had undergone, or the fatigues of the day, or his glimpse of the Invisible World, or the dull conversation of the Ghost, or the lateness of the hour, much in need of repose, went straight to bed, without undressing, and fell asleep upon the instant.

HANS CHRISTIAN ANDERSEN

The Ugly Duckling

(1845)

It was so delightful in the country. The air was full of summer; the corn was yellow; the oats were ripe; the haystacks in the meadows looked like little hills of grass, and there the stork strutted about on his long red legs. All round the open fields were woods and forests, and within these were deep cool lakes. Yes, it was really delightful in the countryside. And there, in the bright sunshine, stood an old manor house surrounded by a moat. Great dock leaves grew from the wall as far down as the water; some of them so big that little children could stand upright underneath them. In their shade, you might think yourself in a tiny secret forest of your own.

This was where a duck sat on her nest and waited for her ducklings to hatch out. She was becoming rather tired of sitting there, though, for the ducklings took so long to come; as for visitors, she hardly ever had any; the other ducks preferred swimming in the moat to dropping in under the dock leaves for a chat.

But at last the eggs began to crack, one after another. 'Peep, peep!' The nest was full of little birds poking their heads from the shell.

'Quack, quack!' said the mother. 'Quick, quick!' So the little things came out as fast as they could, and stared all round their leafy green shelter; and their mother let them look as much as they liked, for green is good for the eyes.

'How big the world is!' the young ones said. And certainly they had much more space now than they had had inside the egg.

'Do you suppose that this is all the world, you foolish little creatures?' said their mother. 'Why – the world stretches out far beyond the other side of the garden, right into the parson's field. Though, to be sure, I have never been there myself. You *are* all here now, aren't you?' She got up from the nest. 'No, you're not. There's still the biggest egg. How much longer is it going to be? I'm really tired of this business, I can tell you.' And down she sat again.

'Well, how are things going?' asked an old duck, who had come to pay a call.

'This egg is taking a dreadfully long time,' said the mother duck. 'It just won't hatch! But do look at the others; they are the prettiest little ducklings I have ever seen, the living image of their father, too – that wretch, who never comes to visit me!'

'Let me look at the egg,' said the old duck. 'Ah! Take my word for it, that's a turkey's egg. I was once played the same trick, and the trouble I had with the young ones! Being turkeys, they were afraid of the water, and I *couldn't* get them to go in. I quacked and scolded, but it was no use. Let me see. Yes, that's a turkey's egg. Just let it be, and go off and teach the rest to swim.'

'Well, I'll sit on it a bit longer,' said the duck. 'As I have sat so long, I may as well finish off the job.'

'Oh, well, please yourself,' said the old duck, and she went away.

At last the big egg cracked. 'Peep, peep,' said the young one as he tumbled out. But how big and ugly he was! The mother looked at him. 'That's a terribly big duckling,' she thought. 'Can he be a turkey chick after all? Well, we shall soon find out; into the water he shall go, even if I have to push him in myself.'

The next day the weather was beautiful, and the mother duck came out with all her young ones and went down to the moat. Splash! In she went. 'Quack, quack!' she called, and one after another the ducklings plopped in. The water went over their heads, but they rose up again in a moment, and were soon swimming busily. Their feet moved of their own accord, and there they all were, out in the water – even the ugly grey one was swimming with them.

'No, that's no turkey,' the mother said. 'Look how well he uses his legs, and how straight he holds himself. He's my own child, no doubt about it. Really, he is quite handsome if you look at him properly. Quack, quack! Come along with me, children; I'll take you into the world and introduce you to the other farm birds; but mind you stay close to me, so that no one treads on you. And keep a careful look out for the cat.'

So they went into the poultry-yard. There was a hor-rible noise and commotion there, for two families were squabbling over the head of an eel – and then the cat got it after all.

'That's the way of the world,' said the mother duck. Her own beak watered a little, for she too would have liked the eel's head. 'Now, then, use your legs; hurry along and make a bow to the old duck over there! She is our most distinguished resident; her ancestors came from Spain, and, as you see, she has a piece of red cloth tied round her leg. That is something very special; it means that no one will get rid of her, and both man and beast must treat her with respect. Come along! Don't turn your toes in! A well-bred duckling walks with feet well apart, like father and mother. Now then! Make a bow and say "Quack!"'

The little birds did as they were told; but the other ducks in the yard looked at them and said quite loudly: 'Now we shall have to put up with all that mob, as if there weren't enough of us already. And – my goodness! What an odd-looking duckling that one is! We certainly don't want *him*!' And a duck flew at the grey one and pecked him in the neck.

'Leave him alone,' said the mother. 'He's not doing anyone any harm.'

'Yes, but he's too big, and peculiar-looking,' said the duck who had pecked at him. 'He has to be put in his place.'

'There's a fine family,' said the old duck with a piece of red cloth round her leg. 'All the children are pretty – except *that* one; he won't do at all. I do wish that the mother could make him all over again.'

'That can't be done, Your Grace,' said the mother duck. 'To be sure, he isn't handsome, but he has a nice disposition, and he swims quite as prettily as any of the others. I venture to say, he may even grow to be better-looking, and perhaps, in time, a bit smaller. He has lain too long in the egg, and that has spoilt his shape.' And she tidied the fluff on the back of his neck, and smoothed him down here and there. 'Besides,' she said, 'he's a drake, so it doesn't matter quite as much about looks. He is healthy, I'm sure, and he'll make his way in the world well enough.'

'Anyhow, the other ducklings are charming,' said the old duck. 'Well, make yourselves at home – and if you happen to come across an eel's head, you can bring it to me.'

That was only the first day; after that the grey one's plight grew worse. How wretched he felt to be so ugly! He was chased about by everyone. The ducks snapped at him; the hens too; and the girl who came to feed them shoved him with her foot. Even his brothers and sisters were against him, and kept saying: 'You ugly thing! We hope that the cat will get you!' His mother, too, would murmur: 'I wish you were far away.'

So away he went. First, he flew over the fence – and the little birds in the bushes rose up into the air with alarm. 'That's because I am so ugly,' the duckling thought, and shut his eyes. But he went on all the same. At last, he reached the wide marshes where the wild ducks lived, and he lay there all the night, for he was so tired and sad.

In the morning the wild ducks flew up and considered their new companion. 'What kind of creature are you?' they asked, and the duckling turned from one to another and greeted them as politely as he could.

'You're certainly ugly, that's a fact!' said the wild duck. 'Still, that doesn't matter so long as you don't marry into the family.'

Poor little outcast! The idea of marriage had never even entered his head. All he wanted was to lie and rest in the reeds, and to have a drink of marsh water.

There he lay for two whole days; then he was visited by a pair of wild geese – young ganders, really, for both were cock-birds. They were only recently hatched, and were as lively and saucy as could be. 'Listen, friend,' they said.

'You're so ugly that we rather like you. What about coming with us when we fly further afield? In another marsh not far from here there are some charming young wild geese, lovely girls, whose "Quack!" is worth hearing. With your funny looks, you might be quite a success with them.'

At that moment there was a Bang! Bang! and both the gay young ganders fell down dead in the reeds. The water became quite red with blood. Again, Bang! Bang! – and a great flock of wild geese flew up from the rushes. A big shoot was going on. The sportsmen were stationed all round the marsh; some were even in the trees overhanging the reeds. Blue smoke drifted like clouds in and out of the dark branches and floated over the water. The dogs went splash! splash! through the mud, treading down the rushes. The poor duckling was terrified; just as he was trying to hide his head under his wing, a huge and frightful dog stood before him, with tongue hanging out of his mouth and eyes gleaming horribly. He thrust his muzzle at the duckling, showed his sharp teeth, and then – splash! He was off without touching the bird.

'Oh, thank goodness,' sighed the duckling. 'I'm so ugly that even the dog thinks twice before biting me.' And he lay quite still while shot after shot whined and banged through the reeds. The day was far on before the noise stopped; but the poor young thing dared not move even then. At last, however, he lifted up his head, peered cautiously round, then hurried away from the marsh as fast as he could. Over fields and meadows he ran, while the wind blew so keenly against him that it was hard work to get along.

Towards evening he reached a miserable hovel; it was in such a crazy state that it couldn't decide which way to tumble down, so it remained standing. The wind howled so fiercely round the duckling that he had to sit down on his tail to avoid being blown over; and the wind grew fiercer still. Then he noticed that the door had lost one of its hinges, and was hanging so crookedly that he could slip inside through the crack, and that is what he did.

In the hovel lived an old woman with a cat and a hen. The cat, whom she called Sonny, could arch his back and purr; he could give out sparks, too, but only when he was stroked the wrong way. The hen had little short legs, and so was called Chicky Short-Legs. She laid well, and the old woman was as fond of her as if she were her own child.

When morning came, the strange little visitor was noticed at once; the cat began to purr and the hen to cluck. 'What's the matter?' said the old woman, looking all about her. But her sight was none too good, so she mistook the little new-comer for a full-grown bird. 'Here's a piece of luck, and no mistake,' said she. 'Now I can have duck eggs – as long as it isn't a drake. Well, we shall see.'

And the duckling was taken in on approval for three weeks; but no eggs appeared.

The cat was the master of the house and the hen the mistress; they were always saying 'We and the world,' for they looked on themselves as half the world, and the better half at that. The duckling thought that there might be other opinions on that matter, but the hen would not hear of it.

'Can you lay eggs?' she asked. 'No? Then kindly keep your views to yourself!'

The cat asked: 'Can you arch your back and purr, or give out sparks? No? Then you had better keep quiet while sensible people are talking.'

So the duckling sat in a corner and moped. Thoughts of fresh air and sunshine came into his mind; and then an extraordinary longing seized him to float on the water. At last, he could not help telling the hen about it.

'What a preposterous notion!' she exclaimed. 'The trouble with you is that you have nothing to do; that's why you get these fancies. Just lay a few eggs or practise purring, and they'll pass off.'

'But it is so delicious to float on the water,' said the duckling. 'It is so lovely to put down your head and dive to the bottom.'

'That *must* be delightful!' said the hen sarcastically. 'You must be out of your mind! Ask the cat — he's the cleverest person I know — if *he* likes floating on the water, or diving to the bottom. Never mind my opinion; ask our mistress, the old woman — there's no one wiser in the whole world. Do you imagine that *she* wants to float or put her head under water?'

'You don't understand,' said the duckling sadly.

'Well, if we don't understand you, nobody will. You'll never be as wise as the cat and the old woman, to say nothing of myself. Don't give yourself airs, child, but be thankful for all the good things that have been done for you. Haven't you found a warm room and elegant company, from whom you can learn plenty if you listen? But all you do is talk nonsense; you're not even cheerful to be with. Believe me, I mean this for your good. Now do make an effort to lay some eggs, or at least learn to purr and give out sparks.'

'I think I had better go out into the wide world,' said the duckling.

'All right, do,' said the hen.

So the duckling went. He floated on the water, and dived below the surface; but it seemed to him that other ducks ignored him because of his ugliness.

Now autumn came: the leaves in the wood turned brown and yellow; the wind caught them and whirled them madly round; the very sky looked chill; the clouds hung heavy with hail and snow; and the raven, perched on the fence, cried 'Caw! Caw!' because of the cold. Even to look at the scene was enough to make you shiver. It was a hard time for the duckling, too.

One evening, as the sky flamed with the setting sun, a flock of marvellous great birds rose out of the rushes. The duckling had never seen any birds so beautiful. They were brilliantly white, with long graceful necks – indeed, they were swans; uttering a strange sound, they spread their splendid wings and flew far away to warmer lands and lakes which did not freeze. High in the air they soared, and the ugly duckling was filled with a wild excitement; he turned round and round in the water like a wheel, and called out in a voice so loud and strange that it quite frightened him. Oh, he would never forget those wonderful birds, those fortunate birds! As soon as the last was out of sight, he dived right down to the bottom of the water, and when he came up again he was almost frantic. He did not know what the birds were called; he did not know where they had come from, nor where they were flying – but he felt more deeply drawn to them than to anything he had ever known.

The winter grew colder still. The duckling had to swim round and round in the water to keep it from freezing over; but every night the ice-free part became smaller. Then he had to use his feet all the time to break up the surface; at last, however, he was quite worn out. He lay still and was frozen fast in the ice.

Early next morning a peasant came by. Seeing the bird, he went out, broke up the ice with his wooden clogs, and carried him home to his wife. Presently the duckling came to life again. The children wanted to play with him, but he thought that they meant to hurt him, and in his fright he flew into the milk-pail. The milk splashed all over the room;

the woman shrieked and threw up her hands – then he flew into the butter tub, then into the flour barrel, and out again. Goodness, what a sight he was! The woman, still screaming, hit out at him with the fire-tongs; the children, laughing and shrieking, tumbled over one another as they tried to grab the little creature. Luckily, the door stood open; out he rushed into the bushes and the new-fallen snow, and lay there in a kind of swoon.

But it would be too sad to tell you of all the hardships and miseries that he had to go through during that cruel winter. One day he was huddling among the reeds in the marsh when the sun began to send down warm rays again; the larks started their song; how glorious! It was spring. The duckling raised his wings. They seemed stronger than before, and carried him swiftly away; before he realized what was happening, he was in a lovely garden full of apple-trees in blossom, and where sweet-smelling lilac hung on its long boughs right down to the winding stream. And then, directly in front of him, out of the leafy shadows, came three magnificent white swans, ruffling their feathers as they floated lightly over the water. The duckling recognized the wonderful birds, and a strange sadness came over him.

'I will fly to those noble birds, even though they may peck me to death for daring to come near them, an ugly thing like me. But I don't care – better to be killed by such splendid creatures than to be pecked by ducks and hens and kicked by the poultry-yard girl – or be left to suffer another winter like the last.' So he flew out to the open water, and swam towards the glorious swans. They saw him, and came speeding towards him, ruffling their plumage.

'Yes, kill me,' said the poor creature, bowing his head right down to the water as he waited for his end. Yet what did he see reflected below? He beheld his own likeness –

but he was no longer an awkward ugly dark grey bird. He was like the proud white birds about him; he was a swan.

It doesn't matter if you are born in a duck-yard, so long as you come from a swan's egg.

He felt glad that he had suffered so much hardship and trouble, for now he could value his good fortune and the home he had found at last. The stately swans swam round him, and stroked him admiringly with their beaks. Some little children came into the garden and threw bread into the water, and the smallest of all cried joyfully: 'There's a new one!' And the others called out in delight: 'Yes, a new swan has come!' They clapped their hands and danced about with pleasure; then they ran to tell their father and mother. More bread and cake were thrown into the water, and everyone said: 'The new one is the most beautiful of all. Look how handsome he is, that young one there.' And the older swans bowed before him.

He felt quite shy, and hid his head under his wing; he did not know what to do. He was almost too happy, yet he was not proud, for a good heart is never proud or vain. He remembered the time when he had been persecuted and scorned, yet now he heard everyone saying that he was the most beautiful of all these beautiful birds. The lilacs bowed their branches down to the water to greet him; the sun sent down its friendly warmth, and the young bird, his heart filled with joy, ruffled his feathers, raised his slender neck, and said: 'I never dreamt that such happiness could ever be when I was the ugly duckling.'

THOMAS HUGHES

FROM *Tom Brown's Schooldays*

(1857)

Then the quarter to ten struck, and the prayer-bell rang. The sixth- and fifth-form boys ranged themselves in their school order along the wall, on either side of the great fires, the middle-fifth and upper-school boys round the long table in the middle of the hall, and the lower-school boys round the upper part of the second long table, which ran down the side of the hall furthest from the fires. Here Tom found himself at the bottom of all, in a state of mind and body not at all fit for prayers, as he thought; and so tried hard to make himself serious, but couldn't, for the life of him, do anything but repeat in his head the choruses of some of the songs, and stare at all the boys opposite, wondering at the brilliancy of their waistcoats, and speculating what sort of fellows they were. The steps of the head-porter are heard on the stairs, and a light gleams at the door. 'Hush!' from the fifth-form boys who stand there, and then in strides the Doctor, cap on head, book in one hand, and gathering up his gown in the other. He walks up the middle, and takes his post by Warner, who begins calling over the names. The Doctor takes no notice of anything, but quietly turns over his book and finds the place, and then stands, cap in hand and finger in book, looking straight before his nose. He knows better than any one when to look, and when to see nothing; tonight is singing night, and there's been lots of noise and no harm done; nothing but beer drunk, and nobody the worse for it; though some of them do look hot and excited. So the Doctor sees nothing, but fascinates Tom in a horrible manner as he stands there, and reads out the Psalm in that deep, ringing, searching voice of his. Prayers are over, and Tom still stares open-mouthed after the Doctor's retiring figure, when he feels a pull at his sleeve, and turning round sees East.

'I say, were you ever tossed in a blanket?'

'No,' said Tom; 'why?'

''Cause there'll be tossing tonight most likely, before the sixth come up to bed. So if you funk, you just come along and hide, or else they'll catch you and toss you.'

'Were you ever tossed? Does it hurt?' inquired Tom.

'Oh, yes, bless you, a dozen times,' said East, as he hobbled along by Tom's side upstairs. 'It don't hurt unless you fall on the floor. But most fellows don't like it.'

They stopped at the fireplace in the top passage, where were a crowd of small boys whispering together, and evidently unwilling to go up into the bed-rooms. In a minute, however, a study door opened and a sixth-form boy came out, and off they all scuttled up the stairs, and then noiselessly dispersed to their different rooms. Tom's heart beat rather quick as he and East reached their room, but he had made up his mind. 'I shan't hide, East,' said he.

'Very well, old fellow,' replied East, evidently pleased; 'no more shall I – they'll be here for us directly.'

The room was a great big one with a dozen beds in it, but not a boy that Tom could see, except East and himself. East pulled off his coat and waistcoat, and then sat on the bottom of his bed, whistling, and pulling off his boots; Tom followed his example.

A noise and steps are heard in the passage, the door opens, and in rush four or five great fifth-form boys, headed by Flashman in his glory.

Tom and East slept in the further corner of the room, and were not seen at first.

'Gone to ground, eh?' roared Flashman; 'push 'em out then, boys! Look under the beds;' and he pulled up the little white curtain of the one nearest him. 'Who-o-op,' he roared, pulling away at the leg of a small boy, who held on tight to the leg of the bed, and sung out lustily for mercy.

'Here, lend a hand, one of you, and help me pull out this young howling brute. Hold your tongue, sir, or I'll kill you.'

'Oh, please, Flashman, please, Walker, don't toss me! I'll fag for you, I'll do anything, only don't toss me.'

'You be hanged,' said Flashman, lugging the wretched boy along. ''twon't hurt you – you! Come along, boys, here he is.'

'I say, Flashey,' sung out another of the big boys, 'drop that; you heard what old Pater Brooke said tonight. I'll be hanged if we'll toss any one against their will – no more bullying. Let him go, I say.'

Flashman, with a oath and a kick, released his prey, who

rushed headlong under his bed again, for fear they should change their minds, and crept along underneath the other beds, till he got under that of the sixth-form boy, which he knew they daren't disturb.

'There's plenty of youngsters don't care about it,' said Walker. 'Here, here's Scud East – you'll be tossed, won't you, young un?' Scud was East's nickname, or Black, as we called it, gained by his fleetness of foot.

'Yes,' said East, 'if you like, only mind my foot.'

'And here's another who didn't hide. Hullo! New boy; what's your name, sir?'

'Brown.'

'Well, Whitey Brown, you don't mind being tossed?'

'No,' said Tom, setting his teeth.

'Come along then, boys,' sung out Walker, and away they all went, carrying along Tom and East, to the intense relief of four or five other small boys, who crept out from under the beds and behind them.

'What a trump Scud is!' said one. 'They won't come back here now.'

'And that new boy too; he must be a good plucked one.'

'Ah, wait till he's been tossed on to the floor; see how he'll like it then!'

Meantime the procession went down the passage to Number 7, the largest room, and the scene of tossing, in the middle of which was a great open space. Here they joined other parties of the bigger boys, each with a captive or two, some willing to be tossed, some sullen, and some frightened to death. At Walker's suggestion all who were afraid were let off, in honour of Brooke's speech.

Then a dozen big boys seized hold of a blanket dragged from one of the beds. 'In with Scud, quick, there's no time to lose.' East was chucked into the blanket. 'Once, twice, thrice, and away!' up he went like a shuttlecock, but not quite up to the ceiling.

'Now, boys, with a will,' cried Walker, 'once, twice, thrice, and away!' This time he went clean up, and kept himself from touching the ceiling with his hand, and so again, a third time, when he was turned out, and up went another boy. And then came Tom's turn. He lay quite still by East's advice, and didn't dislike the 'once, twice, thrice'; but the 'away' wasn't so pleasant. They were in good wind now, and sent him slap up to the ceiling first time, against which his knees came rather sharply. But the moment's pause before descending was the rub, the feeling of utter helplessness, and of leaving his whole inside behind him sticking to the ceiling. Tom was very near shouting to be set down, when he found himself back in the blanket, but thought of East, and didn't; and so took his three tosses without a kick or a cry, and was called a young trump for his pains.

He and East, having earned it, stood now looking on. No catastrophe happened, as all the captives were cool hands, and didn't struggle. This didn't suit Flashman. What your real bully likes in tossing is when the boys kick and struggle, or hold on to the side of the blanket, and so get pitched bodily on to the floor; it's no fun to him when no one is hurt or frightened.

'Let's toss two of them together, Walker,' suggested he.

'What a cursed bully you are, Flashey!' rejoined the other. 'Up with another one.'

And so no two boys were tossed together, the peculiar hardship of which is that it's too much for human nature to lie still then and share troubles; and so the wretched pair of small boys struggle in the air which shall fall a-top in the descent, to the no small risk of both falling out of the blanket, and the huge delight of brutes like Flashman.

But now there's a cry that the praepostor of the room is coming; so the tossing stops, and all scatter to their different rooms; and Tom is left to turn in, with the first day's experience of a public school to meditate upon.

CHARLES KINGSLEY

From *The Water-Babies*

(1863)

A mile off, and a thousand feet down.
So Tom found it; though it seemed as if he could
have chucked a pebble on to the back of the woman in the
red petticoat who was weeding in the garden, or even across
the dale to the rocks beyond. For the bottom of the valley
was just one field broad, and on the other side ran the
stream; and above it, grey crag, grey down, grey stair, grey
moor walled up to heaven.

A quiet, silent, rich, happy place; a narrow crack cut deep
into the earth; so deep, and so out of the way, that the bad
bogies can hardly find it out. The name of the place is
Vendale ...

So Tom went to go down; and first he went down three
hundred feet of steep heather, mixed up with loose brown

gritstone, as rough as a file; which was not pleasant to his poor little heels, as he came bump, stump, jump, down the steep. And still he thought he could throw a stone into the garden.

Then he went down three hundred feet of limestone terraces, one below the other, as straight as if a carpenter had ruled them with his ruler and then cut them out with his chisel. There was no heath there, but –

First, a little grass slope, covered with the prettiest flowers, rockrose and saxifrage, and thyme and basil, and all sorts of sweet herbs.

Then bump down a two-foot step of limestone.

Then another bit of grass and flowers.

Then bump down a one-foot step.

Then another bit of grass and flowers for fifty yards, as steep as the house-roof, where he had to slide down on his dear little tail.

Then another step of stone, ten feet high; and there he had to stop himself, and crawl along the edge to find a crack; for if he had rolled over, he would have rolled right into the old woman's garden, and frightened her out of her wits.

Then, when he had found a dark narrow crack, full of green-stalked fern, and had crawled down through it, with knees and elbows, as he would down a chimney, there was another grass slope, and another step, and so on, till – oh, dear me! I wish it was all over; and so did he …

At last he came to a bank of beautiful shrubs; whitebeam with its great silver-backed leaves, and mountain-ash, and oak; and below them cliff and crag, cliff and crag, with great beds of crown-ferns and wood-sedge; while through the shrubs he could see the stream sparkling, and hear it murmur on the white pebbles. He did not know that it was three hundred feet below.

You would have been giddy, perhaps, at looking down; but Tom was not. He was a brave little chimney-sweep ... and down he went, by stock and stone, sedge and ledge, bush and rush, as if he had been born a jolly little black ape, with four hands instead of two.

And all the while he never saw the Irishwoman coming down behind him.

But he was getting terribly tired now. The burning sun on the fells had sucked him up; but the damp heat of the woody crag sucked him up still more; and the perspiration ran out of the ends of his fingers and toes, and washed him cleaner than he had been for a whole year. But, of course, he dirtied everything terribly as he went. There has been a great black smudge all down the crag ever since ...

At last he got to the bottom. But, behold, it was not the bottom – as people usually find when they are coming down a mountain. For at the foot of the crag were heaps and heaps of fallen limestone of every size from that of your head to that of a stage-waggon, with holes between them full of sweet heath-fern; and before Tom got through them, he was out in the bright sunshine again; and then he felt, once for all and suddenly, as people generally do, that he was b-e-a-t, beat ...

He could not get on. The sun was burning, and yet he felt chill all over. He was quite empty, and yet he felt quite sick. There was but two hundred yards of smooth pasture between him and the cottage, and yet he could not walk down it. He could hear the stream murmuring only one field beyond it, and yet it seemed to him as if it was a hundred miles off.

He lay down on the grass till the beetles ran over him, and the flies settled on his nose. I don't know when he would have got up again, if the gnats and the midges had not taken compassion on him. But the gnats blew their trumpets so loud in his ear, and the midges nibbled so at his hands and face wherever they could find a place free from soot, that at last he woke up, and stumbled away, down over a low wall, and into a narrow road, and up to the cottage door.

And a neat pretty cottage it was, with clipt yew hedges all round the garden, and yews inside too, cut into peacocks and trumpets and teapots and all kinds of queer shapes ...

He came slowly up to the open door, which was all hung round with clematis and roses; and then peeped in, half afraid.

And there sat by the empty fireplace, which was filled with a pot of sweet herbs, the nicest old woman that ever was seen, in her red petticoat, and short dimity bedgown, and clean white cap, with a black silk handkerchief over it, tied under her chin. At her feet sat the grandfather of all the cats; and opposite her sat, on two benches, twelve or four-teen neat, rosy, chubby little children, learning their criss-cross row; and gabble enough they made about it. Such a pleasant cottage it was, with a shiny clean stone floor, and curious old prints on the walls, and an old black oak side-board full of bright pewter and brass dishes, and a cuckoo-clock in the corner, which began shouting as soon as Tom appeared; not that it was frightened at Tom, but that it was just eleven o'clock.

All the children started at Tom's dirty black figure – the girls began to cry, and the boys began to laugh, and all pointed at him rudely enough; but Tom was too tired to care for that.

'What art thou, and what dost want?' cried the old dame. 'A chimney-sweep! Away with thee! I'll have no sweeps here.'

'Water,' said poor Tom, quite faint.

'Water? There's plenty i' the beck,' she said, quite sharply.

'But I can't get there; I'm most clemmed with hunger and drought.' And Tom sank down upon the door-step, and laid his head against the post.

And the old dame looked at him through her spectacles one minute, and two, and three; and then she said, 'He's sick, and a bairn's a bairn, sweep or none.'

'Water,' said Tom.

'God forgive me!' and she put by her spectacles, and rose, and came to Tom. 'Water's bad for thee; I'll give thee milk.' And she toddled off into the next room, and brought a cup of milk and a bit of bread.

Tom drank the milk off at one draught, and then looked up, revived.

'Where didst come from?' said the dame.

'Over Fell, there,' said Tom, and pointed up into the sky.

'Over Harthover? And down Lewthwaite Crag? Art sure thou art not lying?'

'Why should I?' said Tom, and leant his head against the post.

'And how got ye up there?'

'I came over from the Place;' and Tom was so tired and desperate he had no heart or time to think of a story, so he told all the truth in a few words.

'Bless thy little heart! And thou hast not been stealing, then?'

'No.'

'Bless thy little heart! And I'll warrant not. Why, God's guided the bairn, because he was innocent! Away from the Place, and over Harthover Fell, and down Lewthwaite Crag! Who ever heard the like, if God hadn't led him? Why dost not eat thy bread?'

'I can't.'

'It's good enough, for I made it myself.'

'I can't,' said Tom, and he laid his head on his knees, and then asked –

'Is it Sunday?'

'No, then; why should it be?'

'Because I hear the church-bells ringing so.'

'Bless thy pretty heart! The bairn's sick. Come wi' me, and I'll hap thee up somewhere. If thou wert a bit cleaner I'd put thee in my own bed, for the Lord's sake. But come along here.'

But when Tom tried to get up, he was so tired and giddy that she had to help him and lead him.

She put him in an outhouse upon soft sweet hay and an old rug, and bade him sleep off his walk, and she would come to him when school was over, in an hour's time.

And so she went in again, expecting Tom to fall fast asleep at once.

But Tom did not fall asleep.

Instead of it he turned and tossed and kicked about in the strangest way, and felt so hot all over that he longed to get into the river and cool himself; and then he fell half asleep, and dreamt that he heard the little white lady crying to him, 'Oh, you're so dirty; go and be washed;' and then that he heard the Irishwoman saying, 'Those that wish to be clean, clean they will be.' And then he heard the church-bells ring so loud, close to him too, that he was sure it must be Sunday, in spite of what the old dame had said; and he would go to church, and see what a church was like inside, for he had never been in one, poor little fellow, in all his life. But the people would never let him come in, all over soot and dirt like that. He must go to the river and wash first. And he said out loud again and again, though being half asleep he did not know it, 'I must be clean, I must be clean.'

And all of a sudden he found himself, not in the outhouse on the hay, but in the middle of a meadow, over the road, with the stream just before him, saying continually, 'I must be clean, I must be clean.' He had got there on his own legs, between sleep and awake ... But he was not a bit surprised, and went on to the bank of the brook, and lay down on the grass, and looked into the clear, clear limestone water, with every pebble at the bottom bright and clean, while the little silver trout dashed about in fright at the sight of his black face; and he dipped his hand in and found it so cool, cool, cool; and he said, 'I will be a fish; I will swim in the water; I must be clean, I must be clean.'

So he pulled off all his clothes in such haste that he tore some of them, which was easy enough with such ragged old things. And he put his poor hot sore feet into the water; and then his legs; and the farther he went in, the more the church-bells rang in his head.

'Ah!' said Tom, 'I must be quick and wash myself; the bells are ringing quite loud now; and they will stop soon, and then the door will be shut, and I shall never be able to get in at all.' ...

And all the while he never saw the Irishwoman, not behind him this time, but before.

For just before he came to the river-side, she had stepped down into the cool clear water; and her shawl and her petticoat floated off her, and the green water-weeds floated round her sides, and the white water-lilies floated round her head, and the fairies of the stream came up from the bottom and bore her away and down upon their arms; for she was the Queen of them all; and perhaps of more besides.

'Where have you been?' they asked her.

'I have been smoothing sick folk's pillows, and whispering sweet dreams into their ears; opening cottage casements to let out the stifling air; coaxing little children away from the gutters, and foul pools where fever breeds; turning women from the gin-shop door, and staying men's hands as they were going to strike their wives; doing all I can to help those who will not help themselves: and little enough that is, and weary work for me. But I have brought you a new little brother, and watched him safe all the way here.'

Then all the fairies laughed for joy at the thought that they had a little brother coming.

'But mind, maidens, he must not see you, or know that you are here ... You must not play with him, or speak to him, or let him see you; but only keep him from being harmed.'

Then the fairies were sad, because they could not play with their new brother, but they always did what they were told.

And their Queen floated away down the river; and whither she went, thither she came. But all this Tom, of course, never saw or heard: and perhaps if he had it would have made little difference in the story; for he was so hot and thirsty, and longed so to be clean for once, that he tumbled himself as quick as he could into the clear cool stream.

And he had not been in it two minutes before he fell fast asleep, into the quietest, sunniest, cosiest sleep that ever he had in his life; and he dreamt about the green meadows by which he had walked that morning, and the tall elm-trees, and the sleeping cows; and after that he dreamt of nothing at all.

The reason of his falling into such a delightful sleep is very simple; and yet hardly anyone has found it out. It was merely that the fairies took him ...

The kind old dame came back at twelve, when school was

over, to look after Tom; but there was no Tom there. She looked about for his footprints; but the ground was so hard that there was no slot, as they say in dear old North Devon…

So the old dame went in again quite sulky, thinking that little Tom had tricked her with a false story, and shammed ill, and then run away again.

But she altered her mind next day. For, when Sir John and the rest of them had run themselves out of breath, and lost Tom, they went back again, looking very foolish.

And they looked more foolish still when Sir John heard more of the story from the nurse; and more foolish still, again, when they heard the whole story from Miss Ellie, the little lady in white. All she had seen was a poor little black chimney-sweep, crying and sobbing, and going to get up the chimney again. Of course, she was very much frightened; and no wonder. But that was all. The boy had taken nothing in the room; by the mark of his little sooty feet, they could see that he had never been off the hearthrug till the nurse caught hold of him. It was all a mistake.

So Sir John told Grimes to go home, and promised him five shillings if he would bring the boy quietly up to him, without beating him, that he might be sure of the truth. For he took for granted, and Grimes, too, that Tom had made his way home.

But no Tom came back to Mr Grimes that evening; and he went to the police-office, to tell them to look out for the boy. But no Tom was heard of. As for his having gone over those great fells to Vendale, they no more dreamt of that than of his having gone to the moon.

So Mr Grimes came up to Harthover next day with a very sour face; but when he got there, Sir John was over the hills and far away; and Mr Grimes had to sit in the outer servants' hall all day, and drink strong ale to wash away his sorrows; and they were washed away long before Sir John came back.

For good Sir John had slept very badly that night; and he said to his lady, 'My dear, the boy must have got over into the grouse-moors, and lost himself; and he lies very heavily on my conscience, poor little lad. But I know what I will do.'

So, at five the next morning up he got, and into his bath, and into his shooting-jacket and gaiters, and into the stable-yard, like a fine old English gentleman, with a face as red as a rose, and a hand as hard as a table, and a back as broad as a bullock's; and bade them bring his shooting pony, and the keeper to come on his pony, and the huntsman, and the first whip, and the second whip, and the under-keeper with the bloodhound in a leash – a great dog as tall as a calf, of the colour of a gravel-walk, with mahogany ears and nose, and a throat like a church-bell. They took him up to the place where Tom had gone into the wood; and there the hound lifted up his mighty voice, and told them all he knew.

Then he took them to the place where Tom had climbed the wall; and they shoved it down, and all got through.

And then the wise dog took them over the moor, and over the fells, step by step, very slowly; for the scent was a day old, you know, and very light from the heat and drought. But that was why cunning old Sir John started at five in the morning.

And at last he came to the top of Lewthwaite Crag, and there he bayed, and looked up in their faces, as much as to say 'I tell you he is gone down here!'

They could hardly believe that Tom would have gone so far; and when they looked at that awful cliff, they could never believe that he would have dared to face it. But if the dog said so, it must be true.

'Heaven forgive us!' said Sir John. 'If we find him at all, we shall find him lying at the bottom.' And he slapped his great hand upon his great thigh, and said –

'Who will go down over Lewthwaite Crag, and see if that boy is alive? Oh, that I were twenty years younger, and I would go down myself!' And so he would have done, as well as any sweep in the county. Then he said –

'Twenty pounds to the man who brings me that boy alive!' and, as was his way, what he said he meant.

Now among the lot was a little groom-boy, a very little groom indeed; and he was the same who had ridden up the court, and told Tom to come to the Hall; and he said –

'Twenty pounds or none, I will go down over Lewthwaite Crag, if it's only for the poor boy's sake. For he was as civil a spoken little chap as ever climbed a flue.'

So down over Lewthwaite Crag he went: a very smart groom he was at the top, and a very shabby one at the bottom; for he tore his gaiters, and he tore his breeches, and he tore his jacket, and he burst his braces, and he burst his boots, and he lost his hat, and what was worst of all, he lost his shirt pin, which he prized very much, for it was gold, and he had won it in a raffle at Malton, and there was a figure at the top of it, of t'ould mare, noble old Beeswing herself, as natural as life; so it was a really severe loss: but he never saw anything of Tom.

And all the while Sir John and the rest were riding round, full three miles to the right, and back again, to get into Vendale, and to the foot of the crag.

When they came to the old dame's school, all the children came out to see. And the old dame came out too; and when she saw Sir John, she curtsied very low, for she was a tenant of his.

'Well, dame, and how are you?' said Sir John.

'Blessings on you as broad as your back, Harthover,' says she – she didn't call him Sir John, but only Harthover, for that is the fashion in the North country – 'and welcome into Vendale: but you're no hunting the fox this time of the year?'

'I am hunting, and strange game, too,' said he.

'Blessings on your heart, and what makes you look so sad the morn?'

'I'm looking for a lost child, a chimney-sweep, that is run away.'

'Oh, Harthover, Harthover,' says she, 'ye were always a just man and a merciful; and ye'll no harm the poor little lad if I give you tidings of him?'

'Not I, not I, dame. I'm afraid we hunted him out of the house all on a miserable mistake, and the hound has brought him to the top of Lewthwaite Crag, and – '

Whereat the old dame broke out crying, without letting him finish his story.

'So he told me the truth after all, poor little dear! Ah, first thoughts are best, and a body's heart'll guide them right, if they will but hearken to it.' And then she told Sir John all.

'Bring the dog here, and lay him on,' said Sir John, without another word, and he set his teeth very hard.

And the dog opened at once; and went away at the back of the cottage, over the road, and over the meadow, and through a bit of alder copse; and there, upon an alder stump, they saw Tom's clothes lying. And then they knew as much about it all as there was any need to know.

And Tom?

Ah, now comes the most wonderful part of this wonderful story. Tom, when he woke, for of course he woke – children always wake after they have slept exactly as long as is good for them – found himself swimming about in the stream, being about four inches long, and having round the parotid region of his fauces a set of external gills (I hope you understand all the big words) just like those of a sucking eft, which he mistook for a lace frill, till he pulled at them, found he hurt himself, and made up his mind that they were part of himself, and best left alone.

In fact, the fairies had turned him into a water-baby.

LOUISA M. ALCOTT

From *Little Women*

(1868)

'Christmas won't be Christmas without any presents,' grumbled Jo, lying on the rug.

'It's so dreadful to be poor!' sighed Meg, looking down at her old dress.

'I don't think it's fair for some girls to have plenty of pretty things, and other girls nothing at all,' added little Amy, with an injured sniff.

'We've got father and mother and each other,' said Beth, contentedly, from her corner.

The four young faces on which the firelight shone brightened at the cheerful words, but darkened again as Jo said sadly: 'We haven't got father, and shall not have him for a long time.' She didn't say 'perhaps never', but each silently added it, thinking of father far away, where the fighting was.

Nobody spoke for a minute; then Meg said in an altered tone: 'You know the reason mother proposed not having any presents this Christmas was because it is going to be a hard winter for everyone; and she thinks we ought not to spend money for pleasure when our men are suffering so in the army. We can't do much, but we can make our little sacrifices, and ought to do it gladly. But I am afraid I don't'; and Meg shook her head, and she thought regretfully of all the pretty things she wanted.

'But I don't think the little we should spend would do any good. We've each got a dollar, and the army wouldn't be much helped by our giving that. I agree not to expect anything from mother or you, but I do want to buy *Undine and Sintram* for myself; I've wanted it *so* long,' said Jo, who was a bookworm.

'I planned to spend mine on new music,' said Beth, with a little sigh, which no one heard but the hearth-brush and kettle-holder.

'I shall get a nice box of Faber's drawing pencils; I really need them,' said Amy, decidedly.

'Mother didn't say anything about our money, and she won't wish us to give up everything. Let's each buy what we want, and have a little fun; I'm sure we work hard enough to earn it,' cried Jo, examining the heels of her shoes in a gentlemanly manner.

'I know *I* do – teaching those tiresome children nearly all day when I am longing to enjoy myself at home,' began Meg, in the complaining tone again.

'You don't have half such a hard time as I do,' said Jo. 'How would you like to be shut up for hours with a nervous, fussy old lady, who keeps you trotting, is never satisfied, and worries you till you're ready to fly out of the window or cry?'

'It's naughty to fret; but I do think washing dishes and keeping things tidy is the worst work in the world. It makes me cross; and my hands get so stiff, I can't practise well at all'; and Beth looked at her rough hands with a sigh that anyone could hear that time.

'I don't believe any of you suffer as I do,' cried Amy; 'for you don't have to go to school with impertinent girls, who plague you if you don't know your lessons, and laugh at your dresses, and label your father if he isn't rich, and insult you when your nose isn't nice.'

'If you mean *libel*, I'd say so, and not talk about *labels*, as if papa was a pickle-bottle,' advised Jo, laughing.

'I know what I mean, and you needn't be *statirical* about it. It's proper to use good words, and improve your *vocabulary*,' returned Amy, with dignity.

'Don't peck at one another, children. Don't you wish we had the money papa lost when we were little, Jo? Dear me! how happy and good we'd be, if we had no worries!' said Meg, who could remember better times.

'You said, the other day, you thought we were a deal happier than the King children, for they were fighting and fretting all the time, in spite of their money.'

'So I did, Beth. Well, I think we are; for, though we do have to work, we make fun for ourselves, and are a pretty jolly set, as Jo would say.'

'Jo does use such slang words!' observed Amy, with a reproving look at the long figure stretched on the rug. Jo immediately sat up, put her hands in her pockets, and began to whistle.

'Don't, Jo; it's so boyish!'

'That's why I do it.'

'I detest rude, unladylike girls!'

'I hate affected, niminy-piminy chits!'

"'Birds in their little nests agree,'" sang Beth, the peace-maker, with such a funny face that both sharp voices softened to a laugh, and the 'pecking' ended for that time.

'Really, girls, you are both to be blamed,' said Meg, beginning to lecture in her elder-sisterly fashion. 'You are old enough to leave off boyish tricks, and to behave better, Josephine. It didn't matter so much when you were a little girl; but now you are so tall, and turn up your hair, you should remember that you are a young lady.'

'I'm not! And if turning up my hair makes me one, I'll wear it in two tails till I'm twenty,' cried Jo, pulling off her net, and shaking down her chestnut mane. 'I hate to think I've got to grow up, and be Miss March, and wear long gowns, and look as prim as a China-aster! It's bad enough to be a girl, anyway, when I like boys' games and work and manners! I can't get over my disappointment in not being a boy; and it's worse than ever now, for I'm dying to go and fight with papa, and I can only stay at home and knit, like a poky old woman!' And Jo shook the blue army sock till the needles rattled like castanets, and her ball bounded across the room.

'Poor Jo! It's too bad, but it can't be helped; so you must try to be contented with making your name boyish, and playing brother to us girls,' said Beth, stroking the rough head at her knee with a hand that all the dish-washing and dusting in the world could not make ungentle in its touch.

'As for you, Amy,' continued Meg, 'you are altogether too particular and prim. Your airs are funny now; but you'll grow up an affected little goose, if you don't take care. I like your nice manners and refined ways of speaking when you don't try to be elegant; but your absurd words are as bad as Jo's slang.'

'If Jo is a tomboy and Amy a goose, what am I, please?' asked Beth, ready to share the lecture.

'You're a dear, and nothing else,' answered Meg, warmly; and no one contradicted her, for the 'Mouse' was the pet of the family.

As young readers like to know 'how people look', we will take this moment to give them a little sketch of the four sisters, who sat knitting away in the twilight, while the December snow fell quietly without, and the fire crackled cheerfully within. It was a comfortable old room, though the carpet was faded and the furniture very plain; for a good picture or two hung on the walls, books filled the recesses, chrysanthemums and Christmas roses bloomed in the windows, and a pleasant atmosphere of home-peace pervaded it.

Margaret, the eldest of the four, was sixteen, and very pretty, being plump and fair, with large eyes, plenty of soft, brown hair, a sweet mouth, and white hands, of which she was rather vain. Fifteen-year-old Jo was very tall, thin, and brown, and reminded one of a colt; for she never seemed to know what to do with her long limbs, which were very much in her way. She had a decided mouth, a comical nose, and sharp, grey eyes, which appeared to see everything, and were by turns fierce, funny, or thoughtful. Her long, thick hair was her one beauty; but it was usually bundled in a net, to be out of her way. Round shoulders had Jo, big hands and feet, a fly-away look to her clothes, and the uncomfortable appearance of a girl who was rapidly shooting up into a woman, and didn't like it. Elizabeth – or Beth, as everyone called her – was a rosy, smooth-haired, bright-eyed girl of thirteen, with a shy manner, a timid voice, and a peaceful expression, which was seldom disturbed. Her father called her 'Little Tranquillity', and the name suited her excellently; for she seemed to live in a happy world of her own, only venturing out to meet the few whom she trusted and loved.

Amy, though the youngest, was a most important person –
in her own opinion at least. A regular snow maiden, with
blue eyes, and yellow hair, curling on her shoulders, pale
and slender, and always carrying herself like a young lady
mindful of her manners. What the characters of the four
sisters were we will leave to be found out.

The clock struck six; and, having swept up the hearth,
Beth put a pair of slippers down to warm. Somehow the
sight of the old shoes had a good effect upon the girls; for
mother was coming, and everyone brightened to welcome
her. Meg stopped lecturing, and lighted the lamp, Amy got
out of the easy-chair without being asked, and Jo forgot
how tired she was as she sat up to hold the slippers nearer
to the blaze.

'They are quite worn out; Marmee must have a new pair.'

'I thought I'd get her some with my dollar,' said Beth.

'No, I shall!' cried Amy.

'I'm the oldest,' began Meg, but Jo cut in with a decided:
'I'm the man of the family now papa is away, and *I* shall
provide the slippers, for he told me to take special care of
mother while he was gone.'

'I'll tell you what we'll do,' said Beth; 'let's each get her
something for Christmas, and not get anything for ourselves.'

'That's like you, dear! What will we get?' exclaimed Jo.

Every one thought soberly for a minute; then Meg
announced as if the idea was suggested by the sight of her
own pretty hands, 'I shall give her a nice pair of gloves.'

'Army shoes, best to be had,' cried Jo.

'Some handkerchiefs, all hemmed,' said Beth.

'I'll get a little bottle of cologne; she likes it, and it won't
cost much, so I'll have some left to buy my pencils,' added
Amy.

'How will we give the things?' asked Meg.

'Put them on the table, and bring her in and see her open the bundles. Don't you remember how we used to do on our birthdays?' answered Jo.

'I used to be *so* frightened when it was my turn to sit in the big chair with the crown on, and see you all come marching round to give the presents, with a kiss. I liked the things and the kisses, but it was dreadful to have you sit looking at me while I opened the bundles,' said Beth, who was toasting her face and the bread for tea, at the same time.

'Let Marmee think we are getting things for ourselves, and then surprise her. We must go shopping tomorrow afternoon, Meg; there is so much to do about the play for Christmas night,' said Jo, marching up and down, with her hands behind her back and her nose in the air.

'I don't mean to act any more after this time; I'm getting too old for such things,' observed Meg, who was as much a child as ever about 'dressing-up' frolics.

'You won't stop, I know, as long as you can trail round in a white gown with your hair down, and wear gold-paper jewellery. You are the best actress we've got, and there'll be an end of everything if you quit the boards,' said Jo. 'We ought to rehearse tonight. Come here, Amy, and do the fainting scene, for you are as stiff as a poker in that.'

'I can't help it; I never saw anyone faint, and I don't choose to make myself all black and blue, tumbling flat as you do. If I can go down easily, I'll drop; if I can't, I shall fall into a chair and be graceful; I don't care if Hugo does come at me with a pistol,' returned Amy, who was not gifted with dramatic power, but was chosen because she was small enough to be borne out shrieking by the villain of the piece.

'Do it this way; clasp your hands so, and stagger across

the room, crying frantically, "Roderigo! Save me! Save me!"' and away went Jo, with a melodramatic scream which was truly thrilling.

Amy followed, but she poked her hands out stiffly before her, and jerked herself along as if she went by machinery; and her 'Ow!' was more suggestive of pins being run into her than of fear and anguish. Jo gave a despairing groan, and Meg laughed outright, while Beth let her bread burn as she watched the fun with interest.

'It's no use! Do the best you can when the time comes, and if the audience laugh, don't blame me. Come on, Meg.'

Then things went smoothly, for Don Pedro defied the world in a speech of two pages without a single break; Hagar, the witch, chanted an awful incantation over her kettleful of simmering toads, with weird effect; Roderigo rent his chains asunder manfully, and Hugo died in agonies of remorse and arsenic, with a wild 'Ha! Ha!'

'It's the best we've had yet,' said Meg, as the dead villain sat up and rubbed his elbows.

'I don't see how you can write and act such splendid things, Jo. You're a regular Shakespeare!' exclaimed Beth, who firmly believed that her sisters were gifted with won-derful genius in all things.

'Not quite,' replied Jo modestly. 'I do think *The Witch's Curse, an Operatic Tragedy*, is rather a nice thing; but I'd like to try *Macbeth*, if we only had a trap-door for Banquo. I always wanted to do the killing part. "Is that a dagger I see before me?"' muttered Jo, rolling her eyes and clutching at the air, as she had seen a famous tragedian do.

'No, it's the toasting fork, with mother's shoe on it instead of the bread. Beth's stage-struck!' cried Meg, and the rehearsal ended in a general burst of laughter.

'Glad to find you so merry, my girls,' said a cheery voice

at the door, and actors and audience turned to welcome a tall, motherly lady, with a 'can-I-help-you' look about her which was truly delightful. She was not elegantly dressed, but a noble-looking woman, and the girls thought the grey cloak and unfashionable bonnet covered the most splendid mother in the world.

'Well, dearies, how have you got on today? There was so much to do, getting the boxes ready to go tomorrow, that I didn't come home to dinner. Has anyone called, Beth? How is your cold, Meg? Jo, you look tired to death. Come and kiss me, baby.'

While making these maternal inquiries, Mrs March got her wet things off, her warm slippers on, and, sitting down in the easy-chair, drew Amy to her lap, preparing to enjoy the happiest hour of her busy day. The girls flew about, trying to make things comfortable, each in her own way. Meg arranged the tea-table; Jo brought wood and set chairs, dropping, overturning, and clattering everything she touched; Beth trotted to and fro between parlour and kitchen, quiet and busy; while Amy gave directions to everyone, as she sat with her hands folded.

As they gathered about the table, Mrs March said, with a particularly happy face, 'I've got a treat for you after supper.'

A quick, bright smile went round like a streak of sunshine. Beth clapped her hands, regardless of the biscuit she held, and Jo tossed up her napkin, crying, 'A letter! A letter! Three cheers for father!'

'Yes, a nice long letter. He is well, and thinks he shall get through the cold season better than we feared. He sends all sorts of loving wishes for Christmas, and an especial message to you girls,' said Mrs March, patting her pocket as if she had got a treasure there.

'Hurry and get done! Don't stop to quirk your little

finger, and simper over your plate, Amy,' cried Jo, choking in her tea, and dropping her bread, butter side down, on the carpet in her haste to get at the treat.

Beth ate no more, but crept away, to sit in her shadowy corner and brood over the delight to come, till the others were ready.

'I think it was so splendid of father to go as chaplain when he was too old to be drafted, and not strong enough for a soldier,' said Meg, warmly.

'Don't I wish I could go as a drummer, a *vivan* – what's its name? Or a nurse, so I could be near him and help him,' exclaimed Jo, with a groan.

'It must be very disagreeable to sleep in a tent, and eat all sorts of bad-tasting things, and drink out of a tin mug,' sighed Amy.

'When will he come home, Marmee?' asked Beth, with a little quiver in her voice.

'Not for many months, dear, unless he is sick. He will stay and do his work faithfully as long as he can, and we won't ask for him back a minute sooner than he can be spared. Now come and hear the letter.'

They all drew to the fire, mother in the big chair, with Beth at her feet, Meg and Amy perched on either arm of the chair, and Jo leaning on the back, where no one would see any sign of emotion if the letter should happen to be touching. Very few letters were written in those hard times that were not touching, especially those which fathers sent home. In this one little was said of the hardships endured, the dangers faced, or the home-sickness conquered; it was a cheerful, hopeful letter, full of lively descriptions of camp life, marches, and military news; and only at the end did the writer's heart overflow with fatherly love and longing for the little girls at home.

'Give them all my dear love and a kiss. Tell them I think of them by day, pray for them by night, and find my best comfort in their affection at all times. A year seems very long to wait before I see them, but remind them that while we wait we may all work, so that these hard days need not be wasted. I know they will remember all I said to them, that they will be loving children to you, will do their duty faithfully, fight their bosom enemies bravely, and conquer themselves so beautifully that when I come back to them I may be fonder and prouder than ever of my little women.'

Everybody sniffed when they came to that part; Jo wasn't ashamed of the great tear that dropped off the end of her nose, and Amy never minded the rumpling of her curls as she hid her face on her mother's shoulder and sobbed out, 'I *am* a selfish girl! But I'll truly try to be better, so he mayn't be disappointed in me by and by.'

'We all will!' cried Meg. 'I think too much of my looks, and hate to work, but won't any more, if I can help it.'

'I'll try and be what he loves to call me, "a little woman", and not be rough and wild; but do my duty here instead of wanting to be somewhere else,' said Jo, thinking that keeping her temper at home was a much harder task than facing a rebel or two down South.

Beth said nothing, but wiped away her tears with the blue army sock, and began to knit with all her might, losing no time in doing the duty that lay nearest her, while she resolved in her quiet little soul to be all that father hoped to find her when the year brought round the happy coming home.

Mrs March broke the silence that followed Jo's words, by saying in her cheery voice, 'Do you remember how you used to play *Pilgrim's Progress* when you were little things? Nothing delighted you more than to have me tie my piece-bags on your backs for burdens, give you hats and sticks and rolls of paper, and let you travel through the house from the cellar, which was the City of Destruction, up, up, to the housetop, where you had all the lovely things you could collect to make a Celestial City.'

'What fun it was, especially going by the lions, fighting Apollyon, and passing through the Valley where the hobgoblins were!' said Jo.

'I liked the place where the bundles fell off and tumbled downstairs,' said Meg.

'My favourite part was when we came out on the flat roof where our flowers and arbours and pretty things were, and all stood and sang for joy up there in the sunshine,' said Beth, smiling, as if that pleasant moment had come back to her.

'I don't remember much about it, except that I was afraid of the cellar and the dark entry, and always liked the cake and milk we had up at the top. If I wasn't too old for such things, I'd rather like to play it over again,' said Amy, who began to talk of renouncing childish things at the mature age of twelve.

'We never are too old for this, my dear, because it is a play we are playing all the time in one way or another. Our burdens are here, our road is before us, and the longing for goodness and happiness is the guide that leads us through many troubles and mistakes to the peace which is a true Celestial City. Now, my little pilgrims, suppose you begin again, not in play, but in earnest, and see how far on you can get before Father comes home.'

'Really, Mother? Where are our bundles?' asked Amy, who was a very literal young lady.

'Each of you told what your burden was just now, except Beth; I rather think she hasn't got any,' said her mother.

'Yes, I have; mine is dishes and dusters, and envying girls with nice pianos, and being afraid of people.'

Beth's bundle was such a funny one that everybody wanted to laugh; but nobody did, for it would have hurt her feelings very much.

'Let us do it,' said Meg, thoughtfully. 'It is only another name for trying to be good, and the story may help us; for though we do want to be good, it's hard work, and we forget, and don't do our best.'

'We were in the Slough of Despond tonight, and Mother came and pulled us out as Help did in the book. We ought to have our roll of directions, like Christian. What shall we do about that?' asked Jo, delighted with the fancy which lent a little romance to the very dull task of doing her duty.

'Look under your pillows, Christmas morning, and you will find your guide-book,' replied Mrs March.

They talked over the new plan while old Hannah cleared the table; then out came the four little work-baskets, and the needles flew as the girls made sheets for Aunt March. It was uninteresting sewing, but tonight no one grumbled. They adopted Jo's plan of dividing the long seams into four parts, and calling the quarters Europe, Asia, Africa, and America, and in that way got on capitally, especially when they talked about the different countries, as they stitched their way through them.

At nine they stopped work, and sang, as usual, before they went to bed. No one but Beth could get much music out of the old piano; but she had a way of softly touching the yellow keys, and making a pleasant accompaniment to the simple songs they sang. Meg had a voice like a flute, and she and her mother led the little choir. Amy chirped like a cricket, and Jo wandered through the airs at her own sweet will, always coming out at the wrong place with a croak or a quaver that spoilt the most pensive tune. They had always done this from the time they could lisp

'Crinkle, crinkle, 'ittle 'tar.'

and it had become a household custom, for the mother was a born singer. The first sound in the morning was her voice, as she went about the house singing like a lark; and the last sound at night was the same cheery sound, for the girls never grew too old for that familiar lullaby.

LEWIS CARROLL

FROM *Through the Looking-Glass*

(1871)

'It was a glorious victory, wasn't it?' said the White
Knight, as he came up panting.

'I don't know,' Alice said doubtfully. 'I don't want to be
anybody's prisoner. I want to be a Queen.'

'So you will, when you've crossed the next brook,' said
the White Knight. 'I'll see you safe to the end of the wood –
and then I must go back, you know. That's the end of my
move.'

'Thank you very much,' said Alice. 'May I help you off
with your helmet?' It was evidently more than he could
manage by himself; however, she managed to shake him out
of it at last.

'Now one can breathe more easily,' said the Knight,
putting back his shaggy hair with both hands, and turning

his gentle face and large mild eyes to Alice. She thought she had never seen such a strange-looking soldier in all her life.

He was dressed in tin armour, which seemed to fit him very badly, and he had a queer-shaped little deal box fastened across his shoulders, upside-down, and with the lid hanging open. Alice looked at it with great curiosity.

'I see you're admiring my little box,' the Knight said in a friendly tone. 'It's my own invention – to keep clothes and sandwiches in. You see I carry it upside-down, so that the rain ca'n't get in.'

'But the things can get *out*,' Alice gently remarked. 'Do you know the lid's open?'

'I didn't know it,' the Knight said, a shade of vexation passing over his face. 'Then all the things must have fallen out! And the box is no use without them.' He unfastened it as he spoke, and was just going to throw it into the bushes, when a sudden thought seemed to strike him, and he hung it carefully on a tree. 'Can you guess why I did that?' he said to Alice.

Alice shook her head.

'In hopes some bees may make a nest in it – then I should get the honey.'

'But you've got a bee-hive – or something like one – fastened to the saddle,' said Alice.

'Yes, it's a very good bee-hive,' the Knight said in a discontented tone, 'one of the best kind. But not a single bee has come near it yet. And the other thing is a mouse-trap. I suppose the mice keep the bees out – or the bees keep the mice out, I don't know which.'

'I was wondering what the mouse-trap was for,' said Alice. 'It isn't very likely there would be any mice on the horse's back.'

'Not very likely, perhaps,' said the Knight; 'but, if they *do* come, I don't choose to have them running all about.'

'You see,' he went on after a pause, 'it's as well to be pro-vided for *everything*. That's the reason the horse has all those anklets round his feet.'

'But what are they for?' Alice asked in a tone of great curiosity.

'To guard against the bites of sharks,' the Knight replied. 'It's an invention of my own. And now help me on. I'll go with you to the end of the wood – What's that dish for?'

'It's meant for plum-cake,' said Alice.

'We'd better take it with us,' the Knight said. 'It'll come in handy if we find any plum-cake. Help me to get it into this bag.'

This took a long time to manage, though Alice held the bag open very carefully, because the knight was so *very* awk-ward in putting in the dish: the first two or three times that he tried he fell in himself instead. 'It's rather a tight fit, you see,' he said, as they got it in at last; 'there are so many candlesticks in the bag.' And he hung it to the saddle, which was already loaded with bunches of carrots, and fire-irons, and many other things.

'I hope you've got your hair well fastened on?' he contin-ued, as they set off.

'Only in the usual way,' Alice said, smiling.

'That's hardly enough,' he said, anxiously. 'You see the wind is so *very* strong here. It's as strong as soup.'

'Have you invented a plan for keeping the hair from being blown off?' Alice enquired.

'Not yet,' said the Knight. 'But I've got a plan for keeping it from *falling* off.'

'I should like to hear it, very much.'

'First you take an upright stick,' said the Knight. 'Then you make your hair creep up it, like a fruit-tree. Now the reason hair falls off is because it hangs *down* – things never fall *upwards*, you know. It's a plan of my own invention. You may try it if you like.'

It didn't sound a comfortable plan, Alice thought, and for a few minutes she walked on in silence, puzzling over the idea, and every now and then stopping to help the poor Knight, who certainly was *not* a good rider.

Whenever the horse stopped (which it did very often), he fell off in front; and, whenever it went on again (which it generally did rather suddenly), he fell off behind. Otherwise he kept on pretty well, except that he had a habit of now and then falling off sideways; and, as he generally did this on the side on which Alice was walking, she soon found that it was the best plan not to walk *quite* close to the horse.

'I'm afraid you've not had much practice in riding,' she ventured to say, as she was helping him up from his fifth tumble.

The Knight looked very much surprised, and a little offended at the remark. 'What makes you say that?' he asked, as he scrambled back into the saddle, keeping hold of Alice's hair with one hand, to save himself from falling over on the other side.

'Because people don't fall off quite so often, when they've had much practice.'

'I've had plenty of practice,' the Knight said very gravely; 'plenty of practice!'

Alice could think of nothing better to say than 'Indeed?' but she said it as heartily as she could. They went on a little way in silence after this, the Knight with his eyes shut, muttering to himself, and Alice watching anxiously for the next tumble.

'The great art of riding,' the Knight suddenly began in a loud voice, waving his right arm as he spoke, 'is to keep —' Here the sentence ended as suddenly as it had begun, as the

Knight fell heavily on the top of his head exactly in the path where Alice was walking. She was quite frightened this time, and said in an anxious tone, as she picked him up, 'I hope no bones are broken?'

'None to speak of,' the Knight said, as if he didn't mind breaking two or three of them. 'The great art of riding, as I was saying, is – to keep your balance properly. Like this, you know –'.

He let go the bridle, and stretched out both his arms to show Alice what he meant, and this time he fell flat on his back, right under the horse's feet.

'Plenty of practice!' he went on repeating, all the time that Alice was getting him on his feet again. 'Plenty of practice!'

'It's too ridiculous!' cried Alice, losing all her patience this time. 'You ought to have a wooden horse on wheels, that you ought!'

'Does that kind go smoothly?' the Knight asked in a tone of great interest, clasping his arms round the horse's neck as he spoke, just in time to save himself from tumbling off again.

'Much more smoothly than a live horse,' Alice said, with a little scream of laughter, in spite of all she could do to prevent it.

'I'll get one,' the Knight said thoughtfully to himself. 'One or two – several.'

There was a short silence after this, and then the Knight went on again. 'I'm a great hand at inventing things. Now, I daresay you noticed, the last time you picked me up, that I was looking rather thoughtful?'

'You *were* a little grave,' said Alice.

'Well, just then I was inventing a new way of getting over a gate – would you like to hear it?'

'Very much indeed,' Alice said, politely.

'I'll tell you how I came to think of it,' said the Knight. 'You see, I said to myself "The only difficulty is with the feet; the *head* is high enough already." Now, first I put my head on the top of the gate – then the head's high enough – then I stand on my head – then the feet are high enough, you see – then I'm over, you see.'

'Yes, I suppose you'd be over when that was done,' Alice said thoughtfully; 'but don't you think it would be rather hard?'

'I haven't tried it yet,' the Knight said, gravely; 'so I ca'n't tell for certain – but I'm afraid it *would* be a little hard.'

He looked so vexed at the idea that Alice changed the subject hastily. 'What a curious helmet you've got!' she said, cheerfully. 'Is that your invention, too?'

The Knight looked down proudly at his helmet, which hung from the saddle. 'Yes,' he said; 'but I've invented a better one than that – like a sugar-loaf. When I used to wear it, if I fell off the horse, it always touched the ground directly. So I had a *very* little way to fall, you see – But there *was* the danger of falling *into* it, to be sure. That happened to me once – and the worst of it was, before I could get out again, the other White Knight came and put it on. He thought it was his own helmet.'

The Knight looked so solemn about it that Alice did not dare to laugh. 'I'm afraid you must have hurt him,' she said in a trembling voice, 'being on the top of his head.'

'I had to kick him, of course,' the Knight said, very seriously. 'And then he took the helmet off again – but it took hours and hours to get me out. I was as fast as – as lightning, you know.'

'But that's a different kind of fastness,' Alice objected.

The Knight shook his head. 'It was all kinds of fastness with me, I can assure you!' he said. He raised his hands in some excitement as he said this, and instantly rolled out of the saddle, and fell headlong into a deep ditch.

Alice ran to the side of the ditch to look for him. She was rather startled by the fall, as for some time he had kept on very well, and she was afraid that he really *was* hurt this time. However, though she could see nothing but the soles of his feet, she was much relieved to hear that he was talking on in his usual tone. 'All kinds of fastness,' he repeated; 'but it was careless of him to put another man's helmet on – with the man in it, too.'

'How *can* you go on talking so quietly, head downwards?' Alice asked, as she dragged him out by the feet, and laid him in a heap on the bank.

The Knight looked surprised at the question. 'What does it matter where my body happens to be?' he said. 'My mind goes on working all the same. In fact, the more head-downwards I am, the more I keep inventing new things.'

'Now the cleverest thing of the sort that I ever did,' he went on after a pause, 'was inventing a new pudding during the meat-course.'

'In time to have it cooked for the next course?' said Alice. 'Well, that *was* quick work, certainly!'

'Well, not the *next* course,' the Knight said in a slow thoughtful tone; 'no, certainly not the next *course*.'

'Then it would have to be the next day. I suppose you wouldn't have two pudding-courses in one dinner?'

'Well, not the *next* day,' the Knight repeated as before; 'not the next *day*. In fact,' he went on, holding his head down, and his voice getting lower and lower, 'I don't believe that pudding ever *was* cooked! In fact, I don't believe that pudding ever *will* be cooked! And yet it was a very clever pudding to invent.'

'What did you mean it to be made of?' Alice asked,

hoping to cheer him up, for the poor Knight seemed quite low-spirited about it.

'It began with blotting-paper,' the Knight answered with a groan.

'That wouldn't be very nice, I'm afraid – '

'Not very nice *alone*,' he interrupted, quite eagerly; 'but you've no idea what a difference it makes, mixing it with other things – such as gunpowder and sealing-wax. And here I must leave you.' They had just come to the end of the wood.

Alice could only look puzzled; she was thinking of the pudding.

'You are sad,' the Knight said in an anxious tone; 'let me sing you a song to comfort you.'

'Is it very long?' Alice asked, for she had heard a good deal of poetry that day.

'It's long,' said the Knight, 'but it's very, *very* beautiful. Everybody that hears me sing it – either it brings the *tears* into their eyes, or else – '

'Or else what?' said Alice, for the Knight had made a sudden pause.

'Or else it doesn't, you know. The name of the song is called "Haddocks' Eyes".'

'Oh, that's the name of the song, is it?' Alice said, trying to feel interested.

'No, you don't understand,' the Knight said, looking a little vexed. 'That's what the name is *called*. The name really *is* "The Aged Aged Man".'

'Then I ought to have said: "That's what the *song* is called"?' Alice corrected herself.

'No, you oughtn't; that's quite another thing! The song is called "Ways and Means"; but that's only what it's *called*, you know!'

'Well, what *is* the song, then?' said Alice, who was by this time completely bewildered.

'I was coming to that,' the Knight said. 'The song really *is* "A-sitting On a Gate"; and the tune's my own invention.'

So saying, he stopped his horse and let the reins fall on its neck; then, slowly beating time with one hand, and with a faint smile lighting up his gentle foolish face, as if he enjoyed the music of his song, he began.

Of all the strange things that Alice saw in her journey Through the Looking-Glass, this was the one that she always remembered most clearly. Years afterwards she could bring the whole scene back again, as if it had been only yesterday – the mild blue eyes and kindly smile of the Knight – the setting sun gleaming through his hair, and shining on his armour in a blaze of light that quite dazzled her – the horse quietly moving about, with the reins hanging loose on his neck, cropping the grass at her feet – and the black shadows of the forest behind – all this she took in like a picture, as, with one hand shading her eyes, she leant against a tree, watching the strange pair, and listening, in a half-dream, to the melancholy music of the song.

'But the tune *isn't* his own invention,' she said to herself; 'it's "I give thee all, I can no more".' She stood and listened very attentively, but no tears came into her eyes.

> *I'll tell thee everything I can:*
> *There's little to relate.*
> *I saw an aged aged man,*
> *A-sitting on a gate.*
> *"Who are you, aged man?" I said.*
> *"And how is it you live?"*
> *And his answer trickled through my head,*
> *Like water through a sieve.*

He said: "I look for butterflies
   That sleep among the wheat;
I make them into mutton-pies,
   And sell them in the street.
I sell them unto men," he said,
   "Who sail on stormy seas;
And that's the way I get my bread —
   A trifle, if you please."

But I was thinking of a plan
   To dye one's whiskers green,
And always use so large a fan
   That they could not be seen.
So, having no reply to give
   To what the old man said,
I cried: "Come, tell me how you live!"
   And thumped him on the head.

His accents mild took up the tale;
   He said: "I go my ways,
And when I find a mountain-rill,
   I set it in a blaze;
And thence they make a stuff they call
   Rowlands' Macassar-Oil —
Yet twopence-halfpenny is all
   They give me for my toil."

But I was thinking of a way
   To feed oneself on batter,
And so go on from day to day
   Getting a little fatter.
I shook him well from side to side,
   Until his face was blue;
"Come, tell me how you live," I cried,
   "And what it is you do!"

He said: "I hunt for haddocks' eyes
  Among the heather bright,
And work them into waistcoat-buttons
  In the silent night.
And these I do not sell for gold
  Or coin of silvery shine,
But for a copper halfpenny,
  And that will purchase nine."

"I sometimes dig for buttered rolls,
  Or set limed twigs for crabs;
I sometimes search the grassy knolls
  For wheels of Hansom-cabs.
And that's the way" (he gave a wink)
  "By which I get my wealth —
And very gladly will I drink
  Your Honour's noble health."

I heard him then, for I had just
  Completed my design
To keep the Menai bridge from rust
  By boiling it in wine.
I thanked him much for telling me
  The way he got his wealth,
But chiefly for his wish that he
  Might drink my noble health.

And now, if e'er by chance I put
  My fingers into glue,
Or madly squeeze a right-hand foot
  Into a left-hand shoe,
Or if I drop upon my toe
  A very heavy weight,
I weep, for it reminds me so
Of that old man I used to know —

> *Whose look was mild, whose speech was slow*
> *Whose hair was whiter than the snow,*
> *Whose face was very like a crow,*
> *With eyes, like cinders, all aglow,*
> *Who seemed distracted with his woe,*
> *Who rocked his body to and fro,*
> *And muttered mumblingly and low,*
> *As if his mouth were full of dough,*
> *Who snorted like a buffalo —*
> *That summer evening long ago,*
>   *A-sitting on a gate.'*

As the Knight sang the last words of the ballad, he gathered up the reins, and turned his horse's head along the road by which they had come. 'You've only a few yards to go,' he said, 'down the hill and over that little brook, and then you'll be a Queen — But you'll stay and see me off first?' he added as Alice turned with an eager look in the direction to which he pointed. 'I sha'n't be long. You'll wait and wave your handkerchief when I get to that turn in the road! I think it'll encourage me, you see.'

'Of course I'll wait,' said Alice; 'and thank you very much for coming so far — and for the song — I liked it very much.'

'I hope so,' the Knight said doubtfully; 'but you didn't cry so much as I thought you would.'

So they shook hands, and then the Knight rode slowly away into the forest. 'It wo'n't take long to see him *off*, I expect,' Alice said to herself, as she stood watching him. 'There he goes! Right on his head as usual! However, he gets on again pretty easily — that comes of having so many things hung round the horse — ' So she went on talking to herself, as she watched the horse walking leisurely along the road, and the Knight tumbling off, first on one side and then on the other. After the fourth or fifth tumble he reached the turn, and then she waved her handkerchief to him, and waited till he was out of sight.

'I hope it encouraged him,' she said, as she turned to run down the hill; 'and now for the last brook, and to be a Queen! How grand it sounds!' A very few steps brought her to the edge of the brook. 'The Eighth Square at last!' she cried as she bounded across,

    *   *   *   *   *

       *   *   *   *

    *   *   *   *   *

and threw herself down to rest on a lawn as soft as moss, with little flower-beds dotted about it here and there. 'Oh, how glad I am to get here! And what *is* this on my head?' she exclaimed in a tone of dismay, as she put her hands up to something very heavy, that fitted tight all around her head.

'But how *can* it have got there without my knowing it?' she said to herself, as she lifted it off, and set it on her lap to make out what it could possibly be.

It was a golden crown.

GEORGE MACDONALD

FROM *The Princess and the Goblin*

(1871)

I have said the Princess Irene was about eight years old when my story begins. And this is how it begins.

One very wet day, when the mountain was covered with mist which was constantly gathering itself together into raindrops, and pouring down on the roofs of the great old house, whence it fell in a fringe of water from the eaves all round about it, the princess could not of course go out. She got very tired, so tired that even her toys could no longer amuse her. You would wonder at that if I had time to describe to you one half of the toys she had. But then you wouldn't have the toys themselves, and that makes all the difference: you can't get tired of a thing before you have it. It was a picture, though, worth seeing – the princess sitting in the nursery with the sky-ceiling over her head, at a great table covered with her toys. If the artist would like to draw this, I should advise him not to meddle with the toys. I am afraid of attempting to describe them, and I think he had better not try to draw them. He had better not. He can do a thousand things I can't, but I don't think he could draw those toys. No man could better make the princess herself than he could, though – leaning with her back bowed into the back of the chair, her head hanging down, and her hands in her lap, very miserable as she would say herself, not even knowing what she would like, except it were to go out and get thoroughly wet, and catch a particularly nice cold, and have to go to bed and take gruel. The next moment after you see her sitting there, her nurse goes out of the room.

Even that is a change, and the princess wakes up a little, and looks about her. Then she tumbles off her chair, and runs out of the door, not the same door the nurse went out of, but one which opened at the foot of a curious old stair of worm-eaten oak, which looked as if never anyone had set foot upon it. She had once before been up six steps, and that was sufficient reason, in such a day, for trying to find out what was at the top of it.

Up and up she ran – such a long way it seemed to her! – until she came to the top of the third flight. There she found the landing was the end of a long passage. Into this she ran. It was full of doors on each side. There were so many that she did not care to open any, but ran on to the end, where she turned into another passage, also full of doors. When she had turned twice more, and still saw doors and only doors about her, she began to get frightened. It was so silent! And all those doors must hide rooms with nobody in them! That was dreadful. Also the rain made a great trampling noise on the roof. She turned and started at

full speed, her little footsteps echoing through the sounds
of the rain – back for the stairs and her safe nursery. So she
thought, but she had lost herself long ago. It doesn't follow
that she *was* lost, because she had lost herself, though.

She ran for some distance, turned several times, and then
began to be afraid. Very soon she was sure that she had lost
the way back. Rooms everywhere, and no stair! Her little
heart beat as fast as her little feet ran, and a lump of tears
was growing in her throat. But she was too eager and perhaps too frightened to cry for some time. At last her hope
failed her. Nothing but passages and doors everywhere! She
threw herself on the floor, and burst into a wailing cry
broken by sobs.

She did not cry long, however, for she was as brave as
could be expected of a princess of her age. After a good cry,
she got up, and brushed the dust from her frock. Oh, what
old dust it was! Then she wiped her eyes with her hands, for
princesses don't always have their handkerchiefs in their
pockets, any more than some other little girls I know of.
Next, like a true princess, she resolved on going wisely to
work to find her way back: she would walk through the passages, and look in every direction for the stair. This she did,
but without success. She went over the same ground again
and again without knowing it, for the passages and doors
were all alike. At last, in a corner, through a half-open door,
she did see a stair. But alas! It went the wrong way: instead
of going down, it went up. Frightened as she was, however,
she could not help wishing to see where yet further the stair
could lead. It was very narrow, and so steep that she went
on like a four-legged creature on her hands and feet.

When she came to the top, she found herself in a little
square place, with three doors, two opposite each other, and
one opposite the top of the stair. She stood for a moment,

without an idea in her little head what to do next. But as she stood, she began to hear a curious humming sound. Could it be the rain? No. It was much more gentle, and even monotonous than the sound of the rain, which now she scarcely heard. The low sweet humming sound went on, sometimes stopping for a little while and then beginning again. It was more like the hum of a very happy bee that had found a rich well of honey in some globular flower than anything else I can think of at this moment. Where could it come from? She laid her ear first to one of the doors to hearken if it was there – then to another. When she laid her ear against the third door, there could be no doubt where it came from: it must be from something in that room. What could it be? She was rather afraid, but her curiosity was stronger than her fear, and she opened the door very gently and peeped in. What do you think she saw? A very old lady who sat spinning.

Perhaps you will wonder how the princess could tell that the old lady was an old lady, when I inform you that not only was she beautiful, but her skin was smooth and white. I will tell you more. Her hair was combed back from her forehead and face, and hung loose far down and all over her back. That is not much like an old lady – is it? Ah! But it was white almost as snow. And although her face was so smooth, her eyes looked so wise that you could not have helped seeing she must be old. The princess, though she could not have told you why, did think her very old indeed – quite fifty – she said to herself. But she was rather older than that, as you shall hear.

SUSAN COOLIDGE

From *What Katy Did*

(1872)

'Tomorrow I will begin,' thought Katy, as she dropped asleep that night. How often we all do so! And what a pity it is that when morning comes and tomorrow is today we so frequently wake up feeling quite differently; careless or impatient, and not a bit inclined to do the fine things we planned overnight...

You know how, if we begin the day in a cross mood, all sorts of unfortunate accidents seem to occur to add to our vexations. The very first thing Katy did this morning was to break her precious vase – the one Cousin Helen had given her.

It was standing on the bureau with a little cluster of blush-roses in it. The bureau had a swing-glass. While Katy was brushing her hair, the glass tipped a little so that she could not see ... She gave the glass a violent push. The lower part swung forward, there was a smash, and the first thing Katy knew, the blush-roses lay scattered all over the floor, and Cousin Helen's pretty present was ruined.

Katy just sat down on the carpet and cried as hard as if she had been Phil himself. Aunt Izzie heard her lamenting, and came in.

'I'm very sorry,' she said, picking up the broken glass, 'but it's no more than I expected. You're so careless, Katy. Now don't sit there in that foolish way! Get up and dress your-self. You'll be late to breakfast.'

'What's the matter?' asked Papa, noticing Katy's red eyes as she took her seat at the table.

'I've broken my vase,' said Katy, dolefully ...

'What are you all going to do today?' asked Dr Carr, hoping to give things a more cheerful turn.

'Swing!' cried John and Dorry both together. 'Alexander's put us up a splendid one in the wood-shed.'

'No, you're not,' said Aunt Izzie, in a positive tone. 'The swing is not to be used till tomorrow. Remember that, children. Not till tomorrow. And not then, unless I give you leave.'

This was unwise of Aunt Izzie. It would have been better had she explained further. The truth was that Alexander, in putting up the swing, had cracked one of the staples which fastened it to the roof. He meant to get a new one in the course of the day, and meantime, he had cautioned Miss Carr to let no one use the swing, because it really was not safe. If she had told this to the children, all would have been right; but Aunt Izzie's theory was that young people must obey their elders without explanation.

John, and Elsie, and Dorry all pouted when they heard this order. Elsie recovered her good-humour first.

'I don't care,' she said, ''cause I'm going to be very busy;

I've got to write a letter to Cousin Helen about somefing.' (Elsie never could quite pronounce the *th*.)

'What?' asked Clover.

'Oh, somefing,' answered Elsie, wagging her head mysteriously. 'None of the rest of you must know, Cousin Helen said so; it's a secret she and me has got.'

'I don't believe Cousin Helen said so at all,' said Katy, crossly. 'She wouldn't tell secrets to a silly little girl like you.'

'Yes, she would too,' retorted Elsie, angrily. 'She said I was just as good to trust as if I were ever so big. And she said I was her pet. So there! Katy Carr!'

'Stop disputing,' said Aunt Izzie. 'Katy, your top drawer is all out of order. I never saw anything look so badly. Go upstairs at once and straighten it, before you do anything else. Children, you must keep in the shade this morning. It's too hot for you to be running about in the sun. Elsie, go into the kitchen and tell Debby I want to speak to her.'

'Yes,' said Elsie, in an important tone. 'And afterwards I'm coming back to write my letter to Cousin Helen.'

Katy went slowly upstairs, dragging one foot after the other. It was a warm, languid day. Her head ached a little, and her eyes smarted and felt heavy from crying so much … She pulled the top drawer open with a disgusted groan.

It must be confessed that Miss Izzie was right. A bureau drawer could hardly look worse than this one did … All sorts of things were mixed together, as if somebody had put in a long stick and stirred them well up … Stocking-legs had come unrolled, and twisted themselves about pocket-handkerchiefs, and ends of ribbons and linen collars. Ruffles, all crushed out of shape, stuck up from under the heavier things, and sundry little paper boxes lay empty on top, the treasures they once held having sifted down to the bottom of the drawer and disappeared beneath the general mass.

It took much time and patience to bring order out of this confusion. But Katy knew that Aunt Izzie would be up by-and-by, and she dared not stop till all was done. By the time it was finished she was very tired. Going downstairs she met Elsie coming up with a slate in her hand, which, as soon as she saw Katy, she put behind her.

'You mustn't look,' she said; 'it's my letter to Cousin Helen. Nobody but me knows the secret. It's all written, and I'm going to send it to the post-office. See – there's a stamp on it' – and she exhibited a corner of the slate. Sure enough, there was a stamp stuck on the frame.

'You little goose!' said Katy, impatiently; 'you can't send *that* to the post-office. Here, give me the slate; I'll copy what you've written on paper, and Papa'll give you an envelope.'

'No, no,' cried Elsie, struggling, 'you mustn't! You'll see what I've said, and Cousin Helen said I wasn't to tell. It's a secret. Let go of my slate, I say! I'll tell Cousin Helen what a mean girl you are, and then she won't love you a bit.'

'There, then, take your old slate!' said Katy, giving her a push. Elsie slipped, screamed, caught at the banisters, missed them, and, rolling over and over, fell with a thump on the hall floor.

It wasn't much of a fall, only half a dozen steps, but the bump was a hard one, and Elsie roared as if she had been half killed. Aunt Izzie and Mary came rushing to the spot.

'Katy – pushed – me,' sobbed Elsie. 'She wanted me to tell my secret, and I wouldn't. She's a bad naughty girl!'

'Well, Katy Carr, I *should* think you'd be ashamed of yourself,' said Aunt Izzie … 'There, there, Elsie! Don't cry any more, dear. Come upstairs with me. I'll put on some arnica, and Katy shan't hurt you again.'

So they went upstairs. Katy, left below, felt very miserable: repentant, defiant, discontented, and sulky all at once ...

'I don't care!' she murmured, choking back her tears. 'Elsie is a real cry-baby, anyway. And Aunt Izzie always takes her part. Just because I told the little silly not to go and send a great heavy slate to the post-office.'

She went by the side-door into the yard. As she passed the shed the new swing caught her eye.

'How exactly like Aunt Izzie,' she thought, 'ordering the children not to swing till she gives them leave. I suppose she thinks it's too hot, or something. *I* shan't mind her, anyhow.'

She seated herself in the swing. It was a first-rate one, with a broad comfortable seat and thick new ropes. The seat hung just the right distance from the floor. Alexander was a capital hand at putting up swings, and the wood-shed the nicest possible spot in which to have one.

It was a big place, with a very high roof. There was not much wood left in it just now, and the little there was, was piled neatly about the sides of the shed, so as to leave plenty of room. The place felt cool and dark, and the motion of the swing seemed to set the breeze blowing. It waved Katy's hair like a great fan, and made her dreamy and quiet. All sorts of sleepy ideas began to flit through her brain. Swinging to and fro like the pendulum of a great clock, she gradually rose higher and higher, driving herself along by the motion of her body, and striking the floor smartly with her foot at every sweep. Now she was at the top of the high-arched door. Then she could almost touch the cross-beam above it, and through the small square window could see pigeons sitting and pluming themselves on the eaves of the barn and white clouds blowing over the blue sky. She had never swung so high before. It was like flying she thought, as she bent and curved more strongly in the seat, trying to send herself yet higher and graze the roof with her toes.

Suddenly at the very highest point of the sweep there was a sharp noise of cracking. The swing gave a violent twist, spun half round and tossed Katy into the air. She clutched the rope – felt it dragged from her grasp – then down – down – she fell. All grew dark, and she knew no more.

When she opened her eyes she was lying on the sofa in the dining-room. Clover was kneeling beside her with a pale, scared face, and Aunt Izzie was dropping something cold and wet on her forehead.

'What's the matter?' said Katy, faintly.

'Oh, she's alive – she's alive!' and Clover put her arms round Katy's neck and sobbed.

'Hush, dear!' Aunt Izzie's voice sounded unusually gentle. 'You've had a bad tumble, Katy. Don't you recollect?'

'A tumble? Oh, yes – out of the swing,' said Katy, as it all came slowly back to her. 'Did the rope break, Aunt Izzie? I can't remember about it.'

'No, Katy, not the rope. The staple drew out of the roof. It was a cracked one, and not safe. Don't you recollect my telling you not to swing today? Did you forget?'

'No, Aunt Izzie – I didn't forget. I –' but here Katy broke down. She closed her eyes, and big tears rolled from under the lids.

'Don't cry,' whispered Clover, crying herself; 'please don't. Aunt Izzie isn't going to scold you.' But Katy was too weak and shaken not to cry.

'I think I'd like to go upstairs and lie on the bed,' she said. But when she tried to get off the sofa everything swam before her, and she fell back again on the pillow.

'Why, I can't stand up!' she gasped, looking very much frightened.

'I'm afraid you've given yourself a sprain somewhere,' said Aunt Izzie, who looked rather frightened herself. 'You'd better lie still a while, dear, before you try to move. Ah, here's the doctor! Well, I *am* glad.' And she went forward to meet him. It wasn't Papa, but Dr Alsop, who lived quite near them.

'I am so relieved that you could come,' Aunt Izzie said. 'My brother has gone out of town, not to return till tomorrow, and one of the little girls has had a bad fall.'

Dr Alsop sat down beside the sofa and counted Katy's pulse. Then he began feeling all over her.

'Can you move this leg?' he asked.

Katy gave a feeble kick.

'And this?'

The kick was a good deal more feeble.

'Did that hurt you?' asked Dr Alsop, seeing a look of pain on her face.

'Yes, a little,' replied Katy, trying hard not to cry.

'In your back, eh? Was the pain high up or low down?' and the doctor punched Katy's spine for some minutes, making her squirm uneasily.

'I'm afraid she's done some mischief,' he said, at last, 'but it is impossible to tell yet exactly what. It may only be a twist or a slight sprain,' he added, seeing the look of terror on Katy's face. 'You'd better get her upstairs and undress her as soon as you can, Miss Carr. I'll leave a prescription to rub her with.' And Dr Alsop took out a bit of paper and began to write.

'Oh, must I go to bed?' said Katy. 'How long will I have to stay there, doctor?'

'That depends on how fast you get well,' replied the doctor; 'not long, I hope. Perhaps only a few days.'

'A few days!' repeated Katy in a despairing tone.

After the doctor was gone, Aunt Izzie and Debby lifted Katy and carried her slowly upstairs. It was not easy, for every motion hurt her, and the sense of being helpless hurt most of all. She couldn't help crying after she was undressed and put into bed. It all seemed so dreadful and strange. If only Papa was here, she thought. But Dr Carr had gone into the country to see somebody who was very sick, and couldn't possibly be back till tomorrow.

Such a long, long afternoon as that was! Aunt Izzie sent up some dinner, but Katy couldn't eat. Her lips were parched and her head ached violently. The sun began to pour in; the room grew warm. Flies buzzed in the window and tormented her by lighting on her face. Little prickles of pain ran up and down her back. She lay with her eyes shut, because it hurt to keep them open, and all sorts of uneasy thoughts went rushing through her mind ...

Suddenly she became conscious that the glaring light from the window was shaded, and that the wind seemed to be blowing freshly over her. She opened her heavy eyes. The blinds were shut, and there beside the bed sat little Elsie, fanning her with a palm-leaf fan.

'Did I wake you up, Katy?' she asked in a timid voice.

Katy looked at her with startled, amazed eyes.

'Don't be frightened,' said Elsie, 'I won't disturb you. Johnny and me are *so* sorry you're sick,' and her little lips trembled. 'But we mean to keep real quiet, and never bang the nursery door, or make noises on the stairs, till you're all well again.' ...

Katy tried to speak, but began to cry instead, which frightened Elsie very much.

'Does it hurt you so bad?' she asked, crying too from sympathy.

'Oh, no! It isn't *that*,' sobbed Katy, 'but I was so cross to you this morning Elsie, and pushed you. Oh, please forgive me, please do!'

'Why, it's got well,' said Elsie, surprised. 'Aunt Izzie put a fing out of a bottle on it, and the bump all went away. Shall I go and ask her to put some on you too? – I will.' And she ran towards the door.

'Oh, no!' cried Katy, 'don't go away, Elsie. Come here and kiss me, instead.'

Elsie turned, as if doubtful whether this invitation could be meant for her. Katy held out her arms. Elsie ran right into them, and the big sister and the little exchanged an embrace which seemed to bring their hearts closer together than they had ever been before.

'You're the most *precious* little darling,' murmured Katy, clasping Elsie tight. 'I've been real horrid to you, Elsie. But I'll never be again. You shall play with me and Clover and Cecy just as much as you like, and write notes in all the post-offices, and everything else.'

'Oh, goody, goody!' cried Elsie, executing little skips of transport. 'How sweet you are, Katy! I mean to love you next best to Cousin Helen and Papa! And' – racking her brains for some way of repaying this wonderful kindness – 'I'll tell you the secret, if you want me to so *very* much. I guess Cousin Helen would let me.'

'No,' said Katy; 'never mind about the secret. I don't want you to tell it to me. Sit down by the bed and fan me some more instead.'

'No!' persisted Elsie, who, now that she had made up her mind to part with the treasured secret, could not bear to be stopped. 'Cousin Helen gave me a half-dollar, and told me to give it to Debby, and tell her she was much obliged to her making such nice things to eat. And I did. And Debby was real pleased. And I wrote Cousin Helen a letter, and told her that Debby liked the half-dollar. That's the secret! Isn't it a nice one? Only you mustn't tell anybody about it, ever – just as long as you live.'

'No!' said Katy, smiling faintly, 'I won't.'

All the rest of the afternoon Elsie sat beside the bed with her palm-leaf fan, keeping off the flies and 'shueing' away the other children when they peeped in at the door. 'Do you really like to have me here?' she asked more than once, and smiled, oh *so* triumphantly, when Katy said 'Yes!' But though Katy said 'Yes,' I am afraid it was only half the truth, for the sight of the dear little forgiving girl whom she had treated unkindly gave her more pain than pleasure.

'I'll be *so* good to her when I get well,' she thought to herself, tossing uneasily to and fro.

Aunt Izzie slept in her room that night. Katy was feverish. When morning came and Dr Carr returned, he found her in a good deal of pain, hot and restless, with wide-open anxious eyes.

'Papa!' she cried the first thing, 'must I lie here as much as a week?'

'My darling, I'm afraid you must,' replied her father, who looked worried and very grave.

'Dear, dear!' sobbed Katy, 'how can I bear it?'

JULES VERNE

FROM *Around the World in Eighty Days*

(1873)

The train, on leaving Great Salt Lake at Ogden, passed northward for an hour as far as Weber River, having completed nearly nine hundred miles from San Francisco. From this point it took an easterly direction towards the jagged Wahsatch Mountains. It was in the section included between this range and the Rocky Mountains that the American engineers found the most formidable difficulties in laying the road, and that the government granted a subsidy of forty-eight thousand dollars per mile, instead of sixteen thousand allowed for the work done on the plains. But the engineers, instead of violating nature, avoided its difficulties by winding around, instead of penetrating the rocks. One tunnel only, fourteen thousand feet in length, was pierced in order to arrive at the great basin.

The track up to this time had reached its highest elevation at the Great Salt Lake. From this point it described a long curve, descending towards Bitter Creek Valley, to rise again to the dividing ridge of the waters between the Atlantic and the Pacific. There were many creeks in this mountainous region, and it was necessary to cross Muddy Creek, Green Creek and others, upon culverts.

Passepartout grew more and more impatient as they went on, while Fix longed to get out of this difficult region, and was more anxious than Phileas Fogg himself to be beyond the danger of delays and accidents, and set foot on English soil.

At ten o'clock at night the train stopped at Fort Bridger station, and twenty minutes later entered Wyoming Territory, following the valley of Bitter Creek throughout. The next day, December 7th, they stopped for a quarter of an hour at Green River station. Snow had fallen abundantly during the night, but, being mixed with rain, it had half melted, and did not interrupt their progress. The bad weather, however, annoyed Passepartout; for the accumulation of snow, by blocking the wheels of the cars, would certainly have been fatal to Mr Fogg's tour.

'What an idea!' he said to himself. 'Why did my master make this journey in winter? Couldn't he have waited for the good season to increase his chances?'

While the worthy Frenchman was absorbed in the state of the sky and the depression of the temperature, Aouda was experiencing fears from a totally different cause.

Several passengers had got off at Green River, and were walking up and down the platforms; and among these Aouda recognized Colonel Stamp Proctor, the same who had so grossly insulted Phileas Fogg at the San Francisco meeting. Not wishing to be recognized, the young woman drew back from the window, feeling much alarm at her

discovery. She was attached to the man who, however coldly, gave her daily evidences of the most absolute devotion.
She did not comprehend, perhaps, the depth of the senti-
ment with which her protector inspired her, which she
called gratitude, but which, though she was unconscious of
it, was really more than that. Her heart sank within her when
she recognized the man whom Mr Fogg desired, sooner or
later, to call to account for his conduct. Chance alone, it was
clear, had brought Colonel Proctor on this train; but there
he was, and it was necessary, at all hazards, that Phileas
Fogg should not perceive his adversary.

Aouda seized a moment when Mr Fogg was asleep to tell
Fix and Passepartout whom she had seen.

'That Proctor on this train!' cried Fix. 'Well, reassure
yourself, madam: before he settles with Mr Fogg, he has got
to deal with me! It seems to me that I was the more insulted
of the two.'

'And besides,' added Passepartout, 'I'll take charge of him,
colonel as he is.'

'Mr Fix,' resumed Aouda, 'Mr Fogg will allow no one to
avenge him. He said that he would come back to America
to find this man. Should he perceive Colonel Proctor, we
could not prevent a collision which might have terrible
results. He must not see him.'

'You are right, madam,' replied Fix; 'a meeting between
them might ruin all. Whether he were victorious or beaten,
Mr Fogg would be delayed, and – '

'And,' added Passepartout, 'that would play the game of
the gentlemen of the Reform Club. In four days we shall be
in New York. Well, if my master does not leave this car during those four days, we may hope that chance will not bring
him face to face with this confounded American. We must,
if possible, prevent his stirring out of it.'

The conversation dropped. Mr Fogg had just woken up, and was looking out of the window. Soon after Passepartout, without being heard by his master or Aouda, whispered to the detective, 'Would you really fight for him?'

'I would do anything,' replied Fix, in a tone which betrayed determined will, 'to get him back living to Europe!'

Passepartout felt something like a shudder shoot through his frame, but his confidence in his master remained unbroken.

Was there any means of detaining Mr Fogg in the car, to avoid a meeting between him and the colonel? It ought not to be a difficult task, since that gentleman was naturally sedentary and little curious. The detective, at least, seemed to have found a way; for, after a few moments, he said to Mr Fogg, 'These are long and slow hours, sir, that we are passing on the railway.'

'Yes,' replied Mr Fogg; 'but they pass.'

'You were in the habit of playing whist,' resumed Fix, 'on the steamers.'

'Yes; but it would be difficult to do so here. I have neither cards nor partners.'

'Oh, but we can easily buy some cards, for they are sold on all the American trains. And as for partners, if madam plays – '

'Certainly, sir,' Aouda quickly replied; 'I understand whist. It is part of an English education.'

'I myself have some pretensions to playing a good game. Well, here are three of us, and a dummy – '

'As you please, sir,' replied Phileas Fogg, heartily glad to resume his favourite pastime – even on the railway.

Passepartout was despatched in search of the steward, and soon returned with two packs of cards, some pins, counters, and a shelf covered with cloth.

The game commenced. Aouda understood whist sufficiently well, and even received some compliments on her playing from Mr Fogg. As for the detective, he was simply an adept, and worthy of being matched against his present opponent.

'Now,' thought Passepartout, 'we've got him. He won't budge.'

At eleven in the morning the train had reached the dividing ridge of the waters at Bridger Pass, seven thousand five hundred and twenty-four feet above the level of the sea, one of the highest points attained by the track in crossing the Rocky Mountains. After going about two hundred miles, the travellers at last found themselves on one of those vast plains which extend to the Atlantic, and which nature has made so propitious for laying the iron road.

On the declivity of the Atlantic basin the first streams, branches of the North Platte River, already appeared. The whole northern and eastern horizon was bounded by the immense semicircular curtain which is formed by the southern portion of the Rocky Mountains, the highest being Laramie Peak. Between this and the railway extended vast plains, plentifully irrigated. On the right rose the lower spurs of the mountainous mass which extends southward to the sources of the Arkansas River, one of the great tributaries of the Missouri.

At half-past twelve the travellers caught sight for an instant of Fort Halleck, which commands that section; and in a few more hours the Rocky Mountains were crossed. There was reason to hope, then, that no accident would mark the journey through this difficult country. The snow had ceased falling, and the air became crisp and cold. Large birds, frightened by the locomotive, rose and flew off in the distance. No wild beast appeared on the plain. It was a desert in its vast nakedness.

After a comfortable breakfast, served in the car, Mr Fogg and his partners had just resumed whist when a violent whistling was heard, and the train stopped. Passepartout put his head out of the door, but saw nothing to cause the delay; no station was in view.

Aouda and Fix feared that Mr Fogg might take it into his head to get out; but that gentleman contented himself with saying to his servant, 'See what is the matter.'

Passepartout rushed out of the car. Thirty or forty passengers had already descended, amongst them Colonel Stamp Proctor.

The train had stopped before a red signal which blocked the way. The engineer and conductor were talking excitedly with a signal-man, whom the station-master at Medicine Bow, the next stopping place, had sent on before. The passengers drew around and took part in the discussion, in which Colonel Proctor, with his insolent manner, was conspicuous.

Passepartout, joining the group, heard the signal-man say, 'No! you can't pass. The bridge at Medicine Bow is shaky, and would not bear the weight of the train.'

This was a suspension-bridge thrown over some rapids, about a mile from the place where they now were. According to the signal-man, it was in a ruinous condition, several of the iron wires being broken; and it was impossible to risk the passage. He did not in any way exaggerate the condition of the bridge. It may be taken for granted that, rash as the Americans usually are, when they are prudent there is good reason for it.

Passepartout, not daring to apprise his master of what he heard, listened with set teeth, immovable as a statue.

'Hum!' cried Colonel Proctor; 'but we are not going to stay here, I imagine, and take root in the snow?'

'Colonel,' replied the conductor, 'we have telegraphed to

Omaha for a train, but it is not likely that it will reach Medicine Bow in less than six hours.'

'Six hours!' cried Passepartout.

'Certainly,' returned the conductor. 'Besides, it will take us as long as that to reach Medicine Bow on foot.'

'But it is only a mile from here,' said one of the passengers.

'Yes, but it's on the other side of the river.'

'And can't we cross that in a boat?' asked the colonel.

'That's impossible. The creek is swelled by the rains. It is a rapid, and we shall have to make a circuit of ten miles to the north to find a ford.'

The colonel launched a volley of oaths, denouncing the railway company and the conductor; and Passepartout, who was furious, was not disinclined to make common cause with him. Here was an obstacle, indeed, which all his master's bank-notes could not remove.

There was a general disappointment among the passengers, who, without reckoning the delay, saw themselves compelled to trudge fifteen miles over a plain covered with snow. They grumbled and protested, and would certainly have thus attracted Phileas Fogg's attention if he had not been completely absorbed in his game.

Passepartout found that he could not avoid telling his master what had occurred, and, with hanging head, he was turning towards the car when the engineer – a true Yankee, named Forster – called out, 'Gentlemen, perhaps there is a way, after all, to get over.'

'On the bridge?' asked a passenger.

'On the bridge.'

'With our train?'

'With our train.'

Passepartout stopped short, and eagerly listened to the engineer.

'But the bridge is unsafe,' urged the conductor.

'No matter,' replied Forster; 'I think that by putting on the very highest speed we might have a chance of getting over.'

'The devil!' muttered Passepartout.

But a number of the passengers were at once attracted by the engineer's proposal, and Colonel Proctor was especially delighted, and found the plan a very feasible one. He told stories about engineers leaping their trains over rivers without bridges, by putting on full steam; and many of those present avowed themselves of the engineer's mind.

'We have fifty chances out of a hundred of getting over,' said one.

'Eighty! Ninety!'

Passepartout was astounded, and, though ready to attempt anything to get over Medicine Creek, thought the experiment proposed a little too American. 'Besides,' thought he, 'there's a still more simple way, and it does not even occur to any of these people! Sir,' said he aloud to one of the passengers, 'the engineer's plan seems to me a little dangerous, but – '

'Eighty chances!' replied the passenger, turning his back on him.

'I know it,' said Passepartout, turning to another passenger, 'but a simple idea – '

'Ideas are no use,' returned the American, shrugging his shoulders, 'as the engineer assures us that we can pass.'

'Doubtless,' urged Passepartout, 'we can pass, but perhaps it would be more prudent – '

'What! Prudent!' cried Colonel Proctor, whom this word seemed to excite prodigiously. 'At full speed, don't you see, at full speed!'

'I know – I see,' repeated Passepartout; 'but it would be,

if not more prudent, since that word displeases you, at least more natural – '

'Who! What! What's the matter with this fellow?' cried several.

The poor fellow did not know to whom to address himself.

'Are you afraid?' asked Colonel Proctor.

'I afraid! Very well; I will show these people that a Frenchman can be as American as they!'

'All aboard!' cried the conductor.

'Yes, all aboard!' repeated Passepartout, and immediately. 'But they can't prevent me from thinking that it would be more natural for us to cross the bridge on foot, and let the train come after!'

But no one heard this sage reflection, nor would anyone have acknowledged its justice. The passengers resumed their places in the cars. Passepartout took his seat without telling what had passed. The whist-players were quite absorbed in their game.

The locomotive whistled vigorously; the engineer, reversing the steam, backed the train for nearly a mile – retiring, like a jumper, in order to take a longer leap. Then, with another whistle, he began to move forward; the train increased its speed, and soon its rapidity became frightful; a prolonged screech issued from the locomotive; the piston worked up and down twenty strokes to the second. They perceived that the whole train, rushing on at the rate of a hundred miles an hour, hardly bore upon the rails at all.

And they passed over! It was like a flash. No one saw the bridge. The train leaped, so to speak, from one bank to the other, and the engineer could not stop it until it had gone five miles beyond the station. But scarcely had the train passed the river, when the bridge, completely ruined, fell with a crash into the rapids of Medicine Bow.

MARK TWAIN

FROM *The Adventures of Tom Sawyer*

(1876)

Saturday morning was come, and all the summer world was bright and fresh, and brimming with life. There was a song in every heart; and if the heart was young the music issued at the lips. There was cheer in every face, and a spring in every step. The locust trees were in bloom, and the fragrance of the blossoms filled the air.

Cardiff Hill, beyond the village and above it, was green with vegetation, and it lay just far enough away to seem a Delectable Land, dreamy, reposeful, and inviting.

Tom appeared on the side-walk with a bucket of white-wash and a long-handled brush. He surveyed the fence, and the gladness went out of nature, and a deep melancholy settled down upon his spirit. Thirty yards of broad fence nine feet high! It seemed to him that life was hollow, and existence but a burden. Sighing, he dipped his brush and passed it along the topmost plank; repeated the operation; did it again; compared the insignificant whitewashed streak with the far-reaching continent of unwhitewashed fence, and sat down on a tree-box discouraged. Jim came skipping out at the gate with a tin pail, and singing 'Buffalo Gals'. Bringing water from the town pump had always been hateful work in Tom's eyes before, but now it did not strike him so. He remembered that there was company at the pump. White, mulatto, and Negro boys and girls were always there waiting their turns, resting, trading playthings, quarrelling, fighting, skylarking. And he remembered that although the pump was only a hundred and fifty yards off Jim never got back with a bucket of water under an hour; and even then somebody generally had to go after him. Tom said: 'Say, Jim; I'll fetch the water if you'll whitewash some.'

Jim shook his head, and said: 'Can't, Mar's Tom. Ole missis she tole me I got to go an' git dis water an' not stop foolin' 'roun' wid anybody. She say she spec' Ma'rs Tom gwyne to ax me to whitewash, an' so she tole me go 'long an' 'tend to my own business – she 'lowed *she'd* 'tend to de whitewashin'.'

'Oh, never you mind what she said, Jim. That's the way she always talks. Gimme the bucket – I won't be gone only a minute. *She* won't ever know.'

'Oh, I dasn't, Ma'rs Tom. Ole missis she'd take an' tar de head off'n me. 'Deed she would.'

'*She!* She never licks anybody – whacks 'em over the head with her thimble, and who cares for that, I'd like to know? She talks awful, but talk don't hurt – anyways, it don't if she don't cry. Jim, I'll give you a marble. I'll give you a white alley!'

Jim began to waver.

'White alley, Jim; and it's a bully tow.'

'My; dat's a mighty gay marvel, *I* tell you. But, Ma'rs Tom, I's powerful 'fraid ole missis.'

But Jim was only human – this attention was too much for him. He put down his pail, took the white alley. In another minute he was flying down the street with his pail and a tingling rear, Tom was whitewashing with vigour, and Aunt Polly was retiring from the field with a slipper in her hand and triumph in her eye.

But Tom's energy did not last. He began to think of the fun he had planned for this day, and his sorrows multiplied. Soon the free boys would come tripping along on all sorts of delicious expeditions, and they would make a world of fun of him for having to work – the very thought of it burnt him like fire. He got out his worldly wealth and examined it – bits of toys, marbles, and trash; enough to buy an exchange of work maybe, but not enough to buy so much as half an hour of pure freedom. So he returned his straitened means to his pocket, and gave up the idea of trying to buy the boys. At this dark and hopeless moment an inspiration burst upon him. Nothing less than a great, magnificent inspiration. He took up his brush and went tranquilly to work. Ben Rogers hove in sight presently; the very boy of all boys whose ridicule he had been dreading. Ben's gait was the hop, skip, and jump – proof enough that his heart was light and his anticipations high. He was eating an apple, and giving a long melodious whoop at intervals, followed by a deep-toned ding dong dong, ding dong dong, for he was personating a steamboat! As he drew near he slackened speed, took the middle of the street, leaned far over to starboard, and rounded-to ponderously, and with laborious pomp and circumstance, for he was personating the *Big Missouri*, and considered himself to be drawing nine feet of water. He was boat, and captain, and engine-bells combined, so he had to imagine himself standing on his own hurricane-deck giving the orders and executing them.

'Stop her, sir! Ling-a-ling-ling.' The headway ran almost out, and he drew up slowly towards the side-walk. 'Ship up to back! Ling-a-ling-ling!' His arms straightened and stiffened down his sides. 'Set her back on the stabboard! Ling-a-ling-ling! Chow! Ch-chow-wow-chow!' his right hand meantime describing stately circles, for it was representing a forty-foot wheel. 'Let her go back on the labboard! Ling-a-ling-ling! Chow-ch-chow-chow!' The left hand began to describe circles.

'Stop the stabboard! Ling-a-ling-ling! Stop the labboard! Come ahead on the stabboard! Stop her! Let your outside turn over slow! Ling-a-ling-ling! Chow-ow-ow! Get out that head-line! Lively, now! Come – out with your spring-line – what're you about there? Take a turn round that stump with the bight of it! Stand by that stage now – let her go! Done with the engines, sir! Ling-a-ling-ling!

'Sht! s'sht! sht!' (Trying the gauge-cocks.)

Tom went on whitewashing – paid no attention to the steamer. Ben stared a moment, and then said: 'Hi-yi! You're up a stump, ain't you!'

No answer. Tom surveyed his last touch with the eye of an artist; then he gave his brush another gentle sweep, and surveyed the result as before. Ben ranged up alongside of him. Tom's mouth watered for the apple, but he stuck to his work. Ben said: 'Hello, old chap; you got to work, hey?'

'Why, it's you, Ben! I warn't noticing.'

'Say, I'm going in a swimming, I am. Don't you wish you could? But of course, you'd druther work, wouldn't you? 'Course you would!'

Tom contemplated the boy a bit, and said: 'What do you call work?'

'Why, ain't that work?'

Tom resumed his whitewashing, and answered carelessly: 'Well, maybe it is, and maybe it ain't. All I know is, it suits Tom Sawyer.'

'Oh, come now, you don't mean to let on that you like it?'

The brush continued to move.

'Like it? Well, I don't see why I oughtn't to like it. Does a boy get a chance to whitewash a fence every day?'

That put the thing in a new light. Ben stopped nibbling his apple. Tom swept his brush daintily back and forth – stepped back to note the effect – added a touch here and there – criticized the effect again, Ben watching every move, and getting more and more interested, more and more absorbed. Presently he said: 'Say, Tom, let me whitewash a little.'

Tom considered; was about to consent; but he altered his mind: 'No, no; I reckon it wouldn't hardly do, Ben. You see, Aunt Polly's awful particular about this fence – right here on the street, you know – but if it was the back fence I wouldn't mind, and she wouldn't. Yes, she's awful particular about this fence; it's got to be done very careful; I reckon there ain't one boy in a thousand, maybe two thousand, that can do it the way it's got to be done.'

'No – is that so? Oh, come now; lemme just try, only just a little. I'd let you, if you was me, Tom.'

'Ben, I'd like to, honest injun; but Aunt Polly – well, Jim wanted to do it, but she wouldn't let him. Sid wanted to do it, but she wouldn't let Sid. Now, don't you see how I am fixed? If you was to tackle this fence, and anything was to happen to it – '

'Oh, shucks; I'll be just as careful. Now lemme try. Say – I'll give you the core of my apple.'

'Well, here. No, Ben; now don't; I'm afeard – '

'I'll give you all of it!'

Tom gave up the brush with reluctance in his face, but alacrity in his heart. And while the late steamer *Big Missouri* worked and sweated in the sun, the retired artist sat on a barrel in the shade close by, dangled his legs, munched his apple, and planned the slaughter of more innocents. There was no lack of material; boys happened along every little while; they came to jeer, but remained to whitewash. By the time Ben was fagged out, Tom had traded the next chance to Billy Fisher for a kite in good repair; and when he played out, Johnny Miller bought in for a dead rat and a string to swing it with; and so on, and so on, hour after hour. And when the middle of the afternoon came, from being a poor poverty-stricken boy in the morning Tom was literally rolling in wealth. He had, besides the things I have mentioned, twelve marbles, part of a jew's harp, a piece of blue bottle-glass to look through, a spool-cannon, a key that wouldn't unlock anything, a fragment of chalk, a glass stopper of a decanter, a tin soldier, a couple of tadpoles, six firecrackers, a kitten with only one eye, a brass door-knob, a dog-collar – but no dog – the handle of a knife, four pieces of orange-peel, and a dilapidated old window-sash. He had had a nice, good, idle time all the while – plenty of company – and the fence had three coats of whitewash on it! If he hadn't run out of whitewash he would have bankrupted every boy in the village.

Tom said to himself that it was not such a hollow world after all. He had discovered a great law of human action, without knowing it, namely, that, in order to make a man or a boy covet a thing, it is only necessary to make the thing difficult to attain. If he had been a great and wise philosopher, like the writer of this book, he would now have comprehended that work consists of whatever a body is obliged to do, and that play consists of whatever a body is not obliged to do. And this would help him to understand why constructing artificial flowers, or performing on a tread-mill, is work, whilst rolling nine-pins or climbing Mont Blanc is only amusement. There are wealthy gentlemen in England who drive four-horse passenger-coaches twenty or thirty miles on a daily line, in the summer, because the privilege costs them considerable money; but if they were offered wages for the service that would turn it into work, then they would resign.

ANNA SEWELL

From *Black Beauty*

(1877)

Later on in the evening, a traveller's horse was brought in by the second ostler, and whilst he was cleaning him, a young man with a pipe in his mouth lounged into the stable to gossip.

'I say, Towler,' said the ostler, 'just run up the ladder into the loft and put some hay down into this horse's rack, will you? Only lay down your pipe.'

'All right,' said the other, and went up through the trap door; and I heard him step across the floor overhead and put down the hay. James came in to look at us the last thing, and then the door was locked.

I cannot say how long I had slept, nor what time in the night it was, but I woke up very uncomfortable, though I hardly knew why. I got up; the air seemed all thick and choking. I heard Ginger coughing and one of the other horses moved about restlessly; it was quite dark, and I could see nothing, but the stable was very full of smoke, and I hardly knew how to breathe.

The trap door had been left open, and I thought that was the place it came through. I listened and heard a soft rushing sort of noise, and a low crackling and snapping. I did not know what it was, but there was something in the sound so strange that it made me tremble all over. The other horses were now all awake; some were pulling at their halters, others were stamping.

At last I heard steps outside, and the ostler who had put up the traveller's horse burst into the stable with a lantern, and began to untie the horses, and try to lead them out; but he seemed in such a hurry, and so frightened himself that he frightened me still more. The first horse would not go with him; he tried the second and third, they too would not stir. He came to me next and tried to drag me out of the stall by force; of course that was no use. He tried us all by turns and then left the stable.

No doubt we were very foolish, but danger seemed to be all round, and there was nobody we knew to trust in, and all was strange and uncertain. The fresh air that had come in through the open door made it easier to breathe, but the rushing sound overhead grew louder, and as I looked upward, through the bars of my empty rack, I saw a red light flickering on the wall. Then I heard a cry of 'Fire' outside, and the old ostler quietly and quickly came in; he got one horse out, and went to another, but the flames were playing round the trap door, and the roaring overhead was dreadful.

The next thing I heard was James's voice, quiet and cheery, as it always was.

'Come, my beauties, it is time for us to be off, so wake up and come along.' I stood nearest the door, so he came to me first, patting me as he came in.

'Come, Beauty, on with your bridle, my boy, we'll soon be out of this smother.' It was on in no time; then he took the scarf off his neck, and tied it lightly over my eyes, and patting and coaxing he led me out of the stable. Safe in the yard, he slipped the scarf off my eyes, and shouted, 'Here, somebody! Take this horse while I go back for the other.'

A tall broad man stepped forward and took me, and James darted back into the stable. I set up a shrill whinny as I saw him go. Ginger told me afterwards that whinny was the best thing I could have done for her, for had she not heard me outside, she would never have had the courage to come out.

There was much confusion in the yard; the horses being got out of other stables, and the carriages and gigs being pulled out of houses and sheds, lest the flames should spread further. On the other side of the yard, windows were thrown up, and people were shouting all sorts of things; but I kept my eye fixed on the stable door, where the smoke poured out thicker than ever, and I could see flashes of red light; presently I heard above all the stir and din a loud clear voice, which I knew was master's.

'James Howard! James Howard! Are you there?' There was no answer, but I heard a crash of something falling in the stable, and the next moment I gave a loud joyful neigh, for I saw James coming through the smoke leading Ginger with him; she was coughing violently and he was not able to speak.

'My brave lad!' said master, laying his hand on his shoulder. 'Are you hurt?'

James shook his head, for he could not yet speak.

'Aye,' said the big man who held me, 'he is a brave lad, and no mistake.'

'And now,' said master, 'when you have got your breath, James, we'll get out of this place as quickly as we can,' and we were moving towards the entry, when from the Market Place there came a sound of galloping feet and loud rumbling wheels.

''Tis the fire engine! The fire engine!' shouted two or three voices. 'Stand back, make way!' and clattering and thundering over the stones two horses dashed into the yard with the heavy engine behind them. The firemen leaped to the ground; there was no need to ask where the fire was – it was torching up in a great blaze from the roof.

We got out as fast as we could into the broad quiet Market Place; the stars were shining, and, except the noise behind us, all was still. Master led the way to a large hotel on the other side, and as soon as the ostler came, he said, 'James, I must now hasten to your mistress; I trust the horses entirely to you, order whatever you think is needed,' and with that he was gone. The master did not run, but I never saw mortal man walk so fast as he did that night.

There was a dreadful sound before we got into our stalls; the shrieks of those poor horses that were left burning to death in the stable – it was very terrible, and made both Ginger and me feel very bad. We, however, were taken in and well done by.

The next morning the master came to see how we were and to speak to James. I did not hear much, for the ostler was rubbing me down, but I could see that James looked very happy, and I thought the master was proud of him. Our mistress had been so much alarmed in the night that the journey was put off till the afternoon, so James had the morning on hand, and went first to the inn to see about our harness and the carriage, and then to hear more about the fire. When he came back, we heard him tell the ostler about it. At first no one could guess how the fire had been caused, but at last a man said he saw Dick Towler go into the stable with a pipe in his mouth, and when he came out he had not one, and went to the tap for another. Then the under-ostler said he had asked Dick to go up the ladder to put down some hay, but told him to lay down his pipe first. Dick denied taking the pipe with him, but no one believed him. I remember our John Manly's rule, never to allow a pipe in the stable, and thought it ought to be the rule everywhere.

James said the roof and floor had all fallen in, and that only the black walls were standing; the two poor horses that could not be got out were buried under the burnt rafters and tiles.

JOHANNA SPYRI

FROM *Heidi*

(1881)

Heidi was awakened next morning by a shrill whistle and as she opened her eyes a beam of sunlight came through the hole in the wall, making the hay shine like gold. At first she could not think where she was, then she heard her grandfather's deep voice outside and remembered joyfully that she had come to live in the mountains. She had been glad to leave old Ursula, who was very deaf and felt the cold so much that she sat all day by the kitchen fire or the living-room stove. Heidi had had to stay indoors where the old woman could see her, though she often longed to run outside and play. Now she jumped out of bed, full of excitement at all the new experiences awaiting her. She dressed herself as quickly as possible, then climbed down the ladder and hurried outside. Peter was waiting there with his herd and her grandfather was just bringing Daisy and Dusky from their stall. She went to say good morning to them all.

'Do you want to go up to the pasture with Peter?' asked the old man. This idea clearly delighted her. 'You must have a wash first, or the sun will laugh to see you look so black.'

He pointed to a tub full of water, standing in the sun beside the door, and Heidi went over to it at once and began to splash about. The Alm-Uncle went indoors, calling to Peter: 'Come here, General of the goats, and bring your knapsack with you.' Peter held out the little bag which contained his meagre lunch, and watched with big eyes as the old man put in a piece of bread and a piece of cheese, both twice as big as his own.

'Take this mug too, and fill it for her twice at dinner time. She doesn't know how to drink straight from the goat as you do. She'll stay with you all day, and mind you look after her and see she doesn't fall down the ravine.'

Heidi came running in. 'The sun can't laugh at me now,' she said. Her grandfather smilingly agreed. In her desire to please the sun, she had rubbed her face with the hard towel until she looked like a boiled lobster.

'When you come home tonight, you'll have to go right inside the tub like a fish, for you'll get black feet running about with the goats. Now off you go.'

It was very beautiful on the mountain that morning. The night wind had blown all the clouds away and the sky was deep blue. The sun shone brilliantly on the green pasture land and on the flowers which were blooming everywhere. There were primroses, blue gentian, and dainty yellow rock-roses. Heidi rushed to and fro, wild with excitement at sight of them. She quite forgot Peter and the goats, and kept stopping to gather flowers and put them in her apron. She wanted to take them home to stick among the hay in her bedroom, to make it look like a meadow.

Peter needed eyes all round his head. It was more than one pair could do to keep watch on Heidi as well as the goats, for they too were running about in all directions. He had to whistle and shout and swing his stick in the air to bring the wandering animals together.

'Where have you got to now, Heidi?' he called once rather crossly.

'Here,' came her voice from behind a little hillock some distance back. It was covered with primulas which had a most delicious scent. Heidi had never smelt anything so lovely before and had sat down among them to enjoy it to the full.

'Come on,' called Peter. 'Uncle said I wasn't to let you fall over the ravine.'

'Where's that?' she called, without moving.

'Right up above. We've still a long way to go, so do come on. Hear the old hawk croaking away up there?'

Heidi jumped up at this last remark and ran to him with her apron full of flowers.

'You've got enough now,' he said, as they started to climb again. 'Don't pick any more, otherwise you'll always be lagging behind, and besides, if you keep on, there won't be any left for tomorrow.'

Heidi saw the sense of this, and anyway her apron was almost full. She kept close to Peter after that, and the goats went on in a more orderly fashion too, for now they could smell the fragrant herbs they loved which grew on their grazing ground, and were anxious to reach them.

Peter usually took up his quarters for the day at the very foot of a rocky mountain peak. On the steep slopes above, there were only a few bushes and stunted fir trees, and the summit itself was just bare rock. On one side was the sheer drop over the ravine which the Alm-Uncle had spoken of. When they reached this place Peter took off his knapsack and laid it, for safety, in a little hollow, for there were sometimes strong gusts of wind and he had no wish to see his precious food go bowling down the mountain. Then he lay down in the sun to rest after the strenuous climb. Heidi put her apronful of flowers in the same little hollow. Then she sat down beside Peter and looked around her. The valley below was bathed in sunlight. In front of them a snowclad mountain stood out against the blue sky and to the left of this was a huge mass of rock, with jagged twin peaks. Everything was very still. Only a gentle breeze set the blue and yellow flowers nodding on their slender stems.

Peter fell asleep and the goats climbed about among the bushes. Heidi sat quite still, enjoying it all. She gazed so intently at the mountain peaks that soon they seemed to her to have faces and to be looking at her like old friends. Suddenly she heard a loud noise. Looking up, she saw an enormous bird, circling overhead with outstretched wings and croaking harshly as it flew. 'Peter, Peter, wake up!' she cried. 'Here's the hawk.' Peter sat up and together they watched as the great bird soared higher and higher into the sky and finally disappeared over the grey peaks.

'Where's it gone to?' asked Heidi, who had never seen a bird as big as that before and had watched its flight with great interest.

'Home to its nest,' replied Peter.

'Does it live right up there? How wonderful! Why does it make such a noise?'

'Because it has to,' explained Peter briefly.

'Let's climb up and see where it lives,' she proposed.

'Oh, no, we won't! Even the goats can't climb as high as

that, and don't forget Uncle told me to look after you,' he said with marked disapproval. To Heidi's surprise he then began whistling and shouting, but the goats recognized the familiar sounds and came towards him from all directions, though some lingered to nibble a tasty blade of grass, while others butted one another playfully. Heidi jumped up and ran among them, delighted to see them so obviously enjoying themselves. She spoke to each one, and every one was different and easily distinguishable from the others.

Meanwhile Peter opened his bag and spread its contents out in a square on the ground, two large portions for Heidi and two smaller ones for himself. Then he filled the mug with milk from Daisy and placed it in the middle of the square. He called to Heidi, but she was slower to come than the goats had been. She was so busy with her new playmates that she had ears and eyes for nothing else. He went on calling till his voice re-echoed from the rocks and at last she appeared. When she saw the meal laid out so invitingly, she skipped up and down with pleasure.

'Stop jigging about,' said Peter, 'it's dinner-time. Sit down and begin.'

'Is the milk for me?'

'Yes, and those huge pieces of bread and cheese. I'll get you another mugful from Daisy when you've drunk that one. Then I'll have a drink myself.'

'Where will you get yours from?' she inquired.

'From my own goat, Spot. Now start eating.'

She drank the milk, but ate only a small piece of bread and passed the rest over to Peter, with the cheese. 'You can have that,' she said. 'I've had enough.' He looked at her with amazement for he had never in his life had any food to give away. At first he hesitated, thinking she must be joking, but she went on holding it out to him and finally put it on his knee. This convinced him that she really meant what she said, so he took it, nodded his thanks and settled down to enjoy the feast. Heidi meanwhile sat watching the goats.

'What are they all called, Peter?' she asked presently.

Peter did not know a great deal, but this was a question he could answer without difficulty. He told her all the names, pointing to each animal in turn. She listened attentively and soon knew one from the other. Each had little tricks by which it could easily be recognized by anyone looking at them closely, as she was doing. Big Turk had strong horns, and was always trying to butt the others, so they kept out of his way as much as possible. The only one to answer him back was a frisky little kid called Finch, with sharp little horns, and Turk was generally too astonished at such impudence to make a fight of it. Heidi was particularly attracted to a little white goat called Snowflake, which was bleating most pitifully. She had tried earlier to comfort it. Now she ran up to it again, put her arm round its neck, and asked fondly, 'What's the matter, Snowflake? What are you crying for?' At that, the goat nestled against her and stopped bleating.

Peter had not yet finished his meal, but he called out between mouthfuls, 'She's crying because her mother doesn't come up here any more. She's been sold to someone in Mayenfeld.'

'Where's her grandmother then?'

'Hasn't got one.'

'Or her grandfather?'

'Hasn't one.'

'Poor Snowflake,' said Heidi, hugging the little animal again. 'Don't cry any more. I shall be up here every day now, and you can always come to me if you feel lonely.' Snowflake rubbed her head on the little girl's shoulder, and seemed to be comforted.

Peter had now finished eating and came up to Heidi, who was making fresh discoveries all the time. She noticed that Daisy and Dusky seemed more independent than the other goats and carried themselves with a sort of dignity. They led the way as the herd went up to the bushes again. Some of them stopped here and there to sample a tasty herb, others went straight up, leaping over any small obstacles in their path. Turk was up to his tricks as usual, but Daisy and Dusky ignored him completely and were soon nibbling daintily at the leaves of the two thickest bushes. Heidi watched them for some time. Then she turned to Peter, who was lying full length on the grass.

'Daisy and Dusky are the prettiest of all the goats,' she said.

'I know. That's Uncle – he keeps them very clean and gives them salt and he has a fine stall for them,' he replied. Then he suddenly jumped up and ran after his herd, with Heidi close behind, anxious not to miss anything. He had noticed that inquisitive little Finch was right at the edge of the ravine, where the ground fell away so steeply that if it went any farther, it might go over and would certainly break its legs. Peter stretched out his hands to catch hold of the little kid, but he slipped and fell, though he managed to grasp one of its legs and Finch, highly indignant at such treatment, struggled wildly to get away. 'Heidi, come here,' called Peter, 'come and help.'

He couldn't get up unless he let go of Finch's leg – which he was nearly pulling out of its socket already. Heidi saw at once what to do, and pulled up a handful of grass which she held under Finch's nose.

'Come on, don't be silly,' she said. 'You don't want to fall down there and hurt yourself.'

At that the little goat turned round and ate the grass from her hand, and Peter was able to get up. He took hold of the cord, on which a little bell was hung round Finch's neck. Heidi took hold of it, too, on the other side, and together they brought the runaway safely back to the herd. Then Peter took up his stick to give it a good beating, and, seeing what was coming, Finch tried to get out of the way.

'Don't beat him,' pleaded Heidi. 'See how frightened he is.'

'He deserves it,' Peter replied, raising his arm, but she caught hold of him and exclaimed: 'No, you're not to! It will hurt him. Leave him alone!' She looked at him so fiercely that he was astonished and dropped the stick.

'I won't beat him if you'll give me some of your cheese again tomorrow,' he said, feeling he ought to have some compensation after the fright the little goat had given him.

'You can have it all, tomorrow and every day,' promised Heidi. 'I shan't want it. And I'll give you some of my bread as well, but then you must never beat Finch or Snowflake or any of them.'

'It's all the same to me,' said Peter, which was his way of saying that he promised. He let Finch go and it bounded back to the herd.

It was getting late and the setting sun spread a wonderful golden glow over the grass and the flowers, and the high peaks shone and sparkled. Heidi sat for a while, quietly enjoying the beautiful scene, then all at once she jumped up, crying, 'Peter, Peter! A fire, a fire! The mountains are on fire, and the snow and the sky too. Look, the trees and the rocks are all burning, even up there by the hawk's nest. Everything's on fire!'

'It's always like this in the evening,' Peter said calmly, whittling away at his stick. 'It's not a fire.'

'What is it then?' she cried, rushing about to look at the wonderful sight from all sides. 'What is it, Peter?'

'It just happens,' he said.

'Oh, just see, the mountains have got all rosy red! Look at the one with the snow on it, and that one with the big rocks at the top. What are their names, Peter?'

'Mountains don't have names,' he answered.

'How pretty the rosy snow looks, and the red rocks. Oh dear,' she added, after a pause, 'now the colour's going and everything's turning grey. Oh, it's all over.' She sat down, looking as upset as if it was indeed the end of everything.

'It'll be the same again tomorrow,' explained Peter. 'Now it's time to go home.' He whistled and called the goats together and they started the downward journey.

'Is it always like this up here?' asked Heidi hopefully.

'Usually.'

'Will it really be the same tomorrow?'

'Yes, it will,' he assured her.

With this she was content and as she had so much to think about, she didn't say another word till they reached the hut and saw her grandfather sitting under the fir trees, on the seat he had fixed there so that he could watch for the return of his animals. The little girl ran towards him, followed by Daisy and Dusky, and Peter called 'Good night, Heidi. Come again tomorrow.' She ran back to say goodbye and promised to go with him next day. Then she put her arms around Snowflake's neck and said, 'Sleep well, Snowflake. Remember I'll be coming with you again tomorrow and you're not to cry any more.' Snowflake gave her a trusting look and scampered off after the other goats.

'Oh, Grandfather,' Heidi cried, as she ran back to him, 'it was lovely up there, with all the flowers and then the fire and the rosy rocks. And see what I've brought you.' She shook out the contents of her little apron in front of him, but the poor flowers had all faded and looked like so much hay. She was terribly upset.

'What's happened to them? They weren't like that when I picked them.'

'They wanted to stay in the sun and didn't like being shut up in your apron,' he explained.

'Then I'll never pick any more. Grandfather, why does the hawk croak so loudly?'

'You go and jump in the washtub, while I milk the goats,' he replied. 'Then we'll have supper together indoors and I'll tell you about the hawk.'

As soon as Heidi was settled on her new high chair with her grandfather beside her and a mug of milk in front of her, she repeated her question.

'He's jeering at all the people who live in the villages down below and make trouble for one another. You can imagine he's saying, "If only you would all mind your own business and climb up to the mountain tops as I do, you'd be a lot better off."' The old man spoke these words so fiercely that it really reminded Heidi of the croaking of the great bird.

'Why haven't mountains got names?' she asked next.

'But they have,' he told her, 'and if you can describe one to me so that I can recognize it, I'll tell you its name.'

So she told him about the mountain with the twin peaks and described it very well. Her grandfather looked pleased. 'That's called Falkniss,' he said. Then she described the one covered with snow and he told her its name was Scesaplana.

'You enjoyed yourself, then?' he asked.

'Oh, yes,' she cried, and told him all the wonderful things that had happened during the day. 'The fire in the evening was the best of all. Peter said it wasn't a fire, but he couldn't tell me what it really was. You can though, Grandfather, can't you?'

'It's the sun's way of saying goodnight to the mountains,'

he explained. 'He spreads that beautiful light over them so that they won't forget him till he comes back in the morning.'

Heidi liked this explanation very much, and longed for another day to begin so that she could go up and watch the sun's goodnight again. But first she had to go to bed, and all night long she slept peacefully on her mattress of hay, dreaming of mountains and flowers and of Snowflake bounding happily about in the midst of it all.

CARLO COLLODI

FROM *Pinocchio*

(1883)

Geppetto goes home and makes his puppet; he calls him Pinocchio; the puppet gets into mischief.

Geppetto's little room on the ground floor was lit by a window under the stairs. His furniture could not have been simpler. An old chair, a tottering bed, and a broken-down table. At the back of the room you could see a fireplace, with the fire lit; but the fire was painted, and over the fire was painted a kettle boiling merrily, with a cloud of steam that was just like real steam.

As soon as he arrived home, Geppetto took his tools and began to make his puppet.

'What shall I call him?' he asked himself. 'I think I shall call him Pinocchio. That name will bring him good luck. I once knew a whole family of Pinocchios: there was Pinocchio the father, and Pinocchia the mother, and Pinocchii the children, and they all got along splendidly. The richest of them was a beggar.'

Having thought out a name for his puppet, he started his work with great determination. He made his hair, his forehead, and his eyes in a very short time.

As soon as the eyes were finished, imagine his bewilderment when he saw them moving and looking at him!

When Geppetto saw those two wooden eyes looking at him, he did not like it at all, and he said angrily, 'Naughty wooden eyes, why are you staring at me?'

But no one answered.

After the eyes, he made the nose; but as soon as it was finished, it began to grow. It grew, and it grew, and in a few minutes' time it was as long as if there was no end to it.

Poor Geppetto worked fast to shorten it; but the more he cut it off, the longer that insolent nose became.

After the nose, he made the mouth; but before he had finished it, it began to laugh and poke fun at him.

'Stop laughing!' said Geppetto; but he might as well have spoken to the wall.

'Stop laughing, I say!' he shouted, menacingly.

The mouth stopped laughing, and stuck out its tongue.

However, as Geppetto did not want to spoil the puppet, he pretended not to see it, and continued his work.

After the mouth, he made the chin, then the neck, the shoulders, the stomach, the arms, and the hands.

As soon as the hands were finished, Geppetto's wig was snatched from his head. He looked up, and what should he see but his yellow wig in the puppet's hands.

'Pinocchio! Give me back my wig at once!'

But Pinocchio, instead of giving back the wig, put it on his own head, and was almost hidden under it.

This cheeky, mocking behaviour made Geppetto feel sadder than ever before in his life. He turned to Pinocchio, and said: 'You scoundrel of a son! You are not even finished, and you already disobey your father! That's bad, my boy – very bad!' And he wiped away a tear.

There were still the legs and feet to make.

When Geppetto had finished the feet, he received a kick on the nose.

'It serves me right,' he said to himself. 'I should have thought of it before. Now it is too late.'

He took the puppet in his hands, and put him down on the floor to see if he could walk; but Pinocchio's legs were stiff, and he did not know how to move them. So Geppetto led him by the hand, and showed him how to put one foot before the other.

When the stiffness went out of his legs, Pinocchio started to walk alone, and run around the room; and finally he slipped through the door into the street and ran away.

Poor old Geppetto ran after him as quickly as he could, but he did not catch him, for the little rascal jumped like a rabbit, and his wooden feet clattered on the pavement, making as much noise as twenty pairs of wooden shoes.

'Catch him! Catch him!' cried Geppetto.

But when the people saw that wooden puppet running as fast as a racehorse, they looked at him in amazement, and then laughed, and laughed, and laughed, until their sides were aching.

At last, by some lucky chance, a policeman came and when he heard the clatter, he thought somebody's horse had run away from its master. So he courageously stood in the middle of the street with his legs apart, in order to stop it, and prevent any more trouble.

From far away, Pinocchio saw the policeman barricading

the street, and he decided to run between his legs; but he failed dismally.

The policeman, without moving from his place, picked him up by the nose – that ridiculous, long nose, that seemed made on purpose to be caught by policemen – and returned him to Geppetto, who wanted to pull his ears to punish him for his naughtiness. Imagine what he felt when he could not find any ears! And do you know why? Because he had made him in such a hurry that he had forgotten his ears.

So he took him by the nape of his neck, and as they walked away he said, shaking his head menacingly: 'You just come home, and I'll settle your account when we get there!'

At this threatening remark, Pinocchio threw himself down on the ground, and refused to walk.

A crowd of idle and inquisitive people gathered around him. Some said one thing, some another.

'The poor puppet,' said some of them, 'is right, not wanting to go home! Who knows how horribly that bad Geppetto might beat him?'

And others added, with evil tongues: 'Geppetto *seems* to be a good man, but he is a perfect tyrant with children. If we leave that poor marionette in his hands, he may tear him to pieces.'

In short, so much was said and done that the policeman let Pinocchio go, and decided to take poor Geppetto to prison.

He could not, for the time being, say anything in his own defence, but he cried like a calf and, as they walked towards the prison, he whimpered, 'Wretched son! And to think that I worked so hard to make a fine puppet! But serve me right. I ought to have known what would happen!'

What happened afterwards is almost too much to believe; and I shall tell you about it in the following chapters.

ROBERT LOUIS STEVENSON

From *Treasure Island*

(1883)

Now, just after sundown, when all my work was over,
and I was on my way to my berth, it occurred to me
that I should like an apple. I ran on deck. The watch was all
forward looking out for the island. The man at the helm
was watching the luff of the sail, and whistling away gently
to himself; and that was the only sound excepting the swish
of the sea against the bows and around the sides of the ship.

In I got bodily into the apple barrel, and found there was
scarce an apple left; but, sitting down there in the dark,
what with the sound of the waters and the rocking movement of the ship, I had either fallen asleep, or was on the
point of doing so, when a heavy man sat down with rather a
clash close by. The barrel shook as he leaned his shoulders
against it, and I was just about to jump up when the man

began to speak. It was Silver's voice, and, before I had heard a dozen words, I would not have shown myself for all the world, but lay there, trembling and listening, in the extreme of fear and curiosity; for from these dozen words I understood that the lives of all the honest men aboard depended upon me alone.

'No, not I,' said Silver. 'Flint was cap'n; I was quartermaster, along of my timber leg. The same broadside I lost my leg, old Pew lost his deadlights. It was a master surgeon, him that ampytated me – out of college and all – Latin by the bucket, and what not; but he was hanged like a dog, and sun-dried like the rest, at Corso Castle. That was Roberts' men, that was, and comed of changing names of their ships – *Royal Fortune* and so on. Now, what a ship was christened, so let her stay, I says. So it was with the *Cassandra*, as brought us all safe home from Malabar, after England took the Viceroy of the Indies; so it was with the old *Walrus*, Flint's old ship, as I've seen a'muck with the red blood and fit to sink with gold.'

'Ah!' cried another voice, that of the youngest hand on board, and evidently full of admiration, 'he was the flower of the flock, was Flint!'

'Davis was a man, too, by all accounts,' said Silver. 'I never sailed along of him; first with England, then with Flint, that's my story; and now here on my own account, in a manner of speaking. I laid by nine hundred safe, from England, and two thousand after Flint. That ain't bad for a man before the mast – all safe in bank. 'Tain't earning now, it's saving does it, you may lay to that. Where's all England's men now? I dunno. Where's Flint's? Why, most on 'em aboard here, and glad to get the duff – been begging before that, some on 'em. Old Pew, as had lost his sight, and might have thought shame, spends twelve hundred pounds in a

year, like a lord in Parliament. Where is he now? Well, he's
dead now and under hatches; but for two year before that,
shiver my timbers, the man was starving! He begged, and he
stole, and he cut throats, and starved at that, by the powers!'

'Well, it ain't much use, after all,' said the young seaman.

''Tain't much use for fools, you may lay to it – that, nor
nothing,' cried Silver. 'But now, you look here: you're young,
you are, but you're as smart as paint. I see that when I set
my eyes on you, and I'll talk to you like a man.'

You may imagine how I felt when I heard this abomi-
inable old rogue addressing another in the very same words
of flattery as he had used to myself. I think, if I had been
able, that I would have killed him through the barrel.
Meantime, he ran on, little supposing he was overheard.

'Here it is about gentlemen of fortune. They lives rough,
and they risk swinging, but they eat and drink like fighting-
cocks, and when a cruise is done, why it's hundreds of
pounds instead of hundreds of farthings in their pockets.
Now, the most goes for rum and a good fling, and to sea
again in their shirts. But that's not the course I lay. I puts it
all away, some here, some there, and none too much any-
wheres, by reason of suspicion. I'm fifty, mark you; once
back from this cruise, I set up gentleman in earnest. Time
enough, too, says you. Ah, but I've lived easy in the meantime; never denied myself o' nothing heart desires, and slep'
soft and ate dainty all my days, but when at sea. And how
did I begin? Before the mast, like you!'

'Well,' said the other, 'but all the other money's gone now,
ain't it? You daren't show face in Bristol after this.'

'Why, where might you suppose it was?' asked Silver,
derisively.

'At Bristol, in banks and places,' answered his companion.

'It were,' said the cook; 'it were when we weighed anchor.

But my old missis has it all by now. And the "Spy-glass" is sold, lease and goodwill and rigging; and the old girl's off to meet me. I would tell you where, for I trust you; but it 'ud make jealousy among the mates.'

'And can you trust your missis?' asked the other.

'Gentlemen of fortune,' returned the cook, 'usually trust little among themselves, and right they are, you may lay to it. But I have a way with me, I have. When a mate brings a slip on his cable – one as knows me, I mean – it won't be in the same world with old John. There was some that was feared of Pew, and some that was feared of Flint; but Flint his own self was feared of me. Feared he was, and proud. They was the roughest crew afloat, was Flint's; the devil himself would have been feared to go to sea with them. Well, now, I tell you, I'm not a boasting man, and you seen yourself how easy I keep company; but when I was quartermaster, *lambs* wasn't the word for Flint's old buccaneers. Ah, you may be sure of yourself in old John's ship.'

'Well, I tell you now,' replied the lad, 'I didn't half a quarter like the job till I had this talk with you, John; but there's my hand on it now.'

'And a brave lad you were, and smart, too,' answered Silver, shaking hands so heartily that all the barrel shook, 'and a finer figurehead for a gentleman of fortune I never clapped my eyes on.'

By this time I had begun to understand the meaning of their terms. By a 'gentleman of fortune' they plainly meant neither more nor less than a common pirate, and the little scene that I had overheard was the last act in the corruption of one of the honest hands – perhaps of the last one left aboard. But on this point I was soon to be relieved, for Silver giving a little whistle, a third man strolled up and sat down by the party.

'Dick's square,' said Silver.

'Oh, I know'd Dick was square,' returned the voice of the coxswain, Israel Hands. 'He's no fool, is Dick.' And he turned his quid and spat. 'But, look here,' he went on, 'here's what I want to know, Barbecue: how long are we a-going to stand off and on like a blessed bumboat? I've had a'most enough o' Cap'n Smollett; he's hazed me long enough, by thunder! I want to go into that cabin, I do. I want their pickles and wines, and that.'

'Israel,' said Silver, 'your head ain't much account, nor ever was. But you're able to hear, I reckon; leastways, your ears is big enough. Now, here's what I say: you'll berth forward, and you'll live hard, and you'll speak soft, and you'll keep sober, till I give the word; and you may lay to that, old son.'

'Well, I don't say no, do I?' growled the coxswain. 'What I say is, when? That's what I say.'

'When! By the powers!' cried Silver. 'Well, now, if you want to know, I'll tell you when. The last moment I can manage; and that's when. Here's a first-rate seaman, Cap'n Smollett, sails the blessed ship for us. Here's this squire and doctor with a map and such – I don't know where it is, do I? No more do you, says you. Well, then, I mean this squire and doctor shall find the stuff, and help us to get it aboard, by the powers. Then we'll see. If I was sure of you all, sons of double Dutchmen, I'd have Cap'n Smollett navigate us half-way back again before I struck.'

'Why, we're all seamen aboard here, I should think,' said the lad Dick.

'We're all foc's'le hands, you mean,' snapped Silver. 'We can steer a course, but who's to set one? That's what all you gentlemen split on, first and last. If I had my way, I'd have Cap'n Smollett work us back into the trades at least; then we'd have no blessed miscalculations and a spoonful of water a day. But I know the sort you are. I'll finish with 'em at the island, as soon's the blunt's on board, and a pity it is. But you're never happy till you're drunk. Split my sides, I've a sick heart to sail with the likes of you!'

'Easy all, Long John,' cried Israel. 'Who's a-crossin' of you?'

'Why, how many tall ships, think ye, now, have I seen laid aboard? And how many brisk lads drying in the sun at Execution Dock?' cried Silver. 'And all for this same hurry and hurry and hurry. You hear me? I seen a thing or two at sea, I have. If you would on'y lay your course, and a p'int to windward, you would ride in carriages, you would. But not you! I know you. You'll have your mouthful of rum tomorrow, and go hang.'

'Everybody know'd you was a kind of a chapling, John; but there's others as could hand and steer as well as you,' said Israel. 'They liked a bit of fun, they did. They wasn't so high and dry, nohow, but took their fling, like jolly companions every one.'

'So?' says Silver. 'Well, and where are they now? Pew was that sort, and he died a beggar-man. Flint was, and he died of rum at Savannah. Ah, they was a sweet crew, they was! On'y, where are they?'

'But,' asked Dick, 'when we do lay 'em athwart, what are we to do with 'em, anyhow?'

'There's the man for me!' cried the cook, admiringly. 'That's what I call business. Well, what would you think? Put 'em ashore like maroons? That would have been England's way. Or cut 'em down like that much pork? That would have been Flint's or Billy Bones's.'

'Billy was the man for that,' said Israel. '"Dead men don't bite," says he. Well, he's dead now hisself; he knows the long and short of it now; and if ever a rough hand come to port, it was Billy.'

'Right you are,' said Silver, 'rough and ready. But mark you here: I'm an easy man – I'm quite the gentleman, says you; but this time it's serious. Dooty is dooty, mates. I give my vote – death. When I'm in Parlyment, and riding in my coach, I don't want none of these sea-lawyers in the cabin a-coming home, unlooked for, like the devil at prayers. Wait is what I say; but when the time comes, why let her rip!'

'John,' cries the coxswain, 'you're a man!'

'You'll say so, Israel, when you see,' said Silver. 'Only one thing I claim – I claim Trelawney. I'll wring his calf's head off his body with these hands. Dick!' he added, breaking off, 'you just jump up, like a sweet lad, and get me an apple, to wet my pipe like.'

'You may fancy the terror I was in! I should have leaped out and run for it, if I had found the strength; but my limbs and heart alike misgave me. I heard Dick begin to rise, and then someone seemingly stopped him, and the voice of Hands exclaimed: 'Oh, stow that! Don't you get sucking of that bilge, John. Let's have a go of the rum.'

'Dick,' said Silver, 'I trust you. I've a gauge on the keg, mind. There's the key; you fill a pannikin and bring it up.'

Terrified as I was, I could not help thinking to myself that this must have been how Mr Arrow got the strong waters that destroyed him.

Dick was gone but a little while, and during his absence Israel spoke straight on in the cook's ear. It was but a word or two that I could catch, and yet I gathered some important news; for, besides other scraps that tended to the same purpose, this whole clause was audible: 'Not another man of them'll jine.' Hence there were still faithful men on board.

When Dick returned, one after another of the trio took the pannikin and drank – one 'To luck'; another with a 'Here's to old Flint'; and Silver himself saying, in a kind of song, 'Here's to ourselves, and hold your luff, plenty of prizes and plenty of duff.'

Just then a sort of brightness fell upon me in the barrel, and, looking up, I found the moon had risen, and was silvering the mizzen-top and shining white on the luff of the foresail; and almost at the same time the voice of the look-out shouted: 'Land ho!'

FRANCES HODGSON BURNETT

From *Little Lord Fauntleroy*

(1885)

It was late in the afternoon when the carriage containing little Lord Fauntleroy and Mr Havisham drove up the long avenue which led to the Castle. The Earl had given orders that his grandson should arrive in time to dine with him, and for some reason best known to himself he had also ordered that the child should be sent alone into the room in which he intended to receive him. As the carriage rolled up the avenue, Lord Fauntleroy sat leaning comfortably against the luxurious cushions, and regarded the prospect with great interest ...

When the carriage reached the great gates of the park, he looked out of the window to get a good view of the huge stone lions ornamenting the entrance. The gates were opened by a motherly, rosy-looking woman, who came out of a pretty ivy-covered lodge. Two children ran out of the house and stood looking with round wide-open eyes at the little boy in the carriage, who looked at them also. Their mother stood curtsying and smiling, and the children, on receiving a sign from her, made bobbing little curtsies too.

'Does she know me?' asked Lord Fauntleroy. 'I think she must think she knows me.' And he took off his black velvet cap to her and smiled.

'How do you do?' he said brightly. 'Good afternoon!'

The woman seemed pleased, he thought. The smile broadened on her rosy face and a kind look came into her blue eyes.

'God bless your lordship!' she said. 'God bless your pretty face! Good luck and happiness to your lordship! Welcome to you!'

Lord Fauntleroy waved his cap and nodded to her again as the carriage rolled by her.

'I like that woman,' he said. 'She looks as if she liked boys. I should like to come here and play with her children. I wonder if she has enough to make up a company?'

Mr Havisham did not tell him that he would scarcely be allowed to make playmates of the gate-keeper's children. The lawyer thought there was time enough for giving him that information.

The carriage rolled on and on between the great beautiful trees which grew on each side of the avenue and stretched their broad swaying branches in an arch across it. Cedric had never seen such trees, they were so grand and stately, and their branches grew so low down on their huge trunks. He did not then know that Dorincourt Castle was one of the most beautiful in all England; that its park was one of the broadest and finest, and its trees and avenue almost without rivals. But he did know that it was all very beautiful. He liked the big, broad-branched trees, with the late afternoon sunlight striking golden lances through them. He liked the perfect stillness which rested on everything. He felt a great, strange pleasure in the beauty of which he caught glimpses under and between the sweeping boughs – the great, beautiful spaces of the park, with still other trees, standing sometimes stately and alone, and sometimes in groups …

'It's a beautiful place, isn't it?' he said to Mr Havisham. 'I never saw such a beautiful place. It's prettier even than Central Park.'

He was rather puzzled by the length of time they were on their way.

'How far is it,' he said at length, 'from the gate to the front door?'

'It is between three and four miles,' answered the lawyer.

'That's a long way for a person to live from his gate,' remarked his lordship.

Every few moments he saw something new to wonder at and admire. When he caught sight of the deer, some couched in the grass, some standing with their pretty antlered heads turned with a half-startled air towards the avenue as the carriage wheels disturbed them, he was enchanted.

'Has there been a circus' he cried, 'or do they live here always? Whose are they?'

'They live here,' Mr Havisham told him. 'They belong to the Earl, your grandfather.'

It was not long after this that they saw the Castle. It rose up before them stately and beautiful and grey, the last rays of the sun casting dazzling lights on its many windows. It had turrets and battlements and towers; a great deal of ivy grew upon its walls; all the broad open space about it was laid out in terraces and lawns and beds of brilliant flowers.

'It's the most beautiful place I ever saw!' said Cedric, his round face flushing with pleasure. 'It reminds anyone of a king's palace. I saw a picture of one once in a fairy-book.'

He saw the great entrance door thrown open and many servants standing in two lines looking at him. He wondered why they were standing there, and admired their liveries very much. He did not know that they were there to do honour to the little boy to whom all this splendour would one day belong – the beautiful Castle like the fairy king's palace, the magnificent park, the grand old trees, the dells full of ferns and bluebells where the hares and rabbits played, the dappled, large-eyed deer couching in the deep grass. It was only a couple of weeks since he had sat with Mr Hobbs among the potatoes and canned peaches, with his legs dangling from the high stool; it would not have been possible for him to realize that he had very much to do with all this grandeur. At the head of the line of servants there stood an elderly woman in a rich, plain, black silk gown; she had grey hair and wore a cap. As he entered the hall she stood nearer than the rest, and the child thought from the look in her eyes that she was going to speak to him. Mr Havisham, who held his hand, paused a moment.

'This is Lord Fauntleroy, Mrs Mellon,' he said. 'Lord Fauntleroy, this is Mrs Mellon, who is the housekeeper.'

Cedric gave her his hand, his eyes lighting up.

'Was it you who sent the cat?' he said. 'I'm much obliged to you, ma'am.'

Mrs Mellon's handsome old face looked as pleased as the face of the lodge-keeper's wife had done.

'I should know his lordship anywhere,' she said to Mr Havisham. 'He has the Captain's face and way. It's a great day, this, sir.'

Cedric wondered why it was a great day. He looked at Mrs Mellon curiously. It seemed to him for a moment as if there were tears in her eyes, and yet it was evident she was not unhappy. She smiled down at him.

'The cat left two beautiful kittens here,' she said. 'They shall be sent up to your lordship's nursery.'

Mr Havisham said a few words to her in a low voice.

'In the library, sir,' Mrs Mellon replied. 'His lordship is to be taken there alone.'

A few minutes later the very tall footman in livery, who had escorted Cedric to the library door, opened it and announced: 'Lord Fauntleroy, my lord,' in quite a majestic tone. If he was only a footman, he felt it was rather a grand occasion when the heir came home to his own land and possessions, and was ushered into the presence of the old Earl, whose place and title he was to take.

Cedric crossed the threshold into the room. It was a very large and splendid room, with massive carven furniture in it, and shelves upon shelves of books ... For a moment Cedric thought there was nobody in the room, but soon he saw that by the fire burning on the wide hearth there was a large easy chair, and that in that chair someone was sitting – someone who did not at first turn to look at him.

But he had attracted attention in one quarter at least. On the floor, by the armchair, lay a dog, a huge tawny mastiff with body and limbs almost as big as a lion's; and this great creature rose majestically and slowly, and marched towards the little fellow with a heavy step.

Then the person in the chair spoke. 'Dougal,' he called, 'come back, sir.' ...

Cedric put his hand on the big dog's collar in the most natural way in the world, and they strayed forward together, Dougal sniffing as he went.

And then the Earl looked up. What Cedric saw was a large old man with shaggy white hair and eyebrows, and a nose like an eagle's beak between his deep fierce eyes. What the Earl saw was a graceful childish figure in a black velvet suit, with a lace collar, and with love-locks waving about the handsome, manly little face, whose eyes met his with a look of innocent good-fellowship …

Cedric looked at him just as he had looked at the woman at the lodge and at the housekeeper, and came quite close to him.

'Are you the Earl?' he said. 'I'm your grandson, you know, that Mr Havisham brought. I'm Lord Fauntleroy.'

He held out his hand because he thought it must be the polite and proper thing to do even with earls. 'I hope you are very well,' he continued, with the utmost friendliness. 'I'm very glad to see you.'

The Earl shook hands with him, with a curious gleam in his eyes; just at first he was so astonished that he scarcely knew what to say. He stared at the picturesque little apparition from under his shaggy brows, and took it all in from head to foot.

'Glad to see me, are you?' he said.

'Yes,' answered Lord Fauntleroy, 'very.'

There was a chair near him, and he sat down on it; it was a high-backed, rather tall chair, and his feet did not touch the floor when he had settled himself in it, but he seemed to be quite comfortable as he sat there and regarded his august relative intently and modestly.

'I've kept wondering what you would look like,' he remarked. 'I used to lie in my berth in the ship and wonder if you would be anything like my father.'

'Am I?' asked the Earl.

'Well,' Cedric replied, 'I was very young when he died, and I may not remember exactly how he looked, but I don't think you are like him.'

'You are disappointed, I suppose?' suggested his grand-father.

'Oh, no!' responded Cedric politely. 'Of course you would like anyone to look like your father; but of course you would enjoy the way your grandfather looked, even if he wasn't like your father. You know how it is yourself about admiring your relations.'

The Earl leaned back in his chair and stared. He could not be said to know how it was about admiring his relations. He had employed most of his noble leisure in quarrelling violently with them, in turning them out of his house, and applying abusive epithets to them; and they all hated him cordially.

'Any boy would love his grandfather,' continued Lord Fauntleroy, 'especially one that had been as kind to him as you have been.'

Another queer gleam came into the old nobleman's eyes.

'Oh,' he said, 'I have been kind to you, have I?'

'Yes,' answered Lord Fauntleroy brightly; 'I'm ever so much obliged to you about Bridget and the apple-woman and Dick!'

'Bridget!' exclaimed the Earl. 'Dick! The apple-woman!'

'Yes,' explained Cedric; 'the ones you gave me all that money for – the money you told Mr Havisham to give me if I wanted it.'

'Ha!' ejaculated his lordship. 'That's it, is it! The money you were to spend as you liked. What did you buy with it? I should like to hear something about that.'

He drew his shaggy eyebrows together and looked at the child sharply. He was secretly curious to know in what way the lad had indulged himself.

'Oh,' said Lord Fauntleroy, 'perhaps you didn't know about Dick and the apple-woman and Bridget. I forgot you lived such a long way off from them. They were particular friends of mine. And you see Michael had the fever – '

'Who's Michael?' asked the Earl.

'Michael is Bridget's husband, and they were in great trouble. When a man is sick and can't work and has twelve children you know how it is. And Michael had always been a sober man. And Bridget used to come to our house and cry. And the evening Mr Havisham was there, she was in the kitchen crying because they had almost nothing to eat and couldn't pay the rent; and I went in to see her, and Mr Havisham sent for me and he said you had given him some money for me. And I ran as fast as I could into the kitchen and gave it to Bridget; and that made it all right; and Bridget could scarcely believe her eyes. That's why I'm so obliged to you.'

'Oh,' said the Earl in his deep voice, 'that was one of the things you did for yourself, was it? What else?

Dougal had been sitting by the tall chair; the great dog had taken its place there when Cedric sat down ... And, just as this moment, the big dog gave little Lord Fauntleroy a look of dignified scrutiny, and deliberately laid its huge, lion-like head on the boy's black-velvet knee.

The small hand went on stroking this new friend as Cedric answered: 'Well, there was Dick,' he said. 'You'd like Dick, he's so square.'

This was an Americanism the Earl was not prepared for.

'What does that mean?' he inquired.

Lord Fauntleroy paused a moment to reflect. He was not very sure himself what it meant. He had taken it for granted as meaning something very creditable because Dick had been fond of using it.

'I think it means that he wouldn't cheat anyone,' he exclaimed, 'or hit a boy who was under his size, and that he blacks people's boots very well and makes them shine as much as he can. He's a professional boot-black.'

'And he's one of your acquaintances, is he?' said the Earl.

'He's an old friend of mine,' replied his grandson. 'Not quite as old as Mr Hobbs, but quite old. He gave me a present before the ship sailed.'

He put his hand into his pocket and drew forth a neatly folded red object and opened it with an air of affectionate pride. It was the red silk handkerchief with the large purple horseshoes and heads on it.

'He gave me this,' said his young lordship. 'I shall keep it always. You can wear it round your neck or keep it in your pocket. He bought it with the first money he earned after I bought Jake out and gave him the new brushes. It's a keepsake. I put some poetry in Mr Hobbs's watch. It was, "When this you see, remember me." When this I see I shall always remember Dick.'

The sensations of the Right Honourable the Earl of Dorincourt could scarcely be described. He was not an old nobleman who was very easily bewildered, because he had seen a great deal of the world; but here was something he found so novel that it almost took his lordly breath away, and caused him some singular emotions. He had never cared for children; he had been so occupied with his own pleasures that he had never had time to care for them. His own sons had not interested him when they were very young – though sometimes he remembered having thought Cedric's father a handsome and strong little fellow … A boy had always seemed to him a most objectionable little animal, selfish and greedy and boisterous when not under strict restraint … It had never once occurred to him that he should like his grandson; he had sent for the little Cedric because his pride impelled him to do so …

And then their talk began; and he was still more curiously moved and more and more puzzled. In the first place he was so used to seeing people rather afraid and embarrassed before him, that he had expected nothing else but that his grandson would be timid or shy. But Cedric was no more afraid of the Earl than he had been of Dougal. He was not bold; he was only innocently friendly, and he was not conscious that there should be any reason why he should be awkward or afraid. The Earl could not help seeing that the little boy took him for a friend and treated him as one, without having any doubt of him at all. It was quite plain as the little fellow sat there in his tall chair and talked in his friendly way that it had never occurred to him that this large, fierce-looking old man could be anything but kind to him, and rather pleased to see him there. And it was plain, too, that in his childish way he wished to please and interest his grandfather. Cross and hard-hearted and worldly as the old Earl was, he could not help feeling a secret and novel pleasure in this very confidence. After all, it was not disagreeable to meet someone who did not distrust or shrink from him, or seem to detect the ugly part of his nature; someone who looked at him with clear, unsuspecting eyes – if it was only a little boy in a black-velvet suit.

So the old man leaned back in his chair, and led his young companion on to telling him still more of himself, and with that odd gleam in his eyes watched the little fellow as he talked. Lord Fauntleroy was quite willing to answer all his questions and chatted on in his genial little way quite composedly. He told him all about Dick and Jerry and the apple-woman and Mr Hobbs; he described the Republican rally in all the glory of its banners and transparencies, torches and rockets. In the course of the conversation he reached the Fourth of July and the Revolution, and was just becoming enthusiastic, when he suddenly remembered something and stopped very abruptly.

'What is the matter?' demanded his grandfather. 'Why don't you go on?'

Lord Fauntleroy moved rather uneasily in his chair. It was evident to the Earl that Lord Fauntleroy was embarrassed by the thought which had just occurred to him.

'I was just thinking that perhaps you mightn't like it,' he replied. 'Perhaps someone belonging to you might have been there. I forgot you were an Englishman.'

'You can go on,' said my lord. 'No one belonging to me was there. You forgot you were an Englishman too.'

'Oh, no,' said Cedric quickly. 'I'm an American!'

'You are an Englishman,' said the Earl grimly. 'Your father was an Englishman.' ...

The lad had never thought of such a development as this. He felt himself grow quite hot up to the roots of his hair.

'I was born in America,' he protested. 'You have to be an American if you are born in America.' ...

They had not time to go very deep into the Revolution again before dinner was announced.

Cedric left his chair and went to his noble kinsman. He looked down at his gouty foot.

'Would you like me to help you?' he said politely. 'You could lean on me, you know. Once when Mr Hobbs hurt his foot with a potato barrel rolling on it, he used to lean on me.'

The big footman almost perilled his reputation and his situation by smiling. He was an aristocratic footman who had always lived in the best of noble families, and he had never smiled ... He only just saved himself by staring straight over the Earl's head at a very ugly picture.

The Earl looked his valiant young relative over from head to foot.

'Do you think you could do it?' he asked gruffly.

'I *think* I could,' said Cedric. 'I'm strong. I'm seven, you know. You could lean on your stick on one side, and on me on the other. Dick says I've a good deal of muscle for a boy that's only seven.'

He shut his hand and moved it upwards to his shoulder, so that the Earl might see the muscle Dick had kindly approved of, and his face was so grave and earnest that the footman found it necessary to look very hard indeed at the ugly picture.

'Well,' said the Earl, 'you may try.'

Cedric gave him his stick, and began to assist him to rise. Usually the footman did this, and was violently sworn at when his lordship had an extra twinge of gout. The Earl was not a very polite person as a rule, and many a time the huge footmen about him quaked inside their imposing liveries.

But this evening he did not swear, though his gouty foot gave him more twinges than one. He chose to try an experiment. He got up slowly and put his hand on the small shoulder presented to him with so much courage. Little Lord Fauntleroy made a careful step forward, looking down at the gouty foot.

'Just lean on me,' he said with encouraging good cheer. 'I'll walk very slowly.' …

'Does your foot hurt very much when you stand on it?' he asked. 'Did you ever put it in hot water and mustard? Mr Hobbs used to put his in hot water. Arnica is a very nice thing, they tell me.'

The big dog stalked slowly beside them, and the big footman followed; several times he looked very queer as he watched the little figure making the very most of all its strength, and bearing its burden with such goodwill. The Earl too looked rather queer, once, as he glanced sideways down at the flushed little face.

When they entered the room where they were to dine, Cedric saw it was a very large and imposing one, and that the footman who stood behind the chair at the head of the table stared very hard as they came in.

But they reached the chair at last. The hand was removed from his shoulder and the Earl was fairly seated.

Cedric took out Dick's handkerchief and wiped his forehead.

'It's a warm night, isn't it?' he said. 'Perhaps you need a fire because – because of your foot, but it seems just a little warm to me.'

His delicate consideration for his noble relative's feelings was such that he did not wish to seem to intimate that any of his surroundings were unnecessary.

'You have been doing some rather hard work,' said the Earl.

'Oh, no!' said Lord Fauntleroy, 'it wasn't exactly hard, but I got a little warm. A person will get warm in summer time.'

And he rubbed his damp curls rather vigorously with the gorgeous handkerchief. His own chair was placed at the other end of the table, opposite his grandfather's ...

Perhaps he had never looked so little a fellow as when seated now in his great chair, at the end of the table. Notwithstanding his solitary existence, the Earl chose to live in considerable state. He was fond of his dinner, and he dined in a formal style. Cedric looked at him across a glitter of splendid glass and plate, which to his unaccustomed eyes seemed quite dazzling ...

'You don't wear your coronet all the time?' remarked Lord Fauntleroy respectfully.

'No,' replied the Earl with his grim smile; 'it is not becoming to me.'

'Mr Hobbs said you always wore it,' said Cedric; 'but after he thought it over, he said he supposed you must sometimes take it off to put your hat on.'

'Yes,' said the Earl, 'I take it off occasionally.'

And one of the footmen suddenly turned aside and gave a singular little cough behind his hand.

Cedric finished his dinner first, and then he leaned back in his chair and took a survey of the room.

'You must be very proud of your house,' he said, 'it's such a beautiful house. I never saw anything so beautiful; but of course as I'm only seven, I haven't seen much.'

'And you think I must be proud of it, do you?' said the Earl.

'I should think anyone would be proud of it,' replied Lord Fauntleroy. 'I should be proud of it if it were my house. Everything about it is beautiful. And the park, and those trees, how beautiful they are and how the leaves rustle!'

Then he paused an instant and looked across the table rather wistfully.

'It's a very big house for just two people to live in, isn't it?' he said.

'It is quite large enough for two,' answered the Earl. 'Do you find it too large?'

His little lordship hesitated a moment.

'I was only thinking,' he said, 'that if two people lived in it who were not very good companions, they might feel lonely sometimes.'

'Do you think I shall make a good companion?' inquired the Earl.

'Yes,' replied Cedric, 'I think you will.'

ROBERT LOUIS STEVENSON

FROM *Kidnapped*

(1886)

Sometimes we walked, sometimes ran; and as it drew on to morning, walked ever the less and ran the more. Though, upon its face, that country appeared to be a desert, yet there were huts and houses of the people, of which we must have passed more than twenty, hidden in quiet places of the hills. When we came to one of these, Alan would leave me in the way, and go himself and rap upon the side of the house and speak a while at the window with some sleeper awakened. This was to pass the news; which, in that country, was so much of a duty that Alan must pause to attend to it even while fleeing for his life; and so well attended to by others that in more than half of the houses where we called they had heard already of the murder. In the others, as well as I could make out (standing back at a distance and hearing a strange tongue) the news was received with more of consternation than surprise.

For all our hurry, day began to come in while we were still far from any shelter. It found us in a prodigious valley, strewn with rocks and where ran a foaming river. Wild mountains stood around it; there grew there neither grass nor trees ...

The first peep of morning, then, showed us this horrible place, and I could see Alan knit his brow.

'This is no fit place for you and me,' he said. 'This is a place they're bound to watch.'

And with that he ran harder than ever down to the water side, in a part where the river was split in two among three rocks. It went through with a horrid thundering that made my belly quake; and there hung over the lynn a little mist of spray. Alan looked neither to the right nor to the left, but jumped clean upon the middle rock and fell there on his hands and knees to check himself, for that rock was small and he might have pitched over on the far side. I had scarce time to measure the distance or to understand the peril, before I had followed him, and he had caught and stopped me.

So there we stood, side by side upon a small rock slippery with spray, a far broader leap in front of us, and the river dinning upon all sides. When I saw where I was, there came on me a deadly sickness of fear, and I put my hand over my eyes. Alan took me and shook me; I saw he was speaking, but the roaring of the falls and the trouble of my mind prevented me from hearing; only I saw his face was red with anger, and that he stamped upon the rock. The same look showed me the water raging by, and the mist hanging in the air; and with that, I covered my eyes again and shuddered.

The next minute Alan had set the brandy bottle to my lips, and forced me to drink about a gill, which sent the blood into my head again. Then, putting his hands to his mouth and his mouth to my ear, he shouted, 'Hang or drown!' and turning his back upon me, leaped over the farther branch of the stream, and landed safe.

I was now alone upon the rock, which gave me the more room; the brandy was singing in my ears; I had this good example fresh before me, and just wit enough to see that if I did not leap at once, I should never leap at all. I bent low on my knees and flung myself forth, with that kind of anger of despair that has sometimes stood me in stead of courage. Sure enough, it was but my hands that reached the full length; these slipped, caught again, slipped again; and I was sliddering back into the lynn, when Alan seized me, first by the hair, then by the collar, and with a great strain dragged me into safety.

Never a word he said, but set off running again for his life, and I must stagger to my feet and run after him. I had been weary before, but now I was sick and bruised, and partly drunken, with the brandy; I kept stumbling as I ran, I had a stitch that came near to overmaster me; and when at last Alan paused under a great rock that stood there among a number of others, it was none too soon for David Balfour.

A great rock, I have said; but by rights it was two rocks leaning together at the top, both some twenty feet high, and at first sight inaccessible. Even Alan (though you may say he had as good as four hands) failed twice in an attempt to climb them; and it was only at the third trial, and then by standing on my shoulders and leaping up with such force as I thought must have broken my collar-bone, that he secured a lodgement. Once there, he let down his leathern girdle; and with the aid of that and a pair of shallow footholds in the rocks, I scrambled up beside him.

Then I saw why he had come there; for the two rocks, being both somewhat hollow on the top and sloping one to the other, made a kind of dish or saucer, where as many as three or four men might have lain hidden.

All this while Alan had not said a word, and had run and climbed with such a savage, silent frenzy of hurry that I knew he was in mortal fear of some miscarriage. Even now we were on the rock he said nothing, nor so much as relaxed the frowning look upon his face; but clapped flat down, and keeping only one eye above the edge of our place of shelter, scouted all round the compass. The dawn had come quite clear; we could see the stony sides of the valley, and its bottom, which was bestrewed with rocks, and the river, which went from one side to another, and made white falls; but nowhere the smoke of a house, nor any living creature but some eagles screaming round a cliff.

Then at last Alan smiled.

'Ay,' said he, 'now we have a chance'; and then looking at me with some amusement, 'Ye're no very gleg* at the jumping,' said he.

At this I suppose I coloured with mortification, for he added at once: 'Hoots! Small blame to ye! To be feared of a thing and yet to do it is what makes the prettiest kind of a man. And then there was water there, and water's a thing that dauntons even me. No, no,' said Alan, 'it's no you that's to blame, it's me.'

I asked him why.

'Why,' said he, 'I have proved myself a gomeral this night. For first of all I take a wrong road, and that in my own country of Appin; so that the day has caught us where we should never have been; and thanks to that, we lie here in

*brisk

some danger and mair discomfort. And next (which is the worst of the two, for a man that has been so much among the heather as myself) I have come wanting a water-bottle, and here we lie for a long summer's day with naething but neat spirit. Ye may think that a small matter; but before it comes night, David, ye'll give me news of it.'

I was anxious to redeem my character, and offered, if he would pour out the brandy, to run down and fill the bottle at the river.

'I wouldnae waste the good spirit either,' says he. 'It's been a good friend to you this night; or in my poor opinion, ye would still be cocking on yon stone. And what's mair,' says he, 'ye may have observed (you that's a man of so much penetration) that Alan Breck Stewart was perhaps walking quicker than his ordinar'.'

'You!' I cried. 'You were running fit to burst.'

'Was I so?' said he. 'Well, then, ye may depend upon it, there was nae time to be lost. And now here is enough said; gang you to your sleep, lad, and I'll watch.'

Accordingly, I lay down to sleep; a little peaty earth had drifted in between the top of the two rocks, and some bracken grew there, to be a bed to me; the last thing I heard was still the crying of the eagles.

I dare say it would be nine in the morning when I was roughly awakened, and found Alan's hand pressed upon my mouth.

'Wheesht!' he whispered. 'Ye were snoring.'

'Well,' said I, surprised at his anxious and dark face, 'and why not?'

He peered over the edge of the rock, and signed to me to do the like.

It was now high day, cloudless, and very hot. The valley was as clear as in a picture. About half a mile up the water was a camp of red-coats; a big fire blazed in their midst, at which some were cooking; and near by, on the top of a rock about as high as ours, there stood a sentry, with the sun sparkling on his arms. All the way down along the river-side were posted other sentries; here near together, there widelier scattered; some planted like the first, on places of command, some on the ground level and marching and counter-marching, so as to meet half way. Higher up the glen, where the ground was more open, the chain of posts was continued by horse-soldiers, whom we could see in the distance riding to and fro. Lower down, the infantry continued; but as the stream was suddenly swelled by the confluence of a considerable burn, they were more widely set, and only watched the fords and stepping-stones.

I took but one look at them, and ducked again into my place. It was strange indeed to see this valley, which had lain so solitary in the hour of dawn, bristling with arms and dotted with the red coats and breeches.

'Ye see,' said Alan, 'this was what I was afraid of, Davie: that they would watch the burn-side. They began to come in about two hours ago, and, man, but ye're a grand hand at the sleeping! We're in a narrow place. If they get up the sides of the hill, they could easy spy us with a glass; but if they'll only keep in the foot of the valley, we'll do yet. The posts are thinner down the water; and, come night, we'll try our hand at getting by them.'

'And what are we to do till night?' I asked.

'Lie here,' says he, 'and birstle.'

That one good Scotch word, 'birstle,' was indeed the most of the story of the day that we had now to pass. You are to remember that we lay on the bare top of a rock, like scones upon a girdle; the sun beat upon us cruelly; the rock grew so heated, a man could scarce endure the touch of it;

and the little patch of earth and fern, which kept cooler, was only large enough for one at a time. We took turn about to lie on the naked rock, which was indeed like the position of that saint that was martyred on a gridiron; and it ran in my mind how strange it was, that in the same climate and at only a few days' distance, I should have suffered so cruelly, first from cold upon my island, and now from heat upon this rock.

All the while we had no water, only a raw brandy for a drink, which was worse than nothing; but we kept the bottle as cool as we could, burying it in the earth, and got some relief by bathing our breasts and temples.

The soldiers kept stirring all day in the bottom of the valley, now changing guard, now in patrolling parties hunting among the rocks. These lay round in so great a number, that to look for men among them was like looking for a needle in a bottle of hay; and being so hopeless a task, it was gone about with the less care. Yet we could see the soldiers pike their bayonets among the heather, which sent a cold thrill into my vitals; and they would sometimes hang about our rock, so that we scarce dared to breathe.

It was in this way that I first heard the right English speech; one fellow as he went by actually clapping his hand upon the sunny face of the rock on which we lay, and plucking it off again with an oath.

'I tell you it's 'ot,' says he; and I was amazed at the clipping tones and the odd sing-song in which he spoke, and no less at that strange trick of dropping out the letter h. To be sure, I had heard Ransome; but he had taken his ways from all sorts of people, and spoke so imperfectly at the best that I set down the most of it to childishness. My surprise was all the greater to hear that manner of speaking in the mouth of a grown man; and indeed I have never grown used to it;

nor yet altogether with the English grammar, as perhaps a very critical eye might here and there spy out even in these memoirs.

The tediousness and pain of these hours upon the rock grew only the greater as the day went on; the rock getting still the hotter and the sun fiercer. There were giddiness, and sickness, and sharp pangs like rheumatism, to be supported. I minded then, and have often minded since, on the lines in our Scotch psalm:

> The moon by night thee shall not smite,
> Nor yet the sun by day;

and indeed it was only by God's blessing that we were neither of us sun-smitten.

At last, about two, it was beyond men's bearing, and there was now temptation to resist, as well as pain to thole. For the sun being now got a little into the west, there came a patch of shade on the east side of our rock, which was the side sheltered from the soldiers.

'As well one death as another,' said Alan, and slipped over the edge and dropped on the ground on the shadowy side.

I followed him at once, and instantly fell all my length, so weak was I and so giddy with that long exposure. Here, then, we lay for an hour or two, aching from head to foot, as weak as water, and lying quite naked to the eye of any soldier who should have strolled that way. None came, however, all passing by on the other side; so that our rock continued to be our shield even in this new position.

Presently we began again to get a little strength; and as the soldiers were now lying closer along the riverside, Alan proposed that we should try a start. I was by this time afraid of but one thing in the world; and that was to be set back upon the rock; anything else was welcome to me; so we got ourselves at once in marching order, and began to slip from rock to rock one after the other, now crawling flat on our bellies in the shade, now making a run for it, hcart in mouth.

The soldiers, having searched this side of the valley after a fashion, and being perhaps somewhat sleepy with the sultriness of the afternoon, had now laid by much of their vigilance, and stood dozing at their posts or only kept a lookout along the banks of the river; so that in this way, keeping down the valley and at the same time towards the mountains we drew steadily away from their neighbourhood.

OSCAR WILDE

The Happy Prince

(1888)

High above the city, on a tall column, stood the statue of the Happy Prince. He was gilded all over with thin leaves of fine gold, for eyes he had two bright sapphires, and a large red ruby glowed on his sword-hilt.

He was very much admired indeed. 'He is as beautiful as a weathercock,' remarked one of the Town Councillors who wished to gain a reputation for having artistic tastes; 'only not quite so useful,' he added, fearing lest people should think him unpractical, which he really was not.

'Why can't you be like the Happy Prince?' asked a sensible mother of her little boy who was crying for the moon. 'The Happy Prince never dreams of crying for anything.'

'I am glad there is someone in the world who is quite

happy,' muttered a disappointed man as he gazed at the wonderful statue.

'He looks just like an angel,' said the Charity Children as they came out of the cathedral in their bright scarlet cloaks and their clean white pinafores.

'How do you know?' said the Mathematical Master. 'You have never seen one.'

'Ah! But we have, in our dreams,' answered the children; and the Mathematical Master frowned and looked very severe, for he did not approve of children dreaming.

One night there flew over the city a little Swallow. His friends had gone away to Egypt six weeks before, but he had stayed behind, for he was in love with the most beautiful Reed. He had met her early in the spring as he was flying down the river after a big yellow moth, and had been so attracted by her slender waist that he had stopped to talk to her.

'Shall I love you?' said the Swallow, who liked to come to the point at once, and the Reed made him a low bow. So he flew round and round her, touching the water with his wings, and making silver ripples. This was his courtship, and it lasted all through the summer.

'It is a ridiculous attachment,' twittered the other Swallows; 'she has no money, and far too many relations'; and indeed the river was quite full of Reeds. Then, when the autumn came they all flew away.

After they had gone he felt lonely, and began to tire of his lady-love. 'She has no conversation,' he said, 'and I am afraid that she is a coquette, for she is always flirting with the wind.' And certainly, whenever the wind blew, the Reed made the most graceful curtsies. 'I admit that she is domestic,' he continued, 'but I love travelling, and my wife, consequently, should love travelling also.'

'Will you come away with me?' he said finally to her, but the Reed shook her head, she was so attached to her home.

'You have been trifling with me,' he cried. 'I am off to the Pyramids. Good-bye!' and he flew away.

All day long he flew, and at night-time he arrived at the city. 'Where shall I put up?' he said; 'I hope the town has made preparations.'

Then he saw the statue on the tall column.

'I will put up there,' he cried; 'it is a fine position, with plenty of fresh air.' So he alighted just between the feet of the Happy Prince.

'I have a golden bedroom,' he said softly to himself as he looked round, and he prepared to go to sleep; but just as he was putting his head under his wing a large drop of water fell on him. 'What a curious thing!' he cried; 'there is not a single cloud in the sky, the stars are quite clear and bright, and yet it is raining. The climate in the north of Europe is really dreadful. The Reed used to like the rain, but that was merely her selfishness.'

Then another drop fell.

'What is the use of a statue if it cannot keep the rain off?' he said; 'I must look for a good chimney-pot,' and he determined to fly away.

But before he had opened his wings, a third drop fell, and he looked up, and saw – Ah! What did he see?

The eyes of the Happy Prince were filled with tears, and tears were running down his golden cheeks. His face was so beautiful in the moonlight that the little Swallow was filled with pity.

'Who are you?' he said.

'I am the Happy Prince.'

'Why are you weeping then?' asked the Swallow; 'you have quite drenched me.'

'When I was alive and had a human heart,' answered the statue, 'I did not know what tears were, for I lived in the Palace of Sans-Souci, where sorrow is not allowed to enter. In the daytime I played with my companions in the garden, and in the evening I led the dance in the Great Hall. Round the garden ran a very lofty wall, but I never cared to ask what lay beyond it, everything about me was so beautiful. My courtiers called me the Happy Prince, and happy indeed I was, if pleasure be happiness. So I lived, and so I died. And now that I am dead they have set me up here so high that I can see all the ugliness and all the misery of my city, and though my heart is made of lead yet I cannot choose but weep.'

'What! Is he not solid gold?' said the Swallow to himself. He was too polite to make any personal remarks out loud.

'Far away,' continued the statue in a low musical voice, 'far away in a little street there is a poor house. One of the windows is open, and through it I can see a woman seated at a table. Her face is thin and worn, and she has coarse, red hands, all pricked by the needle, for she is a seamstress. She is embroidering passion-flowers on a satin gown for the loveliest of the Queen's maids-of-honour to wear at the next Court ball. In a bed in the corner of the room her little boy is lying ill. He has a fever, and is asking for oranges. His mother has nothing to give him but river water, so he is crying. Swallow, Swallow, little Swallow, will you not bring her the ruby out of my sword-hilt? My feet are fastened to this pedestal and I cannot move.'

'I am waited for in Egypt,' said the Swallow. 'My friends are flying up and down the Nile, and talking to the large lotus-flowers. Soon they will go to sleep in the tomb of the great King. The King is there himself in his painted coffin. He is wrapped in yellow linen, and embalmed with spices.

Round his neck is a chain of pale green jade, and his hands are like withered leaves.'

'Swallow, Swallow, little Swallow,' said the Prince, 'will you not stay with me for one night, and be my messenger? The boy is so thirsty, and the mother so sad.'

'I don't think I like boys,' answered the Swallow. 'Last summer, when I was staying on the river, there were two rude boys, the miller's sons, who were always throwing stones at me. They never hit me, of course; we swallows fly far too well for that, and besides I come of a family famous for its agility; but still, it was a mark of disrespect.'

But the Happy Prince looked so sad that the little Swallow was sorry. 'It is very cold here,' he said; 'but I will stay with you for one night, and be your messenger.'

'Thank you, little Swallow,' said the Prince.

So the Swallow picked out the great ruby from the Prince's sword, and flew away with it in his beak over the roofs of the town.

He passed by the cathedral tower, where the white marble angels were sculptured. He passed by the palace and heard the sound of dancing. A beautiful girl came out on the balcony with her lover. 'How wonderful the stars are,' he said to her, 'and how wonderful is the power of love!'

'I hope my dress will be ready in time for the State ball,' she answered. 'I have ordered passion-flowers to be embroidered on it; but the seamstresses are so lazy.'

He passed over the river, and saw the lanterns hanging to the masts of the ships. He passed over the Ghetto, and saw the old Jews bargaining with each other, and weighing out money in copper scales. At last he came to the poor house and looked in. The boy was tossing feverishly on his bed, and the mother had fallen asleep, she was so tired. In he hopped, and laid the great ruby on the table beside the woman's thimble. Then he flew gently round the bed, fanning the boy's forehead with his wings. 'How cool I feel!' said the boy, 'I must be getting better'; and he sank into a delicious slumber.

Then the Swallow flew back to the Happy Prince, and told him what he had done. 'It is curious,' he remarked, 'but I feel quite warm now, although it is so cold.'

'That is because you have done a good action,' said the Prince. And the little Swallow began to think, and then he fell asleep. Thinking always made him sleepy.

When day broke he flew down to the river and had a bath. 'What a remarkable phenomenon!' said the Professor of Ornithology as he was passing over the bridge. 'A swallow in winter!' And he wrote a long letter about it to the local newspaper. Everyone quoted it, it was full of so many words that they could not understand.

'Tonight I go to Egypt,' said the Swallow, and he was in high spirits at the prospect. He visited all the public monuments, and sat a long time on top of the church steeple. Wherever he went the Sparrows chirruped, and said to each other, 'What a distinguished stranger!' so he enjoyed himself very much.

When the moon rose he flew back to the Happy Prince. 'Have you any commissions for Egypt?' he cried; 'I am just starting.'

'Swallow, Swallow, little Swallow,' said the Prince, 'will you not stay with me one night longer?'

'I am waited for in Egypt,' answered the Swallow. 'Tomorrow my friends will fly up to the Second Cataract. The river-horse couches there among the bulrushes, and on a great granite throne sits the God Memnon. All night long he watches the stars, and when the morning star shines he utters one cry of joy, and then he is silent. At noon the yellow lions come down to the water's edge to drink. They have eyes like green beryls, and their roar is louder than the roar of the cataract.'

'Swallow, Swallow, little Swallow,' said the Prince, 'far away across the city I see a young man in a garret. He is leaning over a desk covered with papers, and in a tumbler by his side there is a bunch of withered violets. His hair is brown and crisp, and his lips are red as a pomegranate, and he has large and dreamy eyes. He is trying to finish a play for the Director of the Theatre, but he is too cold to write any more. There is no fire in the grate, and hunger has made him faint.'

'I will wait with you one night longer,' said the Swallow, who really had a good heart. 'Shall I take him another ruby?'

'Alas! I have no ruby now,' said the Prince; 'my eyes are all that I have left. They are made of rare sapphires, which were brought out of India a thousand years ago. Pluck out one of them and take it to him. He will sell it to the jeweller, and buy firewood, and finish his play.'

'Dear Prince,' said the Swallow, 'I cannot do that'; and he began to weep.

'Swallow, Swallow, little Swallow,' said the Prince, 'do as I command you.'

So the Swallow plucked out the Prince's eye, and flew away to the student's garret. It was easy enough to get in, as there was a hole in the roof. Through this he darted, and came into the room. The young man had his head buried in his hands, so he did not hear the flutter of the bird's wings, and when he looked up he found the beautiful sapphire lying on the withered violets.

'I am beginning to be appreciated,' he cried; 'this is from some great admirer. Now I can finish my play,' and he looked quite happy.

The next day the Swallow flew down to the harbour. He sat on the mast of a large vessel and watched the sailors hauling big chests out of the hold with ropes. 'Heave a-hoy!' they shouted as each chest came up. 'I am going to Egypt!' cried the Swallow, but nobody minded, and when the moon rose he flew back to the Happy Prince.

'I am come to bid you good-bye,' he cried.

'Swallow, Swallow, little Swallow,' said the Prince, 'will you not stay with me one night longer?'

'It is winter,' answered the Swallow, 'and the chill snow will soon be here. In Egypt the sun is warm on the green palm-trees, and the crocodiles lie in the mud and look lazily about them. My companions are building a nest in the Temple of Baalbek, and the pink and white doves are watching them, and cooing to each other. Dear Prince, I must leave you, but I will never forget you, and next spring I will bring you back two beautiful jewels in place of those you have given away. The ruby shall be redder than a red rose, and the sapphire shall be as blue as the great sea.'

'In the square below,' said the Happy Prince, 'there stands a little match-girl. She has let her matches fall in the gutter, and they are all spoiled. Her father will beat her if she does not bring home some money, and she is crying. She has no shoes or stockings, and her little head is bare. Pluck out my other eye, and give it to her, and her father will not beat her.'

'I will stay with you one night longer,' said the Swallow, 'but I cannot pluck out your eye. You would be quite blind then.'

'Swallow, Swallow, little Swallow,' said the Prince, 'do as I command you.'

So he plucked out the Prince's other eye, and darted down with it. He swooped past the match-girl, and slipped the jewel into the palm of her hand. 'What a lovely bit of glass!' cried the little girl; and she ran home, laughing.

Then the Swallow came back to the Prince. 'You are blind now,' he said, 'so I will stay with you always.'

'No, little Swallow,' said the poor Prince, 'you must go away to Egypt.'

'I will stay with you always,' said the Swallow, and he slept at the Prince's feet.

All the next day he sat on the Prince's shoulder, and told him stories of what he had seen in strange lands. He told him of the red ibises, who stand in long rows on the banks of the Nile, and catch goldfish in their beaks; of the Sphinx, who is as old as the world itself, and lives in the desert, and knows everything; of the merchants, who walk slowly by the side of their camels and carry amber beads in their hands; of the King of the Mountains of the Moon, who is as black as ebony, and worships a large crystal; of the great green snake that sleeps in a palm-tree, and has twenty priests to feed it with honey-cakes; and of the pygmies who sail over a big lake on large flat leaves, and are always at war with the butterflies.

'Dear little Swallow,' said the Prince, 'you tell me of marvellous things, but more marvellous than anything is the suffering of men and of women. There is no Mystery so great as Misery. Fly over my city, little Swallow, and tell me what you see there.'

So the Swallow flew over the great city, and saw the rich making merry in their beautiful houses, while the beggars were sitting at the gates. He flew into dark lanes, and saw the white faces of starving children looking out listlessly at the black streets. Under the archway of a bridge two little boys were lying in one another's arms to try and keep themselves warm. 'How hungry we are!' they said. 'You must not lie here,' shouted the watchman, and they wandered out into the rain.

Then he flew back and told the Prince what he had seen.

'I am covered with fine gold,' said the Prince, 'you must take it off, leaf by leaf, and give it to my poor; the living always think that gold can make them happy.'

Leaf after leaf of the fine gold the Swallow picked off, till the Happy Prince looked quite dull and grey. Leaf after leaf of the fine gold he brought to the poor, and the children's faces grew rosier, and they laughed and played games in the street. 'We have bread now!' they cried.

Then the snow came, and after the snow came the frost. The streets looked as if they were made of silver, they were so bright and glistening; long icicles like crystal daggers hung down from the eaves of the houses, everybody went about in furs, and the little boys wore scarlet caps and skated on the ice.

The poor little Swallow grew colder and colder, but he would not leave the Prince, he loved him too well. He picked up crumbs outside the baker's door when the baker was not looking, and tried to keep himself warm by flapping his wings.

But at last he knew that he was going to die. He had just enough strength to fly up to the Prince's shoulder once more. 'Good-bye, dear Prince!' he murmured. 'Will you let me kiss your hand?'

'I am glad that you are going to Egypt at last, little Swallow,' said the Prince. 'You have stayed too long here; but you must kiss me on the lips, for I love you.'

'It is not to Egypt that I am going,' said the Swallow. 'I am going to the House of Death. Death is the brother of Sleep, is he not?'

And he kissed the Happy Prince on the lips, and fell down dead at his feet.

At that moment a curious crack sounded inside the statue, as if something had broken. The fact is that the leaden heart had snapped right in two. It certainly was a dreadfully hard frost.

Early the next morning the Mayor was walking in the square below in company with the Town Councillors. As they passed the column he looked up at the statue. 'Dear me! how shabby the Happy Prince looks!' he said.

'How shabby, indeed!' cried the Town Councillors, who always agreed with the Mayor; and they went up to look at it.

'The ruby has fallen out of his sword, his eyes are gone, and he is golden no longer,' said the Mayor; 'in fact, he is little better than a beggar!'

'Little better than a beggar,' said the Town Councillors.

'And here is actually a dead bird at his feet!' continued the Mayor. 'We must really issue a proclamation that birds are not to be allowed to die here.' And the Town Clerk made a note of the suggestion.

So they pulled down the statue of the Happy Prince. 'As he is no longer beautiful he is no longer useful,' said the Art Professor at the University.

Then they melted the statue in a furnace, and the Mayor held a meeting of the Corporation to decide what was to be done with the metal. 'We must have another statue, of course,' he said, 'and it shall be a statue of myself.'

'Of myself,' said each of the Town Councillors, and they quarrelled. When I last heard of them they were quarrelling still.

'What a strange thing!' said the overseer of the workmen at the foundry. 'This broken lead heart will not melt in the furnace. We must throw it away.' So they threw it on a dust-heap where the dead Swallow was also lying.

'Bring me the two most precious things in the city,' said God to one of His Angels; and the Angel brought Him the leaden heart and the dead bird.

'You have rightly chosen,' said God, 'for in my garden of Paradise this little bird shall sing for evermore, and in my city of gold the Happy Prince shall praise me.'

L. FRANK BAUM

FROM *The Wizard of Oz*

(1900)

She was awakened by a shock, so sudden and severe that if Dorothy had not been lying on the soft bed she might have been hurt. As it was, the jar made her catch her breath and wonder what had happened; and Toto put his cold little nose into her face and whined dismally. Dorothy sat up and noticed that the house was not moving; nor was it dark, for the bright sunshine came in at the window, flooding the little room. She sprang from her bed and with Toto at her heels ran and opened the door.

The little girl gave a cry of amazement and looked about her, her eyes growing bigger and bigger at the wonderful sights she saw.

The cyclone had set the house down, very gently – for a cyclone – in the midst of a country of marvellous beauty.

There were lovely patches of greensward all about, with stately trees bearing rich and luscious fruits. Banks of gorgeous flowers were on every hand, and birds with rare and brilliant plumage sang and fluttered in the trees and bushes. A little way off was a small brook, rushing and sparkling along between green banks, and murmuring in a voice very grateful to a little girl who had lived so long on the dry, grey prairies.

While she stood looking eagerly at the strange and beautiful sights, she noticed coming towards her a group of the queerest people she had ever seen. They were not as big as the grown folk she had always been used to; but neither were they very small. In fact, they seemed about as tall as Dorothy, who was a well-grown child for her age, although they were, so far as looks go, many years older.

Three were men and one a woman, and all were oddly dressed. They wore round hats that rose to a small point a foot above their heads, with little bells around the brims that tinkled sweetly as they moved. The hats of the men were blue; the little woman's hat was white, and she wore a white gown that hung in pleats from her shoulders; over it were sprinkled little stars that glistened in the sun like diamonds. The men were dressed in blue, of the same shade as their hats, and wore well-polished boots with a deep roll of blue at the tops. The men, Dorothy thought, were about as old as Uncle Henry, for two of them had beards. But the little woman was doubtless much older; her face was covered with wrinkles, her hair was nearly white, and she walked rather stiffly.

When these people drew near the house where Dorothy was standing in the doorway they paused and whispered among themselves, as if afraid to come farther. But the little old woman walked up to Dorothy, made a low bow, and said in a sweet voice: 'You are welcome, most noble

Sorceress, to the land of the Munchkins. We are so grateful to you for having killed the Wicked Witch of the East, and for setting our people free from bondage.'

Dorothy listened to this speech with wonder. What could the little woman possibly mean by calling her a sorceress, and saying she had killed the Wicked Witch of the East? Dorothy was an innocent, harmless little girl, who had been carried by a cyclone many miles from home; and she had never killed anything in all her life.

But the little woman evidently expected her to answer; so Dorothy said, with hesitation: 'You are very kind; but there must be some mistake. I have not killed anything.'

'Your house did, anyway,' replied the little old woman, with a laugh, 'and that is the same thing. See!' she continued, pointing to the corner of the house. 'There are her two toes, still sticking out from under a block of wood.'

Dorothy looked, and gave a little cry of fright. There, indeed, just under the corner of the great beam the house rested on, two feet were sticking out, shod in silver shoes with pointed toes.

'Oh, dear! Oh, dear!' cried Dorothy, clasping her hands together in dismay. 'The house must have fallen on her. Whatever shall we do?'

'There is nothing to be done,' said the little woman calmly.

'But who was she?' asked Dorothy.

'She was the Wicked Witch of the East, as I said,' answered the little woman. 'She has held all the Munchkins in bondage for many years, making them slave for her night and day. Now they are all set free, and are grateful to you for the favour.'

'Who are the Munchkins?' inquired Dorothy.

'They are the people who live in this land of the East, where the Wicked Witch ruled.'

'Are you a Munchkin?' asked Dorothy.

'No, but I am their friend, although I live in the land of the North. When they saw the Witch of the East was dead the Munchkins sent a swift messenger to me, and I came at once. I am the Witch of the North.'

'Oh, gracious!' cried Dorothy. 'Are you a real witch?'

'Yes, indeed,' answered the little woman. 'But I am a good witch, and the people love me. I am not as powerful as the Wicked Witch was who ruled here, or I should have set the people free myself.'

'But I thought all witches were wicked,' said the girl, who was half frightened at facing a real witch.

'Oh, no, that is a great mistake. There were only four witches in all the Land of Oz, and two of them, those who live in the North and the South, are good witches. I know this is true, for I am one of them myself, and cannot be mistaken. Those who dwelt in the East and the West were, indeed, wicked witches; but now that you have killed one of them, there is but one Wicked Witch in all the Land of Oz – the one who lives in the West.'

'But,' said Dorothy, after a moment's thought, 'Aunt Em has told me that the witches were all dead – years and years ago.'

'Who is Aunt Em?' inquired the little old woman.

'She is my aunt who lives in Kansas, where I came from.'

The Witch of the North seemed to think for a time, with her head bowed and her eyes upon the ground. Then she looked up and said, 'I do not know where Kansas is, for I have never heard that country mentioned before. But tell me, is it a civilized country?'

'Oh, yes,' replied Dorothy.

'Then that accounts for it. In the civilized countries I believe there are no witches left, nor wizards, nor sorceresses, nor magicians. But, you see, the Land of Oz has never been civilized, for we are cut off from all the rest of the world. Therefore we still have witches and wizards among us.'

'Who are the wizards?' asked Dorothy.

'Oz himself is the Great Wizard,' answered the Witch, sinking her voice to a whisper. 'He is more powerful than all the rest of us together. He lives in the City of Emeralds.'

Dorothy was going to ask another question, but just then the Munchkins, who had been standing silently by, gave a loud shout and pointed to the corner of the house where the Wicked Witch had been lying.

'What is it?' asked the little old woman and looked, and began to laugh. The feet of the dead Witch had disappeared entirely and nothing was left but the silver shoes.

'She was so old,' explained the Witch of the North, 'that she dried up quickly in the sun. That is the end of her. But the silver shoes are yours, and you shall have them to wear.' She reached down and picked up the shoes, and after shaking the dust out of them handed them to Dorothy.

'The Witch of the East was proud of those silver shoes,' said one of the Munchkins, 'and there is some charm connected with them; but what it is we never knew.'

Dorothy carried the shoes into the house and placed them on the table. Then she came out again to the Munchkins and said: 'I am anxious to get back to my aunt and uncle, for I am sure they will worry about me. Can you help me find my way?'

The Munchkins and the Witch first looked at one another, and then at Dorothy, and then shook their heads.

'At the East, not far from here,' said one, 'there is a great desert, and none could live to cross it.'

'It is the same at the South,' said another, 'for I have

been there and seen it. The South is the country of the Quadlings.'

'I am told,' said the third man, 'that it is the same at the West. And that country, where the Winkies live, is ruled by the Wicked Witch of the West, who would make you her slave if you passed her way.'

'The North is my home,' said the old lady, 'and at its edge is the same great desert that surrounds this Land of Oz. I'm afraid, my dear, you will have to live with us.'

Dorothy began to sob at this, for she felt lonely among all these strange people. Her tears seemed to grieve the kind-hearted Munchkins, for they immediately took out their handkerchiefs and began to weep also. As for the little old woman, she took off her cap and balanced the point on the end of her nose, while she counted 'One, two, three' in a solemn voice. At once the cap changed to a slate, on which was written in big, white chalk marks:

LET DOROTHY GO TO THE CITY OF EMERALDS.

The little old woman took the slate from her nose, and having read the words on it, asked: 'Is your name Dorothy, my dear?'

'Yes,' answered the child, looking up and drying her tears.

'Then you must go to the City of Emeralds. Perhaps Oz will help you.'

'Where is this city?' asked Dorothy.

'It is exactly in the centre of the country, and is ruled by Oz, the Great Wizard I told you of.'

'Is he a good man?' inquired the girl anxiously.

'He is a good Wizard. Whether he is a man or not I cannot tell, for I have never seen him.'

'How can I get there?' asked Dorothy.

'You must walk. It is a long journey, through a country that is sometimes pleasant and sometimes dark and terrible. However, I will use all the magic arts I know of to keep you from harm.'

'Won't you go with me?' pleaded the girl, who had begun to look upon the little old woman as her only friend.

'No, I cannot do that,' she replied, 'but I will give you my kiss, and no one will dare injure a person who has been kissed by the Witch of the North.'

She came close to Dorothy and kissed her gently on the forehead. Where her lips touched the girl they left a round, shining mark, as Dorothy found out soon after.

'The road to the City of Emeralds is paved with yellow brick,' said the Witch, 'so you cannot miss it. When you get to Oz do not be afraid of him, but tell your story and ask him to help you. Good-bye, my dear.'

The three Munchkins bowed low to her and wished her a pleasant journey, after which they walked away through the trees. The Witch gave Dorothy a friendly little nod, whirled around on her left heel three times, and straightway disappeared, much to the surprise of little Toto, who barked after her loudly enough when she had gone, because he had been afraid even to growl while she stood by.

But Dorothy, knowing her to be a witch, had expected her to disappear in just that way, and was not surprised in the least.

RUDYARD KIPLING

'The Cat That Walked By Himself'
From *Just So Stories*

(1902)

Hear and attend and listen; for this befell and behappened and became and was, O my Best Beloved, when the Tame animals were wild. The Dog was wild, and the Horse was wild, and the Cow was wild, and the Sheep was wild, and the Pig was wild – as wild as wild could be – and they walked in the Wet Wild Woods by their wild lones. But the wildest of all the wild animals was the Cat. He walked by himself, and all places were alike to him.

Of course the Man was wild, too. He was dreadfully wild. He didn't even begin to be tame till he met the Woman, and she told him that she did not like living in his wild ways. She picked out a nice dry Cave, instead of a heap of wet leaves, to lie down in; and she strewed clean sand on the floor; and she lit a nice fire of wood at the back of the Cave; and she hung a dried wild-horse skin, tail-down, across the opening of the Cave; and she said, 'Wipe your feet, dear, when you come in, and now we'll keep house.'

That night, Best Beloved, they ate wild sheep roasted on the hot stones, and flavoured with wild garlic and wild pepper; and wild duck stuffed with wild rice and wild fenugreek and wild coriander; and marrow-bones of wild oxen; and wild cherries, and wild grenadillas. Then the Man went to sleep in front of the fire ever so happy; but the Woman sat up, combing her hair. She took the bone of the shoulder of mutton – the big flat blade-bone – and she looked at the wonderful marks on it, and she threw more wood on the fire, and she made a Magic. She made the First Singing Magic in the world.

Out in the Wet Wild Woods all the wild animals gathered together where they could see the light of the fire a long way off, and they wondered what it meant.

Then Wild Horse stamped with his wild foot and said, 'O my Friends and O my Enemies, why have the Man and the Woman made that great light in that great Cave, and what harm will it do us?'

Wild Dog lifted up his wild nose and smelled the smell of the roast mutton, and said, 'I will go up and see and look, and say; for I think it is good. Cat, come with me.'

'Nenni!' said the Cat. 'I am the Cat who walks by himself, and all places are alike to me. I will not come.'

'Then we can never be friends again,' said Wild Dog, and he trotted off to the Cave. But when he had gone a little way the Cat said to himself, 'All places are alike to me. Why should I not go too and see and look and come away at my own liking?' So he slipped after Wild Dog softly, very softly, and hid himself where he could hear everything.

When Wild Dog reached the mouth of the Cave he lifted up the dried horse-skin with his nose and sniffed the beautiful smell of the roast mutton, and the Woman, looking at the blade-bone, heard him, and laughed, and said, 'Here comes the first. Wild Thing out of the Wild Woods, what do you want?'

Wild Dog said, 'O my Enemy and Wife of my Enemy, what is this that smells so good in the Wild Woods?'

Then the Woman picked up a roasted mutton-bone and threw it to Wild Dog, and said, 'Wild Thing out of the Wild Woods, taste and try.' Wild Dog gnawed the bone, and it was more delicious than anything he had ever tasted, and he said: 'O my Enemy and Wife of my Enemy, give me another.'

The Woman said, 'Wild Thing out of the Wild Woods, help my Man to hunt through the day and guard this Cave at night, and I will give you as many roast bones as you need.'

'Ah!' said the Cat, listening. This is a very wise Woman, but she is not so wise as I am.'

Wild Dog crawled into the Cave and laid his head on the Woman's lap, and said, 'O my Friend and Wife of my Friend, I will help your Man to hunt through the day, and at night I will guard your Cave.'

'Ah!' said the Cat, listening. 'That is a very foolish Dog.' And he went back through the Wet Wild Woods waving his wild tail, and walking by his wild lone. But he never told anybody.

When the Man waked up he said: 'What is Wild Dog doing here?' And the Woman said, 'His name is not Wild Dog any more, but the First Friend, because he will be our friend for always and always and always. Take him with you when you go hunting.'

Next night the Woman cut great green armfuls of fresh grass from the water-meadows, and dried it before the fire, so that it smelt like new-mown hay, and she sat at the mouth of the Cave and plaited a halter out of horse-hide, and she looked at the shoulder-of-mutton bone – at the big broad blade-bone – and she made a Magic. She made the Second Singing Magic in the world.

Out in the Wild Woods all the wild animals wondered what had happened to Wild Dog, and at last Wild Horse stamped with his foot and said, 'I will go and see and say why Wild Dog has not returned. Cat, come with me.'

'Nenni!' said the Cat. ' I am the Cat who walks by himself, and all places are alike to me. I will not come.' But all the same he followed Wild Horse softly, very softly, and hid himself where he could hear everything.

When the Woman heard Wild Horse tripping and stumbling on his long mane, she laughed and said: 'Here comes the second. Wild Thing out of the Wild Woods, what do you want?'

Wild Horse said, 'O my Enemy and Wife of my Enemy, where is Wild Dog?'

The Woman laughed, and picked up the blade-bone and looked at it, and said, 'Wild Thing out of the Wild Woods, you did not come here for Wild Dog, but for the sake of this good grass.'

And Wild Horse, tripping and stumbling on his long mane, said: 'That is true; give it me to eat.'

The Woman said, 'Wild Thing out of the Wild Woods, bend your wild head and wear what I give you, and you shall eat the wonderful grass three times a day.'

'Ah,' said the Cat, listening, 'this is a clever Woman, but she is not so clever as I am.'

Wild Horse bent his wild head, and the Woman slipped

the plaited hide halter over it, and Wild Horse breathed on the Woman's feet and said, 'O my Mistress and Wife of my Master, I will be your servant for the sake of the wonderful grass.'

'Ah,' said the Cat, listening, 'that is a very foolish Horse.' And he went back through the Wet Wild Woods, waving his wild tail and walking by his wild lone. But he never told anybody.

When the Man and the Dog came back from hunting, the Man said, 'What is Wild Horse doing here?' And the Woman said, 'His name is not Wild Horse any more, but the First Servant, because he will carry us from place to place for always and always and always. Ride on his back when you go hunting.'

Next day, holding her wild head high that her wild horns should not catch in the wild trees, Wild Cow came up to the Cave, and the Cat followed, and hid himself just the same as before; and everything happened just the same as before; and the Cat said the same things as before; and when Wild Cow had promised to give her milk to the Woman every day in exchange for the wonderful grass, the Cat went back through the Wet Wild Woods waving his wild tail and walking by his wild lone, just the same as before. But he never told anybody. And when the Man and the Horse and the Dog came home from hunting and asked the same questions same as before, the Woman said: 'Her name is not Wild Cow any more, but the Giver of Good Food. She will give us the warm white milk for always and always and always, and I will take care of her while you and the First Friend and the First Servant go hunting.'

Next day the Cat waited to see if any other Wild Thing would go up to the Cave, but no one moved in the Wet Wild Woods, so the Cat walked there by himself; and he saw the Woman milking the Cow, and he saw the light of the fire in the Cave, and he smelt the smell of the warm white milk.

Cat said, 'O my Enemy and Wife of my Enemy, where did Wild Cow go?'

The Woman laughed and said, 'Wild Thing out of the Wild Woods, go back to the Woods again, for I have braided up my hair, and I have put away the magic blade-bone, and we have no more need of either friends or servants in our Cave.'

Cat said, 'I am not a friend, and I am not a servant. I am the Cat who walks by himself, and I wish to come into your Cave.'

Woman said, 'Then why did you not come with First Friend on the first night?'

Cat grew very angry and said, 'Has Wild Dog told tales of me?'

Then the Woman laughed and said, 'You are the Cat who walks by himself, and all places are alike to you. You are neither a friend nor a servant. You have said it yourself. Go away and walk by yourself in all places alike.'

Then Cat pretended to be sorry and said, 'Must I never come into the Cave? Must I never sit by the warm fire? Must I never drink the warm white milk? You are very wise and very beautiful. You should not be cruel even to a Cat.'

Woman said, 'I knew I was wise, but I did not know I was beautiful. So I will make a bargain with you. If ever I say one word in your praise, you may come into the Cave.'

'And if you say two words in my praise?' said the Cat.

'I never shall,' said the Woman, 'but if I say two words in your praise, you may sit by the fire in the Cave.'

'And if you say three words?' said the Cat.

'I never shall,' said the Woman, 'but if I say three words in your praise, you may drink the warm white milk three times a day for always and always and always.'

Then the Cat arched his back and said, 'Now let the Curtain at the mouth of the Cave, and the Fire at the back of the Cave, and the Milk-pots that stand beside the Fire, remember what my Enemy and the Wife of my Enemy has said.' And he went away through the Wet Wild Woods waving his wild tail and walking by his wild lone.

That night when the Man and the Horse and the Dog came home from hunting, the Woman did not tell them of the bargain that she had made with the Cat, because she was afraid that they might not like it.

Cat went far and far away and hid himself in the Wet Wild Woods by his wild lone for a long time till the Woman forgot all about him. Only the Bat – the little upside-down Bat – that hung inside the Cave knew where Cat hid; and every evening Bat would fly to Cat with news of what was happening.

One evening Bat said, 'There is a Baby in the Cave. He is new and pink and fat and small, and the Woman is very fond of him.'

'Ah,' said the Cat, listening, 'but what is the Baby fond of?'

'He is fond of things that are soft and tickle,' said the Bat. 'He is fond of warm things to hold in his arms when he goes to sleep. He is fond of being played with. He is fond of all those things.'

'Ah,' said the Cat, listening, 'then my time has come.'

Next night Cat walked through the Wet Wild Woods and hid very near the Cave till morning-time, and Man and Dog and Horse went hunting. The Woman was busy cooking that morning, and the Baby cried and interrupted. So she carried him outside the Cave and gave him a handful of pebbles to play with. But still the Baby cried.

Then the Cat put out his paddy paw and patted the Baby on the cheek, and it cooed; and the Cat rubbed against its fat knees and tickled it under its fat chin with his tail. And the Baby laughed; and the Woman heard him and smiled.

Then the Bat – the little upside-down Bat – that hung in the mouth of the Cave said, 'O my Hostess and Wife of my Host and Mother of my Host's Son, a Wild Thing from the Wild Woods is most beautifully playing with your Baby.'

'A blessing on that Wild Thing whoever he may be,' said the Woman, straightening her back, 'for I was a busy woman this morning and he has done me a service.'

That very minute and second, Best Beloved, the dried horse-skin Curtain that was stretched tail-down at the mouth of the Cave fell down – *woosh!* – because it remembered the bargain she had made with the Cat; and when the Woman went to pick it up – lo and behold! – the Cat was sitting quite comfy inside the Cave.

'O my Enemy and Wife of my Enemy and Mother of my Enemy,' said the Cat, 'it is I: for you have spoken a word in my praise, and now I can sit within the Cave for always and always and always. But still I am the Cat who walks by himself, and all places are alike to me.'

The Woman was very angry, and shut her lips tight and took up her spinning-wheel and began to spin.

But the Baby cried because the Cat had gone away, and the Woman could not hush it, for it struggled and kicked and grew black in the face.

'O my Enemy and Wife of my Enemy and Mother of my Enemy,' said the Cat, 'take a strand of the thread that you are spinning and tie it to your spinning-whorl and drag it along the floor, and I will show you a Magic that shall make your Baby laugh as loudly as he is now crying.'

'I will do so,' said the Woman, 'because I am at my wits' end; but I will not thank you for it.'

She tied the thread to the little clay spindle-whorl and drew it across the floor, and the Cat ran after it and patted it with his paws and rolled head over heels, and tossed it backward over his shoulder and chased it between his hind-legs and pretended to lose it, and pounced down upon it again, till the Baby laughed as loudly as it had been crying, and scrambled after the Cat and frolicked all over the Cave till it grew tired and settled down to sleep with the Cat in its arms.

'Now,' said the Cat, 'I will sing the Baby a song that shall keep him asleep for an hour.' And he began to purr, loud and low, low and loud, till the Baby fell fast asleep. The Woman smiled as she looked down upon the two of them, and said, 'That was wonderfully done. No question but you are very clever, O Cat.'

That very minute and second, Best Beloved, the smoke of the Fire at the back of the Cave came down in clouds from the roof – *puff* – because it remembered the bargain she had made with the Cat; and when it had cleared away – lo and behold! – the Cat was sitting quite comfy close to the fire.

'O my Enemy and Wife of my Enemy and Mother of my Enemy,' said the Cat, 'it is I: for you have spoken a second word in my praise, and now I can sit by the warm fire at the back of the Cave for always and always and always. But still I am the Cat who walks by himself, and all places are alike to me.'

Then the Woman was very very angry, and let down her hair and put more wood on the fire and brought out the broad blade-bone of the shoulder of mutton and began to make a Magic that should prevent her from saying a third word in praise of the Cat. It was not a Singing Magic, Best

Beloved, it was a Still Magic; and by and by the Cave grew so still that a little wee-wee mouse crept out of a corner and ran across the floor.

'O my Enemy and Wife of my Enemy and Mother of my Enemy,' said the Cat, 'is that little mouse part of your Magic?'

'Ouh! Chee! No indeed!' said the Woman, and she dropped the blade-bone and jumped upon the footstool in front of the fire and braided up her hair very quick for fear that the mouse should run up it.

'Ah,' said the Cat, watching, 'then the mouse will do me no harm if I eat it?'

'No,' said the Woman, braiding up her hair, 'eat it quickly and I will ever be grateful to you.'

Cat made one jump and caught the little mouse, and the Woman said, 'A hundred thanks. Even the First Friend is not quick enough to catch little mice as you have done. You must be very wise.'

That very moment and second, O Best Beloved, the Milk-pot that stood by the fire cracked in two pieces – *ffft!* – because it remembered the bargain she had made with the Cat; and when the Woman jumped down from the footstool – lo and behold! – the Cat was lapping up the warm white milk that lay in one of the broken pieces.

'O my Enemy and Wife of my Enemy and Mother of my Enemy,' said the Cat, 'it is I: for you have spoken three words in my praise, and now I can drink the warm white milk three times a day for always and always and always. But *still* I am the Cat who walks by himself, and all places are alike to me.'

Then the Woman laughed and set the Cat a bowl of the warm white milk and said, 'O Cat, you are as clever as a man, but remember that your bargain was not made with the Man or the Dog, and I do not know what they will do when they come home.'

'What is that to me?' said the Cat. 'If I have my place in the Cave by the fire and my warm white milk three times a day I do not care what the Man or the Dog can do.'

That evening when the Man and the Dog came into the Cave, the Woman told them all the story of the bargain, while the Cat sat by the fire and smiled. Then the Man said, 'Yes, but he has not made a bargain with *me* or with all proper Men after me.' Then he took off his two leather boots and he took up his little stone axe (that makes three) and he fetched a piece of wood and a hatchet (that is five altogether), and he set them out in a row and he said, 'Now we will make *our* bargain. If you do not catch mice when you are in the Cave for always and always and always, I will throw these five things at you whenever I see you, and so shall all proper Men do after me.'

'Ah,' said the Woman, listening, 'this is a very clever Cat, but he is not so clever as my Man.'

The Cat counted the five things (and they looked very knobby) and he said, 'I will catch mice when I am in the Cave for always and always and always; but *still* I am the Cat who walks by himself, and all places are alike to me.'

'Not when I am near,' said the Man. 'If you had not said that last I would have put all these things away for always and always and always; but now I am going to throw my two boots and my little stone axe (that makes three) at you whenever I meet you. And so shall all proper men do after me!'

Then the Dog said, 'Wait a minute. He has not made a bargain with *me* or with all proper Dogs after me.' And he showed his teeth and said, 'If you are not kind to the Baby while I am in the Cave for always and always and always, I will hunt you till I catch you, and when I catch you I will bite you. And so shall all proper Dogs do after me.'

'Ah,' said the Woman, listening, 'this is a very clever Cat, but he is not so clever as the Dog.'

Cat counted the Dog's teeth (and they looked very pointed) and he said, 'I will be kind to the Baby while I am in the Cave, as long as he does not pull my tail too hard, for always and always and always. But *still* I am the Cat that walks by himself, and all places are alike to me!'

'Not when I am near,' said the Dog. 'If you had not said that last I would have shut my mouth for always and always and always; but *now* I am going to hunt you up a tree whenever I meet you. And so shall all proper Dogs do after me.'

Then the Man threw his two boots and his little stone axe (that makes three) at the Cat, and the Cat ran out of the Cave and the Dog chased him up a tree; and from that day to this, Best Beloved, three proper Men out of five will always throw things at a Cat whenever they meet him, and all proper Dogs will chase him up a tree. But the Cat keeps his side of the bargain too. He will kill mice, and he will be kind to Babies when he is in the house, just as long as they do not pull his tail too hard. But when he has done that, and between times, and when the moon gets up and night comes, he is the Cat that walks by himself, and all places are alike to him. Then he goes out to the Wet Wild Woods or up the Wet Wild Trees or on the Wet Wild Roofs, waving his wild tail and walking by his wild lone.

E. NESBIT

From *Five Children and It*

(1902)

The next morning the children remembered how they had had the luck to find a Psammead, or Sand-fairy; and to receive its promise to grant them a new wish every day. For now they had had two wishes, Beauty and Wealth, and neither had exactly made them happy. But the happening of strange things, even if they are not completely pleasant things, is more amusing than those times when nothing happens but meals, and they are not always completely pleasant, especially on the days when it is cold mutton or hash.

There was no chance of talking things over before breakfast, because everyone overslept itself, as it happened, and it needed a vigorous and determined struggle to get dressed so as to be only ten minutes late for breakfast. During this meal some efforts were made to deal with the question of the Psammead in an impartial spirit, but it is very difficult to discuss anything thoroughly and at the same time to attend faithfully to your baby brother's breakfast needs. The Baby was particularly lively that morning. He not only wriggled his body through the bar of his high chair, and hung by his head, choking and purple, but he collared a tablespoon with desperate suddenness, hit Cyril heavily on the head with it, and then cried because it was taken away from him. He put his fat fist in his bread-and-milk, and demanded 'nam', which was only allowed for tea. He sang, he put his feet on the table – he clamoured to 'go walky'. The conversation was something like this.

'Look here – about that Sand-fairy – Look out! – he'll have the milk over.'

Milk removed to a safe distance.

'Yes – about that Fairy – No, Lamb dear, give Panther the narky poon.'

Then Cyril tried. 'Nothing we've had yet has turned out – He nearly had the mustard that time!'

'I wonder whether we'd better wish – Hullo! – You've done it now, my boy!' And, in a flash of glass and pink baby-paws, the bowl of golden carp in the middle of the table rolled on its side, and poured a flood of mixed water and goldfish into the Baby's lap and into the laps of the others.

Everyone was almost as much upset as the goldfish: the Lamb only remaining calm. When the pool on the floor had been mopped up, and the leaping, gasping goldfish had been collected and put back in the water, the Baby was taken away to be entirely redressed by Martha, and most of the others had to change completely. The pinafores and jackets that had been bathed in goldfish-and-water were hung out to dry, and then it turned out that Jane must either mend the dress she had torn the day before or appear all day in her best petticoat. It was white and soft and frilly, and trimmed with lace, and very, very pretty, quite as pretty as a frock, if not more so. Only it was *not* a frock, and Martha's word was law. She wouldn't let Jane wear her best frock, and she refused to listen for a moment to Robert's suggestion that Jane should wear her best petticoat and call it a dress.

'It's not respectable,' she said. And when people say that, it's no use anyone's saying anything. You will find this out for yourselves some day.

So there was nothing for it but for Jane to mend her frock. The hole had been torn the day before when she happened to tumble down in the High Street of Rochester, just where a water-cart had passed on its silvery way. She had grazed her knee, and her stocking was much more than grazed, and her dress was cut by the same stone which had attended to the knee and the stocking. Of course the others were not such sneaks as to abandon a comrade in misfortune, so they all sat on the grass-plot round the sundial, and Jane darned away for dear life. The Lamb was still in the hands of Martha, having its clothes changed, so conversation was possible.

Anthea and Robert timidly tried to conceal their inmost thought, which was that the Psammead was not to be trusted; but Cyril said: 'Speak out – say what you've got to say – I hate hinting, and "don't know", and sneakish ways like that.' ...

'Well,' said Robert, 'Anthea and I think the Sammyadd is a spiteful brute. If it can give us our wishes, I suppose it can give itself its own, and I feel almost sure it wishes every time that our wishes shan't do us any good. Let's let the tiresome beast alone, and just go and have a jolly good game of forts, on our own, in the chalk-pit.'

(You will remember that the happily situated house where these children were spending their holidays lay between a chalk-quarry and a gravel-pit.)

Cyril and Jane were more hopeful – they generally were.

'I don't think the Sammyadd does it on purpose,' Cyril said; 'and, after all, it *was* silly to wish for boundless wealth. Fifty pounds in two-shilling pieces would have been much more sensible. And wishing to be beautiful as the day was simply donkeyish. I don't want to be disagreeable, but it *was*. We must try to find a really useful wish, and wish it.'

Jane dropped her work and said: 'I think so too; it's too silly to have a chance like this and not use it. I never heard of anyone else outside a book who had such a chance; there must be simply heaps of things we could wish for that wouldn't turn out Dead Sea fish, like these two things have. Do let's think hard, and wish something nice, so that we can have a real jolly day – what there is left of it.' ...

When the frock was darned, the start for the gravel-pit was delayed by Martha's insisting on everybody's washing its hands ...

During the conversation ... it had been decided that fifty pounds in two-shilling pieces was the right wish to have. And the lucky children, who could have anything in the wide world by just wishing for it, hurriedly started for the gravel-pit to express their wishes to the Psammead. Martha caught them at the gate, and insisted on their taking the Baby with them.

'Not want him indeed! Why, everybody 'ud want him, a duck! With all their hearts they would; and you know you promised your ma to take him out every blessed day,' said Martha.

'I know we did,' said Robert in gloom, 'but I wish the Lamb wasn't quite so young and small.' ...

'He'll mend of his youngness with time,' said Martha; 'and as for his smallness, I don't think you'd fancy carrying of him any more, however big he was. Besides he can walk a bit, bless his precious fat legs, a ducky!' …

With this and a kiss, she plumped the Lamb into Anthea's arms, and went back to make new pinafores on the sewing-machine …

The Lamb laughed with pleasure, and said: 'Walky wif Panty,' and rode on Robert's back with yells of joy … and altogether made himself so agreeable that nobody could long be sorry that he was of the party.

The enthusiastic Jane even suggested that they should devote a week's wishes to assuring the Baby's future, by asking such gifts for him as the good fairies give to Infant Princes in proper fairy-tales, but Anthea soberly reminded her that as the Sand-fairy's wishes only lasted till sunset they could not ensure any benefit to the Baby's later years …

Full of high hopes and excellent resolutions, they went round the safe slow cart-road to the gravel-pits, and as they went in between the mounds of gravel a sudden thought came to them … For they remembered that yesterday, when they had asked the Psammead for boundless wealth, and it was getting ready to fill the quarry with the minted gold of bright guineas – millions of them – it had told the children to run along outside the quarry for fear they should be buried alive in the heavy splendid treasure. And they had run. And so it happened that they had not had time to mark the spot where the Psammead was, with a ring of stones, as before …

'Never mind,' said the hopeful Jane, 'we'll soon find him.'

But this, though easily said, was hard in the doing. They looked and they looked, and though they found their sea-side spades, nowhere could they find the Sand-fairy …

The Lamb, as Martha had said, was feeling the benefit of the country air, and he was as frisky as a sandhopper. The elder ones longed to go on talking about the new wishes they would have when (or if) they found the Psammead again. But the Lamb wished to enjoy himself.

He watched his opportunity and threw a handful of sand into Anthea's face, and then suddenly burrowed his own head in the sand and waved his fat legs in the air. Then of course the sand got into his eyes, as it had into Anthea's, and he howled.

The thoughtful Robert has brought one solid brown bottle of ginger-beer with him ... This had to be uncorked hurriedly – it was the only wet thing within reach, and it was necessary to wash the sand out of the Lamb's eyes somehow. Of course the ginger hurt horribly, and he howled more than ever. And, amid his anguish of kicking, the bottle was upset and the beautiful ginger-beer frothed out into the sand and was lost for ever.

It was then that Robert, usually a very patient brother, so far forgot himself as to say: 'Anybody would want him, indeed! Only they don't; Martha doesn't, not really, or she'd jolly well keep him with her. He's a little nuisance, that's what he is. It's too bad. I only wish everybody *did* want him with all their hearts; we might get some peace in our lives.'

The Lamb stopped howling now, because Jane had suddenly remembered that there is only one safe way of taking things out of little children's eyes, and that is with your own soft wet tongue ...

Then there was a little silence. Robert was not proud of himself for having been so cross, and the others were not proud of him either ...

The silence was broken by a sigh – a breath suddenly let out. The children's heads turned as if there had been a string tied to each nose, and someone had pulled all the strings at once.

And everyone saw the Sand-fairy sitting quite close to them, with the expression which it used as a smile on its hairy face.

'Good-morning,' it said; 'I did that quite easily! Everyone wants him now.'

'It doesn't matter,' said Robert sulkily, because he knew he had been behaving rather like a pig. 'No matter who wants him – there's no one here to – anyhow.'

'Ingratitude,' said the Psammead, 'is a dreadful vice.'

'We're not ungrateful,' Jane made haste to say, 'but we didn't *really* want that wish. Robert only just said it. Can't you take it back and give us a new one?'

'No – I can't,' the Sand-fairy said shortly; 'chopping and changing – it's not business. You ought to be careful what you *do* wish.' ...

Suddenly the Lamb perceived that something brown and furry was near him.

'Poof, poof, poofy,' he said, and made a grab.

'It's not a pussy,' Anthea was beginning, when the Sand-fairy leaped back.

'Oh, my left whisker!' it said; 'don't let him touch me. He's wet.'

Its fur stood on end with horror – and indeed a good deal of the ginger-beer had been spilt on the blue smock of the Lamb.

The Psammead dug with its hands and feet, and vanished in an instant and a whirl of sand.

The children marked the spot with a ring of stones.

'We may as well get along home,' said Robert. 'I'll say I'm sorry; but anyway if it's no good it's no harm, and we know where the sandy thing is for to-morrow.'

The others were noble. No one reproached Robert at all. Cyril picked up the Lamb, who was now quite himself again, and off they went by the safe cart-road.

The cart-road from the gravel-pits joins the road almost directly.

At the gate into the road the party stopped to shift the Lamb from Cyril's back to Robert's. And as they paused a very smart open carriage came in sight, with a coachman and a groom on the box, and inside the carriage a lady – very grand indeed, with a dress all white lace and red ribbons and a parasol all red and white – and a white fluffy dog on her lap with a red ribbon round its neck. She looked at the children, and particularly at the Baby, and she smiled at him. The children were used to this, for the Lamb was, as all the servants said, a 'very taking child'. So they waved their hands politely to the lady and expected her to drive on. But she did not. Instead she made the coachman stop. And she beckoned to Cyril, and when he went up to the carriage she said: 'What a dear darling duck of a baby! Oh, I *should* so like to adopt it! Do you think its mother would mind?'

'She'd mind very much indeed,' said Anthea shortly.

'Oh, but I should bring it up in luxury, you know. I am Lady Chittenden. You must have seen my photograph in the illustrated papers. They call me a beauty, you know, but of course that's all nonsense. Anyway – '

She opened the carriage door and jumped out. She had the wonderfullest red high-heeled shoes with silver buckles. 'Let me hold him a minute,' she said. And she took the Lamb and held him very awkwardly, as if she was not used to babies.

Then suddenly she jumped into the carriage with the Lamb in her arms and slammed the door and said: 'Drive on!'

The Lamb roared, the little white dog barked, and the coachman hesitated.

'Drive on, I tell you!' cried the lady; and the coachman did, for, as he said afterwards, it was as much as his place was worth not to.

The four children looked at each other, and then with one accord they rushed after the carriage and held on behind. Down the dusty road went the smart carriage, and after it, at double-quick time, ran the twinkling legs of the Lamb's brothers and sisters.

The Lamb howled louder and louder, but presently his howls changed by slow degree to hiccupy gurgles, and then all was still and they knew he had gone to sleep.

The carriage went on, and the eight feet that twinkled through the dust were growing quite stiff and tired before the carriage stopped at the lodge of a grand park. The children crouched down behind the carriage, and the lady got out. She looked at the Baby as it lay on the carriage seat, and hesitated.

'The darling – I won't disturb it,' she said, and went into the lodge to talk to the woman there …

The coachman and footman sprang from the box and bent over the sleeping Lamb …

'Wonder at her now – I do really!' said the coachman. 'Hates kids. Got none of her own, and can't abide other folkses'.'

The children, crouching in the white dust under the carriage, exchanged uncomfortable glances.

'Tell you what,' the coachman went on firmly, 'blowed if I don't hide the little nipper in the hedge and tell her his brothers took 'im! Then I'll come back for him afterwards.'

'No, you don't,' said the footman. 'I've took to that kid so as never was. If anyone's to have him, it's me – so there!'

'Stow your gab!' the coachman rejoined. 'You don't want no kids, and, if you did, one kid's the same as another to you. But I'm a married man and a judge of breed. I knows a first-rate yearling when I sees him. I'm a-goin' to 'ave him, an' least said soonest mended.'

'I should 'a' thought,' said the footman sneeringly, 'you'd a'most enough. What with Alfred, an' Albert, an' Louise, an' Victor Stanley, and Helena Beatrice, and another – '

The coachman hit the footman in the chin – the footman hit the coachman in the waistcoat – the next minute the two were fighting here and there, in and out, up and down, and all over everywhere, and the little dog jumped on the box of the carriage and began barking like mad.

Cyril, still crouching in the dust, went to the side of the carriage farthest from the battlefield. He unfastened the door of the carriage – the two men were far too much occupied with their quarrel to notice anything – took the Lamb in his arms, and, still stooping, carried the sleeping baby a dozen yards along the road to where a stile led into a wood. The others followed, and there among the hazels and young oaks and sweet chestnuts, covered by high strong-scented bracken, they all lay hidden till the angry voices of the men were hushed at the angry voice of the red-and-white lady, and, after a long and anxious search, the carriage at last drove away.

'My only hat!' said Cyril, drawing a deep breath as the sound of wheels at last died away. 'Everyone *does* want him now – and no mistake! That Sammyadd has done us again! Tricky brute! For any sake, let's get the kid safe home.'

So they peeped out, and finding on the right hand only lonely white road, and nothing but lonely white road on the left, they took courage, and the road, Anthea carrying the sleeping Lamb.

Adventures dogged their footsteps. A boy with a bundle of faggots on his back dropped his bundle by the roadside and asked to look at the Baby, and then offered to carry him; but Anthea was not to be caught that way twice. They all walked on, but the boy followed, and Cyril and Robert couldn't make him go away till they had more than once invited him to smell their fists. Afterwards a little girl in a blue-and-white checked pinafore actually followed them for a quarter of a mile crying for 'the precious Baby', and then she was only got rid of by threats of tying her to a tree in the wood with all their pocket-handkerchiefs. 'So that the bears can come and eat you as soon as it gets dark,' said Cyril severely. Then she went off crying. It presently seemed wise, to the brothers and sisters of the Baby, who was wanted by everyone, to hide in the hedge whenever they saw anyone coming, and thus they managed to prevent the Lamb from arousing the inconvenient affection of a milkman, a stone-breaker, and a man who drove a cart with a paraffin barrel at the back of it. They were nearly home when the worst thing of all happened. Turning a corner suddenly they came upon two vans, a tent, and a company of gipsies encamped by the side of the road. The vans were hung all round with wicker chairs and cradles, and flowerstands and feather brushes. A lot of ragged children were industriously making dust-pies in the road, two men lay on the grass smoking, and three women were doing the family washing in an old red watering-can with the top broken off.

In a moment all the gipsies, men, women, and children, surrounded Anthea and the Baby.

'Let *me* hold him, little lady,' said one of the gipsy women, who had a mahogany-coloured face and dust-coloured hair; 'I won't hurt a hair of his head, the little picture!'

'I'd rather not,' said Anthea.

'Let me have him,' said the other woman, whose face was also of the hue of mahogany, and her hair jet-black, in greasy curls. 'I've nineteen of my own, so I have.'

'No,' said Anthea bravely, but her heart beat so that it nearly choked her.

Then one of the men pushed forward.

'Swelp me if it ain't!' he cried, 'my own long-lost cheild! Have he a strawberry mark on his left ear? No? Then he's my own babby, stolen from me in hinnocent hinfancy. 'And 'im over – and we'll not 'ave the law on yer this time.'

He snatched the Baby from Anthea, who turned scarlet and burst into tears of pure rage.

The others were standing quite still; this was much the most terrible thing that had ever happened to them… Cyril was quite white, and his hands trembled a little, but he made a sign to the others to shut up. He was silent a minute, thinking hard. Then he said: 'We don't want to keep him if he's yours. But you see he's used to us. You shall have him if you want him.'

'No, no!' cried Anthea – and Cyril glared at her.

'Of course we want him,' said the women, trying to get the Baby out of the man's arms. The Lamb howled loudly.

'Oh, he's hurt!' shrieked Anthea; and Cyril, in a savage undertone, bade her 'Stow it!'

'You trust to me,' he whispered. 'Look here,' he went on, 'he's awfully tiresome with people he doesn't know very well. Suppose we stay here a bit till he gets used to you, and then when it's bedtime I give you my word of honour we'll go away and let you keep him if you want to. And then when we're gone you can decide which of you is to have him, as you all want him so much.'

'That's fair enough,' said the man who was holding the Baby, trying to loosen the red neckerchief which the Lamb had caught hold of and drawn round his mahogany throat so tight that he could hardly breathe. The gipsies whispered together, and Cyril took the chance to whisper too. He said: 'Sunset! We'll get away then.'

And then his brothers and sisters were filled with wonder and admiration at his having been so clever as to remember this.

'Oh, do let him come to us!' said Jane. 'See we'll sit down here and take care of him for you till he gets used to you.'

'What about dinner?' said Robert suddenly. The others looked at him with scorn ...

'You won't mind my just running home to get our dinner?' Robert said to the gipsy; 'I can bring it out here in a basket.'

His brother and sisters felt themselves very noble, and despised him. They did not know his thoughtful secret intention. But the gipsies did in a minute.

'Oh, yes!' they said; 'and then fetch the police with a pack of lies about it being your baby instead of ours! D'jever catch a weasel asleep?' they asked.

'If you're hungry you can pick a bit along of us,' said the light-haired gipsy woman, not unkindly. 'Here, Levi, that blessed kid'll howl all his buttons off. Give him to the little lady, and let's see if they can't get him used to us a bit.'

So the Lamb was handed back; but the gipsies crowded so closely that he could not possibly stop howling. Then the man with the red handkerchief said: 'Here, Pharaoh, make up the fire; and you girls see to the pot. Give the kid a chanst.' So the gipsies, very much against their will, went off to their work, and the children and the Lamb were left sitting on the grass.

'He'll be all right at sunset,' Jane whispered. 'But, oh, it is awful! Suppose they are frightfully angry when they come to their senses! They might beat us, or leave us tied to trees, or something.'

'No, they won't,' Anthea said. ('Oh, my Lamb, don't cry any more, it's all right ... ') 'They aren't unkind people, or they wouldn't be going to give us any dinner.'

'Dinner?' said Robert. 'I won't touch their nasty dinner. It would choke me!'

The others thought so too then. But when the dinner was ready – it turned out to be supper, and happened between four and five – they were all glad enough to take what they could get. It was boiled rabbit, with onions, and some bird rather like a chicken, but stringier about its legs and with a stronger taste. The Lamb had bread soaked in hot water and brown sugar sprinkled on the top. He liked this very much, and consented to let the two gipsy women feed him with it, as he sat on Anthea's lap. All that long hot afternoon Robert and Cyril and Anthea and Jane had to keep the Lamb amused and happy, while the gipsies looked eagerly on. By the time the shadows grew long and black across the meadows he had really 'taken to' the woman with the light hair, and even consented to kiss his hand to the children, and to stand up and bow, with his hand on his chest – 'like a gentleman' – to the two men. The whole gipsy camp was in raptures with him, and his brothers and sisters could not help taking some pleasure in showing off his accomplishments to an audience so interested and enthusiastic. But they longed for sunset.

'We're getting into the habit of longing for sunset,' Cyril whispered. 'How I do wish we could wish something really sensible, that would be of some use, so that we should be quite sorry when sunset came.'

The shadows got longer and longer, and at last there were no separate shadows any more, but one soft glowing shadow over everything; for the sun was out of sight – behind the hill – but he had not really set yet ...

The gipsies were getting impatient.

'Now, young uns,' the red-handkerchief man said, 'it's time you were laying of your heads on your pillowses – so it is! The kid's all right and friendly with us now – so you just hand him over ...'

The women and children came crowding round the Lamb, arms were held out, fingers snapped invitingly, friendly faces beaming with admiring smiles; but all failed to tempt the loyal Lamb. He clung with arms and legs to Jane, who happened to be holding him, and uttered the gloomiest roar of the whole day.

'It's no good,' the woman said, 'hand the little poppet over, miss. We'll soon quiet him.'

And still the sun would not set.

'Tell her about how to put him to bed,' whispered Cyril; 'anything to gain time – and be ready to bolt when the sun really does make up its silly old mind to set.'

'Yes, I'll hand him over in just one minute,' Anthea began, talking very fast – 'but do let me just tell you he has a warm bath every night ... and he has a crockery rabbit to go into the warm bath with him ... and if you let the soap get into his eyes, the Lamb –'

'Lamb kyes,' said he – he had stopped roaring to listen.

The woman laughed. 'As if I hadn't never bath'd a babby!' she said. 'Come – give us a hold of him. Come to 'Melia, my precious.'

'G'way, ugsie!' replied the Lamb at once.

'Yes, but,' Anthea went on, 'about his meals; you really *must* let me tell you he has an apple or a banana every morning, and bread-and-milk for breakfast, and an egg for his tea sometimes, and –'

'I've brought up ten,' said the black-ringleted woman, 'besides the others. Come, miss, 'and 'im over – I can't bear it no longer. I just must give him a hug.'

'We ain't settled yet whose he's to be, Esther,' said one of the men.

'It won't be you, Esther, with seven of 'em at your tail a'ready.'

'I ain't so sure of that,' said Esther's husband.

'And ain't I nobody, to have a say neither?' said the husband of 'Melia.

Zillah, the girl, said, 'An' me? I'm a single girl – and no one but 'im to look after – I ought to have him.'

'Hold yer tongue!'

'Shut your mouth!'

'Don't you show me no more of your imperence!'

Everyone was getting very angry. The dark gipsy faces were frowning and anxious-looking. Suddenly a change swept over them, as if some invisible sponge had wiped away these cross and anxious expressions, and left only a blank.

The children saw that the sun really *had* set. But they were afraid to move. And the gipsies were feeling so muddled, because of the invisible sponge that had washed all the feelings of the last few hours out of their hearts, that they could not say a word.

The children hardly dared to breathe. Suppose the gipsies, when they recovered speech, should be furious to think how silly they had been all day?

It was an awkward moment. Suddenly Anthea, greatly daring, held out the Lamb to the red-handkerchief man.

'Here he is!' she said.

The man drew back. 'I shouldn't like to deprive you, miss,' he said hoarsely.

'Anyone who likes can have my share of him,' said the other man.

'After all, I've got enough of my own,' said Esther.

'He's a nice little chap, though,' said Amelia. She was the only one who now looked affectionately at the whimpering Lamb.

Zillah said: 'If I don't think I must have had a touch of the sun. *I* don't want him.'

'Then shall we take him away?' said Anthea.

'Well, suppose you do,' said Pharaoh heartily, 'and we'll say no more about it!'

And with great haste all the gipsies began to be busy about their tents for the night. All but Amelia. She went with the children as far as the bend in the road – and there she said: 'Let me give him a kiss, miss – I don't know what made us go for to behave so silly. Us gipsies don't steal babies, whatever they may tell you when you're naughty. We've enough of our own, mostly. But I've lost all mine.'

She leaned towards the Lamb; and he, looking in her eyes, unexpectedly put up a grubby soft paw and stroked her face.

'Poor, poor!' said the Lamb. And he let the gipsy woman kiss him, and, what is more, he kissed her brown cheek in return – a very nice kiss, as all his kisses are, and not a wet one like some babies give. The gipsy woman moved her finger about on his forehead, as if she had been writing something there, and the same with his chest and his hands and his feet; then she said: 'May he be brave, and have the strong head to think with, and the strong heart to love with, and the strong hands to work with, and the strong feet to travel with, and always come safe home to his own.' Then she said something in a strange language no one could understand, and suddenly added: 'Well, I must be saying "so long" – and glad to have made your acquaintance.' And she turned and went back to her home – the tent by the grassy roadside.

The children looked after her till she was out of sight. Then Robert said, 'How silly of her! Even sunset didn't put *her* right. What rot she talked!'

'Well,' said Cyril, 'if you ask me, I think it was rather decent of her –'

'Decent?' said Anthea; 'it was very nice indeed of her. I think she's a dear.'

And they went home – very late for tea and unspeakably late for dinner. Martha scolded, of course. But the Lamb was safe.

'I say – it turned out we wanted the Lamb as much as anyone,' said Robert, later.

'Of course.'

'But do you feel different about it now the sun's set?'

'*No,*' said all the others together.

'Then it's lasted over sunset with us.'

'No, it hasn't,' Cyril explained. 'The wish didn't do anything to *us.* We always wanted him with all our hearts when we were our proper selves, only we were all pigs this morning; especially you, Robert.' Robert bore this much with a strange calm.

'I certainly *thought* I didn't want him this morning,' said he. 'Perhaps I was a pig. But everything looked so different when we thought we were going to lose him.'

JACK LONDON

From *The Call of the Wild*

(1903)

Buck did not read the newspapers, or he would have known that trouble was brewing not alone for himself, but for every tide-water dog, strong of muscle and with warm, long hair, from Puget Sound to San Diego. Because men, groping in the arctic darkness, had found a yellow metal, and because steamship and transportation companies were booming the find, thousands of men were rushing into the Northland. These men wanted dogs, and the dogs they wanted were heavy dogs, with strong muscles by which to toil and furry coats to protect them from the frost.

Buck lived at a big house in the sun-kissed Santa Clara Valley. Judge Miller's place, it was called. It stood back from the road, half-hidden among the trees, through which glimpses could be caught of the wide cool verandah that ran

around its four sides. The house was approached by gravelled driveways which wound about through wide-spreading
lawns and under the interlacing boughs of tall poplars. At
the rear things were on even a more spacious scale than at
the front. There were great stables, where a dozen grooms
and boys held forth, rows of vine-clad servants' cottages, an
endless and orderly array of out-houses, long grape arbours,
green pastures, orchards, and berry patches. Then there was
the pumping plant for the artesian well, and the big cement
tank where Judge Miller's boys took their morning plunge
and kept cool in the hot afternoon.

And over this great demesne Buck ruled. Here he was
born and here he had lived the four years of his life. It was
true, there were other dogs. There could not but be other
dogs on so vast a place, but they did not count. They came
and went, resided in the populous kennels, or lived obscurely
in the recesses of the house after the fashion of Toots, the
Japanese pug, or Ysabel, the Mexican hairless – strange
creatures that rarely put nose out of doors or set foot to
ground. On the other hand, there were the fox terriers, a
score of them at least, who yelped fearful promises at Toots
and Ysabel looking out of the windows at them and pro-
tected by a legion of housemaids armed with brooms and
mops.

But Buck was neither house-dog nor kennel-dog. The
whole realm was his. He plunged into the swimming tank
or went hunting with the Judge's sons; he escorted Mollie
and Alice, the Judge's daughters, on long twilight or early
morning rambles; on wintry nights he lay at the Judge's feet
before the roaring library fire; he carried the Judge's grand-
sons on his back, or rolled them in the grass, and guarded
their footsteps through wild adventures down to the fountain in the stable yard, and even beyond, where the paddocks

were, and the berry patches. Among the terriers he stalked imperiously, and Toots and Ysabel he utterly ignored, for he was king – king over all the creeping, crawling, flying things of Judge Miller's place, humans included.

His father, Elmo, a huge St Bernard, had been the Judge's inseparable companion and Buck did fair to follow in the way of his father. He was not so large – he weighed only one hundred and forty pounds – for his mother, Shep, had been a Scotch shepherd dog. Nevertheless, one hundred and forty pounds, to which was added the dignity that comes of good living and universal respect, enabled him to carry himself in right royal fashion. During the four years since his puppyhood he had lived the life of a sated aristocrat; he had a fine pride in himself, was ever a trifle egotistical, as country gentlemen sometimes become because of their insular situation. But he had saved himself by not becoming a mere pampered house-dog. Hunting and kindred outdoor delights had kept down the fat and hardened his muscles; and to him, as to the cold-tubbing races, the love of water had been a tonic and a health preserver.

And this was the manner of dog Buck in the fall of 1897, when the Klondike strike dragged men from all the world into the frozen North. But Buck did not read the newspapers, and he did not know that Manuel, one of the gardener's helpers, was an undesirable acquaintance. Manuel had one besetting sin. He loved to play Chinese lottery. Also, in his gambling, he had one besetting weakness – faith in a system; and this made his damnation certain. For to play a system requires money, while the wages of a gardener's helper do not lap over the needs of a wife and numerous progeny.

The Judge was at a meeting of the Raisin Growers' Association, and the boys were busy organizing an athletic club, on the memorable night of Manuel's treachery. No one saw him and Buck go off through the orchard on what Buck imagined was merely a stroll. And with the exception of a solitary man, no one saw them arrive at the little flag station known as College Park. This man talked with Manuel, and money clinked between them.

'You might wrap up the goods before you deliver 'm,' the stranger said gruffly, and Manuel doubled a piece of stout rope around Buck's neck under the collar.

'Twist it, an' you'll choke 'm plentee,' said Manuel, and the stranger grunted a ready affirmative.

Buck had accepted the rope with quiet dignity. To be sure, it was an unwonted performance; but he had learned to trust in men he knew, and to give them credit for a wisdom that outreached his own. But when the ends of the rope were placed in the stranger's hands, he growled menacingly. He had merely intimated his displeasure, in his pride believing that to intimate was to command. But to his surprise the rope tightened around his neck, shutting off his breath. In quick rage he sprang at the man, who met him halfway, grappled him close by the throat, and with a deft twist threw him over on his back. Then the rope tightened mercilessly, while Buck struggled in a fury, his tongue lolling out of his mouth and his great chest panting futilely. Never in all his life had he been so vilely treated, and never in all his life had he been so angry. But his strength ebbed, his eyes glazed, and he knew nothing when the train was flagged and the two men threw him into the baggage car.

The next he knew, he was dimly aware that his tongue was hurting and that he was being jolted along in some kind of conveyance. The hoarse shriek of a locomotive whistling a crossing told him where he was. He had travelled too often with the Judge not to know the sensation of riding in a baggage car. He opened his eyes, and into them came the unbridled anger of a kidnapped king. The man sprang for his throat, but Buck was too quick for him. His jaws closed on the hand; nor did they relax till his senses were choked out of him once more.

'Yep, has fits,' the man said, hiding his mangled hand from the baggageman, who had been attracted by the sounds of struggle. 'I'm takin' 'im up for the boss to 'Frisco. A crack dog-doctor there thinks that he can cure 'im.'

Concerning that night's ride the man spoke most eloquently for himself, in a little shed back of a saloon on the San Francisco water front.

'All I get is fifty for it,' he grumbled; 'an' I wouldn't do it over for a thousand, cold cash.'

His hand was wrapped in a bloody handkerchief, and the right trouser leg was ripped from knee to ankle.

'How much did the other mug get?' the saloon-keeper demanded.

'A hundred,' was the reply. 'Wouldn't take a sou less, so help me.'

'That makes a hundred and fifty,' the saloon-keeper calculated, 'and he's worth it, or I'm a squarehead.'

The kidnapper undid the bloody wrappings and looked at his lacerated hand. 'If I don't get the hydrophoby—'

'It'll be because you were born to hang,' laughed the saloon-keeper. 'Here, lend me a hand before you pull your freight,' he added.

Dazed, suffering intolerable pain from throat and tongue, with the life half throttled out of him, Buck attempted to face his tormentors. But he was thrown down and choked repeatedly, till they succeeded in filing the heavy brass collar from off his neck. Then the rope was removed, and he was flung into a cage-like crate.

There he lay for the remainder of the weary night, nursing his wrath and wounded pride. He could not understand what it all meant. What did they want with him, these strange men? Why were they keeping him pent up in this narrow crate? He did not know why, but he felt oppressed by the vague sense of impending calamity. Several times during the night he sprang to his feet when the shed door rattled open, expecting to see the Judge, or the boys at least. But each time it was the bulging face of the saloon-keeper that peered in at him by the sickly light of a tallow candle. And each time the joyful bark that trembled in Buck's throat was twisted into a savage growl.

But the saloon-keeper let him alone, and in the morning four men entered and picked up the crate. More tormentors, Buck decided, for they were evil-looking creatures, ragged and unkempt; and he stormed and raged at them through the bars. They only laughed and poked sticks at him, which he promptly assailed with his teeth till he realized that that was what they wanted. Whereupon he lay down sullenly and allowed the crate to be lifted into a waggon. Then he, and the crate in which he was imprisoned, began a passage through many hands. Clerks in the express office took charge of him; he was carted about in another wagon; a truck carried him, with an assortment of boxes and parcels, upon a ferry steamer; he was trucked off the steamer into a great railway depot, and finally he was deposited in an express car.

For two days and nights this express car was dragged along at the tail of shrieking locomotives; and for two days and nights Buck neither ate nor drank. In his anger he had met the first advances of the express messengers with growls, and they had retaliated by teasing him. When he flung himself against the bars, quivering and frothing, they laughed at him and taunted him. They growled and barked like detestable dogs, mewed, and flapped their arms and crowed. It was all very silly, he knew; but therefore the more outrage to his dignity, and his anger waxed and waxed. He did not mind the hunger so much, but the lack of water caused him severe suffering and fanned his wrath to fever-pitch. For that matter, high-strung and finely sensitive, the ill treatment had flung him into a fever, which was fed by the inflammation of his parched and swollen throat and tongue.

He was glad for one thing: the rope was off his neck. That had given them an unfair advantage; but now that it was off, he would show them. They would never get another rope around his neck. Upon that he was resolved. For two days and nights he neither ate nor drank and during those two days and nights of torment, he accumulated a fund of wrath that boded ill for whoever first fell foul of him. His eyes turned bloodshot, and he was metamorphosed into a raging fiend. So changed was he that the Judge himself would not have recognized him; and the express messengers breathed with relief when they bundled him off the train at Seattle.

Four men gingerly carried the crate from the waggon into a small, high-walled backyard. A stout man, with a red sweater that sagged generously at the neck, came out and signed the book for the driver. That was the man, Buck divined, the next tormentor, and he hurled himself savagely against the bars. The man smiled grimly, and brought a hatchet and a club.

'You ain't going to take him out now?' the driver asked.

'Sure,' the man replied, driving the hatchet into the crate for a pry.

There was an instantaneous scattering of the four men

who had carried it in, and from safe perches on top the wall they prepared to watch the performance.

Buck rushed at the splintering wood, sinking his teeth into it, surging and wrestling with it. Wherever the hatchet fell on the outside, he was there on the inside, snarling and growling, as furiously anxious to get out as the man in the red sweater was calmly intent on getting him out.

'Now, you red-eyed devil,' he said, when he had made an opening sufficient for the passage of Buck's body. At the same time he dropped the hatchet and shifted the club to his right hand.

And Buck was truly a red-eyed devil, as he drew himself together for the spring, hair bristling, mouth foaming, a mad glitter in his bloodshot eyes. Straight at the man he launched his one hundred and forty pounds of fury, surcharged with the pent passion of two days and nights. In mid air, just as his jaws were about to close on the man, he received a shock that checked his body and brought his teeth together with an agonizing clip. He whirled over, fetching the ground on his back and side. He had never been struck by a club in his life, and did not understand. With a snarl that was part bark and more scream he was again on his feet and launched into the air. And again the shock came and he was brought crushingly to the ground. This time he was aware that it was the club, but his madness knew no caution. A dozen times he charged, and as often the club broke the charge and smashed him down.

After a particularly fierce blow, he crawled to his feet, too dazed to rush. He staggered limply about, the blood flowing from nose and mouth and ears, his beautiful coat sprayed and flecked with bloody slaver. Then the man advanced and deliberately dealt him a frightful blow on the nose. All the pain he had endured was as nothing compared with the exquisite agony of this. With a roar that was almost lionlike in its ferocity, he again hurled himself at the man. But the man, shifting the club from right to left, coolly caught him by the under jaw, at the same time wrenching downward and backward. Buck described a complete circle in the air, and half of another, then crashed to the ground on his head and chest.

For the last time he rushed. The man struck the shrewd blow he had purposely withheld for so long, and Buck crumpled up and went down, knocked utterly senseless.

'He's no slouch at dog-breakin', that's wot I say,' one of the men on the wall cried enthusiastically.

'Druther break cayuses any day, and twice on Sundays,' was the reply of the driver, as he climbed on the waggon and started the horses.

Buck's senses came back to him, but not his strength. He lay where he had fallen, and from there he watched the man in the red sweater.

'"Answers to the name of Buck,"' the man soliloquized, quoting from the saloon-keeper's letter which had announced the consignment of the crate and contents. 'Well, Buck, my boy,' he went on in a genial voice, 'we've had our little ruction, and the best thing we can do is to let it go at that. You've learned your place, and I know mine. Be a good dog and all'll go well and the goose hang high. Be a bad dog, and I'll whale the stuffin' outa you. Understand?'

As he spoke he fearlessly patted the head he had so mercilessly pounded, and though Buck's hair involuntarily bristled at touch of the hand, he endured it without protest. When the man brought him water he drank eagerly, and later bolted a generous meal of raw meat, chunk by chunk, from the man's hand.

He was beaten (he knew that); but he was not broken. He saw, once for all, that he stood no chance against a man with a club. He had learned the lesson, and in all his after life he never forgot it. That club was a revelation. It was his introduction to the reign of primitive law, and he met the introduction halfway. The facts of life took on a fiercer aspect; and while he faced that aspect uncowed, he faced it with all the latent cunning of his nature aroused. As the days went by, other dogs came, in crates and at the ends of ropes, some docilely, and some raging and roaring as he had come; and, one and all, he watched them pass under the dominion of the man in the red sweater. Again and again, as he looked at each brutal performance, the lesson was driven home to Buck: a man with a club was a lawgiver, a master to be obeyed, though not necessarily conciliated. Of this last Buck was never guilty, though he did see beaten dogs that fawned upon the man, and wagged their tails, and licked his hand. Also he saw one dog, that would neither conciliate nor obey, finally killed in the struggle for mastery.

Now and again men came, strangers, who talked excitedly, wheedlingly, and in all kinds of fashions to the man in the red sweater. And at such times that money passed between them the strangers took one or more of the dogs away with them. Buck wondered where they went, for they never came back; but the fear of the future was strong upon him, and he was glad each time when he was not selected.

Yet his time came, in the end, in the form of a little weazened man who spat broken English and many strange and uncouth exclamations which Buck could not understand.

'Sacredam!' he cried, when his eyes lit upon Buck. 'Dat one dam bully dog! Eh? How moch?'

'Three hundred, and a present at that,' was the prompt

reply of the man in the red sweater. 'And seein' it's government money, you ain't got no kick coming; eh, Perrault?'

Perrault grinned. Considering that the price of dogs had been boomed skyward by the unwonted demand, it was not an unfair sum for so fine an animal. The Canadian Government would be no loser, nor would its dispatches travel the slower. Perrault knew dogs, and when he looked at Buck he knew that he was one in a thousand – 'One in ten t'ousand,' he commented mentally.

Buck saw money pass between them, and was not surprised when Curly, a good-natured Newfoundland, and he were led away by the little weazened man. That was the last he saw of the man in the red sweater, and as Curly and he looked at receding Seattle from the deck of the *Narwhal*, it was the last he saw of the warm Southland. Curly and he were taken below by Perrault and turned over to a black-faced giant called François. Perrault was a French-Canadian, and swarthy; but François was a French-Canadian half-breed, and twice as swarthy. They were a new kind of men to Buck (of which he was destined to see many more), and while he developed no affection for them, he none the less grew honestly to respect them. He speedily learned that Perrault and François were fair men, calm and impartial in administering justice, and too wise in the way of dogs to be ever fooled by dogs.

In the 'tween-decks of the *Narwhal*, Buck and Curly joined two other dogs. One of them was a big, snow-white fellow from Spitzbergen who had been brought away by a whaling captain, and who had later accompanied a Geological Survey into the Barrens. He was friendly, in a treacherous sort of way, smiling into one's face the while he meditated some underhand trick, as, for instance, when he stole from Buck's food at the first meal. As Buck sprang to punish him, the lash of François's whip sang through the air, reaching the culprit first; and nothing remained to Buck but to recover the bone. That was fair of François, he decided, and the half-breed began to rise in Buck's estimation.

The other dog made no advances, nor received any; also, he did not attempt to steal from the newcomers. He was a gloomy, morose fellow, and he showed Curly plainly that all he desired was to be left alone, and further, that there would be trouble if he were not left alone. 'Dave' he was called, and he ate and slept, or yawned between times, and took interest in nothing, not even when the *Narwhal* crossed Queen Charlotte Sound and rolled and pitched and bucked like a thing possessed. When Buck and Curly grew excited, half wild with fear, he raised his head as though annoyed, favoured them with an incurious glance, yawned, and went to sleep again.

Day and night the ship throbbed to the tireless pulse of the propeller, and though one day was very like another, it was apparent to Buck that the weather was steadily growing colder. At last, one morning, the propeller was quiet, and the *Narwhal* was pervaded with an atmosphere of excitement. He felt it, as did the other dogs, and knew that a change was at hand. François leashed them and brought them on deck. At the first step upon the cold surface, Buck's feet sank into a white mushy something very like mud. He sprang back with a snort. More of this white stuff was falling through the air. He shook himself, but more of it fell upon him. He sniffed it curiously, then licked some up on his tongue. It bit like fire, and the next instant was gone. This puzzled him. He tried it again, with the same result. The onlookers laughed uproariously, and he felt ashamed, he knew not why, for it was his first snow.

E. NESBIT

FROM *The Railway Children*

(1906)

The Russian gentleman was so delighted with the strawberries that the three racked their brains to find some other surprise for him. But all the racking did not bring out any idea more novel than wild cherries. And this idea occurred to them next morning. They had seen the blossom on the trees in the spring, and they knew where to look for wild cherries now that cherry time was here. The trees grew all up and along the rocky face of the cliff out of which the mouth of the tunnel opened. There were all sorts of trees there, birches and beeches and baby oaks and hazels, and among them the cherry blossom had shone like snow and silver.

The mouth of the tunnel was some way from Three Chimneys, so Mother let them take their lunch with them in a basket. And the basket would do to bring the cherries back in if they found any. She also lent them her silver watch so that they should not be late for tea. Peter's Waterbury had taken it into its head not to go since the day when Peter dropped it into the water-butt. And they started.

When they got to the top of the cutting, they leaned over the fence and looked down to where the railway lines lay at the bottom of what, as Phyllis said, was exactly like a mountain gorge.

'If it wasn't for the railway at the bottom, it would be as though the foot of man had never been there, wouldn't it?'

The sides of the cutting were of grey stone, very roughly hewn. Indeed, the top part of the cutting had been a little natural glen that had been cut deeper to bring it down to the level of the tunnel's mouth. Among the rocks, grass and flowers grew, and seeds dropped by birds in the crannies of the stone had taken root and grown into bushes and trees that overhung the cutting. Near the tunnel was a flight of steps leading down to the line – just wooden bars roughly fixed into the earth – a very steep and narrow way, more like a ladder than a stair.

'We'd better get down,' said Peter; 'I'm sure the cherries would be quite easy to get at from the side of the steps. You remember it was there we picked the cherry blossoms that we put on the rabbit's grave.'

So they went along the fence towards the little swing gate that is at the top of these steps. And they were almost at the gate when Bobbie said: 'Hush. Stop! What's that?'

'That' was a very odd noise indeed – a soft noise, but quite plainly to be heard through the sound of the wind in the branches, and the hum and whir of the telegraph wires. It was a sort of rustling, whispering sound. As they listened it stopped and then it began again.

And this time it did not stop, but it grew louder and more rustling and rumbling.

'Look' – cried Peter, suddenly – 'the tree over there!'

The tree he pointed at was one of those that have rough grey leaves and white flowers. The berries, when they come, are bright scarlet, but if you pick them, they disappoint you by turning black before you get them home. And, as Peter pointed, the tree was moving – not just the way trees ought to move when the wind blows through them, but all in one piece, as though it were a live creature and were walking down the side of the cutting.

'It's moving!' cried Bobbie. 'Oh, look! And so are the others. It's like the woods in *Macbeth*.'

'It's magic,' said Phyllis, breathlessly. 'I always knew the railway was enchanted.'

It really did seem a little like magic. For all the trees for about twenty yards of the opposite bank seemed to be slowly walking down towards the railway line, the tree with the grey leaves bringing up the rear like some old shepherd driving a flock of green sheep.

'What is it? Oh, what is it?' said Phyllis; 'it's much too magic for me. I don't like it. Let's go home.'

But Bobbie and Peter clung fast to the rail and watched breathlessly. And Phyllis made no movement towards going home by herself.

The trees moved on and on. Some stones and loose earth fell down and rattled on the railway metals far below.

'It's *all* coming down,' Peter tried to say, but he found there was hardly any voice to say it with. And, indeed, just as he spoke, the great rock, on the top of which the walking trees were, leaned slowly forward. The trees, ceasing to walk, stood still and shivered. Leaning with the rock, they seemed to hesitate a moment, and then rock and trees and grass and bushes, with a rushing sound, slipped right away from the face of the cutting and fell on the line with a blundering crash that could have been heard half a mile off. A cloud of dust rose up.

'Oh,' said Peter, in awestruck tones, 'isn't it exactly like when coals come in? – If there wasn't any roof to the cellar and you could see down.'

'Look what a great mound it's made!' said Bobbie.

'Yes, it's right across the down line,' said Phyllis.

'That'll take some sweeping up,' said Bobbie.

'Yes,' said Peter slowly. He was still leaning on the fence.

'Yes,' he said again, still more slowly.

Then he stood upright.

'The 11.29 down hasn't gone by yet. We must let them know at the station, or there'll be a most frightful accident.'

'Let's run,' said Bobbie, and began.

But Peter cried: 'Come back!' and looked at Mother's watch. He was very prompt and businesslike, and his face looked whiter than they had ever seen it.

'No time,' he said; 'it's ten miles away, and it's past eleven.'

'Couldn't we,' suggested Phyllis, breathlessly, 'couldn't we climb up a telegraph post and do something to the wires?'

'We don't know how,' said Peter.

'They do it in war,' said Phyllis; 'I know I've heard of it.'

'They only *cut* them, silly,' said Peter, 'and that doesn't do any good. And we couldn't cut them even if we got up, and we couldn't get up. If we had anything red, we could go down on the line and wave it.'

'But the train wouldn't see us till it got round the corner, and then it could see the mound just as well as us,' said Phyllis; 'better, because it's much bigger than us.'

'If we only had something red,' Peter repeated, 'we could go round the corner and wave to the train.'

'We might wave, anyway.'

'They'd only think it was just *us*, as usual. We've waved so often before. Anyway, let's get down.'

They got down the steep stairs. Bobbie was pale and shivering. Peter's face looked thinner than usual. Phyllis was red-faced and damp with anxiety.

'Oh, how hot I am!' she said; 'and I thought it was going to be cold; I wish we hadn't put on our – ' she stopped short, and then ended in quite a different tone – 'our flannel petticoats.'

Bobbie turned at the bottom of the stairs.

'Oh, yes,' she cried, '*they're* red! Let's take them off.'

They did, and with the petticoats rolled up under their arms, ran along the railway, skirting the newly fallen mound of stones and rock and earth, and bent, crushed, twisted trees. They ran at their best pace. Peter led, but the girls were not far behind. They reached the corner that hid the mound from the straight line of railway that ran half a mile without curve or corner.

'Now,' said Peter, taking hold of the largest flannel petticoat.

'You're not' – Phyllis faltered – 'you're not going to *tear* them?'

'Shut up,' said Peter, with brief sternness.

'Oh, yes,' said Bobbie, 'tear them into little bits if you like. Don't you see, Phil, if we can't stop the train, there'll be a real live accident, with people *killed*. Oh, horrible! Here, Peter, you'll never tear it through the band!'

She took the red flannel petticoat from him and tore it off an inch from the band. Then she tore the other in the same way.

'There!' said Peter, tearing in his turn. He divided each petticoat into three pieces. 'Now, we've got six flags.' He looked at the watch again. 'And we've got seven minutes. We must have flagstaffs.'

The knives given to boys are, for some odd reason, seldom of the kind of steel that keeps sharp. The young saplings had to be broken off. Two came up by the roots. The leaves were stripped from them.

'We must cut holes in the flags, and run the sticks through the holes,' said Peter. And the holes were cut. The knife was sharp enough to cut flannel with. Two of the flags were set up in heaps of loose stones beneath the sleepers of the down line. Then Phyllis and Roberta took each a flag, and stood ready to wave it as soon as the train came in sight.

'I shall have the other two myself,' said Peter, 'because it was my idea to wave something red.'

'They're our petticoats, though,' Phyllis was beginning, but Bobbie interrupted –

'Oh, what does it matter who waves what, if we can only save the train?'

Perhaps Peter had not rightly calculated the number of minutes it would take the 11.29 to get from the station to the place where they were, or perhaps the train was late. Anyway, it seemed a very long time that they waited.

Phyllis grew impatient. 'I expect the watch is wrong, and the train's gone by,' said she.

Peter relaxed the heroic attitude he had chosen to show off his two flags. And Bobbie began to feel sick with suspense.

It seemed to her that they had been standing there for hours and hours, holding those silly little red flannel flags that no one would ever notice. The train wouldn't care. It would go rushing by them and tear round the corner and go crashing into that awful mound. And everyone would be killed. Her hands grew very cold and trembled so that she could hardly hold the flag. And then came the distant rumble and hum of the metals, and a puff of white steam showed far away along the stretch of line.

'Stand firm,' said Peter, 'and wave like mad! When it gets to that big furze bush step back, but go on waving! Don't stand *on* the line, Bobbie!'

The train came rattling along very, very fast.

'They don't see us! They won't see us! It's all no good!' cried Bobbie.

The two little flags on the line swayed as the nearing train shook and loosened the heaps of loose stones that held them up. One of them slowly leaned over and fell on the line. Bobbie jumped forward and caught it up, and waved it; her hands did not tremble now.

It seemed that the train came on as fast as ever. It was very near now.

'Keep off the line, you silly cuckoo!' said Peter, fiercely.

'It's no good,' Bobbie said again.

'Stand back!' cried Peter, suddenly, and he dragged Phyllis back by the arm.

But Bobbie cried: 'Not yet, not yet!' and waved her two flags right over the line. The front of the engine looked black and enormous. Its voice was loud and harsh.

'Oh, stop, stop, stop!' cried Bobbie. No one heard her. At least Peter and Phyllis didn't, for the oncoming rush of the train covered the sound of her voice with a mountain of sound. But afterwards she used to wonder whether the engine itself had not heard her. It seemed almost as though it had – for it slackened swiftly, slackened and stopped, not twenty yards from the place where Bobbie's two flags waved over the line. She saw the great black engine stop dead, but somehow she could not stop waving the flags. And when the driver and the fireman had got off the engine and Peter and Phyllis had gone to meet them and pour out their excited tale of the awful mound just round the corner, Bobbie still waved the flags but more and more feebly and jerkily.

When the others turned towards her she was lying across the line with her hands flung forward and still gripping the sticks of the little red flannel flags.

The engine-driver picked her up, carried her to the train, and laid her on the cushions of a first-class carriage.

'Gone right off in a faint,' he said, 'poor little woman. And no wonder. I'll just 'ave a look at this 'ere mound of yours, and then we'll run you back to the station and get her seen to.'

It was horrible to see Bobbie lying so white and quiet, with her lips blue, and parted.

'I believe that's what people look like when they're dead,' whispered Phyllis.

'*Don't!*' said Peter, sharply.

They sat by Bobbie on the blue cushions and the train ran back. Before it reached their station Bobbie sighed and opened her eyes, and rolled herself over and began to cry. This cheered the others wonderfully. They had seen her cry before, but they had never seen her faint, nor anyone else, for the matter of that. They had not known what to do when she was fainting, but now she was only crying they could thump her on the back and tell her not to, just as they always did. And presently, when she stopped crying, they were able to laugh at her for being such a coward as to faint.

When the station was reached, the three were the heroes of an agitated meeting on the platform.

The praises they got for their 'prompt action', their 'common sense,' their 'ingenuity', were enough to have turned anybody's head. Phyllis enjoyed herself thoroughly. She had never been a real heroine before, and the feeling was delicious. Peter's ears got very red. Yet he, too, enjoyed himself. Only Bobbie wished they all wouldn't. She wanted to get away.

'You'll hear from the Company about this, I expect,' said the Station Master.

Bobbie wished she might never hear of it again. She pulled at Peter's jacket.

'Oh, come away, come away! I want to go home,' she said.

So they went. And as they went Station Master and Porter and guards and driver and fireman and passengers sent up a cheer.

'Oh, listen,' cried Phyllis; 'that's for *us*!'

'Yes,' said Peter. 'I say, I am glad I thought about something red and waving it.'

'How lucky we *did* put on our red flannel petticoats!' said Phyllis.

Bobbie said nothing. She was thinking of the horrible mound, and the trustful train rushing towards it.

'And it was *us* that saved them,' said Peter.

'How dreadful if they had all been killed!' said Phyllis; 'wouldn't it, Bobbie?'

'We never got any cherries, after all,' said Bobbie.

The others thought her rather heartless.

KENNETH GRAHAME

From *The Wind in the Willows*

(1908)

The sheep ran huddling together against the hurdles, blowing out thin nostrils and stamping with delicate forefeet, their heads thrown back and a light steam rising from the crowded sheep-pen into the frosty air, as the two animals hastened by in high spirits, with much chatter and laughter. They were returning across country after a long day's outing with Otter, hunting and exploring on the wide uplands where certain streams tributary to their own river had their first small beginnings; and the shades of the short winter day were closing in on them, and they had still some distance to go. Plodding at random across the plough, they had heard the sheep and had made for them; and now, leading from the sheep-pen, they found a beaten track that made walking a lighter business, and responded, moreover, to that small inquiring something which all animals carry inside them, saying unmistakably, 'Yes, quite right; *this* leads home!'

'It looks as if we're coming to a village,' said the Mole somewhat dubiously, slackening his pace, as the track, that had in time become a path and then had developed into a lane, now handed them over to the charge of a well-metalled road. The animals did not hold with villages, and their own highways, thickly frequented as they were, took an independent course, regardless of church, post office, or public-house.

'Oh, never mind!' said the Rat. 'At this season of the year they're all safe indoors by this time, sitting round the fire; men, women, and children, dogs and cats and all. We shall slip through all right, without any bother or unpleasantness, and we can have a look at them through their windows if you like, and see what they're doing.'

The rapid nightfall of mid-December had quite beset the little village as they approached it on soft feet over a first thin fall of powdery snow. Little was visible but squares of a dusky orange-red on either side of the street, where the firelight or lamplight of each cottage overflowed through the casements into the dark world without. Most of the low latticed windows were innocent of blinds, and to the lookers-in from outside, the inmates, gathered round the tea-table, absorbed in handiwork, or talking with laughter and gesture, had each that happy grace which is the last thing the skilled actor shall capture – the natural grace which goes with perfect unconsciousness of observation. Moving at will from one theatre to another, the two spectators, so far from home themselves, had something of wistfulness in their eyes as they watched a cat being stroked, a sleepy child picked up and huddled off to bed, or a tired man stretch and knock out his pipe on the end of a smouldering log.

But it was from one little window, with its blind drawn down, a mere blank transparency on the night, that the sense of home and the little curtained world within walls — the larger stressful world of outside Nature shut out and forgotten — most pulsated. Close against the white blind hung a bird-cage, clearly silhouetted, every wire, perch, and appurtenance distinct and recognizable, even to yesterday's dull-edged lump of sugar. On the middle perch the fluffy occupant, head tucked well into feathers, seemed so near to them as to be easily stroked, had they tried; even the delicate tips of his plumped-out plumage pencilled plainly on the illuminated screen. As they looked, the sleepy little fellow stirred uneasily, woke, shook himself, and raised his head. They could see the gape of his tiny beak as he yawned in a bored sort of way, looked around, and then settled his head into his back again, while the ruffled feathers gradually subsided into perfect stillness. Then a gust of bitter wind took them in the back of the neck, a small sting of frozen sleet on the skin woke them as from a dream, and they knew their toes to be cold and their legs tired, and their own home distant a weary way.

Once beyond the village, where the cottages ceased abruptly, on either side of the road they could smell through the darkness the friendly fields again; and they braced themselves for the last long stretch, the home stretch, the stretch that we know is bound to end, some time, in the rattle of the door-latch, the sudden firelight, and the sight of familiar things greeting us as long-absent travellers from far oversea. They plodded along steadily and silently, each of them thinking his own thoughts. The Mole's ran a good deal on supper, as it was pitch dark, and it was all a strange country to him as far as he knew, and he was following obediently in the wake of the Rat, leaving the guidance entirely to him. As for the Rat, he was walking a little way ahead, as his habit was, his shoulders humped, his eyes fixed on the straight grey road in front of him; so he did not notice poor Mole when suddenly the summons reached him, and took him like an electric shock.

We others, who have long lost the more subtle of the physical senses, have not even proper terms to express an animal's inter-communications with his surroundings, living or otherwise, and have only the word 'smell', for instance, to include the whole range of delicate thrills which murmur in the nose of the animal night and day, summoning, warning, inciting, repelling. It was one of these mysterious fairy calls from out the void that suddenly reached Mole in the darkness, making him tingle through and through with its very familiar appeal, even while as yet he could not clearly remember what it was. He stopped dead in his tracks, his nose searching hither and thither in its efforts to recapture the fine filament, the telegraphic current, that had so strongly moved him. A moment, and he had caught it again; and with it this time came recollection in fullest flood.

Home! That was what they meant, those caressing appeals, those soft touches wafted through the air, those invisible little hands pulling and tugging, all one way! Why, it must be quite close by him at that moment, his old home that he had hurriedly forsaken and never sought again, that day when he first found the river! And now it was sending out its scouts and its messengers to capture him and bring him in. Since his escape on that bright morning he had hardly given it a thought, so absorbed had he been in his new life, in all its pleasures, its surprises, its fresh and captivating experiences. Now, with a rush of old memories, how clearly it stood up before him, in the darkness! Shabby indeed, and small and poorly furnished, and yet his, the home he had made for himself, the home he had been so happy to get back to after his day's work. And the home had been happy with him, too, evidently, and was missing him, and wanted him back, and was telling him so, through his nose, sorrowfully, reproachfully, but with no bitterness or anger; only with plaintive reminder that it was there, and wanted him.

The call was clear, the summons was plain. He must obey it instantly, and go. 'Ratty!' he called, full of joyful excitement, 'hold on! Come back! I want you, quick!'

'O, *come* along, Mole, do!' replied the Rat cheerfully, still plodding along.

'*Please* stop, Ratty!' pleaded the poor Mole, in anguish of heart. 'You don't understand! It's my home, my old home! I've just come across the smell of it, and it's close by here, really quite close. And I *must* go to it, I must, I must! O, come back, Ratty! Please, please come back!'

The Rat was by this time very far ahead, too far to hear clearly what the Mole was calling, too far to catch the sharp note of painful appeal in his voice. And he was much taken up with the weather, for he too could smell something – something suspiciously like approaching snow.

'Mole, we mustn't stop now, really!' he called back. 'We'll come for it tomorrow, whatever it is you've found. But I daren't stop now – it's late, and the snow's coming on again, and I'm not sure of the way! And I want your nose, Mole, so come on quick, there's a good fellow!' And the Rat pressed forward on his way without waiting for an answer.

Poor Mole stood alone in the road, his heart torn asunder, and a big sob gathering, gathering, somewhere low down inside him, to leap up to the surface presently, he knew, in passionate escape. But even under such a test as this his loyalty to his friend stood firm. Never for a moment did he dream of abandoning him. Meanwhile, the wafts from his old home pleaded, whispered, conjured, and finally claimed him imperiously. He dared not tarry longer within their magic circle. With a wrench that tore his very heart-strings he set his face down the road and followed submissively in the track of the Rat, while faint, thin little smells, still dogging his retreating nose, reproached him for his new friendship and his callous forgetfulness.

With an effort he caught up the unsuspecting Rat, who began chattering cheerfully about what they would do when they got back, and how jolly a fire of logs in the parlour would be, and what a supper he meant to eat; never noticing his companion's silence and distressful state of mind. At last, however, when they had gone some considerable way further, and were passing some tree-stumps at the edge of a copse that bordered the road, he stopped and said kindly, 'Look here, Mole, old chap, you seem dead tired. No talk left in you, and your feet dragging like lead. We'll sit down here for a minute and rest. The snow has held off so far, and the best part of our journey is over.'

The Mole subsided forlornly on a tree-stump and tried to control himself, for he felt it surely coming. The sob he had fought with so long refused to be beaten. Up and up, it forced its way to the air, and then another, and another, and others thick and fast; till poor Mole at last gave up the struggle, and cried freely and helplessly and openly, now that he knew it was all over and he had lost what he could hardly be said to have found.

The Rat, astonished and dismayed at the violence of Mole's paroxysm of grief, did not dare to speak for a while. At last he said, very quietly and sympathetically, 'What is it, old fellow? Whatever can be the matter? Tell us your trouble, and let me see what I can do.'

Poor Mole found it difficult to get any words out between the upheavals of his chest that followed one upon another so quickly and held back speech and choked it as it came. 'I know it's a – shabby, dingy little place,' he sobbed forth at last, brokenly; 'not like – your cosy quarters – or Toad's beautiful hall – or Badger's great house – but it was my own little home – and I was fond of it – and I went away and forgot all about it – and then I smelt it suddenly – on the road, when I called and you wouldn't listen, Rat – and everything came back to me with a rush – and I *wanted* it! – O dear, O dear! – and when you *wouldn't* turn back, Ratty – and I had to leave it, though I was smelling it all the time – I thought my heart would break. We might have just gone and had one look at it, Ratty – only one look – it was close by – but you wouldn't turn back, Ratty, you wouldn't turn back! O dear, O dear!'

Recollection brought fresh waves of sorrow, and sobs again took full charge of him, preventing further speech.

The Rat stared straight in front of him, saying nothing, only patting Mole gently on the shoulder. After a time he muttered gloomily, 'I see it all now! What a *pig* I have been! A pig – that's me! Just a pig – a plain pig!'

He waited till Mole's sobs became gradually less stormy and more rhythmical; he waited till at last sniffs were frequent and sobs only intermittent. Then he rose from his seat, and, remarking carelessly, 'Well, now we'd really better be getting on, old chap!' set off up the road again, over the toilsome way they had come.

'Wherever are you (hic) going to (hic), Ratty?' cried the tearful Mole, looking up in alarm.

'We're going to find that home of yours, old fellow,' replied the Rat pleasantly; 'so you had better come along, for it will take some finding, and we shall want your nose.'

'O, come back, Ratty, do!' cried the Mole, getting up and hurrying after him. 'It's no good, I tell you! It's too late, and too dark, and the place is too far off, and the snow's coming! And – and I never meant to let you know I was feeling that way about it – it was all an accident and a mistake! And think of River Bank, and your supper!'

'Hang River Bank, and supper too!' said the Rat heartily. 'I tell you, I'm going to find this place now, if I stay out all night. So cheer up, old chap, and take my arm, and we'll very soon be back there again.'

Still snuffling, pleading, and reluctant, Mole suffered himself to be dragged back along the road by his imperious companion, who by a flow of cheerful talk and anecdote endeavoured to beguile his spirits back and make the weary way seem shorter. When at last it seemed to the Rat that they must be nearing that part of the road where the Mole had been 'held up', he said, 'Now, no more talking. Business! Use your nose, and give your mind to it.'

They moved on in silence for some little way, when suddenly the Rat was conscious, through his arm that was linked in Mole's, of a faint sort of electric thrill that was passing down that animal's body. Instantly he disengaged himself, fell back a pace, and waited, all attention.

The signals were coming through!

Mole stood a moment rigid, while his uplifted nose, quivering slightly, felt the air.

Then a short, quick run forward – a fault – a check – a try back; and then a slow, steady, confident advance.

The Rat, much excited, kept close to his heels as the Mole, with something of the air of a sleep-walker, crossed a dry ditch, scrambled through a hedge, and nosed his way over a field open and trackless and bare in the faint starlight.

Suddenly, without giving warning, he dived; but the Rat

was on the alert, and promptly followed him down the tunnel to which his unerring nose had faithfully led him.

It was close and airless, and the earthy smell was strong, and it seemed a long time to Rat ere the passage ended and he could stand erect and stretch and shake himself. The Mole struck a match, and by its light the Rat saw that they were standing in an open space, neatly swept and sanded underfoot, and directly facing them was Mole's little front door, with 'Mole End' painted, in Gothic lettering, over the bell-pull at the side.

Mole reached down a lantern from a nail on the wall and lit it, and the Rat, looking round him, saw that they were in a sort of fore-court. A garden-seat stood on one side of the door, and on the other, a roller; for the Mole, who was a tidy animal when at home, could not stand having his ground kicked up by other animals into little runs that ended in earth-heaps. On the walls hung wire baskets with ferns in them, alternating with brackets carrying plaster statuary – Garibaldi, and the infant Samuel, and Queen Victoria, and other heroes of modern Italy. Down one side of the fore-court ran a skittle-alley, with benches along it and little wooden tables marked with rings that hinted at beer-mugs. In the middle was a small round pond containing goldfish and surrounded by a cockle-shell border. Out of the centre of the pond rose a fanciful erection clothed in more cockle-shells and topped by a large silvered glass ball that reflected everything all wrong and had a very pleasing effect.

Mole's face beamed at the sight of all these objects so dear to him, and he hurried Rat through the door, lit a lamp in the hall, and took one glance round his old home. He saw the dust lying thick on everything, saw the cheerless, deserted look of the long-neglected house, and its narrow, meagre dimensions, its worn and shabby contents – and collapsed again on a hall-chair, his nose in his paws. 'O, Ratty!' he cried dismally, 'why ever did I do it? Why did I bring you to this poor, cold little place, on a night like this, when you might have been at River Bank by this time, toasting your toes before a blazing fire, with all your own nice things about you!'

The Rat paid no heed to his doleful self-reproaches. He was running here and there, opening doors, inspecting rooms and cupboards, and lighting lamps and candles and sticking them up everywhere. 'What a capital little house this is!' he called out cheerily. 'So compact! So well planned! Everything here and everything in its place! We'll make a jolly night of it. The first thing we want is a good fire; I'll see to that – I always know where to find things. So this is the parlour? Splendid! Your own idea, those little sleeping-bunks in the wall? Capital! Now, I'll fetch the wood and the coals, and you get a duster, Mole – you'll find one in the drawer of the kitchen table – and try and smarten things up a bit. Bustle about, old chap!'

Encouraged by his inspiriting companion, the Mole roused himself and dusted and polished with energy and heartiness, while the Rat, running to and fro with armfuls of fuel, soon had a cheerful blaze roaring up the chimney. He hailed the Mole to come and warm himself; but Mole promptly had another fit of the blues, dropping down on a couch in dark despair and burying his face in his duster.

'Rat,' he moaned, 'how about your supper, you poor, cold, hungry, weary animal? I've nothing to give you – nothing – not a crumb!'

'What a fellow you are for giving in!' said the Rat reproachfully. 'Why, only just now I saw a sardine-opener on the kitchen dresser, quite distinctly; and everybody knows that means there are sardines about somewhere in the neighbourhood. Rouse yourself! Pull yourself together, and come with me and forage.'

They went and foraged accordingly, hunting through every cupboard and turning out every drawer. The result was not so very depressing after all, though of course it might have been better; a tin of sardines – a box of captain's biscuits, nearly full – and a German sausage encased in silver paper.

'There's a banquet for you!' observed the Rat, as he arranged the table. 'I know some animals who would give their ears to be sitting down to supper with us tonight!'

'No bread!' groaned the Mole dolorously; 'no butter, no – '

'No *pâté de foie gras*, no champagne!' continued the Rat, grinning. 'And that reminds me – what's that little door at the end of the passage? Your cellar, of course! Every luxury in this house! Just you wait a minute.'

He made for the cellar door, and presently reappeared, somewhat dusty, with a bottle of beer in each paw and another under each arm. 'Self-indulgent beggar you seem to be, Mole,' he observed. 'Deny yourself nothing. This is really the jolliest little place I ever was in. Now, wherever did you pick up those prints? Make the place look so home-like, they do. No wonder you're so fond of it, Mole. Tell us all about it, and how you came to make it what it is.'

Then, while the Rat busied himself fetching plates, and knives and forks, and mustard which he mixed in an egg-cup, the Mole, his bosom still heaving with the stress of his recent emotion, related – somewhat shyly at first, but with more freedom as he warmed to his subject – how this was planned, and how that was thought out, and how this was got through a windfall from an aunt, and that was a wonderful find and a bargain, and this other thing was bought out of laborious savings and a certain amount of 'going without'. His spirits finally quite restored, he must needs go and caress his possessions, and take a lamp and show off their points to his visitor, and expatiate on them, quite forgetful of the supper they both so much needed; Rat, who was desperately hungry but strove to conceal it, nodding seriously, examining with a puckered brow, and saying, 'Wonderful', and 'Most remarkable', at intervals, when the chance for an observation was given him.

At last the Rat succeeded in decoying him to the table, and had just got seriously to work with the sardine-opener when sounds were heard from the fore-court without – sounds like the scuffling of small feet in the gravel and a confused murmur of tiny voices, while broken sentences reached them – 'No, all in a line – hold the lantern up a bit, Tommy – clear your throats first – no coughing after I say one, two, three. Where's young Bill? – Here, come on, do, we're all a-waiting – '

'What's up?' inquired the Rat, pausing in his labours.

'I think it must be the field-mice,' replied the Mole, with a touch of pride in his manner. 'They go round carol-singing regularly at this time of the year. They're quite an institution in these parts. And they never pass me over – they come to Mole End last of all; and I used to give them hot drinks, and supper too sometimes, when I could afford it. It will be like old times to hear them again.'

'Let's have a look at them!' cried the Rat, jumping up and running to the door.

It was a pretty sight, and a seasonable one, that met their eyes when they flung the door open. In the fore-court, lit by the dim rays of a horn lantern, some eight or ten little field-mice stood in a semicircle, red worsted comforters round their throats, their fore-paws thrust deep into their pockets, their feet jigging for warmth. With bright beady eyes they glanced shyly at each other, sniggering a little, sniffing and applying coat-sleeves a good deal. As the door opened, one of the elder ones that carried the lantern was just saying, 'Now then, one, two, three!' and forthwith their shrill little voices uprose on the air, singing one of the old-time carols that their forefathers composed in fields that were fallow and held by frost, or when snow-bound in chimney corners, and handed down to be sung in the miry street to lamp-lit windows at Yule-time.

Carol

Villagers all, this frosty tide,
Let your doors swing open wide,
Though wind may follow, and snow beside,
Yet draw us in by your fire to bide;
    Joy shall be yours in the morning!

Here we stand in the cold and the sleet,
Blowing fingers and stamping feet,
Come from far away you to greet –
You by the fire and we in the street –
    Bidding you joy in the morning!

For ere one half of the night was gone,
Sudden a star has led us on,
Raining bliss and benison –
Bliss tomorrow and more anon,
    Joy for every morning!

Goodman Joseph toiled through the snow –
Saw the star o'er a stable low;
Mary she might not further go –
Welcome thatch, and litter below!
    Joy was hers in the morning!

And then they heard the angels tell
'Who were the first to cry Nowell?
Animals all, as it befell,
In the stable where they did dwell!
    Joy shall be theirs in the morning!'

The voices ceased, the singers, bashful but smiling, exchanged sidelong glances, and silence succeeded – but for a moment only. Then, from up above and far away, down the tunnel they had so lately travelled was borne to their ears in a faint musical hum the sound of distant bells ringing a joyful and clangorous peal.

'Very well sung, boys!' cried the Rat heartily. 'And now come along in, all of you, and warm yourselves by the fire, and having something hot!'

'Yes, come along, field-mice,' cried the Mole eagerly. 'This is quite like old times! Shut the door after you. Pull up that settle to the fire. Now, you just wait a minute, while we – O, Ratty!' he cried in despair, plumping down on a seat, with tears impending. 'Whatever are we doing? We've nothing to give them!'

'You leave all that to me,' said the masterful Rat. 'Here, you with the lantern! Come over this way. I want to talk to you. Now, tell me, are there any shops open at this hour of the night?'

'Why, certainly, sir,' replied the field-mouse respectfully. 'At this time of the year our shops keep open to all sorts of hours.'

'Then look here!' said the Rat. 'You go off at once, you and your lantern, and you get me –'

Here much muttered conversation ensued, and the Mole only heard bits of it, such as – 'Fresh, mind! – no, a pound of that will do – see you get Buggins's, for I won't have any other – no, only the best – if you can't get it there, try some-where else – yes, of course, home-made, no tinned stuff – well then, do the best you can!' Finally, there was a chink of coin passing from paw to paw, the field-mouse was pro-vided with an ample basket for his purchases, and off he hurried, he and his lantern.

The rest of the field-mice, perched in a row on the settle, their small legs swinging, gave themselves up to enjoyment of the fire, and toasted their chilblains till they tingled; while the Mole, failing to draw them into easy conversation, plunged into family history and made each of them recite the names of his numerous brothers, who were too young, it appeared, to be allowed to go out a-carolling this year, but looked forward very shortly to winning the parental con-sent.

The Rat, meanwhile, was busy examining the label on one of the beer-bottles. 'I perceive this to be Old Burton,' he remarked approvingly. '*Sensible* Mole! The very thing! Now we shall be able to mull some ale! Get the things ready, Mole, while I draw the corks.'

It did not take long to prepare the brew and thrust the tin heater well into the red heart of the fire; and soon every field-mouse was sipping and coughing and choking (for a little mulled ale goes a long way) and wiping his eyes and laughing and forgetting he had ever been cold in all his life.

'They act plays too, these fellows,' the Mole explained to the Rat. 'Make them up all by themselves, and act them afterwards. And very well they do it, too! They gave us a capital one last year, about a field-mouse who was captured at sea by a Barbary corsair, and made to row in a galley; and when he escaped and got home again, his lady-love had gone into a convent. Here, *you*! You were in it, I remember. Get up and recite a bit.'

The field-mouse addressed got up on his legs, giggled shyly, looked round the room, and remained absolutely tongue-tied. His comrades cheered him on, Mole coaxed and encouraged him, and the Rat went so far as to take him by the shoulders and shake him; but nothing could overcome his stage-fright. They were all busily engaged on him like watermen applying the Royal Humane Society's regulations to a case of long submersion, when the latch clicked, the door opened, and the field-mouse with the lantern reappeared, staggering under the weight of his basket.

There was no more talk of play-acting once the very real and solid contents of the basket had been tumbled out on the table. Under the generalship of Rat, everybody was set to do something or to fetch something. In a very few minutes supper was ready, and Mole, as he took the head of the table in a sort of dream, saw a lately barren board set thick with savoury comforts; saw his little friends' faces brighten and beam as they fell to without delay; and then let himself loose – for he was famished indeed – on the provender so magically provided, thinking what a happy home-coming this had turned out, after all. As they ate, they talked of old times, and the field-mice gave him the local gossip up to date, and answered as well as they could the hundred questions he had to ask them. The Rat said little or nothing, only taking care that each guest had what he wanted, and plenty of it, and that Mole had no trouble or anxiety about anything.

They clattered off at last, very grateful and showering wishes of the season, with their jacket pockets stuffed with remembrances for the small brothers and sisters at home. When the door had closed on the last of them and the chink of the lanterns had died away, Mole and Rat kicked the fire up, drew their chairs in, brewed themselves a last nightcap of mulled ale, and discussed the events of the long day. At last the Rat, with a tremendous yawn, said, 'Mole, old chap, I'm ready to drop. Sleepy is simply not the word. That your own bunk over on that side? Very well, then, I'll take this. What a ripping little house this is! Everything so handy!'

He clambered into his bunk and rolled himself well up in the blankets, and slumber gathered him forthwith, as a swath of barley is folded into the arms of the reaping-machine.

The weary Mole also was glad to turn in without delay, and soon had his head on his pillow, in great joy and contentment. But ere he closed his eyes he let them wander round his old room, mellow in the glow of the firelight that played or rested on familiar and friendly things which had long been unconsciously a part of him, and now smilingly received him back, without rancour.

L. M. MONTGOMERY

FROM *Anne of Green Gables*

(1908)

Matthew Cuthbert and the sorrel mare jogged comfortably over the eight miles to Bright River. It was a pretty road, running along between snug farmsteads, with now and again a bit of balsamy fir wood to drive through, or a hollow where wild plums hung out their filmy bloom. The air was sweet with the breath of many apple orchards, and the meadows sloped away in the distance to horizon mists of pearl and purple; while

> The little birds sang as if it were
> The one day of summer in all the year.

…When he reached Bright River there was no sign of any train; he thought he was too early, so he tied his horse in the yard of the small Bright River hotel and went over to the station-house. The long platform was almost deserted; the only living creature in sight being a girl who was sitting on a pile of shingles at the extreme end. Matthew, barely noting that it *was* a girl, sidled past her as quickly as possible without looking at her. Had he looked he could hardly have failed to notice the tense rigidity and expectation of her attitude and expression. She was sitting there waiting for something or somebody, and, since sitting and waiting was the only thing to do just then, she sat and waited with all her might and main.

Matthew encountered the station-master locking up the ticket-office preparatory to going home for supper, and asked him if the five-thirty train would soon be along.

'The five-thirty train has been in and gone half an hour ago,' answered that brisk official. 'But there was a passenger dropped off for you – a little girl. She's sitting out there on the shingles. I asked her to go into the ladies' waiting-room, but she informed me gravely that she preferred to stay outside. "There was more scope for imagination," she said. She's a case, I should say.'

'I'm not expecting a girl,' said Matthew blankly. 'It's a boy I've come for. He should be here. Mrs Alexander Spencer was to bring him over from Nova Scotia for me.'

The station-master whistled. 'Guess there's some mistake,' he said. 'Mrs Spencer came off the train with that girl and gave her into my charge. Said you and your sister were adopting her from an orphan asylum and that you would be along for her presently. That's all *I* know about it – and I haven't got any more orphans concealed hereabouts.'

'I don't understand,' said Matthew helplessly, wishing that Marilla was at hand to cope with the situation.

'Well, you'd better question the girl,' said the station-master carelessly. 'I dare say she'll be able to explain – she's got a tongue of her own, that's certain. Maybe they were out of boys of the brand you wanted.'

He walked jauntily away, being hungry, and the unfortunate Matthew was left to do that which was harder for him than bearding a lion in its den – walk up to a girl – a strange girl – an orphan girl – and demand of her why she wasn't a boy. Matthew groaned in spirit as he turned about and shuffled gently down the platform towards her.

She had been watching him ever since he had passed her and she had her eyes on him now. Matthew was not looking at her and would not have seen what she was really like if he had been, but an ordinary observer would have seen this:

A child of about eleven, garbed in a very short, very tight, very ugly dress of yellowish white wincey. She wore a faded brown sailor hat, and beneath the hat, extending down her back, were two braids of very thick, decidedly red hair. Her face was small, white, and thin, also much freckled; her mouth was large and so were her eyes, that looked green in some lights and moods and grey in others.

So far, the ordinary observer; an extraordinary observer might have seen that the chin was very pointed and pronounced; that the big eyes were full of spirit and vivacity; that the mouth was sweet-lipped and expressive; that the forehead was broad and full; in short, our discerning extraordinary observer might have concluded that no commonplace soul inhabited the body of this stray woman-child of whom shy Matthew Cuthbert was so ludicrously afraid.

Matthew, however, was spared the ordeal of speaking first, for as soon as she concluded that he was coming to her she stood up, grasping with one thin, brown hand the handle of a shabby, old-fashioned carpet-bag; the other she held out to him.

'I suppose you are Mr Matthew Cuthbert of Green

Gables?' she said in a peculiarly clear, sweet voice. 'I'm very glad to see you. I was beginning to be afraid you weren't coming for me and I was imagining all the things that might have happened to prevent you. I had made up my mind that if you didn't come for me tonight I'd go down the track to that big wild cherry-tree at the bend, and climb up into it to stay all night. I wouldn't be a bit afraid, and it would be lovely to sleep in a wild cherry-tree all white with bloom in the moonshine, don't you think? You could imagine you were dwelling in marble halls, couldn't you? And I was quite sure you would come for me in the morning, if you didn't tonight.'

Matthew had taken the scrawny little hand awkwardly in his; then and there he decided what to do. He could not tell this child with the glowing eyes that there had been a mistake; he would take her home and let Marilla do that. She couldn't be left at Bright River anyhow, no matter what mistake had been made, so all questions and explanations might as well be deferred until he was safely back at Green Gables.

'I'm sorry I was late,' he said shyly. 'Come along. The horse is over in the yard. Give me your bag.'

'Oh, I can carry it,' the child responded cheerfully. 'It isn't heavy. I've got all my worldly goods in it, but it isn't heavy. And if it isn't carried in just a certain way the handle pulls out – so I'd better keep it because I know the exact knack of it. It's an extremely old carpet-bag. Oh, I'm very glad you've come, even if it would have been nice to sleep in a wild cherry-tree … Oh, it seems so wonderful that I'm going to live with you and belong to you. I've never belonged to anybody – not really. But the asylum was the worst. I've only been in it four months, but that was enough. I don't suppose you ever were an orphan in an asylum, so you can't possibly understand what it is like. It's worse than anything you could imagine. Mrs Spencer said it was wicked of me to talk like that, but I didn't mean to be wicked … They were good, you know – the asylum people. But there is so little scope for the imagination in an asylum – only just in the other orphans. It *was* pretty interesting to imagine things about them – to imagine that perhaps the girl who sat next to you was really the daughter of a belted earl, who had been stolen away from her parents in her infancy by a cruel nurse who died before she could confess. I used to lie awake at nights and imagine things like that, because I didn't have time in the day. I guess that's why I'm so thin – I *am* dreadfully thin, ain't I? There isn't a pick on my bones. I do love to imagine I'm nice and plump, with dimples in my elbows.'

With this Matthew's companion stopped talking, partly because she was out of breath and partly because they had reached the buggy. Not another word did she say until they had left the village and were driving down a steep little hill, the road part of which had been cut so deeply into the soft soil that the banks, fringed with blooming wild cherry-trees and slim white birches, were several feet above their heads.

The child put out her hand and broke off a branch of wild plum that brushed against the side of the buggy.

'Isn't that beautiful? What did that tree, leaning out from the bank, all white and lacy, make you think of?' she asked.

'Well now, I dunno,' said Matthew.

'Why, a bride, of course – a bride all in white with a lovely misty veil. I've never seen one, but I can imagine what she would look like. I don't ever expect to be a bride myself. I'm so homely nobody will ever want to marry me – unless it might be a foreign missionary. I suppose a foreign missionary mightn't be very particular. But I do hope that some day I shall have a white dress. That is my highest ideal of earthly bliss. I just love pretty clothes. And I've never had a pretty dress in my life that I can remember … This morning when

I left the asylum I felt so ashamed because I had to wear this horrid old wincey dress. All the orphans had to wear them, you know... When we got on the train I felt as if everybody must be looking at me and pitying me. But I just went to work and imagined that I had on the most beautiful pale blue silk dress – because when you *are* imagining you might as well imagine something worth while – and a big hat all flowers and nodding plumes, and a gold watch, and kid gloves and boots. I felt cheered up right away and I enjoyed my trip to the Island with all my might. I wasn't a bit sick coming over in the boat. Neither was Mrs Spencer, although she generally is. She said she hadn't time to get sick, watching to see that I didn't fall overboard... I wanted to see everything that was to be seen on that boat, because I didn't know whether I'd ever have another opportunity. Oh, there are a lot more cherry-trees all in bloom! This Island is the bloomiest place. I just love it already, and I'm so glad I'm going to live here... But those red roads are so funny. When we got into the train at Charlottetown and the red roads began to flash past I asked Mrs Spencer what made them red and she said she didn't know, and for pity's sake not to ask her any more questions. She said I must have asked her a thousand already. I suppose I had, too, but how are you going to find out about things if you don't ask questions? And what *does* make the roads red?'

'Well now, I dunno,' said Matthew.

'Well, that is one of the things to find out some time. Isn't it splendid to think of all the things there are to find out about? It just makes me feel glad to be alive – it's such an interesting world. It wouldn't be half so interesting if we knew all about everything, would it? There'd be no scope for imagination then, would there? But am I talking too much? People are always telling me I do. Would you rather I didn't talk? If you say so, I'll stop. I *can* stop when I make up my mind to it, although it's difficult.'

Matthew, much to his own surprise, was enjoying himself. Like most quiet folks he liked talkative people when they were willing to do the talking themselves and did not expect him to keep up his end of it. But he had never expected to enjoy the society of a little girl... Although he found it rather difficult for his slower intelligence to keep up with her brisk mental processes he thought that he 'kind of liked her chatter'. So he said as shyly as usual: 'Oh, you can talk as much as you like. I don't mind.'

'Oh, I'm so glad. I know you and I are going to get along together fine. It's such a relief to talk when one wants to, and not be told that children should be seen and not heard. I've had that said to me a million times if I have once. And people laugh at me because I use big words. But if you have big ideas you have to use big words to express them, haven't you?'

'Well now, that seems reasonable,' said Matthew.

'Mrs Spencer said ... your place was named Green Gables. I asked her all about it. And she said there were trees all around it. I was gladder than ever. I just love trees. And there weren't any at all about the asylum, only a few poor weeny-teeny things out in front with little whitewashed cagey things about them. They just looked like orphans themselves, those trees did. It used to make me want to cry to look at them. I used to say to them: "Oh, you *poor* little things! If you were out in a great big wood with other trees all around you and little mosses and Junebells growing over your roots and a brook not far away and birds singing in your branches, you could grow, couldn't you? But you can't where you are. I know just exactly how you feel, little trees." I felt sorry to leave them behind this morning. You do get so attached to things like that, don't you? Is there a brook anywhere near Green Gables? I forgot to ask Mrs Spencer that.'

'Well now, yes, there's one right below the house.'

'Fancy! It's always been one of my dreams to live near a brook. I never expected I would, though. Dreams don't often come true, do they? Wouldn't it be nice if they did? But just now I feel pretty nearly perfectly happy. I can't feel exactly perfectly happy because – well, what colour would you call this?'

She twitched one of her long glossy braids over her thin shoulder and held it up before Matthew's eyes. Matthew was not used to deciding on the tints of ladies' tresses, but in this case there couldn't be much doubt.

'It's red, ain't it?' he said.

The girl let the braid drop back with a sigh that seemed to come from her very toes ...

'Yes, it's red,' she said resignedly. 'Now you see why I can't be perfectly happy. Nobody could who had red hair ... It will be my lifelong sorrow. I read of a girl once in a novel who had a lifelong sorrow, but it wasn't red hair. Her hair was pure gold, rippling back from her alabaster brow. What is an alabaster brow? I never could find out. Can you tell me?'

'Well now, I'm afraid I can't,' said Matthew, who was getting a little dizzy. He felt as he had once felt in his rash youth, when another boy had enticed him on the merry-go-round at a picnic.

'Well, whatever it was it must have been something nice because she was divinely beautiful. Have you ever imagined what it must feel like to be divinely beautiful?'

'Well now, no, I haven't,' confessed Matthew ingenuously.

'I have, often. Which would you rather be if you had the

chance – divinely beautiful or dazzlingly clever or angelically good?'

'Well now, I – I don't know exactly.'

'Neither do I. I can never decide. But it doesn't make much real difference, for it isn't likely I'll ever be either. It's certain I'll never be angelically good. Mrs Spencer says – oh, Mr Cuthbert! Oh, Mr Cuthbert!! Oh, Mr Cuthbert!!!'

That was not what Mrs Spencer had said; neither had the child tumbled out of the buggy, nor had Matthew done anything astonishing. They had simply rounded a curve in the road and found themselves in the 'Avenue'.

The 'Avenue', so called by the Newbridge people, was a stretch of road four or five hundred yards long, completely arched over with huge, wide-spreading apple-trees, planted years ago by an eccentric old farmer. Overhead was one long canopy of snowy, fragrant bloom. Below the boughs the air was full of a purple twilight and far ahead a glimpse of painted sunset sky shone like a great rose window at the end of a cathedral aisle.

Its beauty seemed to strike the child dumb. She leaned back in the buggy, her thin hands clasped before her, her face lifted rapturously to the white splendour above. Even when they had passed out and were driving down the long slope to Newbridge she never moved or spoke. Still with rapt face she gazed afar into the sunset west, with eyes that saw visions trooping splendidly across that glowing background... When three more miles had dropped away behind them the child had not spoken. She could keep silence, it was evident, as energetically as she could talk.

'I guess you're feeling pretty tired and hungry,' Matthew ventured at last, accounting for her long visitation of dumbness with the only reason he could think of. 'But we haven't very far to go now – only another mile.'

She came out of her reverie with a deep sigh and looked at him with the dreamy gaze of a soul that had been wandering afar, star-led.

'Oh, Mr Cuthbert,' she whispered, 'that place we came through – that white place – what was it?'

'Well now, you must mean the Avenue,' said Matthew after a few moments' profound reflection. 'It is a kind of pretty place.'

'Pretty? Oh, *pretty* doesn't seem the right word to use. Nor beautiful, either. They don't go far enough. Oh, it was wonderful – wonderful. It's the first thing I ever saw that couldn't be improved upon by imagination. It just satisfied me here' – she put one hand on her breast – 'it made a queer funny ache and yet it was a pleasant ache. Did you ever have an ache like that, Mr Cuthbert?'

'Well now, I just can't recollect that I ever had.'

'I have it lots of times – whenever I see anything royally beautiful. But they shouldn't call that lovely place the Avenue. There is no meaning in a name like that. They should call it – let me see – the White Way of Delight. Isn't that a nice imaginative name? When I don't like the name of a place or a person I always imagine a new one and always think of them so. There was a girl at the asylum whose name was Hepzibah Jenkins, but I always imagined her as Rosalia De Vere. Other people may call that place the Avenue, but I shall always call it the White Way of Delight. Have we really only another mile to go before we get home? I'm glad and I'm sorry. I'm sorry because this drive has been so pleasant and I'm always sorry when pleasant things end … But I'm glad to think of getting home. You see, I've never had a real home since I can remember. It gives me that pleasant ache again just to think of coming to a really truly home. Oh, isn't that pretty?'

They had driven over the crest of a hill. Below them was a pond, looking almost like a river so long and winding was it … Here and there a wild plum leaned out from the bank like a white-clad girl tiptoeing to her own reflection. From the marsh at the head of the pond came the clear, mournfully sweet chorus of the frogs. There was a little grey house peering around a white apple orchard on a slope beyond, and, although it was not yet quite dark, a light was shining from one of its windows.

'That's Barry's pond,' said Matthew.

'Oh, I don't like that name, either. I shall call it – let me see – the Lake of Shining Waters. Yes, that is the right name for it. I know because of the thrill. When I hit on a name that suits exactly it gives me a thrill. Do things ever give you a thrill?'

Matthew ruminated.

'Well now, yes. It always kind of gives me a thrill to see them ugly white grubs that spade up in the cucumber beds. I hate the look of them.'

'Oh, I don't think that can be exactly the same kind of a thrill. Do you think it can? There doesn't seem to be much connexion between grubs and lakes of shining water, does there? But why do other people call it Barry's pond?'

'I reckon because Mr Barry lives up there in that house.' …

'Has Mr Barry any little girls? Well, not so very little either – about my size?'

'He's got one about eleven. Her name is Diana.'

'Oh!' with a long indrawing of breath. 'What a perfectly lovely name!'

'Well now, I dunno. There's something dreadful heathenish about it, seems to me. I'd rather Jane or Mary or some sensible name like that. But when Diana was born there was a schoolmaster boarding there and they gave him the nam-ing of her and he called her Diana.'

'I wish there had been a schoolmaster like that around when I was born, then. Oh, here we are at the bridge. I'm going to shut my eyes tight. I'm always afraid going over bridges... What a jolly rumble it makes! I always like the rumble part of it. Isn't it splendid there are so many things to like in this world? There, we're over. Now I'll look back. Good night, dear Lake of Shining Waters. I always say good night to the things I love, just as I would to people. I think they like it. That water looks as if it was smiling at me.'

When they had driven up the further hill and around a corner Matthew said: 'We're pretty near home now. That's Green Gables over–'

'Oh, don't tell me,' she interrupted breathlessly, catching at his partially raised arm and shutting her eyes that she might not see his gesture. 'Let me guess. I'm sure I'll guess right.'

She opened her eyes and looked about her. They were on the crest of a hill. The sun had set some time since, but the landscape was still clear in the mellow afterlight. To the west a dark church spire rose up against a marigold sky. Below was a little valley, and beyond a long, gently rising slope with snug farmsteads scattered along it. From one to another the child's eyes darted, eager and wistful. At last they lingered on one away to the left, far back from the road, dimly white with blossoming trees in the twilight of the surrounding woods. Over it, in the stainless south-west sky, a great crystal-white star was shining like a lamp of guidance and promise.

'That's it, isn't it?' she said, pointing.

Matthew slapped the reins on the sorrel's back delightedly.

'Well now, you've guessed it! But I reckon Mrs Spencer described it so's you could tell.'

'No, she didn't – really she didn't. All she said might just as well have been about most of those other places. I hadn't any real idea what it looked like. But just as soon as I saw it I felt it was home. Oh it seems as if I must be in a dream. Do you know, my arm must be black and blue from the elbow up, for I've pinched myself so many times today. Every little while a horrible sickening feeling would come over me and I'd be so afraid it was all a dream. Then I'd pinch myself to see if it was real – until suddenly I remembered that even supposing it was only a dream I'd better go on dreaming as long as I could; so I stopped pinching. But it *is* real, and we're nearly home.'

With a sigh of rapture she relapsed into silence. Matthew stirred uneasily. He felt glad that it would be Marilla and not he who would have to tell this waif of the world that the home she longed for was not to be hers after all … By the time they arrived at the house Matthew was shrinking from the approaching revelation with an energy he did not understand. It was not of Marilla or himself he was thinking or of the trouble this mistake was probably going to make for them, but of the child's disappointment. When he thought of that rapt light being quenched in her eyes he had an uncomfortable feeling that he was going to assist at murdering something – much the same feeling that came over him when he had to kill a lamb or calf or any other innocent little creature.

The yard was quite dark as they turned into it, and the poplar leaves were rustling silkily all round it.

'Listen to the trees talking in their sleep,' she whispered, as he lifted her to the ground. 'What nice dreams they must have!'

Then, holding tightly to the carpet bag which contained 'all her worldly goods', she followed him into the house.

FRANCES HODGSON BURNETT

FROM *The Secret Garden*

(1911)

She looked at the key quite a long time. She turned it over and over, and thought about it. As I have said before, she was not a child who had been trained to ask permission or consult her elders about things. All she thought about the key was that if it was the key to the closed garden, and she could find out where the door was, she could perhaps open it and see what was inside the walls, and what had happened to the old rose-trees. It was because it had been shut up so long that she wanted to see it. It seemed as if it must be different from other places and that something strange must have happened to it during ten years. Besides that, if she liked it she could go into it every day and shut the door behind her, and she could make up some play of her own and play it quite alone, because nobody would ever know where she was, but would think the door was still locked and the key buried in the earth. The thought of that pleased her very much.

Living, as it were, all by herself in a house with a hundred mysteriously closed rooms and having nothing whatever to do to amuse herself, had set her inactive brain to work and was actually awakening her imagination. There is no doubt that the fresh, strong, pure air from the moor had a great deal to do with it. Just as it had given her an appetite, and fighting with the wind had stirred her blood, so the same things had stirred her mind. In India she had always been too hot and languid and weak to care much about anything, but in this place she was beginning to care and to want to do new things. Already she felt less 'contrary', though she did not know why.

She put the key in her pocket and walked up and down her walk. No one but herself ever seemed to come there, so she could walk slowly and look at the wall, or, rather, at the ivy growing on it. The ivy was the baffling thing. Howsoever carefully she looked, she could see nothing but thickly growing, glossy, dark green leaves. She was very much disappointed. Something of her contrariness came back to her as she paced the wall and looked over it at the tree-tops inside. It seemed so silly, she said to herself, to be near it and not be able to get in. She took the key in her pocket when she went back to the house, and she made up her mind that she would always carry it with her when she went out, so that if she ever should find the hidden door she would be ready.

Mrs Medlock had allowed Martha to sleep all night at the cottage, but she was back at her work in the morning with cheeks redder than ever and in the best of spirits.

'I got up at four o'clock,' she said. 'Eh! It was pretty on th' moor with th' birds gettin' up an' th' rabbits scamperin' about an' th' sun risin'. I didn't walk all th' way. A man gave me a ride in his cart an' I can tell you I did enjoy myself.'

She was full of stories of the delights of her day out. Her mother had been glad to see her, and they had got the baking and washing all out of the way. She had even made each of the children a dough-cake with a bit of brown sugar in it.

'I had 'em all pipin' hot when they came in from playin' on th' moor. An' th' cottage all smelt o' nice, clean, hot bakin' an' there was a good fire, an' they just shouted for joy. Our Dickon, he said our cottage was good enough for a king to live in.'

In the evening they had all sat round the fire, and Martha and her mother had sewed patches on torn clothes and mended stockings, and Martha had told them about the little girl who had come from India and who had been waited on all her life by what Martha called 'blacks' until she didn't know how to put on her own stockings.

'Eh! They did like to hear about you,' said Martha. 'They wanted to know all about th' blacks an' about th' ship you came in. I couldn't tell 'em enough.'

Mary reflected a little.

'I'll tell you a great deal more before your next day out,' she said, 'so that you will have more to talk about. I dare say they would like to hear about riding on elephants and camels, and about the officers going to hunt tigers.'

'My word!' cried delighted Martha. 'It would set 'em clean off their heads. Would tha' really do that, Miss? It would be the same as a wild beast show like we heard they had in York once.'

'India is quite different from Yorkshire,' Mary said slowly, as she thought the matter over. 'I never thought of that. Did Dickon and your mother like to hear you talk about me?'

'Why, our Dickon's eyes nearly started out o' his head,

they got that round,' answered Martha. 'But Mother, she was put out about your seemin' to be all by yourself like. She said: "Hasn't Mr Craven got no governess for her, nor no nurse?" and I said: "No, he hasn't, though Mrs Medlock says he will when he thinks of it, but she says he mayn't think of it for two or three years."'

'I don't want a governess,' said Mary sharply.

'But Mother says you ought to be learnin' your book by this time an' you ought to have a woman to look after you, an' she says: "Now, Martha, you just think how you'd feel yourself, in a big place like that, wanderin' about alone, an' no mother. You do your best to cheer her up," she says, an' I said I would.'

Mary gave her a long, steady look.

'You do cheer me up,' she said. 'I like to hear you talk.'

Presently Martha went out of the room and came back with something held in her hands under her apron.

'What does tha' think,' she said, with a cheerful grin. 'I've brought thee a present.'

'A present!' exclaimed Mistress Mary. How could a cottage full of fourteen hungry people give anyone a present!

'A man was drivin' across the moor peddlin',' Martha explained. 'An' he stopped his cart at our door. He had pots an' pans an' odds an' ends, but Mother had no money to buy anythin'. Just as he was goin' away our 'Lizbeth Ellen called out: "Mother, he's got skippin'-ropes with red an' blue handles." An' Mother, she calls out quite sudden: "Here, stop, mister! How much are they?" An' he says "Tuppence," an' Mother she began fumblin' in her pocket, an' she says to me: "Martha, tha's brought thee thy wages like a good lass, an' I've got four places to put every penny, but I'm just goin' to take tuppence out of it to buy that child a skippin'-rope," an' she bought one, an' here it is.'

She brought it out from under her apron and exhibited it quite proudly. It was a strong, slender rope with a striped red and blue handle at each end, but Mary Lennox had never seen a skipping-rope before. She gazed at it with a mystified expression.

'What is it for?' she asked curiously.

'For!' cried out Martha. 'Does tha' mean that they've not got skippin'-ropes in India, for all they've got elephants and tigers and camels? No wonder most of 'em's black. This is what it's for; just watch me.'

And she ran into the middle of the room and, taking a handle in each hand, began to skip, and skip, and skip, while Mary turned in her chair to stare at her, and the queer faces in the old portraits seemed to stare at her, too, and wonder what on earth this common little cottager had the impudence to be doing under their very noses. But Martha did not even see them. The interest and curiosity in Mistress Mary's face delighted her, and she went on skipping and counted as she skipped until she had reached a hundred.

'I could skip longer than that,' she said when she stopped. 'I've skipped as much as five hundred when I was twelve, but I wasn't as fat then as I am now, an' I was in practice.'

Mary got up from her chair beginning to feel excited herself.

'It looks nice,' she said. 'Your mother is a kind woman. Do you think I could ever skip like that?'

'You just try it,' urged Martha, handing her the skipping-rope. 'You can't skip a hundred at first, but if you practise you'll mount up. That's what Mother said. She says: "Nothin' will do her more good than skippin'-rope. It's th' sensiblest toy a child can have. Let her play out in th' fresh air skippin' an' it'll stretch her legs an' arms an' give her some strength in 'em."'

It was plain that there was not a great deal of strength in Mistress Mary's arms and legs when she first began to skip. She was not very clever at it, but she liked it so much that she did not want to stop.

'Put on tha' things and run an' skip out o' doors,' said Martha. 'Mother said I must tell you to keep out o' doors as much as you could, even when it rains a bit, so as tha' wrap up warm.'

Mary put on her coat and hat and took her skipping-rope over her arm. She opened the door to go out, and then suddenly thought of something and turned back rather slowly.

'Martha,' she said, 'they were your wages. It was your twopence really. Thank you.' She said it stiffly because she was not used to thanking people or noticing that they did things for her. 'Thank you,' she said, and held out her hand because she did not know what else to do.

Martha gave her hand a clumsy little shake, as if she was not accustomed to this sort of thing either. Then she laughed.

'Eh! Tha' art a queer, old-womanish thing,' she said. 'If tha'd been our 'Lizabeth Ellen tha'd have given me a kiss.'

Mary looked stiffer than ever.

'Do you want me to kiss you?'

Martha laughed again.

'Nay, not me,' she answered. 'If tha' was different, p'raps tha'd want to thysel'. But tha' isn't. Run off outside an' play with thy rope.'

Mistress Mary felt a little awkward as she went out of the room. Yorkshire people seemed strange, and Martha was always rather a puzzle to her. At first she had disliked her very much, but now she did not.

The skipping-rope was a wonderful thing. She counted and skipped, and skipped and counted, until her cheeks were quite red, and she was more interested than she had ever been since she was born. The sun was shining and a little wind was blowing – not a rough wind, but one which came in delightful little gusts and brought a fresh scent of newly turned earth with it. She skipped round the fountain garden, and up one walk and down another. She skipped at last into the kitchen-garden and saw Ben Weatherstaff digging and talking to his robin, which was hopping about him. She skipped down the walk towards him and he lifted his head and looked at her with a curious expression. She had wondered if he would notice her. She really wanted him to see her skip.

'Well!' he exclaimed. 'Upon my word! P'raps tha' art a young 'un, after all, an' p'raps tha's got child's blood in thy veins instead of sour buttermilk. Tha's skipped red into thy cheeks as sure as my name's Ben Weatherstaff. I wouldn't have believed tha' could do it.'

'I never skipped before,' Mary said. 'I'm just beginning. I can only go up to twenty.'

'Tha' keep on,' said Ben. 'Tha' shapes well enough at it for a young 'un that's lived with heathen. Just see how he's watchin' thee,' jerking his head towards the robin. 'He followed after thee yesterday. He'll be at it again today. He'll be bound to find out what th' skippin'-rope is. He's never seen one. Eh!' shaking his head at the bird. 'Tha' curiosity will be th' death of thee some time if tha' doesn't look sharp.'

Mary skipped round all the gardens and round the orchard, resting every few minutes. At length she went to her own special walk and made up her mind to try if she could skip the whole length of it. It was a good long skip, and she began slowly, but before she had gone half-way down the path she was so hot and breathless that she was obliged to stop. She did not mind much, because she had already

counted up to thirty. She stopped with a little laugh of pleasure, and there, lo and behold, was the robin swaying on a
long branch of ivy. He had followed her, and he greeted her
with a chirp. As Mary had skipped towards him she felt
something heavy in her pocket strike against her at each
jump, and when she saw the robin she laughed again.

'You showed me where the key was yesterday,' she said.
'You ought to show me the door today; but I don't believe
you know!'

The robin flew from his swinging spray of ivy on to the
top of the wall and he opened his beak and sang a loud,
lovely trill, merely to show off. Nothing in the world is quite
as adorably lovely as a robin when he shows off – and they
are nearly always doing it.

Mary Lennox had heard a great deal about Magic in her
Ayah's stories, and she always said what happened almost at
that moment was Magic.

One of the nice little gusts of wind rushed down the
walk, and it was a stronger one than the rest. It was strong
enough to wave the branches of the trees, and it was more
than strong enough to sway the trailing sprays of untrimmed
ivy hanging from the wall. Mary had stepped close to the
robin, and suddenly the gust of wind swung aside some
loose ivy trails, and more suddenly still she jumped towards
it and caught it in her hand. This she did because she had
seen something under it – a round knob which had been
covered by the leaves hanging over it. It was the knob of a
door.

She put her hands under the leaves and began to pull and
push them aside. Thick as the ivy hung, it nearly all was a
loose and swinging curtain, though some had crept over
wood and iron. Mary's heart began to thump and her hands
to shake a little in her delight and excitement. The robin

kept singing and twittering away and tilting his head on one side, as if he were as excited as she was. What was this under her hands which was square and made of iron and which her fingers found a hole in?

It was the lock of the door which had been closed ten years, and she put her hand in her pocket, drew out the key, and found it fitted the keyhole. She put the key in and turned it. It took two hands to do it, but it did turn.

And then she took a long breath and looked behind her up the long walk to see if anyone was coming. No one was coming. No one ever did come, it seemed, and she took another long breath, because she could not help it, and she held back the swinging curtain of ivy and pushed back the door which opened slowly – slowly.

Then she slipped through it, and shut it behind her, and stood with her back against it, looking about her and breathing quite fast with excitement, and wonder, and delight.

She was standing *inside* the secret garden.

NORMAN LINDSAY

FROM *The Magic Pudding*

(1918)

The plain truth was that Bunyip and his Uncle lived in a small house in a tree, and there was no room for the whiskers. What was worse, the whiskers were red ...

Bunyip Bluegum was a tidy bear, and he objected to whisker soup, so he was forced to eat his meals outside, which was awkward, and besides, lizards came and borrowed his soup.

His Uncle refused to listen to reason on the subject of his whiskers. It was quite useless giving him hints, such as presents of razors, and scissors, and boxes of matches to burn them off. On such occasions he would remark—

> 'Shaving may add an air that's somewhat brisker,
> For dignity, commend me to the whisker.'

Or, when more deeply moved, he would exclaim—

> 'As noble thoughts the inward being grace,
> So noble whiskers dignify the face.'

Prayers and entreaties to remove the whiskers being of no avail, Bunyip decided to leave home without more ado. The trouble was that he couldn't make up his mind whether to be a Traveller or a Swagman. You can't go about the world being nothing, but if you are a traveller you have to carry a bag, while if you are a swagman you have to carry a swag, and the question is: Which is the heavier?

At length he decided to put the matter before Egbert Rumpus Bumpus, the poet, and ask his advice. He found Egbert busy writing poems on a slate. He was so busy that he only had time to sing out—

> 'Don't interrupt the poet, friend,
> Until his poem's at an end,'

and went on writing harder than ever. He wrote all down one side of the slate and all up the other, and then remarked –

> 'As there's no time to finish that,
> The time has come to have our chat.
> Be quick, my friend, your business state,
> Before I take another slate.'

'The fact is,' said Bunyip, 'I have decided to see the world, and I cannot make up my mind whether to be a Traveller or a Swagman. Which would you advise?'

Then said the Poet—

> 'As you've no bags it's plain to see
> A traveller you cannot be;
> And as a swag you haven't either
> You cannot be a swagman neither.

For travellers must carry bags,
And swagmen have to hump their swags
  Like bottle-ohs or ragmen.
As you have neither swag nor bag
You must remain a simple wag,
  And not a swag- or bagman.'

'Dear me,' said Bunyip Bluegum, 'I never thought of that. What must I do in order to see the world without carrying swags or bags?'

The Poet thought deeply, put on his eyeglass, and said impressively—

'Take my advice, don't carry bags,
For bags are just as bad as swags;
  They're never made to measure.
To see the world, your simple trick
Is but to take a walking-stick—
  Assume an air of pleasure,
And tell the people near and far
You stroll about because you are
  A Gentleman of Leisure.'

'You have solved the problem,' said Bunyip Bluegum, and, wringing his friend's hand, he ran straight home, took his Uncle's walking-stick, and, assuming an air of pleasure, set off to see the world.

He found a great many things to see, such as dandelions, and ants, and traction engines, and bolting horses, and furniture being removed, besides being kept busy raising his hat, and passing the time of day with people on the road; for he was a very well-bred young fellow, polite in his manners, graceful in his attitudes, and able to converse on a great variety of subjects, having read all the best Australian poets.

Unfortunately, in the hurry of leaving home he had forgotten to provide himself with food, and at lunch time found himself attacked by the pangs of hunger.

'Dear me,' he said, 'I feel quite faint. I had no idea that one's stomach was so important. I have everything I require, except food; but without food everything is rather less than nothing.

> 'I've got a stick to walk with.
> I've got a mind to think with.
> I've got a voice to talk with.
> I've got an eye to wink with.
> I've lots of teeth to eat with,
> A brand new hat to bow with,
> A pair of fists to beat with,
> A rage to have a row with.
> No joy it brings
>   To have indeed
> A lot of things
>   One does not need.
> Observe my doleful plight.
>   For here am I without a crumb
>   To satisfy a raging tum—
> Oh what an oversight!'

As he was indulging in these melancholy reflections he came round a bend in the road, and discovered two people in the very act of having lunch. These people were none other than Bill Barnacle, the sailor, and his friend, Sam Sawnoff, the penguin bold.

Bill was a small man with a large hat, a beard half as large as his hat, and feet half as large as his beard. Sam Sawnoff's feet were sitting down and his body was standing up, because his feet were so short and his body so long that he had to do both together. They had a pudding in a basin, and the smell that arose from it was so delightful that Bunyip Bluegum was quite unable to pass on.

'Pardon me,' he said, raising his hat, 'but am I right in supposing that this is a steak-and-kidney pudding?'

'At present it is,' said Bill Barnacle.

'It smells delightful,' said Bunyip Bluegum.

'It is delightful,' said Bill, eating a large mouthful.

Bunyip Bluegum was too much of a gentleman to invite himself to lunch, but he said carelessly, 'Am I right in supposing that there are onions in this pudding?'

Before Bill could reply, a thick, angry voice came out of the pudding, saying—

> 'Onions, bunions, corns and crabs,
> Whiskers, wheels and hansom cabs,
> Beef and bottles, beer and bones,
> Give him a feed and end his groans.'

'Albert, Albert,' said Bill to the Puddin', 'where's your manners?'

'Where's yours?' said the Puddin' rudely, 'guzzling away there and never so much as offering this stranger a slice.'

'There you are,' said Bill. 'There's nothing this Puddin' enjoys more than offering slices of himself to strangers.'

'How very polite of him,' said Bunyip, but the Puddin' replied loudly—

> 'Politeness be sugared, politeness be hanged,
> Politeness be jumbled and tumbled and banged.
> It's simply a matter of putting on pace,
> Politeness has nothing to do with the case.'

'Always anxious to be eaten,' said Bill, 'that's this Puddin's mania. Well, to oblige him, I ask you to join us at lunch.'

'Delighted, I'm sure,' said Bunyip, seating himself. 'There's nothing I enjoy more than a good go in at steak-and-kidney pudding in the open air.'

'Well said,' remarked Sam Sawnoff, patting him on the back. 'Hearty eaters are always welcome.'

'You'll enjoy this Puddin',' said Bill, handing him a large slice. 'This is a very rare Puddin'.'

'It's a cut-an'-come-again Puddin',' said Sam.

'It's a Christmas steak and apple-dumpling Puddin',' said Bill.

'It's a – Shall I tell him?' he asked, looking at Bill. Bill nodded, and the Penguin leaned across to Bunyip Bluegum and said in a low voice, 'It's a Magic Puddin'.'

'No whispering,' shouted the Puddin' angrily. 'Speak up. Don't strain a Puddin's ears at the meal table.'

'No harm intended, Albert,' said Sam. 'I was merely remarking how well the crops are looking. Call him Albert when addressing him,' he added to Bunyip Bluegum. 'It soothes him.'

'I am delighted to make your acquaintance, Albert,' said Bunyip.

'No soft soap from total strangers,' said the Puddin', rudely.

'Don't take no notice of him, mate,' said Bill. 'That's only his rough and ready way. What this Puddin' requires is politeness and constant eatin'.'

They had a delightful meal, eating as much as possible, for whenever they stopped eating the Puddin' sang out –

'Eat away, chew away, munch and bolt and guzzle,
Never leave the table till you're full up to the muzzle.'

But at length they had to stop, in spite of these encouraging remarks, and, as they refused to eat any more, the Puddin' got out of his basin, remarking, 'If you won't eat any more here's giving you a run for the sake of exercise,' and he set off so swiftly on a pair of extremely thin legs that Bill had to run like an antelope to catch him up.

'My word,' said Bill, when the Puddin' was brought back. 'You have to be as smart as paint to keep this Puddin' in order. He's that artful, lawyers couldn't manage him. Put your hat on, Albert, like a little gentleman,' he added, placing the basin on his head. He took the Puddin's hand, Sam took the other and they all set off along the road. A peculiar thing about the Puddin' was that, though they had all had a great many slices off him, there was no sign of the place whence the slices had been cut.

'That's where the Magic comes in,' explained Bill. 'The more you eats the more you gets. Cut-an'-come-again is his name, an' cut, an' come again is his nature. Me an' Sam has been eatin' away at this Puddin' for years, and there's not a mark on him. Perhaps,' he added, 'you would like to hear how we came to own this remarkable Puddin'.'

'Nothing would please me more,' said Bunyip Bluegum.

'In that case,' said Bill, 'let her go for a song.

> "Ho, the cook of the *Saucy Sausage*,
>   Was a feller called Curry and Rice,
> A son of a gun as fat as a tun
> With a face as round as a hot cross bun,
>   Or a barrel, to be precise.
>
> "One winter's morn we rounds the Horn,
>   A-rollin' homeward bound.
> We strikes on the ice, goes down in a trice,
> And all on board but Curry and Rice
>   And me an' Sam is drowned.

"For Sam an' me an' the cook, yer see,
   We climbs on a lump of ice,
And there in the sleet we suffered a treat
For several months from frozen feet,
With nothin' at all but ice to eat,
   And ice does not suffice.

"And Sam and me we couldn't agree
   With the cook at any price.
We was both as thin as a piece of tin
While that there cook was bustin' his skin
   On nothin' to eat but ice.

"Says Sam to me, 'It's a mystery
   More deep than words can utter;
Whatever we do, here's me an' you,
Us both as thin as Irish stoo,
   While he's as fat as butter.'

"But late one night we wakes in fright
   To see by a pale blue flare,
That cook has got in a phantom pot
A big plum-duff an' a rump-steak hot,
And the guzzlin' wizard is eatin' the lot,
   On top of the iceberg bare."'

'There's a verse left out here,' said Bill, stopping the song, 'owin' to the difficulty of explainin' exactly what happened when me and Sam discovered the deceitful nature of that cook. The next verse is as follows—

"Now Sam an' me can never agree
   What happened to Curry and Rice.
The whole affair is shrouded in doubt,
For the night was dark and the flare went out,

> And all we heard was a startled shout,
> Though I think meself, in the subsequent rout,
> That us bein' thin, an' him bein' stout,
> In the middle of pushin' an' shovin' about,
>   He – MUST HAVE FELL OFF THE ICE."'

'That won't do, you know,' began the Puddin', but Sam said hurriedly, 'It was very dark, and there's no sayin' at this date what happened.'

'Yes, there is,' said the Puddin', 'for I had my eye on the whole affair, and it's my belief that if he hadn't been so round you'd have never rolled him off the iceberg, for you was both singin' out, "Yo heave Ho" for half-an-hour, an' him trying to hold on to Bill's beard.'

'In the haste of the moment,' said Bill, 'he may have got a bit of a shove, for the ice bein' slippy, and us bein' justly enraged, and him bein' as round as a barrel, he may, as I said, have been too fat to save himself from rollin' off the iceberg. The point, however, is immaterial to our story, which concerns this Puddin'; and this Puddin',' said Bill, patting him on the basin, 'was the very Puddin' that Curry and Rice invented on the iceberg.'

'He must have been a very clever cook,' said Bunyip.

'He was, poor feller, he was,' said Bill, greatly affected. 'For plum-duff or Irish stoo there wasn't his equal in the land. But enough of these sad subjects. Pausin' only to explain that me an' Sam got off the iceberg on a homeward-bound chicken coop, landed on Tierra del Fuego, walked to Valparaiso, and so got home, I will proceed to enliven the occasion with "The Ballad of the Bo'sun's Bride".'

And without more ado, Bill, who had one of those beef-and-thunder voices, roared out –

'Ho, aboard the *Salt Junk Sarah*
　　We was rollin' homeward bound,
When the bo'sun's bride fell over the side
　　And very near got drowned.

Rollin' home, rollin' home,
Rollin' home across the foam,
　　She had to swim to save her glim
And catch us rollin' home.'

It was a very long song, so the rest of it is left out here, but there was a great deal of rolling and roaring in it, and they all joined in the chorus. They were all singing away at the top of their pipe, as Bill called it when, round a bend in the road, they came on two low-looking persons, hiding behind a tree. One was a Possum, with one of those sharp, snooting, snouting sort of faces, and the other was a bulbous, boozy-looking Wombat in an old long-tailed coat, and a hat that marked him down as a man you couldn't trust in the fowlyard. They were busy sharpening up a carving knife on a portable grindstone, but the moment they caught sight of the travellers the Possum whipped the knife behind him and the Wombat put his hat over the grindstone.

Bill Barnacle flew into a passion at these signs of treachery.

'I see you there,' he shouted.

'You can't see all of us,' shouted the Possum, and the Wombat added, 'cause why, some of us is behind the tree.'

Bill led the others aside in order to hold a consultation.

'What on earth's to be done?' he said.

'We shall have to fight them, as usual,' said Sam.

'Why do you have to fight them?' asked Bunyip Bluegum.

'Because they're after our Puddin',' said Bill.

'They're after our Puddin',' explained Sam, 'because they're professional puddin'-thieves.'

'And as we're perfessional Puddin'-owners,' said Bill, 'we have to fight them on principle. The fighting,' he added, 'is a mere flea-bite, as the sayin' goes. The trouble is, what's to be done with the Puddin'?'

'While you do the fighting,' said Bunyip bravely, 'I shall mind the Puddin'.'

'The trouble is,' said Bill, 'that this is a very secret, crafty Puddin', an' if you wasn't up to his games he'd be askin' you to look at a spider an' then run away while your back is turned.'

'That's right,' said the Puddin', gloomily. 'Take a Puddin's character away. Don't mind his feelings.'

'We don't mind your feelin's, Albert,' said Bill. 'What we minds is your treacherous 'abits.' But Bunyip Bluegum said, 'Why not turn him upside-down and sit on him?'

'What a brutal suggestion,' said the Puddin'; but no notice was taken of his objections, and as soon as he was turned safely upside-down, Bill and Sam ran straight at the puddin'-thieves and commenced sparring up at them with the greatest activity.

'Put 'em up, ye puddin'-snatchers,' shouted Bill. 'Don't keep us sparrin' up here all day. Come out an' take your gruel while you've got the chance.'

The Possum wished to turn the matter off by saying, 'I see the price of eggs has gone up again,' but Bill gave him a punch on the snout that bent it like a carrot, and Sam caught the Wombat such a flip with his flapper that he gave in at once.

'I shan't be able to fight any more this afternoon,' said the Wombat, 'as I've got sore feet.' The Possum said hurriedly, 'We shall be late for that appointment,' and they took their grindstone and off they went.

But when they were a safe distance away the Possum sang

out, 'You'll repent this conduct. You'll repent bending a man's snout so that he can hardly see over it, let alone breathe through it with comfort,' and the Wombat added, 'For shame, flapping a man with sore feet.'

'We laugh with scorn at threats,' said Bill, and he added as a warning—

> 'I don't repent a snout that's bent,
>   And if again I tap it,
> Oh, with a clout I'll bend that snout
>   With force enough to snap it.'

and Sam added for the Wombat's benefit—

> 'I take no shame to fight the lame
> When they deserve to cop it.
> So do not try to pipe your eye,
> Or with my flip I'll flop it.'

The puddin'-thieves disappeared over the hill and, as the evening happened to come down rather suddenly at that moment, Bill said, 'Business bein' over for the day, now's the time to set about makin' the camp fire.'

RICHMAL CROMPTON

<small>FROM</small> *William the Conqueror*

(1926)

William tramped loudly down the stairs singing lustily:
'I want – to *bee* – happy, but I – can't *bee* – happy –'

'Neither can anyone else while you're making that foul row,' said Robert, his elder brother, coming out of the morning-room and slamming the door behind him.

'D'you think,' said William sternly, 'that no one c'sing in the house but you? D'you think –'

'Shut up,' interrupted Robert, furiously, going into the dining-room and slamming the door behind him.

William went into the garden, continuing his interrupted song:

'''Till I've made you – happy too-hoo.'

His 'too-hoo' ranged from E flat to F sharp.

The dining-room window was thrown open and a book whizzed past William's ear, narrowly missing him.

Robert's infuriated voice followed the book.

'Will you shut up?' he said. 'You're driving me mad.'

'I'm not driving you mad, Robert,' said William, meekly. 'That's nothin' to do with me, Robert.'

Robert leaped over the window-sill and started in pursuit. William was prepared for this, and fled down the drive. Robert returned to the dining-room. At the gate William hesitated, then raised his untuneful voice in a challenging: 'I want – to *bee* – happy – ' He looked expectantly towards the house, but Robert had slammed both window and door and had taken up his novel. William, slightly disappointed, continued his raucous progress down the street.

Here he met the other Outlaws. They joined him and his song. Their ideas of key and actual notes varied. No one, even though he were familiar with the immortal ditty, would have recognized it as rendered by the Outlaws. It had become merely an inferno of untuneful sound.

They made their way to the old barn where they always held their meetings. Their exuberance died away somewhat when they entered the barn and found Violet Elizabeth awaiting them. Violet Elizabeth was the daughter of Mr Bott (of Bott's Digestive Sauce), who lived at the Hall.

Violet Elizabeth was six years old. She possessed bobbing curls, blue eyes, a lisp, and an imperious temper, and she had, without invitation, or even encouragement, attached herself to the Outlaws. The Outlaws had tried to shake her off by every means in their power, but she possessed weapons (chiefly weapons of tears and pertinacity) against which they were defenceless. Violet Elizabeth, following them wherever they went, weeping tears of rage and screaming screams of rage whenever they attempted to send her away, had broken their nerve. They now accepted her presence as an inevitable evil. They let her into all their plans and counsels simply because they had tried every means (except physical violence) to keep her out and all had failed. She accepted their lack of cordiality as part of their charm, and was inordinately proud of her position. She greeted them cheerfully now from her seat on the floor.

'Hello!'

They ignored her and gathered round in a circle which Violet Elizabeth promptly joined. She was no whit abashed.

'Your fathe ith dirty,' she said scornfully to Ginger; and to William: 'D'you call that noith you wath making down the road *thinging*?'

William felt that the dignity of his position as leader of the Outlaws must be upheld. He looked at her sternly.

'If you don't shut up speakin' without bein' spoke to,' he said, 'we'll—we'll chuck you out.'

'If you do,' said Violet Elizabeth serenely, 'I'll thcream an' thcream an' thcream till I'm thick,' and added with pride, 'I can!'

'Well,' said William, hastily turning to the others, 'what we goin' to do?'

A thin drizzle was falling, and the countryside was unusually uninviting.

'Let's go on readin' the book,' said Douglas.

It was found that in anticipation of this demand Ginger had brought the book and William had brought a bottle of liquorice water. The act of reading was in the Outlaws' eyes inseparable from the act of imbibing liquid refreshment. They read aloud in turns, and those who were listening passed from hand to hand the bottle of liquorice water. It was an indispensable rite.

'Who'll read first?' said Ginger, taking the book out of his pocket.

'I will,' piped Violet Elizabeth, with an eager flutter of her bobbing curls.

'You *won't*,' said William sternly; 'you can't read straight, you can't. You can't say words. How old are you?'

'Thix,' said Violet Elizabeth proudly.

'Thix!' jeered William. 'Thix!' Violet Elizabeth only beamed proudly.

'You – you can't – read straight,' ended William, slightly deflated by her complacency.

'I can,' said Violet Elizabeth. 'I'm at Book II, I am, in reading. I've finished Book I. I *muth* be a good reader if I'm in Book II.'

'Well, anyway,' said William, 'who asked you to come here?'

He felt that this was unanswerable, but Violet Elizabeth answered it.

'I athed mythelf,' she said with dignity.

'Oh, come on,' said Douglas impatiently, 'let's get on with the reading. You begin, Ginger.'

'Yes,' said Ginger bitterly, 'you'll get me readin' an' then you'll go an' drink up all the liqu'rice water.'

'No, we won't, Ginger,' William reassured him. 'I've got another in my pocket.'

He took it out and held it up.

'Promise you won't begin that till I've finished readin',' said Ginger.

'Promise,' said William.

'Thay 'croth my throat,' prompted Violet Elizabeth.

'You shut up,' said William rudely.

'Thut up yourthelf,' rejoined Violet Elizabeth with spirit.

The book was the story of Robin Hood, and it made a special appeal to the Outlaws.

'They was Outlaws same as us,' said William with satis-
faction.

'I think that was a jolly good idea,' said Douglas, taking a
deep draught and wiping his mouth with the back of his
hand in conscious imitation of the gardener, whom he
greatly admired. 'It was a jolly fine idea taking money from
rich folks to give it to the poor. I think it was a *jolly* good
idea,' he ended, handing the bottle to Henry, who was sitting next to him. Henry held it gloomily up to the light.

'You've taken a *jolly* long drink,' he said mournfully; 'you've
drunk more'n *half* of it all in one swallow.'

'Well, I bet you cun't do it,' said Douglas. 'I bet *you* cun't
drink all that straight off like that without stoppin' to
breathe.'

'There's nothin' to be *proud* of,' rejoined Henry indignantly,
'in havin' a mouth like a rhinoceros.'

Douglas fell upon him to avenge the insult, but William
separated them.

'There's no room in here,' he said; 'wait till it's finished
rainin' an' then you can have a proper fight outside. An',
anyway, you'll be spillin' the liqu'rice water. Give it to me,
Henry.'

He took it and drained it to the last drop.

'*Well!*' said Ginger in the voice of one who is aghast at
the depravity of the human race. '*Well* – he's drunk it all up
before my turn.'

'Well, there's the other bottle,' said William.

'Yes, but I didn't think you'd go an' drink up all the first
one straight off like that.'

'It had to be drunk up some time, hadn't it?' said William.

'*Well!*' repeated Ginger. 'Fancy sayin' that. Fancy drinkin'
it all up an' then sayin' that – sayin' it had to be drunk up
some time – before it came to my turn –'

''S Douglas' fault,' said Henry, who was still nursing his grievance. 'Douglas drinkin' up all that lot in one drink like – like a rhinoceros – '

'You're thinkin' of camels,' said William; 'it's camels what drink a lot. They've got lots of stomachs an' they can fill them all with water at once an' it takes them over the desert, an' when they get thirsty they jus' drink up one of their stomachs. You're thinkin' of camels.'

''Scuse *me*,' said Henry with dignity, 'I think I oughter know what I'm thinkin' of – an' I'm *not* thinkin' of camels. I – '

It was Violet Elizabeth who put an end to the incipient quarrel.

'I think it would be tho nith,' she said in her shrill little voice, 'if we did that – took thingth from rich people to give to poor people, thame ath they did.'

This suggestion was received in silence. The Outlaws looked at William, the leader. William screwed his freckled countenance into a thoughtful frown and ran his hand through his wiry hair. William's best friends could not have called him a handsome boy. Nor did they. Violet Elizabeth's idea appealed to William's adventure-and-romance-loving soul. But it had one serious drawback. It had been proposed by Violet Elizabeth, for whom William professed a most profound contempt. His contempt for the proposer (which was almost a point of honour with him) struggled hard with his secret delight at the proposal.

'I was jus' goin' to say that,' he said at last rather sternly. 'That's jus' like a girl saying *jus'* what I was goin' to say – not givin' anyone else time to say anythin' – talkin' an' talkin' all the time. Well,' he added, 'what'll we do and how'll we do it?'

'Let's get guns an' shoot all the rich people,' said Ginger ferociously.

'Yes,' said William scornfully, 'an' then get put in prison. No, we've either gotter find some – some unfathable woods where we can attack the travellers an' no one ever be able to find us, or else do it all in secret.'

'Well, there aren't any un – any woods like what you said round here,' said the practical Douglas.

'How can we do it in secret, anyway?' said Henry rather contemptuously.

'Like robbers do, of course,' said William. 'D'you think robbers walk up to people with guns an' shoot them straight off, 'cause if you do, let *me* tell *you* they *don't*. There wun't be any *sense* in it, would there, Ginger?'

'I dunno,' said Ginger gloomily. 'All I say is he might have left a *drop* at the bottom 'stead of drinkin' it *all* up like that.'

'Well, I think,' said William, 'that we oughter do it in turns – each one of us take something from a rich person an' give it to a poor. Not all at once, or else people'd get suspicious.'

'Wath thuthpiciouth?' inquired Violet Elizabeth.

William ignored her.

'Well, who'll do it first?' said William.

'Me firtht,' chanted Violet Elizabeth.

'I should say *not*,' said William severely. 'You're goin' to be last.'

'I'm not – I'm goin' to be firtht,' said Violet Elizabeth.

'Well, let *me* tell *you*, you're *not*,' said William.

Violet Elizabeth's eyes brimmed with tears. Her lip quivered.

'I am,' she said. 'My fatherth rich – I oughter be firtht becauth my fatherth rich.'

The truth of this was irrefutable. Mr Bott, of Bott's Digestive Sauce, was very rich indeed. He lived and breathed and had his being in an atmosphere of all-enveloping plutocracy.

'It's all our money,' said Henry lugubriously. 'We eat his sauce.'

'*We* don't,' said William severely; 'it's made of black-beetles. I once met someone who lived near the works an' they said that you can see carts an' carts full of black-beetles goin' in every mornin' and then carts an' carts of sauce goin' out every night. It's all made out of black-beetles.'

'I don't care if it ith,' said Violet Elizabeth. 'We never uthe it.'

'We once got a bottle,' said Douglas, 'an' it went bad.'

'I don't care if it did,' said Violet Elizabeth, 'an' if you don' let me be firtht, I'll thcream an' thcream an' thcream till I'm thick – I can!'

The Outlaws looked at her in apprehension. William called to his aid his dignity as leader of the Outlaws. He had had experience of Violet Elizabeth's screams.

'Well,' he said judicially, 'we'll give you an hour to get something, an' if you don't we'll put someone else first. We'll stay here an' wait for you, an' if you don't come with somethin' in an hour we'll give someone else a turn.'

'All right!' sang Violet Elizabeth, pirouetting round joyfully, her fair curls bobbing. 'I'm firtht! I'm firtht! I'm goin' to thteal! An' I don' care if it *ith* made out of black beetleth!'

It was still raining. They finished the Robin Hood book while she was away. William took out the second bottle of liquorice water and Ginger's spirits rose. He had the first drink (one swallow only allowed) and claimed that it beat Douglas's swallow by several lengths. Douglas disputed this claim, and, the rain having stopped, they all went out to the field for the fight which was to decide the capacity of their respective swallows. The decision was never reached, for Violet Elizabeth arrived just as they were carrying on an indecisive wrestling match on the ground.

Violet Elizabeth danced gaily up to them. In her hand she held a string of pearls worth several thousand pounds.

'I found theeth in a bocth in Mummyth drawer,' she shrilled excitedly. 'She's left the key in the hole, tho I juth turned it an' took them. Wathn't I clever?'

William took them and looked at them contemptuously.

'Beads!' he said with scorn.

'They're nithe beadth, William,' said Violet Elizabeth, with pleading in her voice, 'they're *pearl* beadth.'

'But *beads* is no good,' said William patiently. 'We don' want to give beads to the poor what are starving for food an' drink.'

'Let's sell 'em,' said Ginger.

This suggestion was considered a good one, and the five of them went down to the village.

At the end of the village was a small and dingy secondhand shop in whose window reposed a dirty collection of old iron, photograph frames, bits of tawdry jewellery and old furniture. This collection was seldom disturbed.

William, as spokesman, entered the shop carrying the string of pearls, followed by the other Outlaws.

Mr Marsh, who owned the shop, was out, and his mother, deaf and almost blind and very old, sat behind the counter.

'We want to sell this, please,' said William, a businesslike scowl upon his freckled countenance.

'Eh?' said the old dame, her hand to her ear.

When he had repeated it four times she seemed to understand, and stretched out a skinny hand for the pearls.

She peered at the pearls through her ancient spectacles.

'What is it, lovey?' she said.

'Beads,' said William.

'Eh?' said the old dame again.

When he had repeated it four times she said: 'What sort of beads, dearie?'

'Pearl beads,' yelled William.

Yes. She remembered. They'd had some pearl beads last week, and Jim had given the owner sixpence, marked them two shillings, and sold them within a week.

She handed William sixpence and the Outlaws filed out of the shop.

'Sixpence!' said William. ''S not much – isn't sixpence.'

'It'll do to start on,' said Ginger optimistically.

'It'll have to,' agreed William.

'Anyway, I thtealed 'em,' squeaked Violet Elizabeth, with pride, 'I thtealed 'em for the poor.'

'Now we've got to find the poor,' said Henry brightly.

They looked up and down the road. One solitary figure was shambling down it – James Finch, the village reprobate. He was a merry, unprincipled, good-for-nothing ne'er-do-well.

'*He* looks poor,' said Ginger pitifully. 'Look at him, poor ole man. He looks awfully poor.'

'He'th got holth in hith booth,' squeaked Violet Elizabeth, 'an' holth in hith clo'th, poor ole man.'

'Give him the money, William,' said Henry. 'Poor old man!'

William stepped forward with the sixpence and accosted the dilapidated figure.

'Are you hungry an' thirsty?' asked William.

'I'm thirsty,' said the old man, with a wink.

'Here you are then,' said William.

'Thank you,' said the old man.

He took the sixpence and went into the 'Blue Lion'.

The Outlaws watched him, their hearts warmed by the glow of virtue.

'Poor man,' said Violet Elizabeth. 'He *mutht* be thirthty. Heth gone for a nithe drink of lemonade.'

'Starvin' for drink,' put in Ginger sententiously.

'Isn't it nice to think what pleasure we've been able to give the poor old man?' said Henry.

'And all with jus' a few beads,' said Douglas.

'Whose turn is it to get something next?' said Ginger.

'Bags me,' said William.

Old Lady Markham, who lived at the Manor House in the next village, was on her way in her carriage to visit Mrs Bott. Beside her was Angela, her six-year-old granddaughter, who had been staying with her, and whose home was a few miles beyond the Bott mansion. The carriage was to drop Lady Markham at the Botts', then proceed to Angela's home to drop Angela, then return to the Bott mansion to pick up Lady Markham.

'Where you goin', Gramma?' said Angela.

'To visit a Mrs Bott, dear,' said Lady Markham.

She sighed as she spoke. The Botts were Lady Markham's pet aversion. She had long known of, and delighted to disappoint, Mrs Bott's frenzied attempts to 'know' her. She had managed for a very long time to escape an introduction to Mrs Bott, but last week she had been caught unawares and introduced at the Vicarage. She had, however, managed to infuse into her greeting a whole refrigerator full of ice.

But suddenly she found that she needed Mrs Bott. She was holding a charity *fête* in her grounds and found herself hampered on all sides by lack of funds.

'Ask Mrs Bott to be on the committee,' said her neighbours. 'She'll stock every stall in the place. She's made of money, and she loves throwing it about as long as it makes a splash.'

At first old Lady Markham had merely laughed scornfully. Finally she had capitulated. She was on her way to the Bott mansion now to ask Mrs Bott to be on the committee.

'I've had a lovely stay with you, Gramma, darling,' sighed Angela.

'So glad, dear,' said Lady Markham absently.

'I meant to buy you a good-bye present, Gramma, darling, but I hadn't time before we came away, so may we stop at the first shop we pass and me buy you something?'

'Oh, no dear,' said Lady Markham. 'You mustn't buy me anything.'

'Oh, I *must*! *Please!*' said Angela in distress.

'Very well,' said Lady Markham with a smile.

'Then we'll stop at the first shop we pass,' said Angela happily.

The first shop was Mr Marsh's.

Angela descended from the carriage and entered the shop importantly, holding a half-crown tightly in her hand.

'Good-afternoon,' she said. 'Please, have you anything for two-and-six?'

The old lady took up the pearl necklace, which was still lying on the counter. 'You can have these beads for two-and-six, missie,' she said.

'Oh, thank you,' said Angela; 'they *are* pretty.'

She danced back to the carriage.

'I've got some beads for you, Gramma,' she said. 'You *will* wear them, won't you?'

'Oh, darling,' said Lady Markham in dismay.

Angela's face fell.

'Oh, *Gramma*!' she said reproachfully. 'They're very *good* beads. They cost two-and-sixpence.'

'Very well, darling,' said Lady Markham with a sigh of resignation, 'put them on.'

Lady Markham was extremely short-sighted. All she knew was that her granddaughter had slipped a string of whitish beads round her neck. She covered them carefully with her scarf, then completely forgot them.

The carriage stopped at the Bott mansion. Lady Markham said good-bye to her granddaughter, slipped a ten-shilling note into her hand, and descended from the carriage.

The carriage proceeded to Angela's home and Lady Markham entered the Bott mansion.

Mrs Bott was so excited at the news that Lady Markham had called that she was afraid she was going to have hysterics and not be able to receive her. But she mastered her emotions and went to the drawing-room, where Lady Markham was waiting.

Mrs Bott was quivering with apprehension lest she should fail to live up to this high honour done her. She had striven long and earnestly to 'get in with' Society as typified by Lady Markham. She felt that the day of her dreams had come at last, with Lady Markham's card on the tray on the hall table she could now die happy.

She hoped that Botty would stay in the study (where he was engaged in studying a novel and a cigar) and not join them in the drawing-room. Botty was a hard-working man and a good husband, but there was no denying that he dropped his aitches. He generally picked them up as quickly as he could, but he dropped them with a bang and the picking up only drew attention to their fall.

Mrs Bott, small and plump, dressed in an expensive dress, was sitting on an expensive chair hoping that Lady Markham guessed how much they'd had to pay for it at an antique dealer's. She moved her hands about frequently to show her rings, and she chattered excitedly, glowing with pride and pleasure.

'Oh, yes, Lady Markham, I'll be on the committee with the greatest pleasure. I'll certainly have a stall. What stall? Oh, any stall at all, Lady Markham ... The provision stall if you like. I could stock it complete out of the garding, you know. The gardeners could see to the cutting of the things and one of the chauffeurs could bring the stuff over in one of the cars.'

It was nice to say 'one of the chauffeurs' and 'one of the cars'. The only drawback to the phrases was that they gave no inkling of how many cars there were. On the other hand, 'one of the three chauffeurs' and 'one of the seven cars' were rather cumbersome for ordinary conversation.

'Or the fancy stall,' went on Mrs Bott, brightly. 'I could stock it complete in Town – jewellery an' leather an' such-like. Regardless, you know. Or I wouldn't mind takin' on one or two stalls. Stockin' 'em both. Regardless. It's such a pleasure to work in the cause of charity, I always think. I say to Botty – '

'Botty?' said her ladyship rather faintly.

'Yes, Botty. My hubby. I say to him, "Why is all this here boundless wealth given to us, I say, except to give others a leg up?" Believe me, Lady Markham, when I had a stall at the *fête* here – crowded it was – of course, our garding holds *hundreds* – I spent six hundred pounds on stuff for the stall. I did, indeed, and didn't take a penny out of the profits for expenses either. Believe me.'

Lady Markham sat upright in her pseudo-Jacobean chair and stared in front of her. Mrs Bott was rather disappointed. Nothing friendly or chatty about her visitor, she thought ... Didn't seem a bit interested in things.

'Of course, the place is a responsibility. Forty acres. Believe me. Twenty indoor servants and ten outdoor ones. A responsibility. Not from the money point of view, of course – oh, no. We don't have to think of that. Botty can do things regardless – but it's the *feeling* of responsibility. Why, last week I was quite queer and I put it down to that.'

'Queer?' said Lady Markham.

'Yes, liver,' said Mrs Bott.

'Oh, queer … You mean ill.'

'That's right,' said Mrs Bott. No, she wasn't easy to talk to, thought Mrs Bott with an inward sigh. Funny how stiff some of these Society people were. Really difficult to entertain. Nothing to say for themselves.

'Of course,' went on Mrs Bott, 'it was a relief and no mistake to get the furnishin' of this place off our minds. You'd hardly believe me if I told you what Botty had to fork out for the furnishing of the place.'

She paused, but Lady Markham asked no question. Again Mrs Bott sighed to herself. Like mummies these people were. Took no interest in anything.

'Guess how much I've paid for that chair you're sitting on now.'

'I've no idea,' said Lady Markham, without even looking at the chair.

'A hundred quid. Down.'

'Did you?' said Lady Markham, without the slightest interest.

Perhaps, thought Mrs Bott, she took no interest because she didn't believe that it was a real antique. Perhaps she didn't believe that her diamonds were real. That was a horrid thought, when Botty had paid so much for them. Then for the first time she began to notice the visitor's jewellery. She had thrown open her scarf and revealed a string of pearls.

Very good pearls, thought Mrs Bott.

Very like her own upstairs. Very, very like her own pearls upstairs.

In her own string of pearls there was a peal near the middle of a much darker colour than the others. There was a similar pearl here. In her own string of pearls upstairs (they were graduated in size) there was one which always seemed to Mrs Bott to be not quite the right size. There was just such a one here. A small diamond was missing from the clasp of her own string of pearls upstairs.

'Allow me to draw that curting,' said Mrs Bott. 'The sun's on your back.'

She slipped behind her visitor's back to the window and drew the curtain, her eyes fastened on her visitor's neck. Yes, the same diamond was missing. It was all Mrs Bott could do not to scream for help. It must be – it couldn't be – it couldn't be – it must be – She must at all costs go up to her room and see if her pearls were there. She collected her faculties as best she could.

'Er – I'm sure you'd like to meet my little girl, Lady Markham,' she said. 'Er – I'll – I'll go and try to find her.'

She ran upstairs panting, her fat little face purple. Heaven's alive! it couldn't be – it couldn't be – She opened her drawer and – there lay the open case where she kept her pearls – empty. It was – it couldn't be. But it *was* – With a firm hand she repressed another incipient attack of hysterics and went down to her husband in the study.

'B-B-B-B-Botty!' she gasped. 'She's stolen my pearls.'

Mr Bott stared at her in amazement. He, too, was short and stout and, as a rule, amiable-looking.

' 'Oo – Who 'as – has, love?' inquired Mr Bott.

'That Lady Markham has,' sobbed his wife. 'She c-c-c-called and I was in the garden and she m-m-m-m-must have slipped upstairs and t-t-t-taken them. They're g-g-g-g-gone.'

''Ow – how do you know *she's* taken them, love?' said Mr Bott.

'She's w-w-w-w-*wearing* them, Botty,' sobbed Mrs Bott. 'She's g-g-g-g-got them on. I've -s-s-s-*seen* them. The diamond's gone out of the c-c-c-c-clasp an' *all*!'

'Now don't 'ave – have – 'ysterics – hysterics, love,' said Mr Bott soothingly.

'B-but it *can't* be true, Botty, can it?' she pleaded, wiping her eyes. The sight of the real lace on her handkerchief and the thought of what it had cost soothed her somewhat. 'She c-c-c-*can't* have taken them.'

Mr Bott shook his head wisely. 'I'm afraid it's true, love,' he said sadly. 'I was readin' an article in last week's Sunday paper, and it said there that practically all these haristocrats – aristocrats – are dec – ' (he hunted the elusive word a minute in silence, then gave it up –) 'decayed. Most of 'em thieves. Some of 'em – brilliant figures in Society an' secretly the 'eads – heads – of gangs of thieves. She must be one of them.'

'Oh, but, Botty, why should she w-w-w-w-*wear* them?'

'Nerve,' said Mr Bott solemnly. 'She thought you'd never notice them. Nerve. Now, look here, old lady, go in and talk to her agreeable-like, you know, seem quite 'appy – happy, and keep her there and I'll send for a policeman.'

'Oh, *Botty*!' screamed Mrs Bott. 'You mustn't.'

'Yes, I must,' said Mr Bott firmly. 'If you'd read that article you'd feel the same as what I do now. They ought to be exposed. That's what I feel. Decent citizens same as what I am – ham – am – ought to show 'em up. Now you go back to her, old lady, and leave all the rest to me.'

Mrs Bott went back.

Lady Markham tried to stifle a yawn. Really, these people were amazing. The woman goes out of the room in a most peculiar and abrupt manner, stays away nearly twenty minutes and then returns in a state that her ladyship can only diagnose as partially inebriated – red in the face and talking in a strange and disconnected fashion. Lady Markham began to wish that she had not come. After all, they could have managed without Mrs Bott's money. She'd had no idea these people were so peculiar.

Then suddenly the door opened and the village policeman appeared.

Now the village policeman was a youth who had lived on Lady Markham's estate all his life and looked up to her as lower in rank (and only *just* a little lower, even so) to the Queen alone. It was Lady Markham who had kept his grandmother out of the workhouse, had provided his mother with nurses and nourishment in her recent illness, and had been instrumental in getting him into his present position.

He looked round the room blankly. He'd been sent in to arrest a lady who was in the drawing-room and had stolen Mrs Bott's pearls. He looked round and round the room, gaping. It happened that Lady Markham had sent for him that morning, but the messenger had not been able to find him.

'Oh, Higgs,' said her ladyship kindly, 'you shouldn't have come here after me. It was nothing important – only the orchard's been robbed again. If you'll call at the Manor at half-past six I'll give you all details.' She turned to Mrs Bott. 'Excuse his coming here after me,' she said graciously. 'I sent for him about a small matter this morning and he probably thought it was urgent.'

Outside in the passage the unhappy Higgs faced a furious Mr Bott.

''Aven't – haven't – you *done* it?' stormed Mr Bott.

'No, sir,' gasped Higgs. 'There was no one there, sir. No one but Mrs Bott an' Lady Markham, sir.'

'But it is Lady Markham,' stormed Mr Bott, 'it is Lady Markham, I tell you. Didn't you 'ear – hear – me sayin' it was the lady with Mrs Bott. I've got *proof*!'

'Oh, no, sir,' protested young Higgs earnestly, 'I couldn't do that sir. Honestly I couldn't do that, sir.'

For answer, Mr Bott opened the drawing-room door and pushed Higgs into the room.

'Well, Higgs?' said her ladyship.

The miserable Higgs put his hand to his collar as if to loosen it.

'D-d-did you say six or half-past six, your lady-ship?' he stammered.

'Half-past six,' said her ladyship coldly.

Higgs returned to the impatient Mr Bott.

'Well?' said Mr Bott.

Higgs took out a handkerchief and wiped the perspiration from his brow.

'I can't, sir,' he gasped. 'Honest, I can't.'

'You can and you will,' said little Mr Bott. 'Come in with me.'

He entered, holding Higgs by the arm. Higgs looked wildly round for escape. Lady Markham looked from one to the other in amazement.

'Now, Higgs,' prompted Mr Bott; but at this point a diversion took place.

Violet Elizabeth entered, followed by the four Outlaws. The four Outlaws looked sheepish. This was Violet Elizabeth's stunt, not theirs. They had been in the wood for the last hour lying in wait for unwary travellers, but no travellers, wary or unwary, had passed. Their sole 'bag' had been a tin box deposited by a naturalist in what he thought was a safe hiding place while he went into the village for a drink.

Violet Elizabeth addressed herself to her father.

'Do you want a thnake to make into thauth?' she said, 'becauth we'll thell you one for three shillingth.'

'What!' bellowed Mr Bott.

'William thayth,' lisped Violet Elizabeth placidly, 'that you make thauth out of black beetleth.'

Mr Bott turned a red and ferocious eye upon William. 'Tho we thought that perhapth you'd like a thnake, too.'

'WHAT!' boomed Mr Bott.

He looked as if he were going to burst with fury. Mrs Bott wondered whether to have hysterics now or wait till later. She decided to wait till later. Lady Markham pinched herself to see whether she was awake, and found, rather to her surprise, that she was.

'We thought,' continued Violet Elizabeth unabashed, 'that a thnake might do ath well. Ith a nithe thnake. Ith athleep now.'

She took off the lid of the box and peeped in. But the snake was apparently no longer asleep. With a strong untwisting of its coils it came out upon the carpet. It was of the grass-snake variety, but rather unusually large in size and unusually light in colour, and for that reason had been collected by its collector, the naturalist.

Mr Bott leapt upon the grand piano.

'Send for the gamekeepers!' he shouted. 'Tell them to bring their guns.'

Higgs stepped forward, took up the snake and dropped it out of the window.

Mrs Bott could restrain her hysterics no longer. She burst into tears, leaning for comfort upon Lady Markham's breast and flinging her arms round her neck.

'Oh, you wicked woman!' she sobbed. 'Why did you steal my pearls?'

Of course there were explanations. There were explanations between Mrs Bott and Lady Markham, between the Outlaws and Lady Markham, between Higgs and Mr Bott, between Violet Elizabeth and everyone, and (later and far less pleasant) between the Outlaws and their respective parents. But explanations are wearisome things and best left to the imagination. As William said: ''Straordinary how some people in this world like to make a fuss over every *single* little thing!'

ERICH KÄSTNER

FROM *Emil and the Detectives*

(1929)

The man in the bowler hat got off the tram at the first stop after it turned out of Kaiser Avenue into Trautenau Street. Emil immediately picked up his suitcase and the bunch of flowers, murmured another 'Thank you' to the man who had paid his fare, and got off too. The thief walked in front of the tram, crossed the lines, and proceeded to the other side of the road. When the tram had moved on, Emil saw him standing on the opposite pavement, hesitating, then he went up some steps to a terrace outside a café.

Emil's next move had to be cautious, like a real detective following a suspect. He glanced about him quickly and noticed a newspaper stand at the street corner. It would give him just the right sort of cover, and he hurried over to it.

He put down his heavy case, took off his cap and considered what to do next.

The man had taken a seat close to the railing looking down on the street. He was smoking a cigarette, and appeared very pleased with himself. Emil was disgusted to find that a thief could have all the fun, while the person who had been robbed was in such trouble. It made him furious that he – and not the thief – should have to hang about behind a newspaper stand. And it did not make him feel any better when he saw the man ordering himself a drink and lighting another cigarette. But it would be worse still if he got up to go, for there would be nothing for it but to snatch up the suitcase and chase after him again. As long as he sat there, Emil had only to stay where he was – and that he would do even if he had to stay until his beard sprouted! But long before that of course, a policeman would stop and ask him what he was up to.

'Loitering,' he'd say, 'Suspicious behaviour,' and probably, 'You'd better come along with me, and come quietly or I'll have to put the bracelets on you.'

These miserable reflections were interrupted by a motor horn which honked loudly just behind him. It made him jump, but when he looked round there was only a boy standing there, laughing.

'All right, don't get the wind up,' he said.

'It sounded as though there was a motor right behind me,' Emil said.

'Silly chump, that was me. You can't belong round here or you'd know that. I always carry a motor horn in my trouser pocket. Everyone knows me and my motor horn.'

'I live in Neustadt,' Emil explained. 'I've only just come from the station.'

'Oh, up from the country!' said the boy. 'I suppose that's why you're wearing those awful clothes.'

'You take that back,' said Emil furiously, 'or I'll knock you down.'

'Keep your hair on,' said the boy with the motor horn good-naturedly. 'It's too hot to fight ... though if you really want to, I'm willing.'

'I don't specially,' Emil said. 'Let's put it off. I've no time now,' and he glanced quickly up at the café to make sure that Mr Grundeis was still there.

'I should have thought you had plenty of time,' the boy retorted, 'hanging about here with your outsize suitcase and that great cauliflower! You looked as though you were play-ing hide-and-seek with yourself. I can't say you seem to me in much of a hurry.'

'As a matter of fact,' said Emil, 'I'm keeping my eye on a thief.'

'What!' exclaimed the boy with the motor horn. 'A thief? What has he stolen? Who from?'

'Me,' said Emil, feeling quite important again. 'He took seven pounds out of my pocket while I was asleep in the train. I was bringing it to my grandmother here in Berlin. After he'd stolen it, he left our carriage and got into another farther down the train. But I saw him get out at the Zoological Gardens station, and I've been following him ever since. He got on a tram, and now he's sitting over in that café. Look, that's him, looking as pleased as anything with himself ... that man in the bowler hat.'

'Gosh, what a lark!' said the other boy. 'Just like the pic-tures! What are you going to do next?'

'I don't know,' Emil admitted, 'just keep on following him.'

'There's a policeman over there. Why don't you go and tell him about it? He'd look after him for you all right.'

'I don't like to do that,' Emil confessed. 'The police at Neustadt may be after me by now for something I did at home.'

'I see.'

'And Grandma will still be waiting for me at Friedrich Street station.'

The boy with the motor horn thought hard for a minute, then he said, 'Going after a real thief and catching him would be something! Coo! I think I'll help you, if you don't mind.'

'I'd be awfully glad,' Emil replied warmly.

'That's settled then. By the way, my name's Gustav.'

'Mine's Emil.'

They shook hands, liking each other tremendously.

'We must get busy,' Gustav said. 'It's no use just standing about here. We might lose the blighter. Have you any money left?'

'Not a bean.'

Gustav gave a little toot on his horn because as a rule that helped him to think, but this time it did not.

'What about getting some of your friends to help too?' suggested Emil.

'Good idea,' cried Gustav briskly. 'I've only got to go honking round the streets, and the gang will come tearing along to see what's up.'

'Go on then,' said Emil. 'And don't be long in case that chap moves on. I should have to follow him if he did, and you might not be able to pick us up again then.'

'Right you are. I'll be as quick as I can,' said Gustav. 'Trust me. He's eating an egg now, so he can't be leaving just yet. Cheerio, Emil. Gosh, I'm looking forward to this. It's going to be smashing!'

And with that he dashed off.

Emil felt much better after that. Of course it was bad luck about the money – but it could have happened to anyone. Having friends now to help him made all the difference. He kept his eyes resolutely on the thief, who was plainly enjoying the meal – paid for no doubt out of the money Mrs Tischbein had worked so hard to earn. Emil's only fear now was that he would get up and go before Gustav came back.

However, Mr Grundeis obliged him by remaining at the café table, though if he had had the slightest idea of what was being prepared for him, he would probably have ordered a private plane (if that were possible) to get him away.

Ten minutes later Emil heard the horn again and looked over his shoulder. Quite two dozen boys were coming down the street towards him, headed by Gustav.

'Halt!' he cried, as they arrived at the news stand. 'How's that?' he asked Emil, grinning all over his face.

'Gosh, it's great,' said Emil, giving Gustav a delighted dig in the ribs.

'Well, chaps, this is Emil from Neustadt,' Gustav then announced, 'and that's the rotter who stole his money – over there, sitting by the railings in a black bowler hat. It'd be a nice thing if he was allowed to get away with it, so it's up to us, see?'

'We'll catch him all right, Gustav,' said a boy in horn-rimmed spectacles.

'That's the Professor,' said Gustav, and introduced Emil to each of them in turn.

'Now let's get a move on,' said the Professor. 'And the first thing is to see what money we've got.'

Each of the boys turned out his pockets and threw all the money he'd got into Emil's cap. One very small boy, whom they called Tuesday, had a whole shilling, and was hopping from one foot to the other with excitement because he was the one to count the money.

'We've got five shillings and eightpence,' he reported. 'That's our funds, and we ought to divide it among three of us, in case we get separated.'

'Right-o,' said the Professor, so he and Emil were given two shillings each, and Gustav took the remaining one and eightpence.

'Thanks awfully,' said Emil. 'I'll be able to pay you back as soon as we've caught him. What do we do next? I wish I could get rid of my suitcase and these flowers. They're a frightful nuisance when I run.'

'Give them to me,' said Gustav. 'I'll take them over to the café and leave them at the counter. And I'll take a good look at our man at the same time.'

'Mind how you go,' said the Professor. 'If the scoundrel finds out he's being followed, it will make things more difficult for us.'

'What do you take me for?' growled Gustav, and went off with Emil's things.

'That chap's face is a sight,' he said when he came back. 'Your things will be OK there, Emil. We can pick them up again when we feel like it.'

'I think we ought to have a council of war,' said Emil. 'But not here, with all these people looking on.'

'Let's go to Nicholas Square,' said the Professor. 'That's quite near. Two of us can stay here to keep an eye on the chap, and we'll have five or six scouts along the road. They can relay any news along to us in no time. If he moves, we'll all come dashing back at top speed.'

'Leave all that to me!' said Gustav. 'I'll stay here myself and keep watch,' he told Emil. 'Don't worry. We won't let him get away. You'd better get a move on. It's gone seven already.'

Gustav had the boys organized very quickly. The scouts went to their posts along the street, and the rest of the gang, led by Emil and the Professor, ran off to Nicholas Square.

ALISON UTTLEY

From *The Country Child*

(1931)

One morning Susan looked out of her window and saw that spring had really come. She could smell it and she put her head far out, until she could touch the budding elm twigs. She pressed her hands on the rough stone of the window-sill to keep herself from falling as she took in deep draughts of the wine-filled air.

It was the elder; the sap was rushing up the pithy stems, the young leaves had pierced the buds, and now stuck out like green ears listening to the sounds of spring. The rich heady smell from the pale speckled branches came in waves borne by soft winds, mixed with the pungent odour of young nettles and dock.

She wrinkled her nose with pleasure and a rabbit with her little one directly below the window, on the steep slope, wrinkled her nose, too, as she sat up among the nettles and borage.

Miss Susanna Dickory, Susan's godmother, had stayed at the farm a fortnight, and now Susan felt lost without her. It had been a time of delight to meet lavender in pockets of air on the stairs. Such delicious smells hovered about the house, such rustlings of silken skirts, and yap-yaps of the little be-ribboned, long-haired dog, Twinkle, as unlike Roger as a toy boat is unlike a man-o'-war.

'Twinkle, Twinkle, Twinkle,' she called in her high silvery voice, which made Dan laugh up his sleeve. It was for all the world like the harness bells, he told Becky.

She had come to visit her dear friend, Margaret, and to see her little god-child, Susan, and if she was disappointed in the child and found her a shy young colt, she said nothing.

She was a frail old lady, delicate-looking and fastidious, but she walked in the cowsheds and sat down in the barns with her silk petticoats trailing in the dust, so that Joshua ran for the besom to sweep before her, and he actually took off his coat for her to step upon, like Sir Walter Raleigh, but Miss Dickory wouldn't.

Every day the Garlands had dinner and tea in the parlour, and every day the Worcester china was used. Becky put on a clean white cap and apron, and Dan brushed his coat and changed his collar and scrubbed all the manure off his boots before he sat down in the kitchen, lest she should come in.

She slept in the big four-poster in the parlour bedroom and wore a lace night-cap, for Susan saw it when Becky took up her breakfast on a tray. Twinkle slept in a basket lined with silk at the foot of her bed. It was all most astonishing, like being in church all the time, and Christmas every day.

But now she had gone and only a few little corners of sweet smells remained. Susan sighed as she thought of her, and laughed at the rabbit, and then ran downstairs. It was Good Friday and she had a holiday for a week.

Her mother met her in the hall, running excitedly to call her. There was a parcel addressed to Mr, Mrs, and Miss Garland. Susan had never been called Miss before, except by the old man at the village who said, 'You're late, Missie,' when she ran past his cottage on the way to school.

With trembling fingers Susan and Margaret untied the knots, for never, never had any one at Windystone been so wasteful as to cut a piece of string!

Inside was a flower-embroidered table-cloth for Margaret, a book of the Christian Saints and Martyrs of the Church for Tom, which he took with wondering eyes, and a box containing six Easter eggs.

There were three chocolate eggs, covered with silver paper, a wooden egg painted with pictures round the edge, a red egg with a snake inside, and a beautiful pale blue velvet egg lined with golden starry paper. It was a dream. Never before had Susan seen anything so lovely. Only once had she ever seen an Easter egg (for such luxuries were not to be found in the shops at Broomy Vale), and then it had been associated with her disgrace.

Last Easter Mrs Garland had called at the vicarage with her missionary box and taken Susan with her. Mrs Stone had asked Margaret to make some shirts for the heathen, and whilst they had gone in the sewing-room to look at the pattern, Susan, who had been sitting silent and shy on the edge of her chair, was left alone.

The room chattered to her; she sprang up, wide-awake, and stared round. She had learnt quite a lot about the habits of the family from the table and chairs, when her eye unfortunately spied a fat chocolate egg, a bloated enormous egg, on a desk before the window. Round its stomach was tied a blue ribbon, like a sash.

Susan gazed in astonishment. What was it for? She put out a finger and stroked its glossy surface. Then she gave it a tiny press of encouragement, and, oh, her finger went through and left a little hole. The egg must have been soft with the sunshine. But who would have thought it was hollow, a sham?

She ran and sat down again, deliberating whether to say something at once or to wait till she was alone with her mother. Mrs Stone returned with Margaret saying, 'Yes, Mrs Stone, of course I won't forget the gussets. The heathen jump about a good deal, they will need plenty of room.' But before Susan could speak, a long-haired, beaky-nosed girl ran into the room, stared at Susan and went straight to the Easter egg.

'Who's been touching *my* Easter egg?' she cried, just like the three bears.

They all looked at Susan, and with deep blushes she whispered, 'I did.'

They all talked at once; Margaret was full of apologies and shame, Mrs Stone said it didn't matter, but of course you could see it did, and the bear rumbled and growled.

When she got home Susan had to kneel down at once and say a prayer of forgiveness, although it was the middle of the morning. 'You know, Susan, it's very wrong to touch what isn't yours.'

But this perfect blue egg! There was never one like it. She put it in her little drawer in the table where her treasures were kept, the book of pressed flowers, the book of texts in the shape of a bunch of violets, the velvet Christmas card with the silk fringe, and the card that came this Christmas.

Tenderly she touched them all. In the egg she placed her ring with the red stone, and a drop of quicksilver which had come from the barometer. She closed the drawer and went off to tell any one who would listen, the trees, Dan, the clock, Roger, Duchess, or Fanny.

But what a tale to tell the girls at school! She wouldn't take the egg there or it might get hurt, a rough boy might snatch it from her, or the teacher might see her with it and put it in her desk.

'Mother, may I ask some one to tea to see my egg?' she asked, fearing in her heart that no one would come so far.

'Yes, my dear,' and Margaret smiled at her enthusiasm, 'ask whoever you like.'

She hurried through the woods and along the lanes to school, saying to herself, 'Do you know what I had at Easter? No. Guess what I had at Easter. No. My god-mother, who is a real lady, sent me such a lovely Easter present. It was a box of eggs, and one was made of sky-blue velvet and lined with golden stars.'

She was late and had to run, and when she passed the little cottage with the brass door-knocker and a canary in the window, the nice old man with a beard said, 'You are going to be late this morning, Missie,' as he looked at his turnip watch. It was very kind of him, and Susan thanked him politely before she took to her heels.

She toiled up the hill, a stitch in her side, and her face wet with perspiration, past the cottages with babies at the open doors and cats by the fire, past the silent gabled house where two old ladies lived, and the old cottage where the witch pottered about, and the lovely farm where she some-times went to tea with her mother, and where she sat very still listening to the ancient man who lived there.

The bell stopped ringing and she was late. She would be

caned, she had no excuse. She heard the Lord's Prayer and
the hymn as she took off her hat and cape, and hung them
on the hook. She listened to the high voices and watched
the door handle, waiting to slip in at the sound of Amen.
Her little red tongue glided over the palm of her hand to
prepare for the inevitable pain. There was a shuffle of feet
and she turned the knob. All eyes switched her way as she
walked up to the desk.

'Any excuse, Susan Garland?'

She dumbly held out her hand. Down came the cane
three times on the soft flesh. Biting her lip and keeping
back her tears she walked to her place, and bound her handkerchief round the hot stinging palm. Yes, there were three
marks, three red stripes across it.

Curious eyes watched her to see if she would cry, and she
smiled round and whispered, 'It didn't hurt a bit,' but her
hand throbbed under her pinafore, and the fingers curled
protectingly round it as if they were sorry. It was an honour
to be caned and to bear the strokes unflinchingly. Susan
showed her marks to the girls round her, and then whispered,
'I've got a blue velvet egg. Tell you about it at playtime.'

At break the children walked orderly to the door and then
flung themselves out into the playground, to jump and
'twizzle', hop and skip, to dig in their gardens, or play hide-
and-seek.

Susan had a circle of girls round her looking at the weals
and listening to the tale of the egg. They strolled under the
chestnut trees with their arms round each other.

'It's blue velvet, sky-blue, and inside it is lined with paper
covered with gold stars. It's the most beautiful egg I ever
saw.' The girls opened their eyes and shook their curls in
amazement.

'Bring it to school for us to see,' said Anne Frost, her friend.

'I daren't, Mother wouldn't let me, but you can come to tea and see it.'

'Can I?' asked one. 'Can I?' asked another.

Susan felt a queen and invited them all. Big girls came to her, and she invited them. The rumour spread that Susan Garland was having a lot of girls to tea. Tiny little girls ran up and she said they might come too. She didn't know where to draw the line, and in the end the whole school of girls invited themselves.

They ran home to Dangle and Raddle at dinnertime to say that Susan Garland was having a party, and they were brushed and washed and put into clean pinafores and frocks, with blue necklaces and Sunday hair-ribbons.

Susan sat on a low stone wall eating her sandwiches, excited and happy. She was sure they would all be welcome and she looked forward to the company in the Dark Wood.

After school she started off with a crowd of fifty girls, holding each other's hands, arms entwined round Susan's waist, all pressed up close to her. They filled the narrow road like a migration, or the Israelites leaving the bondage of Egypt.

Mothers came to their doors to see them pass, and waved their hands to their little daughters. 'Those Garlands must have plenty of money,' said they.

Susan was filled with pride to show her beautiful home, the fields and buildings, the haystacks, the bull, and her kind mother and father, and Becky and Joshua who would receive them.

They went noisily through the wood, chattering and gay, astonished at the long journey and the darkness of the trees, clinging to one another on the little path lest an adder or fox should come out, giggling and pushing each other into the leaves. The squirrels looked down in wonder, and all ghostly things fled.

Margaret happened to stand on the bank that day to watch for Susan's appearance at the end of the wood; she always felt slightly anxious if the child were late.

She could scarcely believe her eyes. There was Susan in her grey cape and the new scarlet tam-o'-shanter, but with her came a swarm of children. She had forgotten all about the vague invitation.

Was the child bringing the whole school home?

She ran back to the house and called Becky and Joshua. They stood dumbfounded, looking across the fields.

'We shall have to give them all something to eat, coming all that way,' she gasped.

'It will be like feeding the five thousand in the Bible,' exclaimed Becky, and Joshua stood gaping. He had never known such a thing. What had come over the little maid to ask such a rabble?

'What will her father say?' was every one's thought.

They went to the kitchen and dairy to take stock. There was Becky's new batch of bread, the great earthenware crock full to the brim, standing on the larder floor. There was a dish of butter ready for the shops, and baskets of eggs counted out, eighteen a shilling. There was a tin of ginger snaps to last for months, some enormous jam pasties, besides three plum cakes.

They set to work, cutting and spreading on the big table, filling bread and butter plates with thick slices.

Joshua filled the copper kettles and put them on the fire, and counted out four dozen eggs, which he put on to boil. 'We can boil more when we've counted the lasses.'

Roger nearly went crazy when he saw the tribe come straggling and tired up the path to the front of the house.

Susan left them resting on the wall and went in to her mother.

'I've brought some girls to tea, Mother,' she said, opening her eyes at the preparations.

'Oh, indeed,' said Mrs Garland. 'How many have you brought?'

'A lot,' answered Susan. 'Where's my egg, they want to see it?'

'Susan Garland,' said Margaret severely, taking her by the shoulders, 'whatever do you mean by bringing all those girls home with you? Don't talk about that egg. Don't you see that they must all be fed? We can't let them come all this way without a good tea. You mustn't think of the egg, you will have to work.'

Susan stood aghast, she realized what she had done and began to cry.

'Never mind. Dry your eyes at once and smile. I don't know what your father will say, but we will try to get them fed before he comes.'

Margaret began to enjoy herself; she was a born hostess and here was a chance to exercise her hospitality.

She went out to the children and invited them to have a wash at the back door, where she had put a pancheon of hot water and towels. Then they were to sit orderly on the low walls, along the front of the house, and wait for tea which would come out in a few minutes. She chose four girls to help carry the things, and then she returned, leaving smiles and anticipation.

The fifty trooped round the house and washed their hands and faces, with laughter and glee. They peeped at the troughs, and admired the pig-cotes, but Susan shepherded them back to the walls, where they sat in their white pinafores like swallows ready for flight.

Becky and Joshua carried out the great copper tea-urn, which was used at farm suppers and sometimes lent for church parties. Margaret collected every cup and mug, basin and bowl in the house, from the capacious kitchen cupboards and tallboy, the parlour cupboards, the shelves, the dressers, from corner cupboards upstairs, from china cabinet stand and what-not, from brackets and pedestals.

There were Jubilee mugs and gold lustre mugs, an old china mug with 'Susan Garland, 1840', on it, and several with, 'A present for a Good Girl'. There were mugs with views and mugs with wreaths of pink and blue flowers, with mottoes and proverbs, with old men in high hats and women in wide skirts. There were tin mugs which belonged to the Irishmen, and Sheffield plated mugs from the mantelpiece, pewter and earthenware. There were delicate cups of lovely china, decorated with flowers and birds, blue Worcester, and some Spode breakfast cups, besides little blue basins and fluted bowls.

Margaret gave out the cups and mugs herself, choosing clean, careful-looking girls for her best china. The social position of each girl could be detected at once from the kind of cup she had, which was unlike Margaret's usual procedure, but this was an exceptional occasion. If only they had been round a table she would have trusted them, but now she had to use her judgment.

Becky poured out the tea, and Susan took it to each girl, with new milk and brown sugar. Old Joshua, wearing an apron, walked along the rows with a clothes-basket of bread and butter and a basket of eggs. As soon as he got to the end he began again.

Margaret took over the tea, and sent Becky to cut more and more. Susan's legs ached and an immense hunger seized her, she had eaten nothing but sandwiches since her breakfast at half-past seven. But there was no time, the girls clamoured for more, and she ran backwards and forwards with her four helpers, who had their own tea in between.

A clothes-basket was filled with cut-up pieces of cake, pastry, slabs of the men's cake, apple pasty, and currant slices. Then the box of ginger-snaps was taken round, and some girls actually refused. The end was approaching, but still Joshua walked up and down the line with food.

Dan came from out of the cowhouses with the milk, and Tom followed. Nobody had been in the smaller cowhouses. What was Joshua doing in an apron, and Becky, too, when she should be milking?

He stared at the rows of chattering children and walked in the house. Margaret ran in to explain.

'Don't be cross with her,' she said.

He said nothing till Susan came in for more cake.

Then he stood up and looked at her, and Susan quailed.

'Dang my buttons, Susan Garland, if you are not the most silly soft lass I ever knew! Are you clean daft crazy to bring all that crowd of cackling childer here?'

Then he stamped out to the byres and Susan walked back with her slices of cake, thankful she had not been sent to bed.

At last the feast was finished and Becky and Margaret washed up the cups and mugs, and collected the egg-shells, whilst Joshua went milking, and Susan ran for a ball to give them a game in the field before they went home. They ran races and played hide-and-seek, and lerky, they played ticky-ticky-touch-stone round the great menhir, and swarmed over its surface.

At the end of an hour Margaret rang a bell and they came racing to her. 'Put on your coats now, my dears, and go home; your mothers will expect you, and you have a long walk before you.'

So they said good-bye, and ran off singing and happy, down the hill. Two little girls had come shyly up to Susan with a parcel before they went.

'Mother said if it was your birthday we were to give you this,' and they held out a ball like a pineapple. But Susan had to confess it wasn't her birthday and they took it home.

She went indoors and sat down, tired and famished, at the table. 'And, mother, I never showed them my sky-blue egg after all! But they did enjoy themselves.'

NOEL STREATFEILD

FROM *Ballet Shoes*

(1936)

Pauline had a cold, and she was left at home when Nana took Petrova and Posy for their walk. She was in that state of having a cold when nothing is very nice to do. Sylvia had got her a piece of linen and some coloured thread, and she could have started on the dressing-table cover she was going to give Nana for her birthday. Cook had invited her to come to the kitchen and make toffee. Clara brought in a page of transfers, and suggested she stuck them on a book to 'give to a poor child in hospital'. Nana, who remembered how one felt with colds, gave her some brass polish and the sets of brass out of the dolls' house.

'I expect those to shine when we get in,' she said firmly. 'Much better to have something to do. No good sitting around thinking how miserable you feel.'

The last being an order, and as Nana expected things done when she said they were to be, Pauline finished them first. She found them quite fun to do, but she worked at them so hard that in half an hour they could not shine more than they did. Pauline put them back in the dolls' house, and thought for a moment of rearranging the drawing-room, but decided it would not be any fun without the others. She looked at the clock and wished it was tea-time, but it was only three. She took out the linen, and even threaded a bit of thread; but somehow she did not feel sewish, so she put it back in her drawer. She decided as there was not anything else to do she had better go and make toffee; but she felt hot, and not very much like eating toffee, and what is the fun of making toffee unless you want to eat it. She sat down on the landing of the second floor and sniffed and thought how beastly colds were. At that moment the door behind her opened and a head popped out. It had a shawl round it, and for a moment Pauline was not sure who it was. Then she recognized that it was one of the lady doctors – the one whose surname was Jakes. Doctor Jakes looked at Pauline.

'My dear child, what are you doing there by yourself?'

'I'b god a coad,' Pauline explained stuffily, for she had come down without her handkerchief. 'And the others hab god out withoud me, and I habbent god edythig to do.'

Doctor Jakes laughed.

'You sound as though you *have* got a cold. So have I, as a matter of fact. Come in. I've got a lovely fire, and I'll lend you a large silk handkerchief, and I'll give you some ginger drink which is doing me good.'

Pauline came in at once. She liked the sound of the whole of the invitation. Besides, she had not seen the inside of the two doctors' rooms since they had been boarders' rooms instead of homes for Gum's fossils. As a matter of fact, this one had changed so she felt it was a new room altogether. It had owned a rather shabby wall-paper; but when the boarder idea started it was distempered a sort of pale primrose all over. But the primrose hardly showed now, for the whole walls were covered with books.

'My goodness!' said Pauline, walking round and blowing her nose on the scarlet silk handkerchief Doctor Jakes had provided. 'You must read an awful lot. We have a big book-shelf in the nursery, but that's for all of us and Nana. Fancy all these just for you!'

Doctor Jakes came over to the shelves.

'Literature is my subject.'

'Is it? Is that what you're a doctor of?'

'More or less. But apart from that, books are very orna-mental things to have about.'

Pauline looked at the shelves. These books certainly were grand-looking – all smooth shiny covers, and lots of gold on them.

'Ours aren't very,' she said frankly. 'Yours are more all one size. We have things next to each other like *Peter Rabbit* and *Just So Stories*, and they don't match very well.'

'No, but very good reading.'

Pauline came to the fire. It was a lovely fire; she stood looking at the logs on it.

'Do you think *Peter Rabbit* good reading? I would have thought a person who taught literature was too grand for it.'

'Not a bit – very old friend of mine.'

Pauline looked at the shawl.

'Why do you wear that round your head?'

'Because I had earache with my cold. Have you got ear-ache with yours?'

'No. Just my nose.'

Pauline remembered the ginger drink, and looked round

for it. Doctor Jakes remembered it at the same time. She put on the kettle.

'Sit down. This drink is made with boiling water, and takes quite a time. Have you a holiday from school because of your cold?'

Pauline explained that they did not go to Cromwell House any more, and why.

'You see,' she said, 'Gum said he'd be back in five years, and he isn't.'

'And who exactly is Gum?'

Doctor Jakes poured things out of various bottles into two glasses.

Pauline hugged her knees.

'Well, he's called Gum because he's Garnie's Great-Uncle Matthew. He isn't really a great-uncle of ours, because we haven't any relations. I was rescued off a ship, Petrova is an orphan from Russia, and Posy's father is dead, and her mother couldn't afford to have her, so we've made ourselves into sisters. We've called ourselves Fossil because that's what Gum called us. He brought us back instead of them, you see.'

'I see. Rather exciting choosing your own name and your own relations.'

'Yes.' Pauline saw that the kettle was nearly boiling and looked hopefully at the glasses. 'We almost didn't choose Posy to be a Fossil. She was little and stupid then, but she's all right now.'

Doctor Jakes got up and took the kettle off the fire and poured the water on the mixture in the glasses. At once there was the most lovely hot sweet smell. Pauline sniffed.

'That smells good.'

Doctor Jakes put the tumblers into silver frames with handles, and passed one to Pauline.

'I do envy you. I should think it an adventure to have a name like that, and sisters by accident. The three of you might make the name of Fossil really important, really worth while, and if you do, it's all your own. Now, if I make Jakes really worth while, people will say I take after my grandfather or something.'

Pauline sipped her drink. It was very hot, but simply heavenly – the sort of drink certain to make a cold feel better. She looked across at Doctor Jakes over the rim of the glass, her eyes shining.

'Do you suppose me and Petrova and Posy could make Fossil an important sort of name?'

'Of course. Making your name worth while is a very nice thing to do; it means you must have given distinguished service to your country in some way.'

Pauline gave another gulp at her drink. She frowned thoughtfully.

'I don't think we do the things that make names important. I sew, and Petrova's awfully good at works of things – she can mend clocks and she knows heaps about aeroplanes and motor-cars. Posy doesn't do much yet.'

'There's time. You probably won't develop a talent till you are fourteen or fifteen. Are you good at lessons?'

'Well, we were. Petrova was very good at sums, and I said poetry the best in the class; but it's different now we learn with Garnie. You know, she has to teach Posy too, and she has to do the baby things, like learning her letters and it takes a lot of time. Petrova does sums well still, but Garnie just puts R, R, R; she never teaches her a new one. I say poetry sometimes, but not very often now.'

'What sort of poetry do you like?'

'All sorts. We learnt "Oh to be in England" and "The Ancient Mariner", and I had just started "Hiawatha".'

'Do you ever learn any Shakespeare?'

'No. I should have started *As You Like It* the next term if I had stayed at Cromwell House.'

'You should learn him. He wrote a few good parts for children. If you are fond of reciting, that's the stuff to work at.' She went over to her shelves and picked out a book, and opened it. 'Listen.'

She read the scene in *King John* between Prince Arthur and Hubert. Pauline did not understand it all, but Doctor Jakes was one of those people who really can read out loud. Pauline forgot to drink her ginger, and instead, listened so hard that at last Doctor Jakes vanished, and in her place she saw a cowering little boy pleading for his eyes.

'There.' Doctor Jakes closed the book. 'Learn that. Learn to play Prince Arthur so that we cringe at the hot irons just as he does, and then you can talk about reciting.' She got another book, found the place and passed it to Pauline. 'You read me that.'

It was Puck's speech which begins 'Fairy, thou speak'st aright'. Pauline had never seen it before, and she halted over some of the words, but she got a remarkable amount of the feeling of Puck into it. When she had finished, Doctor Jakes nodded at her in a pleased way.

'Good! We'll read some more one day. I'll make a Shakespearean of you.'

Pauline heard the front door slam and got up.

'There's the others, I must go. Thank you very much for the ginger drink.'

'Goodbye.' Doctor Jakes did not look up; she was studying *A Midsummer Night's Dream*. 'Don't forget, it's fun having a name with no background. Tell the other Fossils.'

After tea Pauline told Petrova and Posy what Doctor Jakes had said. Petrova was most impressed.

'Do you think she meant we could make it a name in history books?'

Pauline was not sure.

'She didn't exactly say history books, but I think that's what she meant. She said making your name worth while means you must have given distinguished service to your country.'

Petrova's eyes shone.

'How lovely if we could! Fancy people learning about us at lessons! Let's make a vow to make Fossil a name like that.'

Pauline looked serious.

'A real vow, do you mean, like at christenings?'

'Yes.' Petrova hopped, she was so excited. 'Like "promise and vow three things ..."'

'What about her?' Pauline pointed at Posy, who, not understanding the conversation, was dressing her Teddy bear.

'Posy' – Petrova knelt down beside her – 'do you know what making a vow is?'

'No.' Posy held out a little pair of blue trousers. 'These don't fit Teddy any more.'

Pauline took Teddy and his clothes from her.

'You must listen, Posy,' she said in a very grown-up voice. 'This is important. A vow is a promise; it's a thing when you've made it you've got to do it. Do you understand?'

'Yes.' Posy held out her hand. 'Give me Teddy.'

'No.' Petrova took her hand. 'Not till we've finished the vowing.' She turned to Pauline. 'You say it, and Posy and I will hold up our hands and say "We vow."'

Pauline put both her feet together and folded her hands.

'We three Fossils,' she said in a church voice, 'vow to try and put our names in history books because it's our very own and nobody can say it's because of our grandfathers.'

She made a face at Petrova, who hurriedly held up her right arm, and grabbed Posy's and held it up, too.

'We vow.' She said this so low down in her inside that it sounded terribly impressive, then she whispered to Posy 'Go on, say "We vow."'

'We vow.'

Posy tried to say it in the same deep voice as Petrova, but she did it wrong, and it sounded rather like a cat meowing. This made them all laugh, and the big vowing, instead of ending seriously, found them laughing so much that they fell on the floor, and their tummies ached.

Pauline was the first to recover.

'Oh, we oughtn't to have laughed!' She wiped her eyes. 'But, Posy, you did sound silly!' She gave another gurgle. 'Shall we make this same vow over again on each of our birthdays?'

'Let's,' agreed Petrova. 'It'll make our birthdays so important.'

'We vow,' Posy said in exactly the same meow.

This time they could not stop laughing, and they were still giggling when it was time to go down to be read to by Sylvia.

Boarders had not settled Sylvia's troubles. It was quite obvious that children with no certain future ought to be brought up with the kind of education that meant they could earn their living later on. The kind of education that she was able to give them could not, as far as she could see, fit them for anything. She kept this worry to herself, but it was such a bad one it kept her awake at nights.

Then one day she had three visitors. The first two came after lunch. She had just sat down to read the paper when there was a knock on her door. She was feeling very tired, for planning food for a lot of boarders as well as giving three children lessons is tiring. She was not in the mood to see anybody; but if you take in boarders you have to put up with seeing them when you do not want to, so she said 'Come in' as politely as she could. It was the two doctors – Doctor Jakes and Doctor Smith. Doctor Jakes wasted no time.

'My dear,' she said, sitting down in the armchair facing Sylvia. 'I doubt if you are qualified to teach those children.'

Sylvia flushed.

'I'm not,' she agreed humbly.

'That's what we thought.' Doctor Smith drew up a small chair and sat down next to Doctor Jakes. 'But, you see, we are.'

'Yes.' Sylvia fiddled with her fingers. 'I know you are, but I can't pay anybody who is.'

'We thought that too.' Doctor Smith looked at Doctor Jakes. 'You tell her.'

Doctor Jakes cleared her throat.

'We should like to teach them. For nothing.'

'For nothing! Why?' asked Sylvia.

'Why not?' said Doctor Smith.

'But they're not your children,' Sylvia protested.

'Nor yours,' Doctor Jakes suggested.

'Mine by adoption,' Sylvia said firmly.

'Mayn't we help?' Doctor Jakes leant forward. 'We thought we should like to retire. It would give us time for research, but we find we miss our teaching. Pauline has a beautiful ear for verse-speaking, I shall enjoy training her.'

'Mathematics is my subject,' Doctor Smith explained. 'I hear Petrova is fond of mathematics.'

Sylvia looked at Doctor Smith as though she were an angel.

'You teach arithmetic?' Her voice was awed. 'You are offering to teach the children?'

'That's right.' Both the doctors spoke at once.

'I think Heaven must have sent you to this house. I accept your offer more gratefully than I can say.' Sylvia turned to Doctor Smith. 'Would you mind starting tomorrow? I simply can't give another arithmetic lesson.'

The two doctors got up.

'Yes, tomorrow,' Doctor Jakes agreed. 'All-round education, specializing in mathematics and literature. The children to be prepared to take the school certificate and matriculation.'

That night after dinner Sylvia had her third visitor. It was Theo Dane. She knocked, and at the same time popped her head round the drawing-room door.

'Can I come in? I want a word with you.' She did not wait for permission, but came in, and sat down on the floor at Sylvia's feet. 'You know I teach dancing at the Children's Academy of Dancing and Stage Training?'

'Yes.' Sylvia went on stitching at the curtains she was hemming.

'The head is Madame Fidolia. She was a big dancer in the years before the 1914 war.'

Sylvia did not know the name, but it seemed rude to say so, so she gave a sort of half cough, half yes.

'Well,' Theo went on, 'I spoke to her today about your three. She'll have them.'

'Have them?' Sylvia looked puzzled. 'How do you mean?'

'Teach them. Take them as pupils.'

'But I couldn't pay the fees.'

'She'll take them free. I told her about them, and what a time you were having, and she'll train them. She'll hope to make something out of them later when they're working.'

'Working! What at?'

'On the stage. It's a stage school.'

Sylvia's mouth opened.

'But I don't want the children to go on the stage.'

'Why not?' Theo half got up in her earnestness. 'Posy has the making of a real dancer. I've tried her out to my gramophone. Pauline is lovely to look at, and she has a good sense of rhythm.'

'Do you mean they should earn money at it?'

'Of course. They have no parents or relations; it's a good thing they should have a career.'

'But I'm instead of parents and relations.'

'But suppose you were run over by a bus. Wouldn't it be a good thing if they were trained to help support themselves?'

'But there's my Great-Uncle Matthew, they are really his wards.'

'Where is he?'

'On a voyage,' Sylvia explained, and then added, 'He's been on it for some years.'

'Quite,' agreed Theo, obviously considering Gum as somebody so unlikely to appear as to matter no more than a ghost. 'Well, what do you say? Isn't it a good idea?'

Sylvia looked worried.

'I don't think Nana would approve; and then there are the doctors upstairs. They are going to educate them. What'll they say?'

'That's easy,' said Theo. 'Let's have them all down and ask them.'

Nana and the two doctors came down and heard Theo's suggestion, then Sylvia said: 'I have told her that I don't think we can consider it.'

'Why not?' asked Nana.

'Oh, Nana' – Sylvia was flushed – 'I thought you'd be certain to agree with me.'

'And for why?' Nana smoothed a crease out of her apron. 'Posy we may say is bound to dance anyway, coming to us with her dancing slippers and all. It might be just the right thing for Pauline too – never any good at her books, only fond of that reciting.'

'How about Petrova?' said Sylvia.

'Well, she won't be no good at it to my way of thinking, but it might be just the thing for her – turn her more like a little lady; always messing about with the works of clocks and that just like a boy; never plays with dolls, and takes no more interest in her clothes than a scarecrow.'

'What do you think?' Sylvia turned to the two doctors.

Doctor Jakes looked at Doctor Smith and they nodded to each other. Then Doctor Jakes cleared her throat.

'It's a great responsibility, my dear, for you to undertake, but we do feel Miss Dane's suggestion is good. It may be that you may find later that dancing is not the career for all of them, but the training will have done them good, and you will at least have taken a step towards trying to make them self-supporting.'

Sylvia looked round at them all; she felt she must take their advice, but she was worried.

'They are such little children,' she exclaimed.

Nana got up.

'Little children grow up. I suppose that Anna Pavlova was a little child once. I'll be going back to my nurseries, if you'll excuse me, Miss Sylvia dear. Good-night.'

J. R. R. TOLKIEN

FROM *The Hobbit*

(1937)

When Bilbo opened his eyes, he wondered if he had; for it was just as dark as with them shut. No one was anywhere near him. Just imagine his fright! He could hear nothing, see nothing, and he could feel nothing except the stone of the floor.

Very slowly he got up and groped about on all fours, till he touched the wall of the tunnel; but neither up nor down it could he find anything: nothing at all, no sight of goblins, no sign of dwarves. His head was swimming, and he was far from certain even of the direction they had been going in when he had his fall. He guessed as well as he could, and crawled along for a good way, till suddenly his hand met what felt like a tiny ring of cold metal lying on the floor of the tunnel. It was a turning point in his career, but he did not know it. He put the ring in his pocket almost without thinking; certainly it did not seem of any particular use at the moment…

He could not think what to do; nor could he think what had happened; or why he had been left behind; or why, if he had been left behind, the goblins had not caught him; or even why his head was so sore…

After some time he felt for his pipe. It was not broken, and that was something. Then he felt for his pouch, and there was some tobacco in it, and that was something more. Then he felt for matches and he could not find any at all, and that shattered his hopes completely. Just as well for him, as he agreed when he came to his senses. Goodness knows what striking of matches and the smell of tobacco would have brought on him out of dark holes in that horrible place. Still at the moment he felt very crushed. But in slapping all his pockets and feeling all round himself for matches his hand came on the hilt of his little sword – the little dagger that he got from the trolls, and that he had quite forgotten; nor fortunately had the goblins noticed it, as he wore it inside his breeches.

Now he drew it out. It shone pale and dim before his eyes. 'So it is an elvish blade, too,' he thought; 'and goblins are not very near, and yet not far enough.'

But somehow he was comforted. It was rather splendid to be wearing a blade made in Gondolin for the goblin-wars of which so many songs had sung; and also he had noticed that such weapons made a great impression on goblins that came upon them suddenly.

'Go back?' he thought. 'No good at all! Go sideways? Impossible! Go forward? Only thing to do! On we go!' So up he got, and trotted along with his little sword held in front of him and one hand feeling the wall, and his heart all of a patter and a pitter.

Now certainly Bilbo was in what is called a tight place. But you must remember it was not quite so tight for him as it would have been for me or for you. Hobbits are not quite like ordinary people; and after all if their holes are nice cheery places and properly aired, quite different from the tunnels of the goblins, still they are more used to tunnelling than we are, and they do not easily lose their sense of direction underground – not when their heads have recovered from being bumped. Also they can move very quietly, and hide easily, and recover wonderfully from falls and bruises, and they have a fund of wisdom and wise sayings that men have mostly never heard or have forgotten long ago.

I should not have liked to have been in Mr Baggins' place, all the same. The tunnel seemed to have no end ... On and on he went, and down and down; and still he heard no sound of anything except the occasional whirr of a bat by his ears, which startled him at first, till it became too frequent to bother about. I do not know how long he kept on like this, hating to go on, not daring to stop, on, on, until he was tireder than tired. It seemed like all the way to tomorrow and over it to the days beyond.

Suddenly without any warning he trotted splash into water! Ugh! It was icy cold. That pulled him up sharp and short. He did not know whether it was just a pool in the path, or the edge of an underground stream that crossed the passage, or the brink of a deep dark subterranean lake. The sword was hardly shining at all. He stopped, and he could hear, when he listened hard, drops drip-drip-dripping from an unseen roof into the water below; but there seemed no other sort of sound ...

Deep down here by the dark water lived old Gollum, a small slimy creature. I don't know where he came from, nor who or what he was. He was a Gollum – as dark as darkness, except for two big round pale eyes in his thin face. He had a little boat, and he rowed about quite quietly on the lake; for lake it was, wide and deep and deadly cold. He paddled it with large feet dangling over the side, but never a ripple did he make. Not he. He was looking out of his pale lamp-like eyes for blind fish, which he grabbed with his long fingers as quick as thinking. He liked meat too. Goblin he thought good, when he could get it; but he took care they never found him out. He just throttled them from behind, if they ever came down alone anywhere near the edge of the water, while he was prowling about. They very seldom did, for they had a feeling that something unpleasant was lurking down there, down at the very roots of the mountain …

Actually Gollum lived on a slimy island of rock in the middle of the lake. He was watching Bilbo now from the distance with his pale eyes like telescopes. Bilbo could not see him, but he was wondering a lot about Bilbo, for he could see that he was no goblin at all.

Gollum got into his boat and shot off from the island, while Bilbo was sitting on the brink altogether flummoxed and at the end of his way and his wits. Suddenly up came Gollum and whispered and hissed: 'Bless us and splash us, my preciousss! I guess it's a choice feast; at least a tasty morsel it'd make us, gollum!' And when he said *gollum* he made a horrible swallowing noise in his throat. That is how he got his name, though he always called himself 'my precious'.

The hobbit jumped nearly out of his skin when the hiss came in his ears, and he suddenly saw the pale eyes sticking out at him.

'Who are you?' he said, thrusting his dagger in front of him.

'What iss he, my preciouss?' whispered Gollum (who always spoke to himself through never having anyone else to speak to). This is what he had come to find out, for he was not really very hungry at the moment, only curious; otherwise he would have grabbed first and whispered afterwards.

'I am Mr Bilbo Baggins. I have lost the dwarves and I have lost the wizard, and I don't know where I am; and I don't want to know, if only I can get away.'

'What's he got in his handses?' said Gollum, looking at the sword, which he did not quite like.

'A sword, a blade which came out of Gondolin!'

'Sssss' said Gollum, and became quite polite. 'Praps ye sits here and chats with it a bitsy, my preciouss. It like riddles, praps it does, does it?' He was anxious to appear friendly, at any rate for the moment, and until he found out more about the sword and the hobbit, whether he was quite alone really, whether he was good to eat, and whether Gollum was really hungry. Riddles were all he could think of. Asking them, and sometimes guessing them, had been the only game he had ever played with other funny creatures sitting in their holes in the long, long ago, before he lost all his friends and was driven away, alone, and crept down, down, into the dark under the mountains.

'Very well,' said Bilbo, who was anxious to agree, until he found out more about the creature, whether he was quite alone, whether he was fierce or hungry, and whether he was a friend of the goblins.

'You ask first,' he said, because he had not had time to think of a riddle.

So Gollum hissed:

What has roots as nobody sees,
Is taller than trees
    Up, up it goes,
    And yet never grows?

'Easy!' said Bilbo. 'Mountain, I suppose.'

'Does it guess easy? It must have a competition with us, my preciouss! If precious asks, and it doesn't answer, we eats it, my preciouss. If it asks us, and we doesn't answer, then we does what it wants, eh? We shows it the way out, yes!'

'All right!' said Bilbo, not daring to disagree, and nearly bursting his brain to think of riddles that could save him from being eaten.

Thirty white horses on a red hill,
    First they champ,
    Then they stamp,
Then they stand still.

That was all he could think of to ask – the idea of eating was rather on his mind. It was rather an old one, too, and Gollum knew the answer as well as you do.

'Chestnuts, chestnuts,' he hissed. 'Teeth! Teeth, my preciousss; but we has only six!' Then he asked his second:

Voiceless it cries,
Wingless flutters,
Toothless bites,
Mouthless mutters.

'Half a moment!' cried Bilbo, who was still thinking uncomfortably about eating. Fortunately he had once heard something rather like this before, and getting his wits back he thought of the answer. 'Wind, wind of course,' he said, and he was so pleased that he made up one on the spot.

'This'll puzzle the nasty little underground creature,' he thought:

> An eye in a blue face
> Saw an eye in a green face.
> 'That eye is like to this eye'
> Said the first eye,
> 'But in low place
>   Not in high place.'

'Ss, ss, ss,' said Gollum. He had been underground a long long time, and was forgetting this sort of thing. But just as Bilbo was beginning to hope that the wretch would not be able to answer, Gollum brought up memories of ages and ages and ages before, when he lived with his grandmother in a hole in a bank by a river. 'Sss, sss, my preciouss,' he said. 'Sun on the daisies it means, it does.'

But these ordinary above ground everyday sort of riddles were tiring for him. Also they reminded him of days when he had been less lonely and sneaky and nasty, and that put him out of temper. What is more they made him hungry; so this time he tried something a bit more difficult and more unpleasant:

> It cannot be seen, cannot be felt,
> Cannot be heard, cannot be smelt.
> It lies behind stars and under hills,
>   And empty holes it fills.
> It comes first and follows after,
>   Ends life, kills laughter.

Unfortunately for Gollum Bilbo had heard that sort of thing before; and the answer was all round him any way. 'Dark!' he said without even scratching his head or putting on his thinking cap.

> A box without hinges, key or lid,
> Yet golden treasure inside is hid,

he asked to gain time, until he could think of a really hard one. This he thought a dreadfully easy chestnut, though he had not asked it in the usual words. But it proved a nasty poser for Gollum. He hissed to himself, and still he did not answer; he whispered and spluttered.

After some while Bilbo became impatient. 'Well, what is it?' he said. 'The answer's not a kettle boiling over, as you seem to think from the noise you are making.'

'Give us a chance; let it give us a chance, my preciouss – ss – ss.'

'Well,' said Bilbo after giving him a long chance, 'what about your guess?'

But suddenly Gollum remembered thieving from nests long ago, and sitting under the river bank teaching his grand-mother, teaching his grandmother to suck – 'Eggses!' he hissed. 'Eggses it is!' ... Then he thought the time had come to ask something hard and horrible. This is what he said:

> This thing all things devours:
> Birds, beasts, trees, flowers;
> Gnaws iron, bites steel;
> Grinds hard stones to meal;
> Slays king, ruins town,
> And beats high mountain down.

Poor Bilbo sat in the dark thinking of all the horrible names of all the giants and ogres he had ever heard told of in tales, but not one of them had done all these things. He had a feeling that the answer was quite different and that he ought to know it, but he could not think of it. He began to get frightened, and that is bad for thinking. Gollum began

to get out of his boat. He flapped into the water and paddled to the bank; Bilbo could not see his eyes coming
towards him. His tongue seemed to stick in his mouth; he
wanted to shout out: 'Give me more time! Give me time!'
But all that came out with a sudden squeal was: 'Time!
Time!'

Bilbo was saved by pure luck. For that of course was the
answer.

Gollum was disappointed once more; and now he was
getting angry, and also tired of the game. It had made him
very hungry indeed. This time he did not go back to the
boat. He sat down in the dark by Bilbo. That made the hobbit most dreadfully uncomfortable and scattered his wits.

'It's got to ask uss a quesstion, my preciouss, yes, yess,
yesss. Jusst one more quesstion to guess, yes, yess,' said
Gollum.

But Bilbo simply could not think of any question with
that nasty wet cold thing sitting next to him, and pawing
and poking him. He scratched himself, he pinched himself;
still he could not think of anything.

'Ask us! Ask us! said Gollum.

Bilbo pinched himself and slapped himself; he gripped on
his little sword; he even felt in his pocket with his other
hand. There he found the ring he had picked up in the passage and forgotten about.

'What have I got in my pocket?' he said aloud. He was
talking to himself, but Gollum thought it was a riddle, and
he was frightfully upset.

'Not fair! not fair!' he hissed. 'It isn't fair, my precious, is
it, to ask us what it's got in its nassty little pocketses?'

Bilbo seeing what had happened and having nothing better to ask stuck to his question, 'What have I got in my
pocket?' he said louder.

'S-s-s-s-s,' hissed Gollum. 'It must give us three guesseses, my preciouss, three guesseses.'

'Very well! Guess away!' said Bilbo.

'Handses!' said Gollum.

'Wrong,' said Bilbo, who had luckily just taken his hand out again. 'Guess again!'

'S-s-s-s-s,' said Gollum more upset than ever. He thought of all the things he kept in his own pockets: fishbones, goblins' teeth, wet shells, a bit of bat-wing, a sharp stone to sharpen his fangs on, and other nasty things. He tried to think what other people kept in their pockets.

'Knife!' he said at last.

'Wrong!' said Bilbo, who had lost his some time ago. 'Last guess!'

Now Gollum was in a much worse state than when Bilbo had asked him the egg-question. He hissed and spluttered and rocked himself backwards and forwards, and slapped his feet on the floor, and wriggled and squirmed; but still he did not dare to waste his last guess.

'Come on!' said Bilbo. 'I am waiting!' He tried to sound bold and cheerful, but he did not feel at all sure how the game was going to end, whether Gollum guessed right or not.

'Time's up!' he said.

'String, or nothing!' shrieked Gollum, which was not quite fair – working in two guesses at once.

'Both wrong,' cried Bilbo very much relieved; and he jumped at once to his feet, put his back to the nearest wall, and held out his little sword. He knew, of course, that the riddle-game was sacred and of immense antiquity, and even wicked creatures were afraid to cheat when they played at it. But he felt he could not trust this slimy thing to keep any promise at a pinch. Any excuse would do for him to slide

out of it. And after all that last question had not been a genu-
ine riddle according to the ancient laws.

But at any rate Gollum did not at once attack him. He
could see the sword in Bilbo's hand. He sat still, shivering
and whispering. At last Bilbo could wait no longer.

'Well?' he said. 'What about your promise? I want to go.
You must show me the way.'

'Did we say so, precious? Show the nassty little Baggins
the way out, yes, yes. But what has it got in its pocketses,
eh? Not string, precious, but not nothing. Oh, no! Gollum!'

'Never you mind,' said Bilbo. 'A promise is a promise.'

'Cross it is, impatient, precious,' hissed Gollum. 'But it
must wait, yes, it must. We can't go up the tunnels so hasty.
We must go and get some things first, yes, things to help us.'

'Well, hurry up!' said Bilbo, relieved to think of Gollum
going away. He thought he was just making an excuse and
did not mean to come back. What was Gollum talking
about? What useful thing could he keep out on the dark
lake? But he was wrong. Gollum did mean to come back.
He was angry now and hungry. And he was a miserable
wicked creature, and already he had a plan.

Not far away was his island, of which Bilbo knew nothing, and there in his hiding-place he kept a few wretched
oddments, and one very beautiful thing, very beautiful, very
wonderful. He had a ring, a golden ring, a precious ring.

'My birthday-present!' he whispered to himself, as he had
often done in the endless dark days. 'That's what we wants
now, yes; we wants it!'

He wanted it because it was a ring of power, and if you
slipped that ring on your finger, you were invisible; only in
the full sunlight could you be seen, and then only by your
shadow, and that would be shaky and faint.

'My birthday-present! It came to me on my birthday, my

precious.' So he had always said to himself. But who knows how Gollum came by that present, ages ago in the old days when such rings were still at large in the world? ...

'Quite safe, yes,' he whispered to himself. 'It won't see us, will it, my precious? No. It won't see us, and its nasty little sword will be useless, yes quite.'

That is what was in his wicked little mind, as he slipped suddenly from Bilbo's side, and flapped back to his boat, and went off into the dark. Bilbo thought he had heard the last of him. Still he waited a while; for he had no idea how to find his way out alone.

Suddenly he heard a screech. It sent a shiver down his back. Gollum was cursing and wailing away in the gloom, not very far off by the sound of it. He was on his island, scrabbling here and there, searching and seeking in vain.

'Where is it? Where iss it?' Bilbo heard him crying. 'Losst it is, my precious, lost, lost! Curse us and crush us, my precious is lost!'

'What's the matter?' Bilbo called. 'What have you lost?'

'It mustn't ask us,' shrieked Gollum. 'Not its business, no, gollum! It's losst, gollum, gollum, gollum.'

'Well, so am I,' cried Bilbo, 'and I want to get unlost. And I won the game, and you promised. So come along! Come and let me out, and then go on with your looking!' Utterly miserable as Gollum sounded, Bilbo could not find much pity in his heart, and he had a feeling that anything Gollum wanted so much could hardly be something good. 'Come along!' he shouted.

'No, not yet, precious!' Gollum answered. 'We must search for it, it's lost, gollum.'

'But you never guessed my last question, and you promised,' said Bilbo.

'Never guessed!' said Gollum. Then suddenly out of the gloom came a sharp hiss. 'What has it got in its pocketses? Tell us that. It must tell first.'

As far as Bilbo knew, there was no particular reason why he should not tell. Gollum's mind had jumped to a guess quicker than his; naturally, for Gollum had brooded for ages on this one thing, and he was always afraid of its being stolen. But Bilbo was annoyed at the delay. After all, he had won the game, pretty fairly, at a horrible risk. 'Answers were to be guessed not given,' he said.

'But it wasn't a fair question,' said Gollum. 'Not a riddle, precious, no.'

'Oh well, if it's a matter of ordinary questions,' Bilbo replied, 'then I asked one first. What have you lost? Tell me that!'

'What has it got in its pocketses?' The sound came hissing louder and sharper, and as he looked towards it, to his alarm Bilbo now saw two small points of light peering at him. As suspicion grew in Gollum's mind, the light of his eyes burned with a pale flame.

'What have you lost?' Bilbo persisted.

But now the light in Gollum's eyes had become a green fire, and it was coming swiftly nearer. Gollum was in his boat again, paddling wildly back to the dark shore; and such a rage of loss and suspicion was in his heart that no sword had any more terror for him.

Bilbo could not guess what had maddened the wretched creature, but he saw that all was up, and that Gollum meant to murder him at any rate. Just in time he turned and ran blindly back up the dark passage down which he had come, keeping close to the wall and feeling it with his left hand.

'What has it got in its pocketses?' he heard the hiss loud behind him, and the splash as Gollum leapt from his boat.

'What have I, I wonder?' he said to himself, as he panted and stumbled along. He put his left hand in his pocket. The ring felt very cold as it quietly slipped on to his groping forefinger.

The hiss was close behind him. He turned now and saw Gollum's eyes like small green lamps coming up the slope. Terrified he tried to run faster, but suddenly he struck his toes on a snag in the floor, and fell flat with his little sword under him.

In a moment Gollum was on him. But before Bilbo could do anything, recover his breath, pick himself up, or wave his sword, Gollum passed by, taking no notice of him, cursing and whispering as he ran.

What could it mean? Gollum could see in the dark. Bilbo could see the light of his eyes palely shining even from behind. Painfully he got up, and sheathed his sword, which was now glowing faintly again, then very cautiously he followed. There seemed nothing else to do. It was no good crawling back down to Gollum's water. Perhaps if he followed him, Gollum might lead him to some way of escape without meaning to.

'Curse it! Curse it! Curse it!' hissed Gollum. 'Curse the Baggins! It's gone! What has it got in its pocketses? Oh we guess, we guess, my precious. He's found it, yes he must have. My birthday-present.'

Bilbo pricked up his ears ...

'My birthday-present! Curse it! How did we lose it, my precious? Yes, that's it. When we came this way last, when we twisted that nassty young squeaker. That's it. Curse it! It slipped from us, after all these ages and ages! It's gone, gollum.'

Suddenly Gollum sat down and began to weep, a whistling and gurgling sound horrible to listen to. Bilbo halted and flattened himself against the tunnel-wall. After a while Gollum stopped weeping and began to talk. He seemed to be having an argument with himself.

'It's no good going back there to search, no. We doesn't remember all the places we've visited. And it's no use. The Baggins has got it in its pocketses; the nassty noser has found it, we says ...

'It's tricksy. It doesn't say what it means. It won't say what it's got in its pocketses. It knows. It knows a way in, it must know a way out, yes. It's off to the back-door. To the back-door, that's it.

'The goblinses will catch it then. It can't get out that way, precious.

'Ssss, sss, gollum! Goblinses! Yes, but if it's got the present, our precious present, then goblinses will get it, gollum! They'll find it, they'll find out what it does. We shan't ever be safe again, never, gollum! One of the goblinses will put it on, and then no one will see him. He'll be there but not seen. Not even our clever eyeses will notice him; and he'll come creepsy and tricksy and catch us, gollum, gollum!

'Then let's stop talking, precious, and make haste. If the Baggins has gone that way, we must go quick and see. Go! Not far now. Make haste!'

With a spring Gollum got up and started shambling off at a great pace. Bilbo hurried after him, still cautiously, though his chief fear now was of tripping on another snag and falling with a noise. His head was in a whirl of hope and wonder. It seemed that the ring he had was a magic ring: it made you invisible! He had heard of such things, of course, in old old tales; but it was hard to believe that he really had found one, by accident. Still there it was: Gollum with his bright eyes had passed him by, only a yard to one side.

On they went, Gollum flip-flapping ahead, hissing and

cursing; Bilbo behind going as softly as a hobbit can. Soon they came to places where, as Bilbo had noticed on the way down, side-passages opened, this way and that. Gollum began at once to count them.

'One left, yes. One right, yes. Two right, yes, yes. Two left, yes, yes.' And so on and on.

As the count grew he slowed down, and be began to get shaky and weepy; for he was leaving the water further and further behind, and he was getting afraid. Goblins might be about, and he had lost his ring. At last he stopped by a low opening, on their left as they went up.

'Seven right, yes. Six left, yes!' he whispered. 'This is it. This is the way to the back-door, yes. Here's the passage!'

He peered in, and shrank back. 'But we dursn't go in, precious, no we dursn't. Goblinses down there. Lots of goblinses. We smells them. Ssss!

'What shall we do? Curse them and crush them! We must wait here, precious, wait a bit and see.'

So they came to a dead stop. Gollum had brought Bilbo to the way out after all, but Bilbo could not get in! There was Gollum sitting humped up right in the opening, and his eyes gleamed cold in his head, as he swayed it from side to side between his knees.

Bilbo crept away from the wall more quietly than a mouse; but Gollum stiffened at once, and sniffed, and his eyes went green. He hissed softly but menacingly. He could not see the hobbit, but now he was on the alert, and he had other senses that the darkness had sharpened: hearing and smell. He seemed to be crouched right down with his flat hands splayed on the floor, and his head thrust out, nose almost to the stone. Though he was only a black shadow in the gleam of his own eyes, Bilbo could see or feel that he was tense as a bowstring, gathered for a spring.

Bilbo almost stopped breathing, and went stiff himself. He was desperate. He must get away, out of this horrible darkness, while he had any strength left. He must fight. He must stab the foul thing, put its eyes out, kill it. It meant to kill him. No, not a fair fight. He was invisible now. Gollum had no sword... All these thoughts passed in a flash of a second. He trembled. And then quite suddenly in another flash, as if lifted by a new strength and resolve, he leaped.

No great leap for a man, but a leap in the dark. Straight over Gollum's head he jumped, seven feet forward and three in the air; indeed, had he known it, he only just missed cracking his skull on the low arch of the passage.

Gollum threw himself backwards, and grabbed as the hobbit flew over him, but too late; his hands snapped on thin air, and Bilbo, falling fair on his sturdy feet, sped off down the new tunnel. He did not turn to see what Gollum was doing. There was a hissing and cursing almost at his heels at first, then it stopped. All at once there came a blood-curdling shriek, filled with hatred and despair. Gollum was defeated. He dared go no further. He had lost: lost his prey, and lost, too, the only thing he had ever cared for, his precious. The cry brought Bilbo's heart to his mouth, but still he held on. Now faint as an echo, but menacing, the voice came behind: 'Thief, thief, thief! Baggins! We hates it, we hates it, we hates it for ever!'

Then there was a silence. But that too seemed menacing to Bilbo. 'If goblins are so near that he smelt them,' he thought, 'then they'll have heard his shrieking and cursing. Careful now, or this way will lead you to worse things.'

The passage was low and roughly made. It was not too difficult for the hobbit, except when, in spite of all care, he stubbed his poor toes again, several times, on nasty jagged stones in the floor...

Soon the passage that had been sloping down began to go up again, and after a while it climbed steeply. That slowed Bilbo down. But at last the slope stopped, the passage turned a corner, and dipped down again, and there, at the bottom of a short incline, he saw, filtering round another corner – a glimpse of light. Not red light, as of fire or lantern, but a pale out-of-doors sort of light. Then Bilbo began to run.

Scuttling as fast as his legs would carry him he turned the last corner and came suddenly right into an open space, where the light, after all that time in the dark, seemed dazzlingly bright. Really it was only a leak of sunshine in through a doorway, where a great door, a stone door, was left standing open.

Bilbo blinked, and then suddenly he saw the goblins: goblins in full armour with drawn swords sitting just inside the door, and watching it with wide eyes, and watching the passage that led to it. They were aroused, alert, ready for anything.

They saw him sooner than he saw them. Yes, they saw him. Whether it was an accident, or a last trick of the ring before it took a new master, it was not on his finger. With yells of delight the goblins rushed upon him.

A pang of fear and loss, like an echo of Gollum's misery, smote Bilbo, and forgetting even to draw his sword he stuck his hands into his pockets. And there was the ring still, in his left pocket, and it slipped on his finger. The goblins stopped short. They could not see a sign of him. He had vanished. They yelled twice as loud as before, but not so delightedly.

'Where is it?' they cried.

'Go back up the passage!' some shouted.

'This way!' some yelled. 'That way!' others yelled.

'Look out for the door,' bellowed the captain ...

Bilbo was dreadfully frightened, but he had the sense to understand what had happened and to sneak behind a big barrel which held drink for the goblin-guards, and so get out of the way and avoid being bumped into, trampled to death, or caught by feel.

'I must get to the door, I must get to the door!' he kept on saying to himself, but it was a long time before he ventured to try. Then it was like a horrible game of blind-man's-buff. The place was full of goblins running about, and the poor little hobbit dodged this way and that, was knocked over by a goblin who could not make out what he had bumped into, scrambled away on all fours, slipped between the legs of the captain just in time, got up, and ran for the door.

It was still ajar, but a goblin had pushed it nearly to. Bilbo struggled but he could not move it. He tried to squeeze through the crack. He squeezed and squeezed, and he stuck! It was awful. His buttons had got wedged on the edge of the door and the doorpost. He could see outside into the open air: there were a few steps running down into a narrow valley between tall mountains; the sun came out from behind a cloud and shone bright on the outside of the door – but he could not get through.

Suddenly one of the goblins inside shouted: 'There is a shadow by the door. Something is outside!'

Bilbo's heart jumped into his mouth. He gave a terrific squirm. Buttons burst off in all directions. He was through, with a torn coat and waistcoat, leaping down the steps like a goat, while bewildered goblins were still picking up his nice brass buttons on the doorstep.

C. S. LEWIS

From *The Voyage of the 'Dawn Treader'*

(1952)

At that very moment the others were washing hands and faces in the river and generally getting ready for dinner and a rest. The three best archers had gone up into the hills north of the bay and returned laden with a pair of wild goats which were now roasting over a fire. Caspian had ordered a cask of wine ashore, strong wine of Archenland which had to be mixed with water before you drank it, so there would be plenty for all. The work had gone well so far and it was a merry meal. Only after the second helping of goat did Edmund say, 'Where's that blighter Eustace?'

Meanwhile Eustace stared round the unknown valley. It was so narrow and deep, and the precipices which surrounded it so sheer, that it was like a huge pit or trench. The floor was grassy though strewn with rocks, and here and there Eustace saw black burnt patches like those you see on the sides of a railway embankment in a dry summer. About fifteen yards away from him was a pool of clear, smooth water. There was, at first, nothing else at all in the valley; not an animal, not a bird, not an insect. The sun beat down and grim peaks and horns of mountains peered over the valley's edge.

Eustace realized of course that in the fog he had come down the wrong side of the ridge, so he turned at once to see about getting back. But as soon as he had looked he shuddered. Apparently he had by amazing luck found the only possible way down – a long green spit of land, horribly steep and narrow, with precipices on either side. There was no other possible way of getting back. But could he do it, now that he saw what it was really like? His head swam at the very thought of it.

He turned round again, thinking that at any rate he'd better have a good drink from the pool first. But as soon as he had turned and before he had taken a step forward into the valley he heard a noise behind him. It was only a small noise but it sounded loud in that immense silence. It froze him dead still where he stood for a second. Then he slewed round his head and looked.

At the bottom of the cliff a little on his left hand was a low, dark hole – the entrance to a cave perhaps. And out of this two thin wisps of smoke were coming. And the loose stones just beneath the dark hollow were moving (that was the noise he had heard) just as if something were crawling in the dark behind them.

Something *was* crawling. Worse still, something was coming out. Edmund or Lucy or you would have recognized it at once, but Eustace had read none of the right books. The thing that came out of the cave was something he had never even imagined – a long lead-coloured snout, dull red eyes, no feathers or fur, a long lithe body that trailed on the ground, legs whose elbows went up higher than its back like a spider's, cruel claws, bat's wings that made a rasping noise on the stones, yards of tail. And the two lines of smoke were coming from its two nostrils. He never said the word *Dragon* to himself. Nor would it have made things any better if he had.

But perhaps if he had known something about dragons he would have been a little surprised at this dragon's behaviour. It did not sit up and clap its wings, nor did it shoot out a stream of flame from its mouth. The smoke from its nostrils was like the smoke of a fire that will not last much longer. Nor did it seem to have noticed Eustace. It moved very slowly towards the pool – slowly and with many pauses. Even in his fear Eustace felt that it was an old, sad creature. He wondered if he dared make a dash for the ascent. But it might look round if he made any noise. It might come more to life. Perhaps it was only shamming. Anyway, what was the use of trying to escape by climbing from a creature that could fly?

It reached the pool and slid its horrible scaly chin down over the gravel to drink; but before it had drunk there came from it a great croaking or clanging cry and after a few twitches and convulsions it rolled round on its side and lay perfectly still with one claw in the air. A little dark blood gushed from its wide-opened mouth. The smoke from its nostrils turned black for a moment and then floated away. No more came.

For a long time Eustace did not dare to move. Perhaps this was the brute's trick, the way it lured travellers to their doom. But one couldn't wait for ever. He took a step nearer, then two steps, and halted again. The dragon remained motionless; he noticed too that the red fire had gone out of its eyes. At last he came up to it. He was quite sure now that it was dead. With a shudder he touched it; nothing happened.

The relief was so great that Eustace almost laughed out loud. He began to feel as if he had fought and killed the dragon instead of merely seeing it die. He stepped over it and went to the pool for his drink, for the heat was getting unbearable. He was not surprised when he heard a peal of thunder. Almost immediately afterwards the sun disappeared and before he had finished his drink big drops of rain were falling.

The climate of this island was a very unpleasant one. In less than a minute Eustace was wet to the skin and half blinded with such rain as one never sees in Europe. There was no use trying to climb out of the valley as long as this lasted. He bolted for the only shelter in sight – the dragon's cave. There he lay down and tried to get his breath.

Most of us know what we should expect to find in a dragon's lair, but, as I said before, Eustace had read only the wrong books. They had a lot to say about exports and imports and governments and drains, but they were weak on dragons. That is why he was so puzzled at the surface on which he was lying. Parts of it were too prickly to be stones and too hard to be thorns, and there seemed to be a great many round, flat things, and it all clinked when he moved. There was light enough at the cave's mouth to examine it by. And of course Eustace found it to be what any of us could have told him in advance – treasure. There were crowns (those were the prickly things), coins, rings, bracelets, ingots, cups, plates and gems.

Eustace (unlike most boys) had never thought much of treasure but he saw at once the use it would be in this new world which he had so foolishly stumbled into through the picture in Lucy's bedroom at home. 'They don't have any tax here,' he said. 'And you don't have to give treasure to the government. With some of this stuff I could have quite a decent time here – perhaps in Calormen. It sounds the least phoney of these countries. I wonder how much I can carry? That bracelet now – those things in it are probably diamonds – I'll slip that on my own wrist. Too big, but not if I push it right up here above my elbow. Then fill my pockets with diamonds – that's easier than gold. I wonder when this infernal rain's going to let up?' He got into a less uncomfortable part of the pile, where it was mostly coins, and settled down to wait. But a bad fright, when once it is over, and especially a bad fright following a mountain walk, leaves you very tired. Eustace fell asleep.

By the time he was sound asleep and snoring the others had finished dinner and become seriously alarmed about him. They shouted, 'Eustace! Eustace! Coo-ee!' till they were hoarse and Caspian blew his horn.

'He's nowhere near or he'd have heard that,' said Lucy with a white face.

'Confound the fellow,' said Edmund. 'What on earth did he want to slink away like this for?'

'But we must do something,' said Lucy. 'He may have got lost, or fallen into a hole, or been captured by savages.'

'Or killed by wild beasts,' said Drinian.

'And a good riddance if he has, *I* say,' muttered Rhince.

'Master Rhince,' said Reepicheep, 'you never spoke a word that became you less. The creature is no friend of mine but he is of the Queen's blood, and while he is one of our fellowship it concerns our honour to find him and to avenge him if he is dead.'

'Of course we've got to find him (if we *can*),' said Caspian wearily. 'That's the nuisance of it. It means a search party and endless trouble. Bother Eustace.'

Meanwhile Eustace slept and slept – and slept. What woke him was a pain in his arm. The moon was shining in at the mouth of the cave, and the bed of treasures seemed to have grown much more comfortable; in fact he could hardly feel it at all. He was puzzled by the pain in his arm at first, but presently it occurred to him that the bracelet which he had shoved up above his elbow had become strangely tight. His arm must have swollen while he was asleep (it was his left arm).

He moved his right arm in order to feel his left, but stopped before he had moved it an inch and bit his lip in terror. For just in front of him, and a little on his right, where the moonlight fell clear on the floor of the cave, he saw a hideous shape moving. He knew that shape: it was a dragon's claw. It had moved as he moved his hand and became still when he stopped moving his hand.

'Oh, what a fool I've been,' thought Eustace. 'Of course, the brute had a mate and it's lying beside me.'

For several minutes he did not dare to move a muscle. He saw two thin columns of smoke going up before his eyes, black against the moonlight; just as there had been smoke coming from the other dragon's nose before it died. This was so alarming that he held his breath. The two columns of smoke vanished. When he could hold his breath no longer he let it out stealthily; instantly two jets of smoke appeared again. But even yet he had no idea of the truth.

Presently he decided that he would edge very cautiously to his left and try to creep out of the cave. Perhaps the creature was asleep – and anyway it was his only chance. But of course before he edged to the left he looked to the left. Oh, horror! There was a dragon's claw on that side too.

No one will blame Eustace if at this moment he shed tears. He was surprised at the size of his own tears as he saw them splashing on to the treasure in front of him. They also seemed strangely hot; steam went up from them.

But there was no good crying. He must try to crawl out from between the two dragons. He began extending his right arm. The dragon's fore-leg and claw on his right went through exactly the same motion. Then he thought he would try his left. The dragon limb on that side moved too.

Two dragons, one on each side, mimicking whatever he did! His nerve broke and he simply made a bolt for it.

There was such a clatter and rasping, and clinking of gold, and grinding of stones, as he rushed out of the cave that he thought they were both following him. He daren't look back. He rushed to the pool. The twisted shape of the dead dragon lying in the moonlight would have been enough to frighten anyone but now he hardly noticed it. His idea was to get into the water.

But just as he reached the edge of the pool two things happened. First of all it came over him like a thunder-clap that he had been running on all fours – and why on earth had he been doing that? And secondly, as he bent towards the water, he thought for a second that yet another dragon was staring up at him out of the pool. But in an instant he realized the truth. That dragon face in the pool was his own reflection. There was no doubt of it. It moved as he moved; it opened and shut its mouth as he opened and shut his.

He had turned into a dragon while he was asleep. Sleeping on a dragon's hoard with greedy, dragonish thoughts in his heart, he had become a dragon himself.

That explained everything. There had been no two dragons beside him in the cave. The claws to right and left had been his own right and left claws. The two columns of smoke had been coming from his own nostrils. As for the pain in his left arm (or what had been his left arm), he could now see what had happened by squinting with his left eye. The bracelet which had fitted very nicely on the upper arm of a boy was far too small for the thick, stumpy foreleg of a dragon. It had sunk deeply into his scaly flesh and there was a throbbing bulge on each side of it. He tore at the place with his dragon's teeth but could not get it off.

In spite of the pain, his first feeling was one of relief. There was nothing to be afraid of any more. He was a terror himself now and nothing in the world but a knight (and not all of those) would dare to attack him. He could get even with Caspian and Edmund now –

But the moment he thought this he realized that he didn't want to. He wanted to be friends. He wanted to get back among humans and talk and laugh and share things. He realized that he was a monster cut off from the whole human race. An appalling loneliness came over him. He began to see that the others had not really been fiends at all. He began to wonder if he himself had been such a nice person as he had always supposed. He longed for their voices. He would have been grateful for a kind word even from Reepicheep.

When he thought of this the poor dragon that had been Eustace lifted up its voice and wept. A powerful dragon crying its eyes out under the moon in a deserted valley is a sight and a sound hardly to be imagined.

At last he decided he would try to find his way back to the shore. He realized now that Caspian would never have sailed away and left him. And he felt sure that somehow or other he would be able to make people understand who he was.

He took a long drink and then (I know this sounds

shocking, but it isn't if you think it over) he ate nearly all the dead dragon. He was half-way through it before he realized what he was doing; for, you see, though his mind was the mind of Eustace, his tastes and his digestion were dragon-ish. And there is nothing a dragon likes so well as fresh dragon. That is why you so seldom find more than one dragon in the same county.

Then he turned to climb out of the valley. He began the climb with a jump and as soon as he jumped he found that he was flying. He had quite forgotten about his wings and it was a great surprise to him – the first pleasant surprise he had had for a long time. He rose high into the air and saw innumerable mountain-tops spread out beneath him in the moonlight. He could see the bay like a silver slab and the *Dawn Treader* lying at anchor and camp fires twinkling in the woods beside the beach. From a great height he launched himself down towards them in a single glide.

Lucy was sleeping very sound for she had sat up till the return of the search party in hope of good news about Eustace. It had been led by Caspian and had come back late and weary. Their news was disquieting. They had found no trace of Eustace but had seen a dead dragon in a valley. They tried to make the best of it and everyone assured everyone else that there were not likely to be more dragons about, and that one which was dead at about three o'clock that afternoon (which was when they had seen it) would hardly have been killing people a very few hours before.

'Unless it ate the little brat and died of him: he'd poison anything,' said Rhince. But he said this under his breath and no one heard it.

But later in the night Lucy was waked, very softly, and found the whole company gathered close together and talking in whispers.

'What is it?' said Lucy.

'We must all show great constancy,' Caspian was saying. 'A dragon has just flown over the tree-tops and lighted on the beach. Yes, I am afraid it is between us and the ship. And arrows are no use against dragons. And they're not at all afraid of fire.'

'With your Majesty's leave – ' began Reepicheep.

'No, Reepicheep,' said the King very firmly, 'you are *not* going to attempt a single combat with it. And unless you promise to obey me in this matter I'll have you tied up. We must just keep close watch and, as soon as it is light, go down to the beach and give it battle. I will lead. King Edmund will be on my right and the Lord Drinian on my left. There are no other arrangements to be made. It will be light in a couple of hours. In an hour's time let a meal be served out and what is left of the wine. And let everything be done silently.'

'Perhaps it will go away,' said Lucy.

'It'll be worse if it does,' said Edmund, 'because then we shan't know where it is. If there's a wasp in the room I like to be able to see it.'

The rest of the night was dreadful, and when the meal came, though they knew they ought to eat, many found that they had very poor appetites. And endless hours seemed to pass before the darkness thinned and birds began chirping here and there and the world got colder and wetter than it had been all night and Caspian said, 'Now for it, friends.'

They got up, all with swords drawn, and formed themselves into a solid mass with Lucy in the middle and Reepicheep on her shoulder. It was nicer than the waiting about and everyone felt fonder of everyone else than at ordinary times. A moment later they were marching. It grew lighter as they came to the edge of the wood. And there on the sand, like a giant lizard, or a flexible crocodile, or a serpent with legs, huge and horrible and humpy, lay the dragon.

But when it saw them, instead of rising up and blowing fire and smoke, the dragon retreated – you could almost say it waddled – back into the shallows of the bay.

'What's it wagging its head like that for?' said Edmund.

'And now it's nodding,' said Caspian.

'And there's something coming from its eyes,' said Drinian.

'Oh, can't you see,' said Lucy. 'It's crying. Those are tears.'

'I shouldn't trust to that, Ma'am,' said Drinian. 'That's what crocodiles do, to put you off your guard.'

'It wagged its head when you said that,' remarked Edmund. 'Just as if it meant No. Look, there it goes again.'

'Do you think it understands what we're saying?' asked Lucy.

The dragon nodded its head violently.

Reepicheep slipped off Lucy's shoulder and stepped to the front.

'Dragon,' came his shrill voice, 'can you understand speech?'

The dragon nodded.

'Can you speak?'

It shook its head.

'Then,' said Reepicheep, 'it is idle to ask you your business. But if you will swear friendship with us raise your left foreleg above your head.'

It did so, but clumsily because that leg was sore and swollen with the golden bracelet.

'Oh, look,' said Lucy, 'there's something wrong with its leg. The poor thing – that's probably what it was crying about. Perhaps it came to us to be cured like in Androcles and the lion.'

'Be careful, Lucy,' said Caspian. 'It's a very clever dragon but it may be a liar.'

Lucy had, however, already run forward, followed by Reepicheep, as fast as his short legs could carry him, and then of course the boys and Drinian came, too.

'Show me your poor paw,' said Lucy. 'I might be able to cure it.'

The dragon-that-had-been-Eustace held out its sore leg gladly enough, remembering how Lucy's cordial had cured him of sea-sickness before he became a dragon. But he was disappointed. The magic fluid reduced the swelling and eased the pain a little but it could not dissolve the gold.

Everyone had now crowded round to watch the treatment, and Caspian suddenly exclaimed, 'Look!' He was staring at the bracelet.

MARY NORTON

From *The Borrowers*

(1952)

It was Pod's hole – the keep of his fortress; the entrance to his home. Not that his home was anywhere near the clock: far from it – as you might say. There were yards of dark and dusty passage-way, with wooden doors between the joists and metal gates against the mice. Pod used all kinds of things for these gates – a flat leaf of a folding cheesegrater, the hinged lid of a small cash-box, squares of pierced zinc from an old meat-safe, a wire fly-swotter … 'Not that I'm afraid of mice,' Homily would say, 'but I can't abide the smell.' In vain Arrietty had begged for a little mouse of her own, a little blind mouse to bring up by hand – 'like Eggletina had had.' But Homily would bang with the pan lids and exclaim: 'And look what happened to Eggletina!' 'What,' Arrietty would ask, 'what did happen to Eggletina?' But no one would ever say.

It was only Pod who knew the way through the intersecting passages to the hole under the clock. And only Pod could open the gates. There were complicated clasps made of hairslides and safety-pins of which Pod alone knew the secret. His wife and child led more sheltered lives in homelike apartments under the kitchen, far removed from the risks and dangers of the dreaded house above. But there was a grating in the brick wall of the house, just below the floor level of the kitchen above, through which Arrietty could see the garden – a piece of gravelled path and a bank where crocus bloomed in spring; where blossom drifted from an unseen tree; and where later an azalea bush would flower; and where birds came – and pecked and flirted and sometimes fought. 'The hours you waste on them birds,' Homily would say, 'and when there's a little job to be done you can never find the time. I was brought up in a house,' Homily went on, 'where there wasn't no grating, and we were all the happier for it. Now go off and get me the potato.'

That was the day when Arrietty, rolling the potato before her from the storehouse down the dusty lane under the floorboards, kicked it ill-temperedly so that it rolled rather fast into their kitchen, where Homily was stooping over the stove.

'There you go again,' exclaimed Homily, turning angrily; 'nearly pushed me into the soup. And when I say "potato" I don't mean the whole potato. Take the scissor, can't you, and cut off a slice.'

'Didn't know how much you wanted,' Arrietty had mumbled, as Homily, snorting and sniffing, unhooked the blade and handle of half a pair of manicure scissors from a nail on the wall, and began to cut through the peel.

'You've ruined this potato,' she grumbled. 'You can't roll it back now in all that dust, not once it's been cut open.'

'Oh, what does it matter?' said Arrietty. 'There are plenty more.'

'That's a nice way to talk. Plenty more. Do you realize,' Homily went on gravely, laying down the half nail scissor, 'that your poor father risks his life every time he borrows a potato?'

'I meant,' said Arrietty, 'that there are plenty more in the store-room.'

'Well, out of my way now,' said Homily, bustling around again, 'whatever you meant – and let me get the supper.'

Arrietty had wandered through the open door into the sitting-room – the fire had been lighted and the room looked bright and cosy. Homily was proud of her sitting-room; the walls had been papered with scraps of old letters out of waste-paper baskets, and Homily had arranged the handwriting sideways in vertical stripes which ran from floor to ceiling. On the walls, repeated in various colours, hung several portraits of Queen Victoria as a girl; these were postage stamps, borrowed by Pod some years ago from the stamp-box on the desk in the morning-room. There was a lacquer trinket-box, padded inside and with the lid open, which they used as a settle; and that useful stand-by – a chest of drawers made of match-boxes. There was a round table with a red velvet cloth, which Pod had made from the wooden bottom of a pill-box supported on the carved pedestal of a knight from the chess-set. (This had caused a great deal of trouble upstairs when Aunt Sophy's eldest son, on a flying mid-week visit, had invited the vicar for 'a game after dinner'. Rosa Pickhatchet, who was housemaid at the time, gave in her notice. Not long after she had left other things were found to be missing and, from that time onwards, Mrs Driver ruled supreme.) The knight itself – its bust, so to speak – was standing on a

column in the corner, where it looked very fine, and lent
that air to the room which only statuary can give.

Beside the fire, in a tilted wooden book-case, stood
Arrietty's library. This was a set of those miniature volumes
which the Victorians loved to print, but which to Arrietty
seemed the size of very large church Bibles. There was
Bryce's *Tom Thumb Gazetteer of the World*, including the last
census; Bryce's *Tom Thumb Dictionary*, with short explanations of scientific, philosophical, literary, and technical
terms; Bryce's *Tom Thumb Edition of the Comedies of William
Shakespeare*, including a foreword on the author; another book,
whose pages were all blank, called *Memoranda*; and, last but
not least, Arrietty's favourite, Bryce's *Tom Thumb Diary and
Proverb Book*, with a saying for each day of the year and, as a
preface, the life story of a little man called General Tom
Thumb, who married a girl called Mercy Lavinia Bump.
There was an engraving of their carriage and pair, with little
horses – the size of mice. Arrietty was not a stupid girl. She
knew that horses could not be as small as mice, but she did
not realize that Tom Thumb, nearly two feet high, would
seem a giant to a Borrower.

Arrietty had learned to read from these books, and to write
by leaning sideways and copying out the writings on the walls.
In spite of this, she did not always keep her diary, although
on most days she would take the book out for the sake of
the saying which sometimes would comfort her. Today it
said: 'You may go farther and fare worse' and, underneath:
'Order of the Garter, instituted 1348.' She carried the book
to the fire and sat down with her feet on the hob.

'What are you doing, Arrietty?' called Homily from the
kitchen.

' 'Writing my diary.'

'Oh,' exclaimed Homily shortly.

'What did you want?' asked Arrietty. She felt quite safe; Homily liked her to write; Homily encouraged any form of culture. Homily herself, poor ignorant creature, could not even say the alphabet. 'Nothing. Nothing,' said Homily crossly, banging away with the pan lids; 'it'll do later.'

Arrietty took out her pencil. It was a small white pencil, with a piece of silk cord attached, which had come off a dance programme, but, even so, in Arrietty's hand, it looked like a rolling-pin.

'Arrietty!' called Homily again from the kitchen.

'Yes?'

'Put a little something on the fire, will you?'

Arrietty braced her muscles and heaved the book off her knees, and stood it upright on the floor. They kept the fuel, assorted slack and crumbled candle grease, in a pewter mustard-pot, and shovelled it out with the spoon. Arrietty trickled only a few grains, tilting the mustard spoon, not to spoil the blaze. Then she stood there basking in the warmth. It was a charming fire-place, made by Arrietty's grandfather, with a cog-wheel from the stables, part of an old cider-press. The spokes of the cog-wheel stood out in starry rays, and the fire itself nestled in the centre. Above there was a chimney-piece made from a small brass funnel, inverted. This, at one time, belonged to an oil-lamp which matched it, and which stood, in the old days, on the hall table upstairs. An arrangement of pipes, from the spout of the funnel, carried the fumes into the kitchen flues above. The fire was laid with matchsticks and fed with assorted slack and, as it burned up, the iron would become hot, and Homily would simmer soup on the spokes, in a silver thimble, and Arrietty would broil nuts. How cosy those winter evenings could be. Arrietty, her great book on her knees, sometimes reading aloud; Pod at his last (he was a shoemaker, and made button-boots out of kid-gloves – now, alas, only for his family); and Homily, quiet at last, with her knitting.

Homily knitted their jerseys and stockings on black head-ed pins, and, sometimes, on darning needles. A great reel of silk or cotton would stand, table high, beside her chair, and sometimes, if she pulled too sharply, the reel would tip up and roll away out of the open door into the dusty passage beyond, and Arrietty would be sent after it, to rewind it carefully as she rolled it back.

The floor of the sitting-room was carpeted with deep red blotting-paper, which was warm and cosy, and soaked up the spills. Homily would renew it at intervals when it became available upstairs, but since Aunt Sophy had taken to her bed, Mrs Driver seldom thought of blotting-paper unless, suddenly, there were guests. Homily liked things which saved washing because drying was difficult under the floor; water they had in plenty, hot and cold, thanks to Pod's father who had tapped the pipes from the kitchen boiler. They bathed in a small tureen, which once had held *pâté de foie gras*. When you had wiped out your bath you were supposed to put the lid back, to stop people putting things in it. The soap, too, a great cake of it, hung on a nail in the scullery, and they scraped pieces off. Homily liked coal tar, but Pod and Arrietty preferred sandalwood.

'What are you doing now, Arrietty?' called Homily from the kitchen.

'Still writing my diary.'

Once again Arrietty took hold of the book and heaved it back on to her knees. She licked the lead of her great pencil, and stared a moment, deep in thought. She allowed herself (when she did remember to write) one little line on each page because she would never – of this she was sure – have another diary, and if she could get twenty lines on each page the diary would last her twenty years. She had kept it for nearly two years already, and today, March 22, she read last year's entry: 'Mother cross.' She thought a while longer then, at last, she put ditto marks under 'mother', and 'worried' under 'cross'.

'What did you say you were doing, Arrietty?' called Homily from the kitchen.

Arrietty closed the book. 'Nothing,' she said.

'Then chop me up this onion, there's a good girl. Your father's late tonight ...'

INDEX OF AUTHORS

BIOGRAPHICAL NOTES

AESOP is said to have been a slave who lived in the mid-sixth century BC. Legend describes him as an ugly little man, whose audiences laughed not only at his strange appearance, but also at his brilliant stories.

LOUISA MAY ALCOTT (1832–88) belonged to an American family much like the one she describes in *Little Women*, except that it was she, rather than her father, who went away to the Civil War, where she was a nurse in a military hospital. She began to write stories to support the family when her father, a philosopher and educationalist, failed to earn money.

HANS CHRISTIAN ANDERSEN (1805–75), the famous Danish writer of fairy stories, was a poor boy who worked as an actor before becoming a writer. Many of his stories can be interpreted as being about their author; he certainly saw himself as an 'ugly duckling' who flourished in the end.

L. FRANK BAUM (1856–1919) was rather like the Wizard of Oz himself: a travelling salesman and performer who toured America with his wares. After the first 'Oz' book, he wrote many sequels, and even made films of some of them – long before the famous Judy Garland film appeared in 1939.

FRANCES HODGSON BURNETT (1849–1924) was a Lancashire ironmonger's daughter who was taken to America in her teens. She married an American and became a successful writer of stories for magazines. *Little Lord Fauntleroy* was based on her son Vivian, who had long ringlets and wore a velvet knickerbocker suit. *The Secret Garden* was partly drawn from her memories of a back garden in her Manchester childhood.

'LEWIS CARROLL' was the pen-name of Charles Lutwidge Dodgson (1832–98), who taught mathematics at Christ Church, Oxford, and made up the first 'Alice' story after he had met Alice Liddell and her sisters, the daughters of the Dean of Christ Church.

'CARLO COLLODI' was really called Carlo Lorenzini (1826–90). He was a campaigner for the independence of his country, Italy, and founded a satirical magazine before he started writing children's stories.

'SUSAN COOLIDGE' was the pen-name of Sarah Chauncy Woolsey (1845–1905), who spent a childhood in Cleveland, Ohio, much like that of her heroine Katy. She worked as a nurse before becoming a writer.

RICHMAL CROMPTON (1890–1969), whose full name was Richmal Crompton Lamburn, was a Lancashire clergyman's daughter. She taught Latin and Greek at a school near London, before contracting polio at the age of thirty-three. She had already begun to write the 'William' stories, which were not originally intended for children and appeared in a women's magazine.

CHARLES DICKENS (1812–70), the most famous and successful of all British novelists, wrote *A Christmas Carol* because the public was not buying enough copies of his current serial, *Martin Chuzzlewit*, and he needed to make money fast. Fortunately for him, *A Christmas Carol* sold very quickly and earned him the money he needed.

KENNETH GRAHAME (1859–1932) had written two books *about* children, *The Golden Age* and *Dream Days*, when he married and had a son; but *The Wind in the Willows* was his first story told *to* a child – his son Alastair. Kenneth Grahame worked as a senior official in the Bank of England.

ROGER LANCELYN GREEN (1918–87) lived in an old manor house in Cheshire, and was an expert on children's literature.

THOMAS HUGHES (1822–96) wrote *Tom Brown's Schooldays* about his own childhood in the Vale of the White Horse, Berkshire, and at Rugby school. He campaigned for better education for the poor, and taught boxing at the Working Men's College in London. Later he became a Member of Parliament and a judge.

JOSEPH JACOBS (1854–1916) became an expert in English folk tales, though he had been born in Australia and, after an education in England, went to America. He was also an expert in Jewish literature, and brought Jewish storytelling skills to his material.

ERICH KÄSTNER (1899–1974) was born in Dresden, Germany. From a poverty-stricken background, he worked as a journalist, but some of his articles caused trouble and he was dismissed. At twenty-eight, penniless and without a job, he went to Berlin to try his luck as a writer and within a year published his first book. *Emil and the Detectives* was highly successful – it was filmed, and translated into twenty-five languages.

CHARLES KINGSLEY (1819–75), English clergyman and novelist, wrote *The Water-Babies* after reading a government report on children being used as chimney sweeps. He was an expert on underwater life.

RUDYARD KIPLING (1865–1936), born in India, was sent to a boarding school in Devon, which he wrote about in *Stalky & Co*. His daughter Josephine, who died in childhood, was the first person to be told the *Just So Stories*. Kipling wrote many stories and poems for adults, receiving the Nobel Prize for Literature in 1907.

C. S. (CLIVE STAPLES) LEWIS (1898–1963) was born in Belfast. He was a distinguished literary scholar and taught English literature at Magdalen College, Oxford, where he became friends with J. R. R. Tolkien. As well as the 'Narnia' stories, he wrote novels and religious books for adults.

NORMAN LINDSAY (1879–1969) was an Australian newspaper cartoonist and painter. He wrote *The Magic Pudding* because he believed that children preferred food to fairy stories.

JACK LONDON (1876–1916) was brought up among poor people in San Francisco and became a sailor and a gold prospector before starting to write books based on his experiences.

GEORGE MACDONALD (1824–1905) was a Congregationalist minister whose unusual ideas about religion lost him his job. He wrote strange, fantastic novels for adults as well as children. The castle in *The Princess and the Goblin* is of a kind found all over Scotland, his native country.

L. M. (LUCY MAUD) MONTGOMERY (1874–1942) was born in a remote part of Canada and, like her heroine Anne, was sent away to live with relatives after her mother died. She became a teacher before making a name for herself as a writer.

E. (EDITH) NESBIT (1858–1924) was born in England, but was taken abroad by her mother after her father's death, when she was three. She was a founder member of the Fabian Society and became a very successful writer of fiction and poetry for adults. However, she is best remembered for her children's stories.

MARY NORTON (1903–92) was brought up in a manor house in Bedfordshire, which became the setting for *The Borrowers*. She worked as an actress, and wrote children's stories after she had married and had four children.

ANNA SEWELL (1820–78) was born in Norfolk into a Quaker family, and was physically disabled from childhood. She wrote *Black Beauty*, her only book, to encourage better treatment of horses.

JOHANNA SPYRI (1827–1901) was a doctor's daughter from a Swiss village, who began to write to earn money for refugees. *Heidi* was her first full-length book.

ROBERT LOUIS STEVENSON (1850–94) was born and brought up in Edinburgh, the son of a civil engineer whose work took him to sea as well as around Scotland. His first book was about travelling across France with a donkey. He made up *Treasure Island* with the help of his stepson.

NOEL STREATFEILD (1895–1986) was the middle sister of the three daughters of a clergyman in the South of England. After the Second World War she trained for the stage, acting professionally before becoming an author.

J. R. R. (JOHN RONALD REUEL) TOLKIEN (1892–1973) was born in South Africa, but was brought up in England after the death of his father. He became Professor of Anglo-Saxon at Oxford University, and began to make up an elaborate saga about 'Middle Earth' before writing *The Hobbit* as a little amusement. *The Hobbit* (1937) and its epic sequel *The Lord of the Rings* (1954–5) achieved worldwide fame.

'MARK TWAIN' was the pen-name of Samuel Langhorne Clemens (1835–1910), who was brought up on the shores of the Mississippi, and worked as a river-pilot before becoming an author.

ALISON UTTLEY (1884–1976), well known for her 'Little Grey Rabbit' books, was born on a farm in Derbyshire. She was one of the first women to take a physics degree at Manchester University.

JULES VERNE (1828–1905), French writer of science fiction, knew very little about actual science, but managed to guess much of what would happen during the twentieth century, including the details of the first landing on the moon.

OSCAR WILDE (1856–1900) was born in Dublin, where he attended Trinity College, and he later went to Magdalen College, Oxford. While in Oxford he cultivated his long hair and unusual mode of dress. His intelligence and wit were famous. In addition to the stories he wrote for his sons, he also wrote several plays, of which the best known is *The Importance of Being Earnest* (1895).

ACKNOWLEDGEMENTS

The editor and publishers gratefully acknowledge the following for permission to reproduce copyright material in this anthology in the form of extracts taken from the following books:

The Ugly Duckling by Hans Christian Andersen from *Hans Andersen's Fairy Tales* translated by Naomi Lewis, copyright © 1981, reprinted by permission of Penguin Books Ltd; *William the Conqueror* by Richmal Crompton, published by Macmillan; *The Wind in the Willows* by Kenneth Grahame, copyright under the Berne Convention, reproduced by permission of Curtis Brown, London; *The Adventures of Robin Hood* retold by Roger Lancelyn Green, copyright © Roger Lancelyn Green 1956, reprinted by permission of Penguin Books Ltd; *Emil and the Detectives* by Erich Kästner, copyright Atrium Verlag AG, Zurich, reproduced by permission of Curtis Brown Group Ltd; 'The Cat That Walked By Himself' from *Just So Stories* by Rudyard Kipling, reprinted by permission of A. P. Watt Ltd on behalf of The National Trust for Places of Historic Interest or Natural Beauty; *The Voyage of the 'Dawn Treader'* by C. S. Lewis, reprinted by permission of HarperCollins *Publishers* Ltd; *The Magic Pudding* by Norman Lindsay, reprinted by permission of HarperCollins *Publishers* Australia; *The Borrowers* by Mary Norton, published by J. M. Dent, reprinted by permission of The Orion Publishing Group Ltd; *Ballet Shoes* by Noel Streatfeild, published by J. M. Dent, reprinted by permission of The Orion Publishing Group Ltd; *The Hobbit* by J. R. R. Tolkien, published by George Allen & Unwin, reprinted by permission of HarperCollins *Publishers* Ltd; *A Country Child* by Alison Uttley, reprinted by permission of Faber and Faber Ltd.